UNBROKEN

BOOK TWO

KAY CAMDEN

UNBROKEN
Unquiet Series, Book 2
Copyright © 2020 Kay Camden

This is a work of fiction. Any similarity to real people, places, or
events is coincidental.

Cover art by Damonza

Interior Design & Typesetting by Ampersand Book Interiors

ISBN 978-1-7336212-2-9 (paperback)
ISBN 978-1-7336212-3-6 (eBook)

For more information about Kay Camden go to kaycamden.com

UNBROKEN

CHAPTER 1

WAAPIKOONA'S MOTEL ROOM had sprung a leak. Rainwater snaked down the wood-paneled wall and hung in fat beads over the bed, ready to drop. With no stain evident on the ceiling it meant this was a first, which was just her luck. It was still the driest place she'd stayed all winter— except when she'd stayed with Mick. But she'd made a personal pledge to stop thinking about that homey apartment and those pillows that smelled like him. He'd given up his bed for her. He'd nearly given up his life.

This was why she had to stay away from Mick.

The rumbling hum of a powerful car passed outside her motel room's window, rattling the panes, rattling her. She peered through the slit in the curtains into the night and found rain pouring straight down, even more persistent than when she'd escaped its frigid grip a few minutes ago. A couple degrees would turn it all to snow. Her stolen motorcycle sat under the halo of white street light, looking defeated

in its parking spot next to a liquid black Nissan 300ZX that had just decided to become its unwelcome neighbor.

If she hadn't felt this coming, she'd be grabbing her coat and bag and sneaking out the bathroom window into the night. It was time to face her hunter. Rather than be backed into the corner of her room, she opened the door and stepped outside, still drenched from her ride. Still tired, still undecided. Still lost.

The last time she saw that Nissan it had a shattered windshield and wicked scrape across the hood thanks to her—and a witness, whom she allowed to think was saving her so she could get him somewhere quiet and kill him. A convenient kill to ease the burden of her quota, she'd thought at the time. Quite the opposite—he'd pulled her straight into an endless unquiet.

The Nissan idled, exhaust humming, four shiny pipes puffing steam into the dusky rain. The windows were too dark to see inside, but she could guess he was on the phone, calling in his position, calling for backup. She needed to speak to him before she brought hell upon him. She had to know why he'd given up the hunt in Wyona, since she hadn't fled that day like she planned, and why he was back on her tail now. There was something new in play she'd be wise not to ignore.

Abruptly, the engine cut off and the door swung open. He angled himself out, hunching broad shoulders and lifting his flannel jacket's inadequate jersey hood. As if he felt her gaze, he looked up at her through the rain. Tucking fingers in the front pockets of her jeans, she watched. He watched back. Rain streamed into her eyes. She refused to blink it away.

He broke the stare first to lean into the car and retrieve an object he quickly tucked inside his jacket under his arm. She'd love to show him what would happen if he tried to shoot one of her Helpers.

The car door slammed. The Nissan chirped. Waapikoona stood her ground in the pouring February rain and watched her hunter cross the parking lot toward her. What he lacked in height he made up for in breadth, and she wondered how all those built muscles even fit inside that car.

"You fixed your windshield," she said as he neared.

"I have good insurance."

His accent was Hispanic, but not Mexican—at least not the one she knew. She didn't know Central or South American countries well enough to identify it. She also didn't have any knowledge of her kind being revived outside of North America. This was definitely something new in play.

"Do you have Native blood?" She couldn't see his face in the shadow from his hood.

"I thought we'd start with names. Going straight to race seems real—"

"I'm not giving you my name."

He chuckled, looking away to survey the building stretching beside them, the parking lot, the street. "That's fine, Sarah. I already have it. But I thought you might want mine, so we could talk like *amigos*." He offered a hand. "Call me Soto."

She ignored his hand. "Why didn't you follow me in Missouri?"

"Can we go inside? This weather is messing up my hair."

His shoulders and hood were drenched. Flannel was warm but not waterproof, and being ill-prepared for this weather meant he was either hot-blooded or not from Oklahoma. She tried to remember where she'd first seen him but retrieved nothing from memories too saturated with things she wanted to forget. And now that he'd mentioned it, she felt the cold crawling under her skin, into her blood, making her straighten her spine against a shiver eager to bend her in two. She could handle cold. Soaked and cold was a dif-

ferent thing. It would be better to release her Helpers in the privacy of her room anyway.

She opened the door and he followed her inside, shrugging out of his wet jacket before she'd even closed the door. The gun he'd stuck under his arm apparently wasn't supposed to be a surprise because there it was, smug in its holster, pretending not to be the affront it was. His sleeves struggled to contain arms so muscled they hung off his body like he was permanently holding something. Prey caught in his grip would have no chance to wriggle free. And the hair he'd been worried about? It didn't exist. His head was shaved to a shine. Dark stubble lined his jaw and upper lip, and his eyes and eyelashes were just as dark. She stood while her hair and clothes dripped and watched him adjust the heat in the room as if it were his, wondering why she had to compare every damn man she met to the tall, blond, all-American blue-collar build of Mick.

"Who are you?"

He dragged a chair next to the heater and sat, rubbing his hands together. A gold wedding band choked his finger. "You want to change? You look cold. I can wait."

"I'm always cold. I'm used to it."

"*Pobrecita*. Or is that a metaphor?"

"I don't have time for this."

"Long list of people to kill tonight?"

"Always. And it just gained one more."

He laughed so loudly she worried who might be on the other side of the wall, now tuned in and listening.

"If you wanted to kill me, you'd have done it in Missouri. Instead I get a hell of an insurance claim and a visit from one of your friends. Too scared to rough me up yourself?"

"I work alone."

"Your two mini demons don't count?"

She had three now, but she didn't want to correct him. Two she carried in her palm, one she'd inherited from Jeremiah's corpse and couldn't carry, but it always found her.

Water from the leak in the ceiling splattered onto the bed. She went into the bathroom for a towel, stopping to dab her hair and collect her thoughts. Too much had happened after she'd trashed this guy's car in Wyona. The mind space she was in that day seemed to be on the opposite side of time than the place she was now. On that day she'd simply wanted to disable his car—creatively, so as to send a message along with it—and get a head start away from him. The whole thing felt like a game back then. Things mattered less, and she didn't know why her every move seemed to matter so much now.

It would help if she could get him to tell her who'd roughed him up. She didn't have any friends, and the person's identity was a clue she'd love to have. After riding so many hours in the cold rain and spending nearly a day without food, she was wrecked. Her brain was on strike, a hopeless help to her now.

A large object thudded against the floor outside the bathroom. She returned to the main room to find Soto shoving the mattress out from under the leak.

He caught her eye. "Might not be worthy of saving, but if we have the chance, why not?"

"Is that a metaphor?"

"You think I'm here to save you?"

"I think you're going to try."

When he bent to give the mattress one final shove she noticed the black ink of a snake slithering around the back of his neck, its horned head peeking out of his collar. A tattoo of a *maneto*—did that mean he was a fan of the creature or a foe? Depending on which one, he was either on her side or

5

against her. The hope he was here on some unrelated business sputtered and died.

At the risk of sounding dense, she had to take a guess. "You've been raised."

He narrowed one eye at her. The suspicion could be real or could be an act. He either knew what she meant but didn't want her to know he knew … or he didn't know and didn't want her to know he didn't know. Her head swirled. She closed her eyes.

"I beg you to sit." He gestured toward the chair he'd pulled against the heater.

"I'm fine."

"I hunt a lot of creatures like you. But you're different. I've seen the pattern of your kills, and it's not random."

If there was a pattern to what she did, it was news to her. Or perhaps he'd invented it, his own confirmation bias on what he wanted to believe. Not that she felt any need to explain this.

"It's not about quantity. You only seem to go after ones who deserve it."

This part could be true, but it certainly wasn't any of his business.

"You're not on my side," he continued. "But I think you should be."

"I told you I work alone."

"Except for the mini demons. And the car mechanic in Missouri."

She felt herself stiffen, wishing she had the strength of mind to have masked it. Mick wasn't just a mechanic, but if that's all this guy knew about him, she needed it to stay that way.

"Who I thought was gonna break my theory. But he's a good guy, right? So you didn't kill him."

"Are you a good guy?"

"*Sí. Muy bueno.*"

"Would you like me to break your theory right now?" She put the effort into making the question sound convincing, but she still hoped he'd see through it. This motel room was supposed to be her hot shower and warm bed, not a crime scene she'd have to flee. Releasing her Helpers now would cost mental energy she couldn't spare. And summoning The Silent One to possess her so she could win against that firearm and make a clean kill? The feat seemed unachievable without a solid block of rest beforehand.

"I get it," he said. "But you don't have to kill me to prove anything, and I don't think I should kill you. It's a waste on both sides."

Again with these sides. So this Soto was a foe of the horned serpent and all creatures from the underworld—including her. Despite being raised from the dead by a great demon and pledging to work for him, she also enjoyed the company of Thunder-Beings—or one particular Thunder-Being, in both his forms. She'd hunted *maneto* with him and had delighted in it. There was no upperworld being more unfit for company than Mick. It was his job to strike all underworld creatures like her from the earth. She wasn't exactly sure which side she was on anymore.

"Then why are you bothering me?"

He wrote something on the pad of paper on the table, ripped off the sheet, and offered it to her. "I'd like to recruit you. Call me when you get tired of working alone."

She didn't take the paper. He folded it and gently set it on the TV table, two fingers holding it in place as he looked up at her. "Until then, I'll keep my eye on you."

"Just one?"

He grinned. "Four, if you're counting."

She had a feeling the other two eyes didn't belong to his inked *maneto*, but she didn't ask as he slid into his jacket and out into the downpour. While she waited to hear the engine start up and drone toward the highway, she collected her things and went to the door, hesitating with her hand on the knob as she stared at his folded piece of paper lying on the table. Even if she didn't want it, it wouldn't be wise to leave behind, so she snatched it up and tucked it into her bag.

The clerk in the motel office had her nose stuck in the same book as when Waapikoona had checked in. On the cover, a dragon's fiery breath curled around the shiny sword of a soldier-princess. Fighting monsters wasn't always so alluring. It was often messy and tedious—except when a Thunder-Being decided to show up.

"Checking out, ma'am?"

"I need a different room. Mine is leaking."

The clerk stared at her, as if connecting a leaking room to Waapikoona's sodden hair and clothes and imagining a full-on downpour inside the room.

"And could you look up a phone number for me?"

The clerk's pointed pause had Waapikoona thinking she rarely got that question.

"I don't have a smart phone."

They exchanged keycards, the clerk found the phone number, and Waapikoona dragged herself back outside toward her new room, trying to talk herself out of making the phone call she finally had an excuse for and was too weak not to make. In tomorrow's light of day, it would feel like the mistake it was, but right now …

She stopped under the motel's overhang to squint through the rain. The Nissan hadn't left its spot next to her motorcycle.

Forget it. Let him stay there all night. He'd already proven he was harmless—for now—and she didn't have an ounce of care in her to handle him tonight. If the car was still there in the morning, she'd wake him up with a freshly broken windshield then make him the next kill applied to her quota, now doubled because she had to cover for Jeremiah's as well as her own. It would've been a worse deal not to accept the blame for Mick. She'd take on more than a doubled quota for him to remain nameless to The Silent One. In the end she'd have her sister back, even if it took longer than she planned. And Mick's involvement would remain concealed.

In her dry room she showered all the cold from her bones. She dried off, dressed, and sat on the sagging mattress until Mick would be on his shift. Then she picked up the phone by the bed and dialed the number, trying to ignore the outrage in her unprepared heart.

"U-Fill."

How she missed his voice. The round vowels and casual tempo, how every word had a soft edge that rolled right into the next. She could hear a layer of exhaustion under that upbeat first syllable, like he'd spared a pull from his drying well of positivity for an unknown caller. That was Mick. Pleasant to a stranger on the phone, even though he spent his nights in eagle form guarding the earth instead of in human form stealing much-needed sleep.

Or perhaps he'd shed his eagle. Cast away his duty to return to his normal life. She had no idea what he'd been doing the past couple months.

But all it took was that one word of his voice to repower a longing so barbed it hooked itself into her with the fury of something tragically betrayed. Here it returned in full force, as damaging as the day she walked away from him.

She swallowed to settle her own voice so it wouldn't reveal all the old grief mixed with the new. "Mick. A guy

named Soto knows about you and me. Hispanic, muscular, tattoo of a *maneto* on his neck."

His pause lasted long enough for her to wonder if he'd already forgotten her.

"Is this your number?"

"Be careful, Mick. He's armed."

"Are you oka—"

She hung up then unplugged the phone from the wall. The many reasons to sever contact outnumbered her one reason not to. It was too bad that single reason haunted her with a weight so heavy she often couldn't remember the others.

CHAPTER
2

MICK REMAINED ON the line long enough for the auto-mated operator message to start. Then he had to ring up a customer's seven different candy bars and seven lottery tickets on seven separate sales, stressed out that somehow the phone number would disappear from the caller ID before he had a chance to input it into his phone.

As soon as the customer left, he jotted the number on a discarded receipt just to be safe. Then he searched the inter-net for the area code—Oklahoma? Right across the border. He clicked the map and zoomed in and out, memorizing fea-tures in the way his eagle mind might recognize, all shapes and colors and details lost on human eyes, like seeing an overhead view and zoomed-in view at the same time layered over one another. The area was well beyond his patrol that had become routine in the months since she'd walked away from him. He wasn't hunting her. He simply wanted to know where she was, if she was okay.

She certainly knew how to disappear. How to avoid catching the eye of a searching thunderbird. If she'd taken to traveling underground, it would explain how he'd failed so far. If she'd been less knowledgeable of his schedule, he'd have found her a long time ago.

He wrote what he remembered of the guy's description under the phone number and stared at it long and hard. If she'd wanted to talk more, she wouldn't have hung up—but maybe she hadn't. Someone might've hung up for her or the line went dead for another reason …

He dialed, his other fingers tapping percussion against the countertop. Since when had he become so neurotic? After four rings he expected voicemail, but he got another ring and another. It went on so long he had to hang up. In four hours he'd be off his shift, and his nightly patrol wouldn't be sweeping arcs in the wide sky guarding the broadest expanse of the land he could manage. It would be as the crow flies straight to the Oklahoma border. Or in his case, the eagle.

MICK ATE A quick midnight meal at home while doing the math. It would be about a four-hour round trip in eagle form, quicker if the wind worked in his favor. That was most of his night. He'd be lucky to get two hours of sleep before he had to get showered and dressed for his shift at Virgil's shop.

"No hunting," he told his eagle self as he stripped off his jeans and hoodie and opened his apartment door. Those 150 mile-per-hour dives would steal too much energy. The horned serpents and winged demons would have to live another night. That range of patrol was too much to ask of one thunderbird anyway, and taking extra territory would set a precedent he didn't want to keep. He had too many jobs already, especially during snow-plow season.

"West-southwest for sixty miles." He'd learned saying it aloud before shifting helped him stay on path. His eagle didn't use human directions or numbers, but somehow a translation occurred as skin became feathers and arms became wings. The one thing that needed no translation was his desire to find Waapikoona. It was a necessity shared by both man and eagle.

This new secret of his had built a wall between himself and every person he knew—a wall only he could see. The wall itself was also a secret, a secret on top of the secret it hid. He hadn't yet figured out if his father's talk of Mighty Eagle and wandering creatures in the woods were attributed to Mick's new reality or his father's own dementia, and Pop's behavior was too inconsistent to make a good case. For now, he had to keep pretending. Keep lying to the ones he loved. Waapikoona was the only one who knew and understood it all. The only one he could talk openly about it to, who shared this world with him. He was drowning in a sky of loneliness without her.

But at least the sky had no walls.

Unclothed, he stepped outside his basement apartment's door and surveyed the silent yard. He couldn't afford to get careless. It wasn't neighbors he worried about—this property was too far from town for anyone to be passing by at such a late hour, and the house sat far enough from the road that a naked man streaking across a yard would go unnoticed. If Old Mae was awake in the house above, he'd trust her to keep his secret. People in Wyona told enough secrets about Old Mae to make her sympathetic to any they told about him. No one would believe a story from her anyway.

What he worried about were Waapikoona's enemies, the ones who knew this house, this driveway, his connection to her. People like Jeremiah, who'd come here, raised Mick's mother from her grave to trap Mick, torture Mick, use Mick as bait for Waapikoona until she somehow managed to stir the eagle from Mick's dying bones. It seemed wrong for his eagle to follow commands from a person raised by the underworld, but he'd learned to stop questioning these things. All it did was keep him from sleep he desperately needed.

His human eyes gathered a sleepy February night in front of him. The hush of winter lay across dead grass and hibernating trees standing stiff and tall in still air. He ducked from under the overhang. Even the moon had gone to bed.

He climbed the steps and slapped his bad leg to wake it up. As if the limp wasn't enough, sometimes it liked to go to sleep on him then wake with renewed pain like it remembered the knife to the shin perfectly and didn't want Mick to forget. As if he could ever forget. The crippling agony, the helplessness, the woman who brought his eagle back. He shook off the stiffness, clenched his teeth through the pain, and took off across the yard, feet pounding rough cold ground in the uneven pattern of his new gait until the air filled the space between skin and earth and he lifted into starry night.

Time was both frozen and endless. The land rolled beneath him. Owls flapped from trees, enforcing their presence, giving a nod, a permission to pass even though they knew he needed none. A she-hawk joined him; he flapped harder, took a superfluous dive, showing off. He remembered his direction, his haste, and left her screeching back to her nest.

The woman who'd called him from death was waiting up ahead. She was his apex, his missing piece. She would heal the weakness growing inside him. If he didn't find her, soon he'd be broken.

Land below him smoothed and flattened as he flew. The glowing human lights on the ground mirrored the stars above. He soared between the matching realms, watching for a clue she might be near. Ahead he spotted the glimmer of a horned serpent's trail through the trees leading away from its sanctuary of water. He couldn't spare a dive now, not before he'd even reached the midpoint of his flight. If the serpent continued its path, it would find a cluster of lights illuminating human shelters—but it didn't matter. This happened every night he wasn't around. This was not his territory to patrol.

Pushing on, he thought of his goal, his long flight home. But as he passed over the serpent's gleaming rainbow scales, instead of flapping away he tilted a wing, circled, took inventory of his stamina. A meal might do him some good.

The sky spit a creature near enough for him to veer fast to the left. His eye never left it—a peregrine falcon diving at top speed. Into the trees it dropped then shot out as fast, with talons full of serpent it tore apart and released midair. Again it dived, snatching the front half and tearing the head off with enough force to fling it at the circling eagle who caught it, squeezed, and released the shredded flesh to the lake below.

The falcon called to him. He called back. He soared down to skim the water, rinse the poisonous serpent blood from his talons. Up again, the sky now empty, he was alone.

When he reached a fat river curling against the land, he banked wide and caught the wind blowing toward home. Frustration made him dip low—if he found no clues for her, he could at least kill a demon and make a night of it. And he was hungry, growing weak. A new type of weakness that

gained intensity with each night he patrolled. Some nights he wasn't sure he could shift back. Tonight would be one of those.

The ground shimmered with fresh rain. Ice grew at the edge of the puddles. He aimed for the mass of human light, hoping to catch a demon out for a hunt itself. Instinct flared; he looked near and far, ahead and behind. He sensed prey nearby but hiding—sentient enough to sense him and take cover. Its energy pulsed strong and large. Circling, he watched. The buildings below him slept. But one car parked with the others sang with life. He located a strong tree and soared down, taking a perch that gave him a view of that car.

A woman exited, leaving the door open. She looked right up at him, into his eyes then quickly away, like she understood his standing. On her hand, a thick glove with a long cuff that covered her halfway to elbow. He'd seen those before. That car—he'd seen that too. Intrigued, he hopped to a different branch that would accommodate his wingspan should he choose to dive.

The night slipped away as he watched the woman breathe her warmth into the cold air. He felt the press of his return flight, of the sun sneaking around the earth. If he didn't leave now, he'd never find the strength to return to human form. So he flapped into the sky and found the wind, grateful for its companionship on his path home.

HE FLEW STRAIGHT under the overhang above his apartment door and flapped to land on the step. Normally he'd have shifted back by now, but he was having trouble remembering what human legs felt like. He should have hunted for food on his flight back. His energy had run out long ago. If he could just get inside, he could rest then shift, but there was no way to get inside except by flying through the window pane, and he had no strength for that, and his human had no desire to fix another broken window.

Back to the woods, then. He'd have to sleep in a tree.

No. C'mon, Mick. It wasn't a thought but a call from his other side struggling upward. Human words could help. Human feelings, human thoughts. The hiss-snap of a cold Coke opening on a summer Saturday afternoon. Breaking the heads off rusted-on bolts underneath cars, busting knuckles. Driving an overpowered GTO fast enough to feel Death in the backseat. Weaving fingers into a woman's hair—Waapikoona's hair. Taking a fistful, stealing a kiss, his body flattening hers against that mausoleum wall.

He fell backward, elbows catching himself against cold stone, the impact jolting through his bones. His bad leg screamed alive, fully human.

"*Damn* it," he said. A human curse, a human voice. He needed to work on this shifting back part.

He dragged his leg inside and fell onto the couch, wondering why every shift began and ended with thoughts of Waapikoona.

Not enough hours later he woke, thought *work*, and got up. Shower, breakfast, pain-reliever for the leg. Keeping his worlds apart proved easier on some days than others. Today, the letdown was too much. That phone call, its nearby area code, her *voice* … and in the end he had nothing but a sorry heap of eagle feathers he stepped in while locking up his apartment on his way out. He took a moment to focus his sleep-deprived brain. If anyone saw this, they'd think a giant bird had been killed there and wonder where the blood was. No one would jump to *Mick Svendsen is a shape-shifter.* He'd clean it up later.

Spot greeted him in the yard with a cold, slobbery nose against his hand. Mick found a stick and chucked it—pitifully. The dog ran anyway, happy for the game no matter how easy. Starting the day this tired, with his leg acting up, and a storm in his head …

He found another stick and flung it so hard and far that Spot uprooted turf to chase it. He rotated his shoulder, felt it click in an unnatural way. He'd feel that later. Wouldn't feel worse than the defeat of the first throw, so he'd gladly take it. Defeat wasn't going to take him anytime soon, no matter how trivial the task.

Old Mae called the dog as he started up the GTO, and Spot tore across the field, stick in mouth, straight into Old Mae's front door. She walked out to the porch railing to catch Mick's eye. He waved as he backed out and turned the car around, not at all missing the look that said, *Get your troubles together, boy. You're upsetting my cats.* It'd been awhile since he'd heard that.

When he entered the shop, Virgil's eyes went straight to his leg.

"That limp's gettin' worse."

Mick tried to ease up, found it impossible. "Nah, just stiff today. It'll loosen up good in a minute."

"You take somethin' for it?"

"Yeah, just waitin' for it to kick in."

He went in the back, grateful to find his coveralls because they hadn't been at home. As he slid them on, he got a flash of memory from the night—the overhead view of a rain-soaked motel parking lot where a woman stood beside a black car that looked very much like the 300ZX Waapikoona vandalized in Wyona the day he met her. Grinding his palms against his closed eyes, he dug into his eagle's mind for more detail. It was there, imagery blurred by bad translation into human sight but clear enough to see the car had the same rims and aftermarket exhaust. That model year was rare enough it had to be the right car. And the woman—hazel-eyed, fair-headed, not Waapikoona. He was thankful his eagle vision picked up that kind of color from one street-light shining on the night below because to his eagle, all human women generally looked the same. If it had been her, he hoped his eagle would know. But his eagle was prone to making split-second decisions sometimes he couldn't follow. He needed to learn to trust his eagle.

"You okay, man?"

Mick lowered his hands from his eyes and found the other morning mechanic standing in front of him.

"Yeah, I'm good."

"Coffee?" Andy held out a cup. "Just poured. Ain't touched it yet."

"Already had some. Don't wanna get the shakes. Thanks, though."

The kid let the slack slip sometimes, but at least he was a decent guy. Not many people could do this job every day and not get sick of it once in a while, especially young guys who weren't so deep in bills and responsibility that chang-ing the twentieth brake pad for the day wasn't some kind of pointless joke.

Mick knew the joke, and it was how much could the world pile on one man before he broke? He pulled some tools and got to work on his project from the day before.

A lot more, so bring it.

After work Mick drove through the ATM to make sure the overtime he'd worked was on yesterday's paycheck and had hit his account in time for him to spend it on a grocery

run. He'd left his coveralls on to avoid having to pry his bad leg out of them in front of an audience at work—another guy was taking his sweet time in the back room, and Mick had to get out of there to check on Pop.

The grocery store parking lot reminded him of Waapikoona every damn week. Tonight it reminded him of that damn car. In the doorway to the store he stopped short—that rain-soaked motel lot holding that 300ZX? She'd been there. *She* was the prey his eagle had sensed, and his eagle had stopped there—

Something hit him from behind.

He turned around and found a woman's startled eyes. Baby on her hip, gripping a set of keys. "Sorry! You—I didn't figure you'd be stoppin'—"

"No, that was my fault. Sorry, ma'am." He stepped aside, allowing her to go in front of him. As she passed, she paused, glancing at his name on his coveralls. Old habit sent his attention straight to her left hand—no ring. He realized what a romantic comedy meetup this was, and he carefully guided his gaze away, locked down the polite Midwestern smile, and tried to grab the tail of the thought that had made him stop like an idiot in the doorway with people behind him.

If that car was there, then she was there … or nearby. It was too much of a coincidence to get a call from her in an area code and find that car parked there too. It seemed he and that car were hunting the same woman. He hadn't planned to go back that way since it had proven so unsuccessful, but tonight was his night off from the U-Fill, and a car like that couldn't hide as easily as a woman who travels through caves and time. He had to go back. But first he had to grab some groceries and check on Pop.

Overtime pay meant he could get something good and hearty so he could shift and find something equally hearty for his eagle before hitting the sky. He also snagged some fresh fruit and a fancy angel food cake from the bakery, half of which would stay with Pop and half would go home with him so he could share it with Dougie and Janie the next time his sister dropped them off. He lingered in the beer aisle, deciding it was too expensive and too risky to schedule in an evening of downtime. If Waapikoona put more distance between them, he'd never find her.

After rounding the end of the aisle and nearly running into the same woman for the third time, he laughed. With each near collision, her smile had gotten more shy—probably a response to his practiced stone-face—but this time, his laugh caused her to look him dead in the eyes. He silently cursed Waapikoona and all her teasing, only to give him nothing and leave him.

But he'd teased back. And it wasn't her fault; he was the one who'd refused to take her to bed. Now he was pathetically hooked on her and running into cute women in stores. Maybe the universe was telling him to move on.

Screw the universe. It never did anything for him.

She pointed to his name tag. "Are you Kari's brother?"

Christ. Of course she knew him. Dang small towns.

"Yep." As much as he tried to ditch the eye contact, manners made it happen.

"I pray for Helen every day."

"Me too." It was a lie. Mick had stopped praying to the god he'd been raised on long ago. If God was responsible for his young mother's death, his father's early dementia, his baby niece's endless medical procedures and hospital stays that no one could afford and wouldn't cure an incurable disease anyway, he was done with faith. Prayer didn't work. What worked was Mick busting his butt to help Kari with the bills. It was Kari driving her baby girl hundreds of

miles to the city where the specialized doctors were. Early in his young adult life he experienced a painful reckoning. He couldn't be abandoned by a god who wasn't there to begin with.

Mick managed to untangle, get through the checkout line, and escape into the night air. He filled his chest with it, tasting the crisp shock of winter, the scent of burning leaves drifting in from a nearby farm. He worried spending so much time in bird form was making him anti-social, claustrophobic, possibly inhuman.

It couldn't be helped.

On the drive to Pop's, he opened the windows in the GTO to feel the deep winter air rushing past. If he ignored the friction from the tires on the road, it was almost like flying.

Pop met him at the front door, looking jumpy and strained. He wished he could go back to the days when he'd show up and find his father absorbed in the same TV program he'd seen twenty times, zoned out and pleasant and not all riled up like he seemed to be every day now. Mick was there to drop off food and do a quick check. He had no time to jump into anything too complex. Tonight he had other duties.

But guilt never really asks. It just barrels in, unwelcome, unhelpful, too stubborn to leave, and even though the stuff in Pop's head was nonsense to Mick, it was real to Pop, and the guilt liked to keep Mick aware of that.

He handed Pop a sack of groceries, working to come up with a way to bring Pop back around to that pleasant distraction. "Check out them grapes I got you. I tasted 'em in the store. Real sweet."

Mick raised his grocery bags away from Spot's curious nose and beating tail. Kari must've brought him over this morning. Since Waapikoona left, the dog had gained a warm

bed at Pop's, Kari's, and Old Mae's. He offered companionship and protection—two things not very useful to Mick's
often empty apartment.

"Listen, Mickey, can you keep a secret?"

"You know I can."

Pop put a hand on Mick's shoulder, steering him inside
so he could shut the door. "Mickey, can you keep a secret?"

Sometimes Mick couldn't determine if the repeated questions were done for emphasis or if they were part of the
dementia. "You know I can, Pop."

Pop's hand remained on Mick's shoulder. "There's a little
Indian girl in my back woods."

This bit of nonsense put a chunk of cold in Mick's gut.
He took a breath, thawed it away. "You been watchin' one
of your history programs today?"

"No, I been watchin' her. She don't speak English, at
least I don't think. Won't come near. She's usin' the blanket
I give her but won't touch the food. I don't think she got
any clothes."

Mick dropped the grocery bags on the floor and went
out Pop's back door.

"Two o'clock," Pop said behind him.

Human vision did Mick no favors especially in the dark,
and the floodlights could only reach into the edge of the
woods. But there, against the hollow of a tree, milky eyes
stared from a gaunt face wrapped in Pop's plaid throw. He
had to get closer, make sure it wasn't some kind of shared
demented illusion. There was a time Mick had thought he
had the dementia too, and that would be a better explanation right now. The truth of this vision was rising, bright
and clear, filling in blanks he'd long forgotten to fill in. On
the day Waapikoona had walked away from him, she'd been
carrying a bag of her sister's bones. Not an easy thing to

travel with. So if she'd gone to Oklahoma, she likely reburied those bones somewhere in Wyona or the surrounding
Ozark mountains. Now he was pretty sure he'd figured out
where. He limped down the steps into the yard.

"You get too close, she'll run," Pop warned behind him.

Sure enough, the girl stiffened, shifting her legs like a
rabbit sensing a predator and prepping to flee. Mick instinc-
tively went for the top button on his coveralls, ready to take
his other form, give chase, and catch her. That wouldn't be
right. It would be inhuman. And he couldn't do it in front
of Pop.

He could catch her as a man, even with his bad leg. She
wasn't any older than Dougie, and even though she'd sensed
him, from the looks of those eyes she had to be blind. He'd
snatch up the blanket she'd surely leave behind, use it to
scoop her up and wrap around her to keep her from fighting. But that would also be inhuman. This was going to be
a long, slow coax from the trees, a complicated, time-con-
suming building of trust. He couldn't leave to track down
Waapikoona tonight, and now he needed her more than ever.

CHAPTER
3

INDECISION WAS A new illness that Waapikoona had no immunity to face. In her first life, every choice had made itself, even the one that led to the foot of the cliff that marked the death of herself and her sister. There was one option, one outcome. Now, she had too many in front of her, too many behind her. None of them agreed. None of them sought harmony.

After collecting Pinepakatwi's bones from the tomb where she and Mick killed Jeremiah, she'd kept watch over them until the next moon phase. She'd moved them from forest to cemetery to the mouth of a cave, staying active during the day when Mick would be working his human jobs, sheltering in at night when his eagle would be patrolling. But the bones remained as cold and lifeless as ever. So she'd packed them up, reburied them in the safest place she knew of, and left Wyona to continue her work for The Silent One. Being in those gentle Missouri mountains and so close to Mick

gave her that most unharmonious option: staying with him. Her work and her life could not allow that.

Before her stretched the highway that led to her people, the ones who raised her in this second life. They'd taken her in as a strange orphan from the woods who had no family, language, or memories. They'd taught her a dying language they were trying to revive, hoping it was close enough to hers that she could find peace in the familiar. She was different. They knew it as clearly as she did, but they accepted her and loved her. Then Jeremiah had found her and she ran away with him, hunting for answers, finding understanding and a surprising solace through his world before it all went bad and she left him behind too.

He was a twisted, cruel, and mutinous pawn of The Silent One. She was glad he was dead. She was glad it was Mick who'd torn out his throat. Death by Thunder-Being was the most fitting end for a spirit raised from the underworld. Maybe she was the mutinous one.

Or maybe Jeremiah had simply been in her way, and now he'd been pushed aside.

If that was all it was, her path would be clear, just as it had been before—satisfy her quota set by The Silent One. Raise her sister from bones, keep her safe, give her the happy life that was stolen from her hundreds of years ago. It seemed so easy until Mick. The path had forked, and with him, she'd taken the wrong side. She needed to get back on the right one. The one without him.

So she had to go home, search for information anyone might have on Jeremiah, who his people were, how she could find the man he'd raised from bones as a gift to her. Gilbert Hammond, headmaster of the Indian school in her first life, with his punishing lye soap and vicious hands. His ways to create new rules on the fly so children could be punished for things they didn't know weren't allowed. She wouldn't find peace until he was gone from this world.

While at home she could find a nice Native man to wash Mick away. Even better—a bad Native man. With bad habits, violent instincts, a criminal record. That was Jeremiah, though, and she'd had him, had enough of him, left him, and he'd found her and tried to make her pay for all of that. She already had a full portion of bad in her. Being linked to The Silent One was enough. She needed a good man for a quick fling, for masculine hands on her body and rough lips on hers that would replace old memories with new ones so she could focus on that quota and forget about Mick.

She had no time for good-natured white men, Thunder-Beings, or love.

If she continued onto this highway to her people, she could find her place again. So she swung her leg over her motorcycle and started it up, breaking in the new winter day like indecision had never plagued her.

The tinted visor on her helmet dimmed the spread of ice blue sky above. The brown winter prairie lay flat below it, too lifeless to compete for space. She sped across the bridge over the river and wondered how many serpents The Silent One had released into its expanse. All that water gave the local Thunder-Beings quite a hunting ground.

As she passed the Tribal administration building, she downshifted, looking for recognizable cars even though she'd been gone too long. The cars would be different. The people would be the same, she hoped, and she hit the gas, compelled by a wave of homesickness this town would ease but never cure. It was her other home she grieved, the one buried by centuries of colonialism. For the first time she felt a stab of dread for what she planned to do. Yanking her sister out of the past, from the peace of death—was it wrong? Was she

homesick and selfish, reviving her sister only to soften her own grief, naïve to think her sister would want to be raised from the earth into this time?

She'd have to ponder that later. Riding down the streets of her childhood brought on a different kind of grief. The flutter in her stomach wasn't just nerves but regret, and it didn't mix well with everything else. She found her foster home's street and turned onto it, slowing her speed. Cracked asphalt driveways branched from the narrow street toward little homes covered in neutral shades of siding, all paled from the sun. The roofs were stained, their shingles curling with age, but the yards were tidy and the windows were clean. One lot had gained a trailer, another, a shiny metal shed. Her foster home was at the end, behind the grove of pines that had doubled in size. She coasted up the driveway and killed the engine, startling a flock of blackbirds from the trees. As she flipped the kickstand, a man came out the storm door and let it slap closed behind him.

It only took a moment for Waapikoona to recognize Sam, now older, grayer, crossing his arms and staring her down like she was unknown trouble in his front yard. She knew that look well, and the process that went along with it. Sized up, questioned, and sentenced—all without him uttering a word.

She took off her helmet. His stare softened at once, and he dropped his arms to make an urgent double knock behind him on the storm door, all while holding on to her gaze as if she'd vanish if he looked away. Josie appeared through the glass behind him, looking annoyed, her words muffled until she caught sight of Waapikoona and then they came through loud and clear.

"Sam! Is that her?"

"You tell me," he said. "I'd guess I'm still asleep and dreaming."

Waapikoona dismounted and propped her helmet on the seat. When she turned around, Josie had joined Sam outside, her hands over her mouth, her eyes wet. Waapikoona wished she'd prepared for this, had come up with something to say on the road because now all language escaped her. She took a deep breath and shut down the tremble in her chest and prickle in her eyes. She didn't expect to cry here, and she wouldn't do it.

"I'm sorry," she began. She didn't want to apologize. No apology would cover it.

Sam had backed up to steer Josie into the house, and he held the door open for Waapikoona, waiting. "It's warmer inside, if you'd like to come in."

No pressure, no obligation. It was almost like he was afraid she'd run away again, right now, and he was making an effort not to scare her. It was that gentle hand that had made her feel so at home as a child. When she'd woken from death, she still remembered the sting of the white man's hand. Of discipline in the Indian school that enforced rules so unfair that failure and punishment was part of the curriculum just as English and religion.

Inside, the house smelled of burned sage and good food. She took off her boots and handed her coat to Sam. He paused as he took it from her, giving her a long look of thinly guarded joy. "We are so very glad to have you here, Waapikoona."

Without a response, the moment stretched into a poignancy she couldn't deal with now. She couldn't hug him. She would break down. So she simply nodded and passed beside him into the kitchen where Josie was putting a kettle on the stove.

"Did you eat lunch yet?"

"I'm not hungry."

"I'll make some sandwiches."

Waapikoona pulled out a chair and sat. She'd had nothing to eat or drink since the gas station coffee and donut when she'd set out at sunrise that morning. After hours on the road she should be starving, but her stomach felt heavy and disinterested.

"Herbal or black?"

"Whatever you have out."

Josie set a mug holding a tea bag in front of her. When she didn't walk away, Waapikoona looked up.

"The world has hardened our girl, Sam."

"She was never ours," he answered, leaning a shoulder against the doorway. "Too much spirit in this girl to belong to anyone. I think it's more that we belong to her."

"Will you come sit and stop with that?" Waapikoona pushed a chair out with her foot. She had to change the subject. "Where's Daniel?"

"Colorado. Married a nice boy and found a great job there."

"Lily?"

"Got a scholarship in Texas."

She *had* been gone long if the youngest of her foster siblings had grown up and left for college. The house was too quiet, too absent of toys, shoes, and backpacks to lead her to believe Sam and Josie had taken on any more orphans. All the things they'd done for her and she couldn't even take the time to call them and find out how they were doing. Years ago she'd have blamed it on Jeremiah for persuading her to run away, but now the only one to blame was herself.

Sam joined Josie at the counter to help with the food, giving Waapikoona a moment to dwell on that blame. She'd run from this haven straight into the darkest places of the world, to mingle with devils—both human and demon. Long ago she'd given up believing they hadn't rubbed off on her. Too many times she'd had to think like them, spend time with them. If she'd kept in touch with her foster home, that illness would've infected the haven contained in these four walls. Growing up here she had the hard memories of her previous life, but she'd made new ones every day, and even though she felt different she never felt unwanted.

The ills she'd witnessed and performed could not be brought back here. Severing contact had been the right thing. Regret she'd take, but not blame.

Pricked by that regret, she got up and gave Josie a long sideways hug. Josie put down her knife to squeeze her back with one arm as if the gaping hole of time had never divided them. This was the woman who'd sat for hours on the edge of her bed convincing her it was safe to fall asleep. She was a mother, teacher, and a friend, always ready to listen. And still ready—but Waapikoona couldn't tell her anything. Coming home wouldn't solve her loneliness. It would compound it.

The tea kettle whistled. Josie took it off the burner and handed it to Waapikoona. She sensed Josie and Sam's stiff dedication to preparing lunch might be busy work to fill in the space of the question they were both dying to ask but afraid might scare her off. She spared them. "I haven't decided how long I'm staying. A couple days, maybe, if you'll have me."

Sam let the statement sit just long enough to keep them from looking too excited. "Love to have you," he said. "Your old room is all yours."

Waapikoona didn't waste the breath to explain they couldn't scare her off now. Staying in touch would be tricky, but not impossible, and this time she was going to try. She should have tried long ago. Back then, and through the years, she'd kept her distance for other reasons—many she couldn't divulge. Explaining all this took too much effort with little payoff. She'd have to prove it to them instead. As she filled their tea mugs with hot water she realized something else they were both probably wanting to know. The last time she'd spoken to them, they'd gently suggested she not become so attached to Jeremiah.

"Jeremiah's dead."

Josie looked at Sam; Sam looked at Waapikoona. And the apprehension on his face gave Waapikoona a need to clarify who killed him. "He messed with the wrong ... man."

"He messed with a lot of men."

He was speaking of himself on that. She restrained another useless apology that would never cover the past. "I took your advice and cut him off years ago, but he came back and ..." Found her with a white man, tried to force her to kill him, got himself killed by that white man's Thunder-Being. She couldn't tell them any of this and didn't want to tread any closer to speaking of Mick. "You were right."

"Had no doubt. His people—"

"Sam." Josie turned from assembling sandwiches to lay a gently scolding hand on his arm.

"Hey, now, I'm not being impolite. It's just that some Blackfeet moved in across the river and they're the nicest folks. I take back everything I said in anger."

Waapikoona sat a bit straighter, her interest piqued. She stirred sugar into her tea and wondered at the reason she'd be offered news so random yet so pointedly helpful. The Silent One could play people in ways such as this, but only if they were part of his ever-expanding shadow. Josie and Sam were not—they were people living in their own time, unaware of the war building underneath them. They knew she'd lost her people, but they didn't know when or where. They thought she was an orphan with amnesia, unmatched to any missing persons list. They didn't know she was out of her time. They didn't know she was undead.

Jeremiah had been Blackfeet. If she could find these people, she could determine if they were fighting the same war he'd been fighting. They might know a contact who'd been working with him, someone who could tell her where Hammond was being held. Jeremiah claimed he'd raised her old headmaster as a gift for her, an incentive to join his group and prove her mutiny against The Silent One. She didn't want mutiny; she wanted out. And she couldn't kill Hammond until she'd met her quota and revived her sister— she wasn't sure what The Silent One would do to her if she killed one of his risen …

Only she had. Jeremiah was dead, and she'd taken the blame. Her punishment had yet to be dealt. She could wait it out, see what The Silent One decided to do.

Or maybe Mick would find Hammond first.

She hoped not. She wanted to tear Hammond's throat out with her teeth.

But first she had a veggie sandwich to eat.

AN HOUR BEFORE dusk Waapikoona set out on foot. Leaving her motorcycle would give Josie and Sam reason to know she was coming back. It would also give her the walk under the sky of her home that she craved, the scuff of dry earth under her boots pulled away on the unforgiving wind. Indian Country could be desolate, but it was familiar and it sang with survival. That Indian survival, though, it was

so cliché. So romanticized by outsiders she wondered if her people would ever be viewed as humans and not relics. The whole thing was bogus. But the truth was her people were here, present, everlasting. She'd crossed time and found a different world on the other side and a people changed by that world, but also similar enough to feel like she was just a few steps away from home.

Some days, the closeness of the similarity was a comfort. Other days, it was a cruel imitation. The constant was her misplaced self, living out of time with the people who were supposed to be hers. Jeremiah had promised to lead her to where she belonged. He had answers she spent years not knowing, and his lure was a promise to finally fit. And here she was, back in her adopted home, as out of place as ever. She'd had decades to acclimate to being misplaced.

Today she found peace in the bleakness of an empty road cutting through town, of the steady quiet, of the big sky hanging so low against the earth it seemed to be the answer to why it was so flat. She crunched through a layer of frost, her steps the only sound besides the wind, her motion given importance by the weight of wide space around her. If time had stopped its unending circle, she'd be blissfully unaware.

And in this solitude, she remembered the frustration of her teenage boredom in this town and the person always willing to talk her out of a slump. It had been so many years, but if he was still here, he was exactly the person who could purge her of Mick.

She crossed the street and took an alley behind a strip of closed shops. Old snow swooped against the rear of the building, a dense arctic blue in the last scraps of daylight. This side faced north, so she cut across the cleared field beside her and found the dry creek bed that would take her to the right plot of land. The last time she'd walked this path was to say goodbye.

It had been hot and dry, the sun baking her hair against the sweat on her neck. The creek had been wet but stagnant, mossy green and swarming with insects. In her haste—recklessness, she recognized now—she'd hopped the water but missed, soaking her sandals. Later, when she'd met Jeremiah at the pick-up spot he'd yelled at her for getting wet shoes in his car. She should have known. Should have gotten out of his car and gone home. But she was blinded by the dream of what lay ahead. The abuses that started that moment had leveled up with each passing day. Its goal was to break her down. But every rough grab of her shoulders and every name call brought back a new memory from her first life. Sarah had been broken. Waapikoona had been raised from her bones.

Waapikoona could not be broken again.

An outsider who came in and stole her away, Jeremiah had never known her real name. Everything he did had been done to Sarah. Waapikoona didn't need to acknowledge the scars if they weren't hers.

She followed the creek bed to the curve where three corpse-sized stones jutted from the steep bank. Above them, what had once been the mouth to a trail was now grown over. Pushing through winter underbrush wouldn't be difficult; gaining purchase to do so on the iced edge of those stones was what gave her pause. She could backtrack and find a better spot where the bank wasn't so steep, but the light was quickly draining away. It wouldn't feel right anyway. This was her path to Rain's trailer. Using any other way after all these years just felt wrong.

One boot on the first stone, she tested for slippage before heaving herself up. Her teenage self could scale these rocks

like a lizard. She made it to the second one and lost a foot over the edge, banging her knee. Up on the top, she stayed low like an animal, ducked her head, and pushed through, snapping limbs that snagged her hood and scratched her cheek. When she made it to Rain's, she'd chide him for letting the trail grow over. He wasn't but a couple years older than her. Did he give up walking the creek? Nothing kept that man from the outdoors, not even the dead of winter.

The brush thinned and she stood up, straightening her coat and shaking out her hair. As she raised her hood against the encroaching night's cold, she realized how many years it had been. She hadn't asked Josie and Sam about Rain. He could have moved away. He could have a wife, a family. He would be no help to her then.

She pushed the remaining way through the woods until it opened against high dry grass and not too far ahead the back of Rain's beige trailer facing a gravel road. A black Jeep Wrangler sat in the dirt nearby, but the trailer's windows were dark, one of them boarded with plywood. And damn it if that didn't remind her of Mick's own boarded apartment window when here she was working so hard to forget him.

Nearing the Jeep, she noticed two tires dangerously low on air. She peered inside, saw a jacket on the seat and a take-out coffee cup in the cupholder. If those were signs of life, the two-by-four across the front door of his trailer was not.

Knocking would be silly; no one lived in a boarded-up trailer. She walked around it, trying to find a window she could see into, but all were covered with shades. She sat on the front step to think.

It would be easy to conclude he'd moved if it weren't for the Jeep. Rain had always driven a Jeep. He'd pick her up from school with the top down and take her for ice cream in the little shop the next town over, his hair and her hair so tangled from the wind and dirt by the time they arrived he'd close the sun visor mirror as she tried to fix her hair and say, "Fuck it. We're savages, right?" And she'd laugh, her mouth gritty from all the gravel dust that had been kicked up in that open-air Jeep. Even though he was a half-breed, he wore his hair long like he was full-blooded Indian, so proud and brazen she wished someday she could be like him. She envied his freedom but not his reason for it. He'd dropped out of high school to work minimum wage. *A life sentence*, he'd called it, both a joke and a warning. But his home life was plagued with drinking, poverty, and bruises, and he told her he had to get out before he contracted the disease. He said kids named after weather like them needed to stick together, and he never tried to kiss her until the day she came to say goodbye.

A light blinked on across the expanse of frosted grass before her, bringing her attention to a new mobile home sitting across the road. She headed toward it, wondering why Rain would abandon this trailer for one that looked smaller, and where he got the money for that nice new pickup sitting against it without trading in his Jeep.

The front door opened and a woman came out in pink pajamas and snow boots. She stopped short when she saw Waapikoona across the road, seemed to determine she was no threat, and clomped over to the mailbox to insert a letter and raise the flag.

"Hello," Waapikoona called as she crossed the road.

The woman stopped to study her more fully.

"Is Rain home?"

"Rain? He's—"

Waapikoona was close enough for conversation now, but the woman wasn't finishing her sentence. Rain's wife, then, wondering what some random woman walking in the chill

of winter could want with her husband. She was younger—mid-twenties—with big dark eyes and thin shoulders braced against the cold.

The woman hugged herself. "I'm sorry, who are you?"

"An old friend of Rain's. I just got back home and hoped to—"

"Rain's dead."

Dead. It fell like a tree in the night, silent until it hit. Unknown, then so utterly final.

"He took his own life."

Waapikoona turned away to stare across the road at Rain's trailer, its boarded front door. The Jeep sitting crooked on two nearly flat tires. All of it made sense but nothing made sense. This wasn't what she came home for, and she didn't want it, couldn't take it, had to get out.

"When?" she whispered into the cold.

"A couple months ago. I'm really sorry. He was such a nice neighbor, always helping out. I—everyone was shocked."

Waapikoona wasn't shocked, she was numb, and so suddenly tired she couldn't even speak. She'd made it to the road when the woman called, "Hey, any chance you're Waapikoona?"

She turned around.

"Hold on, he left you something." The trailer door squeaked open and snapped closed. Then the woman was in front of her again as if time had stopped and restarted in a new spot. "He left a note saying if you ever came back, the Jeep was yours." She passed Waapikoona a key.

Coming back here like this, for what she wanted from Rain, using him like that … she'd been rubbed by evil for so long she had indeed turned wicked.

"Your name, it means 'snow,' right? Rain told me you were just like him, only colder. I get it now." The woman smiled against a glint of tears unrelated to the bitter wind.

Waapikoona wasn't sure that was what her name meant anymore. "Where's his grave?"

"His dad had him cremated. Still has the ashes as far as I know. A real bummer too. Rain hated that guy ..." Her face had gone sour.

Waapikoona turned east, working to remember where Rain's childhood house was. "If those ashes go missing ..." She left it there, hoping to leave it unspoken.

The woman dropped her look of disgust so fast it seemed it was never there. "What ashes?"

Waapikoona didn't follow it with, *And if Rain's father goes missing ...?* She figured it was implied. And when the woman raised her chin, gave a little nod, and went inside without a goodbye, she knew she was being counted on for righting a wrong and would be held to it until Rain's spirit found peace, no matter what. Native woman to Native woman, this was a pact that would never be broken.

Gripping the Jeep key, she crossed the road and assessed the tires. They were drivable but not for long. Mick would scold her—damn him for invading every innocent thought. She turned the key, expecting a dead engine but everything came alive, radio blaring '90s rock. Flipping on the head-lights sent a small, powerful shape in their glare bounding into the shadows. Her third Helper had finally caught up.

After a stop at a gas station to inflate the tires, she drove to the house Rain had left as a young man. It sat far enough off the road a person might miss it, except for at night when the porch light against white siding turned it ghostlike through the trees. She remembered how he'd slow the Jeep and point it out each time they passed by, his eyes linger-

ing on the door. Rapt, seething, full of premeditation. For what, she wasn't sure. Rain wasn't a fighter or a killer, and back then neither was she.

She passed the house, now smaller and grungier than she remembered, and parked the Jeep beside the road a few miles away. This would be tricky. Walk a few miles, kill a man and release her Helpers without alerting the man's wife, steal their dead son's ashes, get out without anyone seeing her. Only The Silent One could pull off a job so silent, so she hopped out of the Jeep and summoned him to possess her.

CHAPTER
4

Food was no lure for the girl. Mick discovered that unhelpful truth after offering one choice after another. So many, that he'd filled his own stomach with bites he took himself to show it wasn't poisoned. Mick had no idea what Indians from the nineteenth century were used to eating, but it sure wasn't lunch meat, potato chips, and angel food cake. Even the fresh grapes Pop was munching on from the back stoop were no help. Gigantic, genetically modified, they probably scared her worst of all.

So he sat in the brittle grass and put his head in his hands. The right thing to do was tell Pop to go to bed, shift into a thunderbird, and destroy her. She was born from the underworld. She was his prey. It was his duty.

He couldn't kill Waapikoona. He couldn't kill her sister either. And if this girl wasn't her sister, then he had a worse moral dilemma of undead children sprouting up all over Wyona County that he'd have to destroy. He wouldn't do it.

Raising his head, he looked at the girl. She looked back. The flood lights from the house lit the night between them in a harsh gray, every object casting a long shadow across the snow-blotted yard. Her eyes, milky white just a moment ago, had turned normal. It hadn't been blindness—she could see the food he was offering her, would move in response to him tossing grapes and granola bars. But now it seemed the cover of death had fully receded, leaving her as human as Waapikoona, and with an understanding—hopefully—that if he was a bad guy he wouldn't be waiting so patiently for her to come to him. Her hair was clipped blunt and level with her chin, but other than that, her eyes and face were a perfect imitation of Waapikoona's. He could prove it. He had a picture on his phone. Unsure if it would help, he had to try, so he got out his phone and opened his photos.

It hurt him to look at it. The two of them, halfway up the big mound in Cahokia, minutes away from a kiss and a union that had changed him in ways he'd never undo. They were together that day. A team, until it all cracked apart. He could blame her. He could blame himself. But it wasn't such a narrow decision made by one person. It was the universe that had determined they didn't fit.

The universe was wrong.

"I got a picture of your sister Waapikoona," he said. "She'd want you to come inside where it's warm." He watched her face for any hint of understanding, but it remained as guarded as ever. The line between her eyebrows folded deeper than it should on any little girl. "Waapikoona," he said again.

She mouthed the word, frowning, like she knew it but couldn't place it. He turned the screen toward her and she jolted, scrambling back the six inches of progress she had made in the last two hours.

Mick spotted his mistake as those six inches were stolen away. Phones, computers, electronic screens—this girl had never seen one. And he's flashing her a digital picture of an unfamiliar relative, a sister who was a child just like her when they died. She wouldn't recognize who Waapikoona was now, and even if she did, she'd never understand how he'd captured her image on a screen.

"Stupid," Mick muttered, straightening out his bad leg. He always thought he was good with kids, but this was a failure. Waapikoona could fix this but she was unreachable. He needed someone more sympathetic to a little girl. Someone she could relate to more than an adult man. Someone she could trust.

He didn't want to bring a sane person into this scene, but after another hour his leg would be dead and he'd be giving up anyway. Wasting that hour seemed as stupid as trying to win over a girl from a history book with a modern smart phone. He dialed his sister's number.

"Hey," Kari answered.

"Can I pick up Dougie? I need his help at Pop's."

"Why—is he okay?"

"Yeah, he's fine. But there's a ... small problem, and I ain't havin' any luck. It needs a kid's touch."

"It's pretty late, Mickey—"

"I'll keep him the night. Have him pack a bag. I'm on my way."

Twenty minutes later Mick's headlights swept across Kari's driveway and Doug came blasting out, coat halfway on, backpack barely hanging on to one shoulder. He hopped in the car and tossed his bag in the backseat.

"Buckle up," Mick said, shifting into reverse and backing out.

"You find another alien?"

Mick checked himself. It was a constant thing, working to remember what people might know and editing his words before they came out of his mouth. Together he and Doug had found Waapikoona's first demon, gutted under the bed in Mick's apartment. His first kill, his first shift into eagle, before he knew what he was, what any of this was. He couldn't remember if he'd corrected Doug and Doug was calling it an alien out of habit or if he really still believed that's what it was.

"You ever tell your mom about that?"

"Not really. I was afraid she'd freak out."

"It ain't good keepin' things from your mom."

Doug sighed, too big and heavy for a ten-year-old kid. "I know. Just didn't want her to have more junk to worry about."

"I hear ya there, bud." Mick thought about asking about baby Helen, but he already knew the answer would be a slight deviation from the last one. *Helen cried all night and Mom called the doctor twelve times.* He couldn't go there right now. "So what's goin' on tonight ain't as weird, but it's a little more ..." Mick couldn't find a word that would work. Secrets weren't bad, but he didn't want to get Doug into the habit of keeping them.

"Scary?" Doug tried.

"... private. And not just from your mom. Though this one won't upset your mom so much. I'm more thinkin' it should stay a family thing."

"Like, family secret? Kinda like them bills from the hospital?"

"Right. So if anyone, like a teacher, or neighbor, or policeman asks about this, you tell 'em nothin' but that they need to talk to your uncle Mick about it."

"Yeah, okay. So what is it?"

Last chance. He could spare the kid from this rift in reality. Without Waapikoona, there was no way to solve this other than giving Doug a try. He'd already seen the gutted demon. He was already a part of this. "There's a girl 'bout your age hidin' in your grandpop's woods, and I need you to help get 'er to come out."

BY THE TIME Mick killed the GTO's engine in Pop's driveway, Doug had already developed a plan. The shark-tooth necklace he was wearing was his second favorite one, not his first, so he'd part with it as a peace offering. Then he'd show her his drawings—only the least scary animal combinations, like the dragonfly bumblebee or chipmunk sparrow. And he'd walk into the edge of the woods by the driveway and come upon her like that instead of from the house. He wanted to win her over as if he were another child lost in the woods, before she knew he was with Mick and Pop. Then he'd bring Mick out to her once he'd gained her trust. It felt like a trick, and Mick told him that. Doug insisted it was most important to make her into a friend, and everything to come after that would work out.

They got out of the car. Mick zipped Doug into his coat, cinched the hood tight, and helped him into his gloves.

"Now if you get too cold, you come on back in, all right? If your toes start to tingle—"

Doug lifted a foot. "I got my snow boots on. I'm good."

"I'll be watchin' you from the house. Be sure to stay where I can see you."

Doug crossed the side yard and walked the lit edge of the woods toward the back of the house, armed with a pack of Skittles he'd been saving in his bag, his sketchbook, and a pencil. As soon as he was out of sight, Mick went in the front of the house and turned off every light inside so he and Pop could spy without being seen. He checked the weather on his phone. Temperature still above freezing, but dropping fast. The kid was bundled, but what he'd just sent him to do would look crazy to anyone but him and Pop. He'd give it fifteen minutes. If Doug made no progress, he'd call him back to the house to create a new plan.

Through the window he could see Doug's neon green snow boots stepping over branches just inside the edge of trees. Mick had lost sight of the girl. She'd retreated too far away from the reach of the floodlight. He wasn't even certain she was still there.

"Hey, Pop, you think she's still out there?"

"Yep." He handed Mick a set of binoculars.

"These got night vision? Ain't that fancy."

Mick lifted the binoculars to his eyes and found Doug in the trees, squatting then sitting. Several yards past him, the low movement of a hunkering girl. He wished he'd been able to mic him to know what he was saying, but whatever it was seemed promising. She hadn't fled.

"Coffee?" Pop asked.

"Yeah. You got decaf?" Caffeine at this time of day would ruin him.

Doug lowered his hood, raised the shark-tooth necklace over his head. He held it in the empty air in front of him for so long Mick marveled at his stamina. His arm had to be well past tired, and he wasn't normally a stubborn kid. His lips moved, on and on, until finally he covered his eyes with his free arm. A shadow moved toward him, snatching that necklace so fast Mick thought Doug would spook, but all he did was rock on his heels from the force and then slowly lower his arm from his eyes.

Mick took a sip of the coffee Pop handed him while resting his vision from the binoculars. "He already made more progress than you and I did in two hours."

"Somethin' special about that boy." Pop lowered himself into a kitchen chair. Spot saw a vacant lap and rested his head, winning an ear rub. "How come you never had any kids?"

"Ain't no time." It was his well-used answer every time someone asked him that. Maybe his own father deserved a better explanation, but he didn't want to get into it and didn't want to tell his father anything deeper when he knew the old man would forget it by tomorrow. The truth had recently gotten more complicated, his answer no longer accurate. He couldn't say 'I haven't met the right woman' and mean it. Just thinking it made his honesty meter tremble.

He'd met a woman so right it hurt. He grieved her absence in his every moment. She'd made everything so clear, his purpose in life so bright. Before her, he'd wandered. With her, he aimed true. Without her, he suffered unending distraction, his every sense seeking, restless, predatory. He was breaking apart.

Pop pushed himself up from the seat he'd just taken, almost as if the restlessness was contagious. "You think we oughta get some food started? That girl's gonna be starved when she finally comes in."

Mick returned to the window. "Problem is I got no clue what to feed her."

"Maybe she needs somethin' hot. Can of chili?"

"Worth a shot, I guess."

Pop turned on the night-light over the stove. "I'll fix a couple cans so you and Doug can eat too."

The front door creaked open and slammed shut. Mick shoved the binoculars at Pop and rounded the wall, collid-

ing straight into Doug on a gust of cold air. He held up his sketchbook. "I got her to draw. Look."

On the page was a U-shaped figure topped with wavy lines. Mick took the book from Doug to study it closer. "What's it—"

"Dunno. She ate a Skittle too. A green one, I think. Spit it out then asked for another but didn't spit that one out. Hard to see out there. Can I have a flashlight?"

Mick was still stuck on the drawing. It couldn't be so simple—but what if it was? "You think this means she wants water?"

Doug took the sketchbook back. Grinned up at Mick. "Duh. Okay, cup of water and flashlight."

"Flashlight might scare her. Let's see if Pop's got any candles."

"Why would a flashlight scare her?"

Lying to Doug was one of Mick's most hated chores. Early in the boy's life it was necessary to avoid hard truths, like why his father was in prison, why his baby sister was always sick, why his grandpop sometimes called him by the wrong name. Then one year ago, Kari dropped the kids off with Mick to work some overtime hours and said, "He knows everything, and I'm not lying to him anymore."

The shock of a sweet nine-year-old being thrown straight into harsh reality had fought against the sudden prize of relief. Mick could finally be real with his nephew. He no longer had to lie to his face. And he'd checked Doug's little face then and had found a tight little smile, a mature, steady gaze. Kari was right. She knew her boy.

So if Mick wasn't lying to Pop about this girl in the woods, he wasn't lying to Dougie either. He'd only have to maintain the bigger lies, the newly discovered truths about himself he kept from them all.

"A flashlight will scare her 'cause she's not from here."

"I figured that since she don't speak English. Unless ... you think she's faking?"

"She ain't faking." Mick limped back to the kitchen and started going through Pop's cabinets. If Pop had candles, he surely wouldn't remember where they were.

"So where's she from?"

There was a way to explain this without having to lie. "You remember my friend Waapikoona who had supper with us a little while ago?"

Doug scrunched his face, and Mick realized his error. Doug didn't know her real name.

"She also goes by Sarah."

"Oh, yeah. The lady who gave you Spot."

"Right. Well, I think this girl's her sister, only ... she hasn't been around people like Sarah has."

"Was she in a hospital or something? Or a cult?"

And how did Doug know about cults? "No, but kind of a similar situation as that. She just don't understand our society like we do."

"Hey, I know something else I can give her." Doug dragged his backpack onto a chair, unzipped it, and retrieved a feather. "Eagle feather I found on your driveway."

Holy shit. Mick nearly said it aloud, but he shut his mouth and kept his cool. "When'd you find that?"

"Last time Mom dropped me off. I found like ten of 'em. Wanna see?"

That pile of feathers he'd left at his apartment door would have to go as soon as he could get back over there. Seeing Doug with a collection of his feathers sent his worlds into a collision he wasn't ready to face. "Nah, I believe you."

Something about it made Mick uneasy, and it wasn't just the idea of his unsuspecting nephew having a collection of

feathers that came from his eagle form. The role of them for the purpose of peace offering to Waapikoona's sister—it didn't seem right, for a reason Mick couldn't get ahold of and couldn't dedicate any thought to it. His brain was still reeling from the damn thing being in Dougie's hand.

Doug filled a tall plastic cup with water. Pop handed him a second one and said, "And one for you, so you can prove our water ain't poisoned."

On a top shelf, Mick spotted a decorative Christmas tin that looked like it might be what he was looking for. He brought it down and found a candle inside, halfway burned so the flame might have enough protection from the wind outside. "You know how to strike a match?"

"Nope."

Kari would probably kill him for teaching her kid to start a fire, but he didn't have much choice. He gave a quick lesson, showing Doug how to keep his fingers back and make sure the match was good and out before he tossed it anywhere. Then he sent him back out the front door, candle tucked in one arm, a cup of water in each hand, matchbox in his pocket. Mick returned to his watch at the back window, binoculars lifted.

This time, Doug didn't bother passing into the trees. He crossed the yard until he reached the spot where the girl was. Then he stepped into the woods, slowed by his full hands unable to help keep balance as he stepped over fallen limbs. Mick couldn't even see the girl with the night vision until Doug squatted. She appeared from under the blanket, shifting back a few inches from Doug's reach. He offered the water. She sat frozen, watchful. Doug poured a small stream out before offering it again. She craned her neck. He set both cups down between them and showed her the Christmas tin, spinning it around, turning it upside down. She pointed to it. He got out the matches. She scooted forward, curious.

"That girl's gotta be freezin'," Mick said under his breath. "C'mon, Dougie, be careful, don't spook 'er."

Maybe the matches were a bad idea.

CHAPTER
5

IN THE BEDROOM Mick had shared with Kari growing up, he took a much-needed break. A sharp headache pulsed behind his eyes as his eagle wrestled impatiently inside him. He couldn't understand why this struggle didn't appear every time he'd been with Waapikoona, and why a little undead girl would create such a reaction. He had a hunch—a fear— he didn't want to admit. The more time he spent as eagle and the more demons his eagle killed, the less human he became.

Or maybe there was just something special about Waapikoona, some reason his eagle was cool with her.

Phone in hand, he tried that Oklahoma number again. Five rings. Ten. He hung up and sent a text, just in case. *It's Mick. Your sister is awake. Call me asap.*

The response dinged in instantly, stating the text failed and to resend to a valid mobile number.

He pocketed his phone and rubbed his face, his temples. Fingers through his hair, digging in. The headache had spread from his eye sockets across his skull to throb at the back of his head. Too many things were pressing for his attention. He got too little sleep to handle it. Now facing the reality that he couldn't fix this alone, that the only answer was to find a woman who'd disappeared and left no trace—it was too much. Before this night, his pledge to find her served him alone. It had no stakes, no teeth. Now, it was urgent and imperative, a burden he couldn't bear because being honest with himself meant he had to admit how impossible it was. How much of his humanity he'd sell off if he gave it his all. Fully committing to the search meant shifting into eagle form and not shifting back until he found her. If, at that point, he could even shift back at all.

The ache coursed through his head, tensing his neck. He stretched, one shoulder and arm, then the other, just like his eagle stretched its wings. He needed a partner, a whole flock of them. Dividing the search in shifts, taking turns. All other thunderbirds would only kill her, though, and his reason to keep her alive wouldn't sit well with them. He'd be aiding and abetting not one but two undead creatures. Other thunderbirds would tear him apart.

He raised his head, catching his reflection in the mirror above the dresser. "I fit nowhere," he said.

He knew this already. But until now it seemed acceptable based on the temporary feel of it. Only alone until he found Waapikoona. Only alone until he no longer needed his eagle. Neither of those would come true. This wasn't temporary. It was a lifelong commitment he never agreed to take on, confining him to secrecy and isolation.

Kari was always telling him he took on too much. Well, maybe that was the problem. If he hadn't met Waapikoona, he wouldn't know this girl was her sister. He'd call the police and let them handle it. If he hadn't come to Pop's tonight, he wouldn't know she was in the woods. Another thunderbird would find her or she'd freeze to death. That was the nature of the undead coming alive in the wintry Missouri woods. It didn't have to be his responsibility.

But if he hadn't met Waapikoona, this girl's bones would never have made it to Pop's backyard.

If he hadn't met Waapikoona …

The thought had too many endings he'd never want to change. So there it was. A reality placed in his hands that he refused to release. He wanted to find an ending that made it all worth it, an ending that outshined them all.

Mick returned to the kitchen. Found a bottle of aspirin in the cabinet, shook two tablets into his palm, and threw them back with a swallow of cold water that chilled him all the way down and landed heavy in his empty stomach. He checked the clock. Dougie had been out there too long, and as much as he didn't want to strong-arm the girl, it became more inevitable with each passing minute.

Waapikoona had dragged him into this world of hers, turned him into an unearthly creature, buried the bones of her undead sister on his father's land, and disappeared without leaving contact info. Fury was the baby brother to whatever emotion was rising from his gut. When he finally found her, this morbid stockpile of longing and anger might unpack and draw him to a place he'd never been.

He joined Pop by the window and nudged his elbow for a turn with the binoculars. Doug knelt facing the girl as he tried to strike a match. Each attempt gave a small spark but burned out too fast to light. After several tries Doug held the match up and scrutinized it before laying it on the ground. He tore off a new one. The girl's bare arm poked from the blanket, reaching.

"No way."

"What's that?" Pop asked.

"I think she's tryin' to help Dougie light the match."

Through the binoculars Doug handed her the whole box of matches and Mick went cold. In the wrong hands that could be a weapon. And if this girl could change like Waapikoona, could give herself over to whatever it was that massacred whole groups of men and summoned carnivorous demons from thin air, who knew what she could do with a match. Mick couldn't wait to react. He had to stop it before it happened. He couldn't stall until the girl's eyes turned glazed and otherworldly like Waapikoona's did when her whole form radiated the essence of the unholy prey Mick's eagle had been born to hunt and kill. And without a group of evil men nearby to steer the eagle away from the undead girl, he wasn't sure he'd be able to stop himself from killing her. His eagle might not find some twisted desire to fight along with her like it wanted to fight along with Waapikoona.

Mick put a hand on the door, bracing himself against the oncoming shift he wasn't sure he should stifle. His bad leg shuddered, wishing for its uncrippled eagle version. Human eyes took in the flash of a bright flame. Shadowy movement played around it—he raised the binoculars to see better. Now Doug was holding the candle on its side as the girl raised a lit match to the wick. Doug righted the candle. The flame held.

Mick blew out a breath. Closed his eyes to find himself and shed his encroaching eagle. It was just long enough to miss the girl moving toward Doug because when Mick looked again she was right by him, pointing to the cup of water he'd set on the ground. Doug picked it up. She pointed to his face.

"Odin could take the form of an eagle, you know," Pop said.

Through the binoculars Doug took a sample drink and then offered the cup to the girl.

"What?"

"You oughta read up on it. It's good stories."

"Read what?" Mick couldn't take one of Pop's out-of-nowhere conversations right now.

"Mind if I have a look?" Pop said at his shoulder.

He handed off the binoculars and went to the pantry, finding crackers for the chili and a jar of applesauce to offer the girl if she remained picky. He couldn't make sense of what Pop had just said and wasn't sure if he should ask him to repeat it. Most often these random mentions were better off left alone. It was different with the word 'eagle' involved, though. "Who were you talkin'—"

"She don't seem to trust that cup, but he got her to hold it—oh, good boy. Handing over the eagle feather now. Kid knows good timing, don't he?"

Mick moved back to the window, his heart thudding hard. His unease with that feather's role in this situation burst into reason. If the girl sensed any hint of thunderbird in that feather, her undead spirit would revolt and she'd run—or attack. He missed his chance to talk Doug out of it. He should have thought it through, should have taken it—

"Oh, shoot. She don't like that feather. And—dang it, I think she just took off."

Mick set the crackers and applesauce on the table. Turned the burner holding the pot of chili to low heat. Then let himself out the front door while Pop was intent on the scene out back and wouldn't notice him stripping off his clothes behind the GTO. As the cold encased his bare skin, he took one final glance at the house, knowing this was the hard way, but the only way. If that girl got any farther away, she'd be frozen to death in an hour.

He stretched his good leg, hopped a few times on his bad one, and took off, the driveway like a runway. A crack of thunder fractured the night, and this time he didn't suppress the sound. He needed to use it the way it was meant to be used—to scare prey into flight so he could spot the movement, analyze speed and direction, and dive.

With wings pumping against silent air, he lifted higher over the trees, their empty branches offering no cover to the fleeing girl below. The boy with the flame called out to her, his voice severed by another thunderstrike that sent the boy's gaze straight up, his mouth dropping open at the sight of what circled above him. He had no reason to fear, but the girl did. The eagle readjusted the dive. Human directive crossed into eagle thought—he was to chase this one to shelter. He should not kill.

From above she looked like any other prey zigzagging through the underwood. Both her trail and her intended path glowed in a fluid rainbow of undulating color. The hot artery in her throat called to him. He could almost taste her underworld-flavored blood; his hunger signaled a dive. A shout from the boy caused him to bank hard just above the trees, shedding his need, remembering his purpose. This girl was that boy's prize, not his.

He flapped higher, circled. His dive had sent her in a new direction, and the boy was on the path to converge. Another dive would force her straight there. His eagle vision found a perfect break in the trees, and he took it, breaching the woody barrier with a cry pulled from the clouds above that brought a flash of light along with it, striking earth just behind her heels. She fell. The boy fell facing her. He grabbed her hand and pulled her up. They ran from the trees across the cleared expanse of ground, her blanket flapping behind her like wings. Toward the human shelter they fled and closed themselves inside.

Gliding into a circular pattern above the house, he watched both openings from all angles, waiting for the girl to break free. Gaining altitude allowed a greater view of the woods and the creatures that roamed the night. The chase had left him unsated, ravenous. Human responsibilities tugged against a drive to make amends with this failure of duty and quench this appetite. Denying this would cost him—distance from underworld prey weakened the eagle. If he neglected upperworld duty and denied the hunger, the eagle would curl away, unneeded.

His human fought. The eagle filled him with its demand, and he left the girl, racing to chase prey he could destroy.

Time stilled as he hunted. Unearthly creatures winged and slithering found their unexpected ends. Every kill powered him for more until the weight of time found his human half, and he coasted to the ground in the woods where he'd first glimpsed the girl. The residue of her underworldness lingered, a gleaming multicolored mist along the forest floor. He landed on a fallen log, digging within himself to find his other half and wake it up.

As he waited he thought of all the creatures he'd ended. And how many more he could kill if he kept going, widened his circle, worked until the sun pushed out the night and the creatures into hiding. He opened his wings and rose in the air to perch in an oak.

No.

Mick struggled, imagining arms not wings, toes not talons. He flapped from the tree back to the log, pacing along it, replacing thoughts of those talons ripping wings from fleeing demons with the feel of the GTO's steering wheel in his hands as he cruised Wyona's curvy backroads. Rainbow serpents gliding under black water mirroring the stars replaced with tears reflecting on Waapikoona's cheeks as he woke her from bad dreams.

Mick fell onto his knees, breaking through a crust of ice sloped against a tree. His mouth was too dry to spit out the rotten tang of demon blood, so he scooped up a handful of the broken ice and let it melt on his tongue, unconcerned about the dirt and tiny leaves mixed in. Eating dirt beat demon blood any day. To his human self, anyway.

The night still black, it gave him no sense of the time. He could have been gone from Pop's for minutes or hours. Either way, someone would be worried. Maybe not Pop but certainly Dougie. He got up, brushed himself off. Closed his eyes to remember this spot the girl had been in and how it related to Pop's house and took off, keeping within the cover of the trees until he reached the side yard where he crossed into the driveway. The motion sensor caught him and light spread across the driveway, blinding him. He squinted against the glare and found his clothes, frozen rigid in the pile where he'd dropped them. He shook them out and put them on, careful with his bad leg, once again a sad mess of inadequate human healing.

But it was the shifting that kept delaying the healing—or so he thought. Maybe he should be blaming it on the eagle.

The windows on the front of the house were dark like he'd left it. He turned the doorknob—unlocked. As he let himself in from dark night to darker house, he heard Spot's collar jangle in the kitchen, paws on tile and then carpet. He lowered both hands to give the dog a greeting satisfying enough to keep him quiet. Cold nose, hot tongue, then the dog moved to sniff Mick's boots where he left them by the door.

A vague scent of food hit him then—chili, he remembered. He wondered if they'd coaxed the girl to the table and all had supper together or if the food still sat on the burner, forgotten. His knee encountered something hard and unforgiving—he reached, finding he'd arrived at the doorway to

the kitchen sooner than expected. The pain from his banged knee struck then, delayed, but no less intense. He hadn't yet fully settled into his human body and needed to pay better attention to his limbs until he did.

Now in the kitchen he got a little help from the microwave's clock spreading blue light across the room. And the flame from a candle on the floor by the back door. Beside it sat the girl, her eyes on him.

Hunkered under Pop's plaid blanket, she was dressed in Doug's dinosaur pajamas and Pop's fleece-lined house slippers. Shadows danced across her face from the flickering flame. She cradled one hand in the other, tight against her stomach, as if she'd hurt herself in the chase. Mick tried to remember if Waapikoona had ever called her by name.

"Hi," Mick whispered, holding up both hands. "I ain't gonna hurt you."

A pallet had been laid beside her, thick with every blanket and pillow in the house. A double blink broke her untrusting stare, giving away how sleepy she was. Fear could keep a person awake—but not forever.

"You get somethin' to eat?" Mick took a careful step farther into the kitchen. Now he could see the digits on the microwave displaying a quarter past midnight. The three bowls in the sink meant three people ate chili—or were at least offered it. He found the pot of leftovers in the fridge and put it on the stove, one eye on the girl to make sure she wouldn't spook.

"You speak any English?"

She said nothing, just continued to watch him. Narrow, high-set eyes and straight black hair, parted in the middle like her sister's but bobbed short against her jaw. She had no idea she'd skipped centuries and landed in a different world, and there was no one here who could help her. Spot wandered over to her pallet, circled, and plopped down. She took no notice, her attention was so glued to Mick.

"Well, it'd sure help me out if you did." He tried to remember the handful of words Waapikoona had spoken of her language. If he could speak one word of it, maybe this girl would understand he wasn't a bad guy.

As he filled a glass with water from the sink, he heard a thump, the scrape of the door. A pile of paper scattered across the table in the wind. Spot sprung to his feet. The back door swayed; the girl was gone.

Mick rounded the table and gave chase. Sock feet on cold steps, bad leg straining under a hard sprint, he gained on her as she fled across the snow-crusted yard. She'd hate him for this, probably never trust him, but he had no other option. He was lucky his eagle was sated—*she* was lucky. He felt his eagle close, like it was swooping down above him ready to carry him away.

Right before she reached the trees, he caught her around the waist, whirling her against him. She was all elbows and feet—heat seared across his forearm—and nails. He didn't have to see it to know she'd drawn blood. A kick to his bad leg, right in the shin that had taken Jeremiah's knife, nearly broke his stance. But he held on and let her fight him, waiting for her to realize she wasn't going to win this, and he wasn't in it to hurt her either.

"Settle down, you're okay." Until he knew otherwise, he had to assume she understood him. It was all he could do. "It's gonna be all right, just settle down."

She kicked for his shin again—he dodged, just in time. Spot barked nearby. Mick got a hand on each shoulder and turned her so she faced him, keeping his grip firm yet gentle. Her frame was so small. Skeletal, almost. The image

of white bones rushed straight to his eagle mind, and he forced it away.

He squatted so his eyes were level with hers. He struggled for the breath to speak. "You gotta quit that. I ain't here to hurt you. Okay?"

She panted, a clump of her hair stuck to her mouth. He wanted to fix it for her, but couldn't risk releasing his hold, and figured she wouldn't want him touching her hair anyway. Gulping air, they watched each other as Spot circled them, whining. Mick's bootless feet ached against the icy grass. Hers had to be just as cold—she'd lost Pop's slippers in the chase and wasn't even wearing socks. He wasn't sure how to get her back in the house without some kind of carrying or dragging and had no clue how to keep her in there once he did. If he took her by the hand—

He noticed then one of her hands was malformed, twisted into itself. Missing fingers—index finger, thumb. He swallowed against the memory of Jeremiah's hammer smashing little bones to dust inside that tomb, of the little skull that had been up next. Sickness washed through him. It was a common feeling when confronted with memories from the torture he'd endured that day. This time, the sickness came for a different reason.

"Uncle Mick!"

He glanced at the house. Dougie stood in outline against the rectangle of kitchen light. Pop came up behind him holding what looked like snow boots. Mick couldn't be such a failure in this to have Dougie bail him out. He returned his attention to the girl, who'd caught her breath but didn't look like she'd given up yet.

"You can't spend the night in the woods. So you gonna walk back or am I gonna have to carry you?"

She stared him down. The thump of snow boots coming down steps carried across the lawn, and Spot took off to meet them. Mick straightened up, testing her by releasing one shoulder and offering a hand instead. Doug clomped up beside them. "Did she run away?"

"Yep. Don't think she wants to come back inside, though."

"Where'd you go before?"

Mick had forgotten about that and had no answer he could give Doug. "I went out to look for her."

"You were gone forever."

"I know. I'm sorry about that."

"Grandpop said not to worry about you."

"He's right."

"Oh man, you shoulda seen this giant bird—"

"You wanna help me get 'er back into the house?"

"—and this lightning, outta nowhere—"

"Let's talk inside where it's warm."

Doug offered the girl his hand from under the blanket wrapped around his shoulders, and Mick withdrew his hold. For a moment he thought she might bolt, but Doug fixed it quickly by stretching his blanket out and taking her inside its warmth. It was a big brother move he'd done to Janie many times when their mother had to be away, and Mick was frustrated to have made no progress yet relieved he didn't have to manhandle the poor girl back into the house.

Mick let them walk ahead but kept close enough to catch her should she decide to run again. He only strayed from their trail to collect Pop's house slippers. When they got inside, Pop closed the door and locked it. "What's all that about?"

"Don't know," Mick said, peeling off his soggy socks. He grabbed a kitchen towel to wipe off his wet feet. "I was

fixin' myself some leftovers when she opened the door and run." He tossed the towel to Doug. "Here, hand 'er this."

"Where'd you get off to?" Pop asked.

Mick had no answer for that. "Where's this girl gonna stay? She can't stay here."

"Looks like she has to, till you can find that lady friend of yours."

"I don't know how soon that's gonna happen." He had no reason to be angry with Pop, but there it was, rising to his head, finding that earlier headache and raising the dial. He glanced at the kids. It seemed Doug had taken the task of drying the girl's feet because she was too engrossed in staring down Mick.

Doug finished, set the towel aside, and followed the girl's gaze. "No offense, Uncle Mick, but I don't think she likes you too much."

Mick held his tongue, knowing the returned headache and pointless anger would cause some snapped comment, and he didn't want to aim that at Doug. He dumped the heated chili into a bowl and sat at the table, distantly grateful Pop had turned the burner down while he'd been outside so he didn't ruin his meal. "You all need to go back to bed."

Doug looked at Pop for help. Pop turned the night-light on over the stove and flipped the main light off. "That enough light for you to eat, Mickey?"

Mick nodded. Doug opened his mouth to object, but Pop raised a hand.

"Dougie, you can hang out there with the girl. I'm headin' back to bed. Mickey, these kids will be okay with me tonight. You go on home when you're done there."

It was so reasonable, so clear-minded, that Mick couldn't even come up with an argument, except that this girl was his problem. Not Pop's. Certainly not Doug's, even though

Mick had commissioned his help. But Pop was down the hall, his door closed, and that was that.

Doug's voice was small across the room. "She just seems scared of you, that's all."

"You don't need to explain. My feelings ain't hurt." Mick's feelings sounded really hurt, but he couldn't figure out how to help that and had no way to describe to Doug the depth of the situation. "I'll be outta here in just a few minutes."

"I feel bad you gotta—"

"Don't feel bad. I just don't much like the idea of leavin' this girl with Pop. He's too old to deal with all this."

By the time Mick finished eating and cleaned up, Doug had split the girl's pallet into two, helped her into one and tucked himself into the other. All would be fine unless she decided to bolt as soon as Doug closed his eyes. And if she did bolt and froze to death, then Mick would lose this new concrete reason to find Waapikoona. It was true he couldn't live without her, but practicality didn't give one care about that. The sun would continue to rise and set, ignorant of the deepening fracture inside him. There was a limit to what he'd do for himself. Now this girl was here, and his search gained new clarity and a gravity he couldn't deny. The girl needed to stay put and give no trouble to Pop so they wouldn't have to figure out a new place to house her. Mick pushed the worries away and climbed into the GTO outside, thinking of only one thing. He had to find Waapikoona.

CHAPTER
6

WAAPIKOONA DIDN'T RETREAT too far as The Silent One filled her head and slid into her bones. She had to stay alert enough to carry him to the ashes they must steal and the man they must send into death. Somewhere in the trees above her a falcon called, the repeating chirp of its mate-call. Inside her The Silent One stilled to listen, pausing their forward motion. Every bird of prey was a suspicion to him. He didn't live in the upperworld like her, didn't know many of them were ordinary birds not out to destroy them.

Beside her, the third Helper lingered in a puddle of darkness. Her own Helpers used the pause to scratch on her palms, anxious to be free. With The Silent One inside, space was tight, and they knew a battle loomed and would soon be needed. She uncurled her fists, and they rolled to the ground—not as gently as they would if she'd been in complete control, but it was all she could manage now. They scampered away on long muscled front limbs, layers of white teeth bared, melting into darkest winter shadow.

The falcon quieted its call. They needed to move.

She forced a word against The Silent One: *run*. Never had she given him such a clear command, but it seemed their relationship had changed since she'd brought Mick and his eagle into the great demon's underground den. To her surprise he chose to accept her idea to move faster. It was more than a run. The road blurred under her boots. Wind whistled past her ears. Miles became heartbeats. Ahead, a path of ghostly white spread across dark earth, leading away from the road. Waapikoona commanded The Silent One to turn, her last call as she retreated into the background and let The Silent One carry them across the gravel driveway to the house.

He chose to hunker beside the porch and wait. Stalking and hunting were part of his game, and he reveled in it, passing the high of it across mind space to Waapikoona so she could share in his joy. If this had been her effort alone, she'd walk up to the front door and knock. But since she wanted The Silent One's help, she had to play along.

A breeze fingered through her hair, but she only felt an odd tingle instead of its cold razor edge cutting away at her warmth. The Silent One wouldn't feel it either. She needed to come back to herself in time before frostbite set in. Cold she could handle, but not the wet deep freeze that was due to hit overnight. Time lost its substance when The Silent One took her over, which made her prompt return tricky.

Kill the man, steal the ashes, she thought at The Silent One as she backed further inside herself and he filled in the vacated space. He needed to be quick and efficient, not stretch this out for his own amusement.

Through shuttered vision she saw headlights approaching through the tunnel of night. Too late she realized Rain's

mother lived here too, and she'd forgotten to tell The Silent One to spare her.

EVERYTHING WAS SIDEWAYS when Waapikoona opened her eyes. The ground was plush, warm—not the ground but some musty piece of furniture making her hot enough to sweat, her clothes damp against her skin, her coat slippery with it.

She sat up, sensing the creased clothes peeling away from the indentions they'd left in her flesh. She covered her face with both hands and filled her lungs, finding herself, wiggling toes and fingers, taking inventory of bones and organs. Her eyes adjusted to the weak light from a table lamp. As her senses returned, color trickled into a room of grays— yellow curtains, a turquoise rug. And her hands ... red. Not sweat but blood. She was covered in it. Smeared down the front of her coat, staining her jeans, sticky on her boots.

If The Silent One had left a mess too big for her Helpers to clean up ...

Standing, she looked around. A toppled end table spilled empty soda cans across the carpet. The TV panel dangled mid-fall, held by its cord wedged behind the table. She found a wall switch and squinted against the onslaught of overhead light. If she'd left blood on the couch, it wasn't showing up against the dark brown material. The carpet— also brown—had too many old stains to worry about any new ones. Thinking she'd dreamed the mess on her clothes, she checked herself again, saw it a second time, and wondered how she'd gotten so covered in gore when her surroundings seemed to be free of it.

All at once she felt eyes on her. She spun around.

"I can't figure it out either."

He stood in the kitchen in shadow. Even though she couldn't clearly see his face, she remembered the gritty voice, the Hispanic accent she couldn't specifically place. She heard his name in her head. *Soto*. She didn't say it.

"Why anyone would leave their TV hanging like that."

"You must not know what could happen to people who sneak up on me."

He raised his hands, palms out. "No sneaking. I tried my best to wake you, but—"

"You need to leave." If this was Rain's father's house she'd woken up in, she needed to find out why she was still inside instead of walking away with Rain's ashes. She had to make sure the kill had been successful, and her Helpers had cleaned up the body. She had to find where Rain's mother was.

Soto zipped himself into a hooded sweatshirt jacket and rummaged through a heaped laundry basket on the kitchen table. He plucked out a sock, then another, and sat in a chair. As he tugged on socks, he caught her gaze. "It's not stealing. It's borrowing. Not sure a dead guy will mind, anyway." He motioned her over with a jerk of his head. "Come. I'm sure there's something to fit you too."

If he was changing clothes, did that mean his had been as bloody as hers? Surely he didn't help in this. Her head spun with the effort of remembering. All she had was a strange blank terrain that refused to fill in with scenery like it should. She found Sam and Josie, Rain's abandoned trailer, the Jeep.

Mick's voice through the phone.

No. It was irrelevant, a distraction hell-bent on yanking her off course. She dropped onto the musty couch, massaging her temples, closing her eyes. It would look weak to

Soto, but she didn't care. She had to get her feet back on the right trail.

Sam and Josie—Rain's trailer—Jeep—

... and filling the tires. Parking on the road. The falcon calling to its mate. Her Helpers rolling off her palm. Her instructions to The Silent One as he possessed her. And then ... nothing.

"You all right, Sarah?"

She looked squarely at him. "No."

"Did that..." he thumbed behind him "...not go as you wanted?"

She stared at him, waiting for him to reveal more. She read him for the kind of guy who preferred talk over any kind of silence, especially if it was his own voice filling the air.

"'Cause as I see it, your target is dead, his body scrubbed off the earth by those little demons. You're good to go. *¿Qué problema hay?*"

"My problem is you."

At that, he laughed. "Without me, you'd be a bloody icicle on that gravel driveway."

Sarcasm wasn't a weapon she selected often, but this exchange demanded it. She couldn't recall a time she'd laid on so much. "*Muchas gracias.*"

"*Ah, español. Me gusta*, even though you're being a smartass. One question, though—why so savage? I'm sure you're capable of a quick neck snap or choke wire. No need to ruin your clothes over one random loser on your death list."

Savage. One of her favorite words. Even though it was a clear retaliation against her smart aleck use of his language, she wasn't going to give him the pleasure of letting it puncture her.

"Wait," he said, standing. "This one was personal. Right? That's why you butchered him into so many pieces."

Now she had enough to fill in the scene. She'd killed Rain's father while possessed by The Silent One, collapsed, and Soto had been there to carry her inside. How long she'd been unconscious could only be gleaned from further conversation with this guy, and she was finished.

She shrugged out of her coat and went to the kitchen sink. Washed her hands, face, and neck, finding a tender knot on her cheekbone and a fat lip she hadn't noticed until now. And one missing golden eagle feather earring. *Mick's* feather. She should leave it here, but she had to find it and didn't have time to analyze why.

The rumble of a sporty car closed in, growing louder until it settled just outside the house. Beyond the thin walls it sat, humming, impatient. Soto returned from the back hallway with a pair of sneakers. "That's my ride."

If Waapikoona cared why he was here—or how he'd found her—she was about to lose her chance to interrogate. It wouldn't change what he wanted from her or her answer to it. So she turned away and helped herself to some ice from the freezer.

"You remember what I said?" he asked.

She pressed the ice against the knot on her face. "No."

His laugh filled the room. That car better not have rolled over her feather. She hunted through the kitchen for a flashlight as Soto laced up his stolen shoes. Then she followed him out the door to the waiting black Nissan, the thick *chug-chug-chug* of the idling engine laying a blanket of sound over the stark night. The inside of the car held too much shadow for Waapikoona to make out who was driving. A ride back to the Jeep would be nice, but no, not from Soto, not from his unidentifiable driver. Definitely not from this living creature of a car that reminded her of Mick's Pontiac and the sanctuary she felt while enclosed inside with him.

A female voice leaked from the car's door as Soto angled himself into the passenger side. The door slammed closed and Waapikoona flipped on her flashlight, ignoring them. A click of gears, a hefty rev of engine, and the car backed out, spreading light across the driveway that consumed Waapikoona's pitiful flashlight. If that was a metaphor of some kind, it could go to the deepest lake and play with the horned serpents.

The feather lay in the middle of the driveway where the car had been sitting, straddled by wheels, unharmed. She clicked off her flashlight and picked it up. The shine it held in its fabric, even in the darkest night, made her heart pinch. It carried a piece of Mick's golden soul, of his fight for good, his sacrifice.

His willing death to save hers, and hers wasn't worth it.

She had to overcome this. Casting away these feathers would help, but not now. Not yet. Deep inside she knew the simple act of destroying this piece of him might break her, and to do what she needed to do—hunt and kill Hammond, raise her sister, sever ties with The Silent One unharmed— she had to remain unbroken.

Back inside the house she checked every room including the basement. She found a better flashlight and circled the yard around the house, checking front to back. Her Helpers had cleaned up well. There was also no sign of Rain's mother. The woman had been an early-to-bed homebody when Waapikoona had known her, so if she wasn't in the house now …

She returned to the basement, tossed all her clothes in the washing machine, and went upstairs to shower. There was no reason to acknowledge the sickening twist in her core. The Silent One had killed Rain's mother, not her.

But she'd failed to tell him not to.

She scrubbed the blood from her hair and fingernails, the dirt from her face. Leaving the water cold helped her get out quickly. She ignored the chatter of her teeth. Clean clothes transferred to the dryer. Cereal in a bowl, bread in the toaster. She found strawberry jam in the fridge and ate a spoonful as she waited for the toast to pop up.

From nowhere, she got a bright image of Mick's adorable niece and wiser-than-his-years nephew giggling over their green beans in Mick's little kitchen. Spot leaning against her leg under the table as she tried not to giggle with them. Kids and dogs lit everything up. Assuming Spot had stuck around, Mick had both, so he was okay. She wished she had time to visit a medicine woman who could purge these memories from her head. Once they were gone, she wouldn't know what she was missing.

Her appetite subdued, she gathered her clothes and dressed. She looked in all the obvious places for a cremation urn before starting a deeper search. In the bedroom closet she found a small metal lockbox that easily surrendered under a sledgehammer she found in the garage. Under the depth of night sky outside she stuffed all the cash in her coat pockets and picked up the lockbox's smashed metal corpse from the stiff grass behind the house.

An upright shimmer drifted from the trees at the edge of the yard. As it moved, it morphed between human features and the vague form of a confused spirit. Unquiet, and very far from its resting grounds, unless there was a graveyard through those trees.

The ghost wasn't wandering. It was floating straight toward her.

She didn't want to spare a few minutes, but she could, and after her negligence tonight she owed some servitude to

the dead. So she dropped the sledgehammer to the ground and stayed put.

"Can you see me?" It was nothing but a whisper, traveling on a tickle of a breeze as if the spirit had cupped hands around lips and spoken straight into Waapikoona's ear.

Waapikoona nodded, knowing her own voice could not overcome space so easily. Unsure how long this might take, she zipped up her coat to conserve warmth and raised her hood over hair still damp from her shower. As the spirit neared, Waapikoona worked to forget what she'd just done—murdered a bad man and his innocent wife, took over their house, ate their food, stole their money. On a larger scale and another context it would be called Westward Expansion or Manifest Destiny … or maybe even The American Dream. She would not feel guilty for it.

The spirit condensed in front of her. A small-statured woman, narrow in shoulders and face. Her features were too vague to identify, but slowly sharpened before Waapikoona's eyes. The ghost worried a string of beads around her neck with skinny fingers and took a long glance past Waapikoona as if looking for someone. "Is he in there?"

"Who?"

"He can't see me. I try to get him to see me, to *tell* him. But he never listens. He never has."

"That man who lives in this house?"

"My husband, yes. I need him to …"

The woman's face had sharpened with Waapikoona's slow memory of her, revealing the Native half of Rain's blood. Remorse swooped so hard and fast upon Waapikoona that she reached for something to hold on to, to brace against, but there was nothing but air around her and an intangible ghost. Swaying, she recovered her balance and swore that if she ever saw Mick again she'd tell him what she really thought of his damn conscience that had somehow infected her. Accidental deaths of innocents never bothered her before and shouldn't bother her now. Soon they'd all be wiped out when the underworld spilled over the earth. Killing them now was nothing but an act of mercy.

It just didn't feel like that anymore.

And all this lingering, this wasting of nights, was doing nothing but giving her extra time to think about right and wrong and her place in all of it. And Mick.

"You need to find your grave and rest. There's nothing I can do …"

Wrongness rushed through Waapikoona. Something here was off. If she—or, actually, The Silent One—had just killed this woman a few hours before, she'd have no grave to return to. She'd be in the belly of one of her Helpers on the way to The Silent One's underground den. It seemed odd for her spirit to have found the way back so soon. Did she even have enough time to decide to become unquiet and return here?

"You must help!" The ghost made a grab, as if to latch on and shake her. Waapikoona felt a frigid wind hollow out the bones in her arms. As quickly as it came, it was gone.

"Help with what?"

"My son is lost, in a place he doesn't want to be—"

"Rain?" It wasn't unusual for spirits to plead for help from the one person who could see them. But for a spirit to ask for help from her own murderer … unless Waapikoona was wrong, and she hadn't killed Rain's mother.

"Yes! You know him? Then you know he shouldn't be stuck here. He'll never find his way."

"Stuck … where?" Waapikoona wasn't sure where he was stuck. If he'd been wandering this house or yard, she'd have seen him. That didn't matter, though. She wasn't here to find Rain's spirit. "Do you remember where his ashes are?"

The ghost shifted her wavering form and headed across the hibernating lawn, making no sound to accompany the crunch of Waapikoona's boots against brittle grass. To the garage they headed, Waapikoona swallowing a suspicion she hoped wouldn't come true in the next moment—Rain's ashes, stored in the same structure where Rain's father had punished him as a child. A detached garage, where his mother wouldn't hear and couldn't save him.

Waapikoona knew how the white man punished children. In the Indian school she'd learned it thoroughly by day and relived it each night as she tried to find a comfortable position in her bunk that avoided the sore spots. Comfort was harder to find with her sister stowing away in her bed, clinging to her to muffle her sobs—but her own comfort mattered little on those nights. She'd often wondered if they used the same barbaric methods on their own children. In her second life Rain had confirmed it. Yes, they did. His father was a monster, but he was not rare. He was one of many. And to his species of monster, a child's skin color would not determine the severity of punishment. On that, all colors of children received equal treatment.

Punishment was the wrong term. It was abuse.

When Waapikoona had searched the garage for the sledgehammer, she hadn't looked around, hadn't lingered. Rain's cold disclosures of the times he'd been dragged into the confines of those walls came at her again like they were days old, not decades old, and she didn't want to relive them. Didn't want to see the glaze in Rain's eyes, the angry quiver of his jaw, the fear that still lived in him years after he'd moved away from it. She couldn't go back and revel in killing that man a second time—or a third. She couldn't even enjoy her memories of the first—she'd let The Silent One do it—and strangely had no recollection to savor.

Now as Rain's mother led her to the door of the garage, her outrage seared along every nerve. She needed that sledge-hammer to smash these walls. If Rain had been dead a day, it would be too long for his ashes to sit in this place. As Rain's mother disappeared through the closed door, Waapikoona took a steadying breath. The woman couldn't know what had been done to her son here, why his soul was so lost. If she didn't know or failed to remember, reminding her would be a new, purposeless wound. Waapikoona would not haunt this woman with knowledge that would help no one now.

Inside the garage, on a high shelf, sat not one urn but two. Waapikoona reached for one, then the other, their inscribed names and dates passing by her eyes as she nestled both in her arm.

"You died just after him," she said to the spirit. Relieved of the burden of this woman's death on her hands, straining under the new one she'd just shouldered.

"Yes, but I can stay here—"

"No, you can't. I'm burning this place to the ground."

Waapikoona found gasoline and a match and lit it up like war.

If she had enough fuel, she'd scorch the whole earth, save The Silent One the trouble.

That was her anger doing her thinking. Anger this primed was a hindrance to clearheaded action, so she had to find a way to get over this. She had too many important things to do.

And the first one was to bury Rain in a place that felt like home.

CHAPTER
7

The two urns rattled against one another on the Jeep ride back to Rain's trailer. Waapikoona hadn't been able to tell Rain's mother where she was taking them—the ghost had disappeared as soon as the fire started. It was better that way. The walk back to the Jeep would have taken much longer at the lazy pace of the dead, and Waapikoona would've had a hard time leaving Rain's mother's spirit alone back there. She also wasn't sure a ghost could ride in a car and didn't care to find out.

The empty road and drone of the engine brought unwelcome thoughts. Like how if Rain's bones were intact instead of in ash, she could've buried him somewhere to raise him back to life after she raised her sister. And how she could've done the same for his mother. And that she didn't have the time, but she needed to visit The Silent One and see if Rain's father's bones could be salvaged so she could smash them to pieces. He only needed the flesh to rebuild those he chose for new life.

She wondered whose flesh she'd been rebuilt from …

No, she didn't care. Because in the end, she was herself, in her own body. The means to get there didn't matter.

She wondered whose flesh her sister would be rebuilt from. For some reason that did seem to matter, even though she had no control over it. She hoped it wasn't anyone she'd killed for her quota, because there were some foul humans on that list.

Turning onto the driveway leading to Rain's boarded trailer filled her with dread. The sadness could be easily stomped down when she was busy killing his father and stealing his ashes. But now, confronted by this empty trailer with the two-by-four nailed over the door, her own spirit cried. She was too late. She was helpless. Useless. She could have done something to stop this tragedy had she been here, but she had run away, broken contact, disappeared.

Not many things startled Waapikoona. But when she gathered her strength and turned off the Jeep's engine, she felt pins and needles scatter across her back. Eyes met hers in the rearview mirror. If not for her seat belt, she'd have jumped hard enough to hit her head on the roof.

"Sorry. Didn't mean to spook you."

Rain's voice. The eyes in the mirror filled in from her memory of him, and she turned around to look into the real things—or the gauzy forms of them she could now somehow see as his.

"Asshole," she said.

"That's fair," he said. "And better than I expected. I figured you'd call me a coward."

"Coward."

"You're all grown-up."

"And you're dead."

"I feel like I should be surprised by … you. Talking to ghosts like this. But everything about you makes a heck of a lot more sense right now." He canted his translucent face toward the urns in the seat beside her. "What's the plan?"

She got out of the Jeep. Went around to the passenger side, unloaded the urns, and slammed the door. She rounded Rain's trailer and headed toward the same opening in the woods she'd come through on her way here. The plan had been to come here and visit a Rain who was alive, to toss a line to her old self and reel it in along with the people she abandoned. To make a promise not to abandon them again. To reorient herself, to reclaim her purpose. She didn't expect this.

She stopped her trek through the high, dead grass, the looming shape of the forest in front of her too dark to make out the place she'd pushed through on her way here. "I didn't want to come here and do this."

Rain stood beside her. He hadn't been there a moment before. "I'm not asking you to do anything."

"Yeah, I know. Your mother—" A gust of wind hissed through the grass, so cold it stole her breath. She spun to face him. "Why?"

His shape flickered like a bad lightbulb. Man-sized ghost, open air, then back to ghost, this time overlaid with his bones. Eyes hollowed by round empty sockets and sharp cheeks, a grille of teeth, bumpy backbone, curved bright ribs. His presence was painted by her own understanding of him, not by anything real. After all, she carried what remained of his bones in her arms. She preferred to see him as she did before, so she looked away, hoping to reimagine his image without the bones.

And then she had to look at him hard, in the kind brown eyes she remembered, because he wasn't answering her question. "Why, Rain?"

He was there again, a lucent version of the Rain she remembered minus all color. No warm-toned skin, no brown eyes. Washed out, a play of light and shadow. "I was sick. Couldn't take the world anymore."

"Depressed."

"Yep, the infamous Indian depression." He chuckled. It sounded more painful than joyous.

"You don't get to give in to that. Remember what you'd always say? 'Oh, how this country loves to romanticize the Indian grief.'"

"Hmm, does that make it ironic?"

"No. It makes it cliché and stupid." She sounded like her teenage self. Déjà vu came in strong, convincing her they'd had this exact conversation fifteen years ago. She'd have been twenty-one then, but still tied to that bitterly impassioned teenage mindset. All grown-up now, for sure.

"You're just mad."

Of course she was mad—at him, at herself. At whatever had turned her land into a place so toxic to her people. She never considered herself a soldier for The Silent One; she only endured his purpose because he had the means to revive her sister, but now, something felt different. The temperature raised on what had been simmering so long. A calling, a way to undo all that had been done. But The Silent One's war wouldn't end where she wanted it to end. His goal was this land under the rule of the underworld. This is what Jeremiah had wanted to head off. To intervene before all that happened, rush in to take control of a ruined land, destroy The Silent One, and reclaim it. Jeremiah's idea of mutiny—maybe he'd been right.

And dealing with all of this by herself ... she feared she might split apart. She was used to working alone. She preferred it. These ideas were bigger than her role, more complex than anything she had planned. Having no living

human to knock these ideas around with made the weight too heavy to carry alone.

It was the sad, overwhelming disconnectedness. Kind of like the Indian depression.

Cliché and stupid.

Whatever simmered inside her would just have to boil out on its own.

She started walking again toward the woods, hoping Rain would stick around and lead the way in the pitch-dark. The sky pressed heavy from above as if overrun by clouds robbing her of moonlight. It didn't take much for her to see in the night, but there was nothing to aid her now. Tired and overwhelmed, she was walking blind. "I'm scattering you in the creek."

"The creek will be too dry here."

"Then take me to the water."

Without a word he led the way, his ghostly light touching the path with enough sheen to help her step over fallen logs and large stones. They found the curve of the creek bed, walking inside the steep bank to avoid the ice gathered along the edge. The earth leveled; a trickle of water carved through the days-old collection of snow. At the next bend the water widened, its lonely babble haunting the night. Its song pressed itself into her memory, promising to haunt her future nights.

She stopped and settled both urns on the ground beside her.

"You need to find someone, Waapikoona. This life is too cold to brave alone."

She picked up Rain's mother's urn and opened the lid. "I don't feel the cold anymore."

"Only because you've turned your back to it."

"Can we not do this?"

"I know what loneliness is, and I wish it on no one. Especially not you."

Here, where the water moved strongest, she could see no threat of ice, but she took care in placing her boots on the slippery rocks just in case. Over the deepest water she tipped the urn, unloading it gently like sand through a closed fist. She wanted to tell Rain she preferred loneliness. It kept things simple, focused her drive toward reviving her sister. Sometimes the chaos of the living grated against her, making her edgy and restless—not unlike the unquiet spirits. When she was younger she blamed the desolation here, thought the only cure was escape. And through leaving she learned she was indeed alive, but different enough from the living not raised from bones. Time among the dead tempered her time in the sunshine among the living. Too much of one or the other left her on edge.

With the urn now fully upside down, she gave it an easy shake before righting it and replacing the lid. "Why aren't you surprised I can see you?"

"Why should I be?"

"Most people can't."

"You aren't most people."

She suspected that was a nod toward what he must see her as now—a woman who walked both upper and lower worlds. It was not something most living people could sense. They were too thoroughly embedded in life to sense the underworld right under their feet. To remain alone wasn't just a choice to Waapikoona, it was unavoidable. She couldn't be with someone who didn't see both worlds.

A voice in her head reminded her Mick could see both worlds. He'd trespassed in the underworld and survived.

Rain said, "There she is."

Past him, a hazy woman-shaped glow drifted through the trees. Rain's mother had come to her new place of rest. As she glided toward the creek, she turned a hollow face toward them, and Waapikoona heard a *thank you* whispered in her ear just as the ghost dissolved into mist that settled softly on the water.

"Ready?" Waapikoona asked Rain.

"Find me here, any time you need to talk."

She wished she could send him off with more ceremony than this, but her people's ceremonies were lost in time. Her new people's rituals often didn't feel like her own. Tonight they would not. "I'll visit soon. Enjoy your quiet."

As the ash cascaded from the urn, Rain's spirit dissolved against the water, tumbling, playful, turning his send-off into a show for her. It dragged a smile out of her from some forgotten place.

She was still smiling as she replaced the urn's lid and planned her next stop: finding Hammond. A monster similar to the one she'd slayed tonight—but more personal.

CHAPTER
8

Mick hit the snooze for an hour before rolling out of bed. Sleep had been both frantic and heavy, a combination that liked to throw his neck or shoulder out. He eased a stretch, felt something about to strain, and backed off. His bad leg tried to buckle on his way to the shower. The hot water unwound his tight neck and woke his leg but did nothing for his head; everything there was beyond twisted up and could only be fixed by ticking off boxes in the list of things he had to do. While he shaved, showered, dressed, and ate, he reviewed his mental list.

Go to Kari's, talk to her about the girl before Kari heard it from Doug and wondered what the hell Mick had used her son for.

Somehow get the girl into his car and settled in his apartment.

Search the mausoleum for clues about Waapikoona or even Jeremiah. There'd be no way to find Waapikoona

without some kind of hint, so something had to be there. It had to be.

Do all this before his U-Fill shift, where he'd go crazy being idle when he had such urgent things to do. But bills weren't going to pay themselves.

"I'm already crazy," he muttered, locking up his apartment.

The sun was out in full force, a warm hand on hair still damp from his shower. Everything around him dripped— gutters, tree branches, the edge of the porch above him. The dripping and sunlight and blue sky made good things feel as possible and expected as the coming spring. Like something was due to change, to wash the land as perfectly and dramatically as a freak rain shower on a sunny, cloudless day. He was ready for a break. So ready.

Fifteen minutes later in Kari's driveway, he hesitated, worried he shouldn't involve her. He could swear Doug to secrecy—but then she'd get the story from Pop, who couldn't be expected to keep it secret. He might not even be capable. Keeping overburdened people in the dark to protect them seemed like a good idea until something leaked. Then there'd be hurt added to the mix, and it wasn't worth it. She'd have already heard his car pull up anyway.

He knocked. No answer. He knocked again, turned the knob, and went in, calling, "It's me."

Instead of Kari's well-lived-in front room spilling with shoes, toys, and half-folded laundry, he found something else. The sofa had been shoved against the wall to make room for blinking equipment and a metal hospital bed—

No, he thought, both hands moving to his head and sticking there. He turned, found an IV stand and a box of labeled bags and bottles. Baby Helen wasn't this bad off. She didn't need this stuff. He heard Janie's sobs then, coming from the kitchen. Kari's soothing voice. He walked in there, wishing he had some way to wipe the shock off his face but it remained, he knew it, knew it would make everything worse but couldn't find any air to breathe it away.

"Mickey—sorry, I didn't hear you come in." Kari gave him the briefest of glances. She had the tight little smile she used when she was trying to keep it all together.

"What's all—"

She gave him a look. *The* look.

Not around the kids.

"Hey, little birdie."

Janie reached for him. Her eyes were wet and red, her chin puckered into the worst frown. He picked her up. She burrowed into his neck, and he held her tight. "It's all right."

"I don't like that stuff in there." The whine in her voice was outraged, helpless, full of a fear that Mick felt knot hard in his throat.

Behind Janie's back, Kari mouthed, *She just woke up and saw it. I should have warned her.*

Mick thought, *You should've warned* me.

Kari squared her shoulders. "We're starting hospice." A word not in most six-year-old's vocabulary, so okay to freely say. Kari's face crumpled, but she fixed it fast, smearing an escapee tear from each eye.

"No," Mick said. Janie pulled back to look him hard in the face, and he realized just how angrily he'd said it.

"Janie," Kari said, "do you want eggs or cereal?"

"I don't want anything."

Mick lowered her to the ground. "Will you eat with me?"

"Are you and Doug both hungry?" Kari asked.

That was right—she expected Doug to be with him. "Doug's still at Pop's." He couldn't get into that now, not with all this. "And I'll just have what Janie's having." He looked at Janie, prompting her to choose.

She did, and Kari got the cereal and milk while Mick got the bowls and spoons. He sat at the table next to Janie and got out his phone, searching for a cute kittens video with a long enough play time to keep Janie occupied so he could yank Kari into the other room and demand more information.

"Did you see this one yet?" He propped his phone against the milk carton. "Be right back. Don't eat my cereal."

He didn't need to yank Kari. She'd already left. He found her in her bedroom, sitting on the edge of the bed that had been built up with pillows at the headboard and boxes along the sides to mimic a hospital bed with guardrails. Helen lay inside, propped up but sleeping, the rasp in her breath too severe to ignore.

A cold prickle ran the length of him; he covered his mouth with both hands. This wasn't happening.

Kari pressed her cheek against Helen's—pink-hued and living against sickly gray.

"What about the medicine?"

"It eases symptoms, that's it. Doesn't stop the disease. You know this, Mick. And it's four thousand dollars a month."

"That don't matter—"

"I know it don't. Only it does. It's not realistic anymore. And it stopped helping and isn't goin' to fix her, so—"

"So?!" He was yelling. He didn't want to be yelling.

Kari steadied herself as if subduing a yell of her own. "Don't. Please don't."

"There's got to be some other—"

She looked him dead in the eye. "There isn't. And when her quality of life—" She choked on the word and her eyes filled. She put a fist against her mouth and shook her head, unable to finish.

Mick felt the world had been torn from under him. Looming finality reached from below, grabbed him with a brutal fist. Kari got up to answer Janie's call from the other room, and Mick took her place on the edge of the bed. He elbowed the boxes out of his way; the commotion roused Helen. The swivel of her head so slight, so lethargic. Baby-soft eyelids slid open just enough for her eyes to find the source of the movement, recognize Mick, then drift closed.

"Hey, sweet thing. Your uncle Mick is here. You warm enough?" He took her hand, found cold fingertips. Kissed them before sandwiching them between his much warmer hands. The blanket was tucked tight around her legs but he knew her feet would be just as cold. He looked around for the heating pad, found it, plugged it in, and settled it against the blanket at her feet.

This could be surrender. He could give in like Kari had and accept reality for what it was. Incurable children's diseases meant children died. Medicine and good care might stall the inevitable, but the end was the end. Time was the enemy and it moved with speed and stealth. No one could fight time. Not even a thunderbird.

Kari stood in the doorway. Her voice was deepened by the work of keeping it steady. "Help me move her?"

Mick slid his arms under Helen and lifted her. She was wilted, lighter than she should be. Her head lolled against his chest. She should be crawling. Walking? Sticking her hands in everything and everything in her mouth. Screaming just for the joy in it, making messes because she could. She shouldn't be this withered, this—dare he even think it? Lifeless.

Her little body should be bursting with toddler energy, but it had given up.

In the living room, Kari lifted the back of the hospital bed to a slight incline. "She can't breathe unless she's propped like this."

Mick laid her down. "How are you goin' to manage this?"

Kari shrugged without looking at him.

"I'll take Janie with me and keep Doug."

"It's better with them here. Otherwise I just sit at her bedside and cry. They keep me busy."

Mick patted his pocket, making sure of keys and phone—phone was missing. Still in the kitchen with Janie. He stood. "Okay then, I'll get him and bring him home."

"No, Mickey, it's ..." She covered her face, took in a trembling breath. "This will probably last months. If we got back on the medicine maybe longer. We don't need to do anything different. If he's hanging with Pop, it's fine."

Then Mick remembered what he'd come here to talk to her about. It all seemed surreal. Trivial, nearly absurd. But it would nag him until he relayed it, and there were certainly more important things to be thinking about. He had to get it out. "Seems a bad time to bring this up now, but ..." He sat down again, raking a hand through his hair. Was everyone's life this much of a mess? And where did he start—should he just blurt it all out? Yes. It was all he had the energy to do. "You remember that woman I met in December?"

"Sarah."

Had he ever told Kari her real name? "She also goes by Waapikoona, for people who know her better anyhow. Last night her little sister shows up in the woods behind Pop's house, all alone. We got her inside with Doug's help—"

"Little sister, how little?"

"A bit younger than Dougie. Maybe eight?"

"Wow, that's ..."

An age difference Mick hadn't thought would be so weird until now. "Yeah. And I got no idea where Waapikoona is. She didn't leave a number or address or nothin'."

"You don't know where she lives?"

When Mick had met her, she was living in an old mausoleum, but Kari didn't need to know that. It wasn't true anymore anyway. "She was … passin' through town. Never mentioned where she lives."

"Did you call the police?"

Mick sat down on the edge of the bed next to Kari. "No, see, this ain't a thing we can call the police about. And we can't go talkin' to *no one*—"

"Mickey …"

"Look, this is serious. I—I mean, Waapikoona isn't—" How to explain what Waapikoona was, without sounding like he'd lost his marbles? He'd have to explain what *he* was too, for any of it to make sense. But that couldn't just be discussed like this. It had to be eased out naturally.

He could also shift right now and show her.

No, he couldn't do that.

"Anyway, the little girl don't speak English and is real afraid of almost everything, except for Dougie. She came from …" *Bones,* he wanted to say. She was raised from death.

In her sleep Helen took in a weak, shaky breath. It lasted long enough that both Mick and Kari turned to look at her drawing deep inside lungs that sounded wet and congested. Mick lost his thought to the image of Waapikoona's sister's disassembled skeleton in that canvas bag. Those dead bones had become a very alive little girl.

An idea, a miracle, sang inside him.

"Kari—" His knuckles against his mouth. He shouldn't say it. Needed to think this through. Needed to talk this over with Waapikoona. Needed to find her right now.

God, yes, he needed her now.

He sprung to standing. Kari had bent to nuzzle Helen's cheek, unaware of Mick pacing like a wild animal. He had to get his thoughts in order. First things first.

"So any chance you got any old clothes that might fit this little girl? She came with nothin'."

Kari raised the side of the hospital bed, making effort to avoid the loud steel click as it found its position. The effort seemed wasted; it would take a lot more to startle Helen. "Where's she gonna stay? Surely not with Pop."

"With me, until I can find Waapikoona."

"You sure you don't want to bring her here? I'm all set up for kids. And she'd have someone to play with."

"Well, I was hopin' you'd let me borrow Dougie for a while. A few days, maybe a week. Just until she learns to trust me."

"You for real with this? The police could find her family. Waapi …"

"Waapikoona."

"Yeah. With such an uncommon name I'm sure they could figure out—"

"Kari, I'm pretty sure that name ain't registered in any records anywhere, and we can't be goin' to the police. This is a real … touchy situation."

Kari gave him the tough-love face, hesitating just long enough to add some suspense to what she was about to drop. "Don't take this the wrong way, but it's an awful lot to take on for a woman who up and left. She didn't even give you her number, Mickey."

"Ain't no other option. I'm the only one who understands what's goin' on here."

"Her family wouldn't understand?"

"Waapikoona's her only family. She's never been around … well, any other people."

Kari stood up a bit straighter at that. "Wow."

"Yeah."

"Okay, if you wanna sit with Janie in the kitchen, I'll find some clothes."

Mick rejoined Janie at the table. Poured milk into his bowl, poked Janie in the belly with his spoon to make her laugh. Tried to lasso his stampeding thoughts while cats fell off window sills in the video on his phone. At least Janie was giggling, though, enough so that milk was dribbling down her chin. He shoveled Cinnamon Toasties into his mouth and rehashed his mental list, adding one item to the very end: make Waapikoona help him raise baby Helen from the dead.

Two things had to be ticked off before that could happen. He had to watch baby Helen die. He had to find Waapikoona. Hopefully in reversed order, because the first one would be a lot easier to stomach if it was actually the second.

BACK AT HIS apartment, Mick stacked the clothes Kari had given him on the couch. It was a mix of Doug's and Janie's—sweatshirts, pants, T-shirts, skirts. Warm pajamas and fuzzy slippers. One pair of snow boots, one pair of Velcro sneakers. Doug's old winter coat Kari was saving for Janie who hadn't yet grown into it. Beside the stack he set a fleece snowflake blanket and a pink floppy-eared stuffed bunny donated by Janie.

He had no idea what he was going to do with the girl during his U-Fill shift. He'd have Dougie too and sure as hell couldn't park them both behind the counter while he worked. Stashing one kid during his shift was pushing it enough. And speaking of the U-Fill, he had a favor to ask of his boss. He got his phone and dialed the number.

"U-Fill."

"Hey, boss. Any chance a woman called there lookin' for me?" Mick's heart did a little stumble at the memory of that phone call and threatened to stumble again if the answer to his question was yes.

"No luck there, man."

That was okay. Just fine. No call didn't mean she wouldn't call, just meant she hadn't yet. "Mind if I ask a favor?"

"Depends. You usin' my landline to pick up women?" After a pause, the man let out a laugh.

Mick couldn't find a laugh to return. "No, it's just she saw me there and don't got my cell—"

"All right, all right, I'm just messin' with ya. Yeah, I'll give her your number if she calls. In fact, I'll do you one better and post it by the phone for Brenda too."

When Mick hung up he made a mental note to tell Brenda in person when she took over at the end of his shift that night, just to make it personal so she wouldn't forget. All shifts needed to be covered. He couldn't risk missing a second call. Or a third, if he'd already missed one.

Next on his list: get the girl settled in his apartment. A trial run was in order. He had to know if the girl and Doug would be okay all evening into the night while he was at work, just the two of them together, with Old Mae upstairs for emergencies. If not, he'd have to use Kari, and he really didn't want to do that.

CHAPTER
9

THE GTO HUMMED along wet roads twisting through trees shedding their week-old coats of frost. The noon sun glared through blue sky, warm through the car windows, making winter feel far away. Mick turned off the heat and cracked his window. It was February-something. Should be deep-freeze cold, even during the day, but he would take this spring fake-out. He felt solar-powered, like for once he had the energy, and the all-too-crucial optimism, to mount this day and spur it into action. Bad luck and unsurmountable circumstance felt as far away as a sleet storm.

He parked in Pop's driveway, killed the engine, and got out, grabbing Doug's old winter coat, the Velcro sneakers, and the pink stuffed bunny he'd brought as a bribe. The sun stroked him, made him want to ruffle his feathers, let it reach him deep down. He knocked on Pop's front door as he let himself in. Pop gave him a nod before turning his attention back to his history program on the little tube TV

on his kitchen table. Past him, Doug and the girl sat cross-legged, bent over Doug's sketchbook.

Mick's shadow fell across them. The girl looked up, her eyes shifting from peace to war and skipping gears in between. Doug, noticing the change in his companion, cut off what he was saying and looked up too. "Hey, Uncle Mick."

"Hey. I need to get you two packed up and over to my place. Think you can help me with that?"

"Um …" Doug glanced at the girl, scrunched his face. "You sure?"

"We're gonna give it a try. You two can't stay here with Pop forever." He held out the stuffed bunny and squatted. "I brought a gift."

The girl's eyes didn't stray from their hard aim on his. Maybe she wasn't the pink bunny type. Heck, if she was anything like her sister, he should've brought her a bone knife or a necklace of demon teeth. And squatting was killing his bad leg, so he took a seat on the far end of the couch while still holding out the bunny.

Spot wriggled over from his place under the kitchen table by Pop's legs. His tail smacked furniture and walls it wagged so hard. Mick shielded his bad leg from the tail while Spot inserted himself between him and the kids, tongue flopping, almost as if he was overcompensating because of the tension in the room. He sat down at Mick's feet, expectant, like the bunny was a toy for him.

"You wanna hand this to her, Doug? See if she wants it?"

Doug raised his eyebrows, smirking and nodding like this was about to get hilarious. He took the bunny and returned to his seat next to the girl. "I don't think Janie's gonna be too happy when she sees this thing's been decapitated."

The girl's glare faltered; the pink plush temptation was too hard to ignore now at such close range. Doug moved it closer so it touched the girl's arm. She flinched and shrunk away, dropping Mick's eye to give all her attention to the impossibly soft, unnaturally pink thing. Mick felt certain she'd never seen any toys that color or texture in her time. She reached out with her good hand, her crippled one tucked close against her belly as if for safety. One finger extended, she tested the fur on the bunny before looking to Doug for some kind of clue.

"Just a toy," he said, making it hop through the air. "You want it?" He offered it to her.

She looked between him and Mick.

"She still thinks you're a bad guy, Uncle Mick."

"Well come over here and gimme a hug. Show her I won't bite."

Doug got up and put his arms around Mick's neck, squeezing as if to prove his unending trust. Mick squeezed back. He hadn't had a hug like this from Doug in months, and he held it longer, knowing it would soon be extinct. Then Doug went back over to the pallet on the floor and handed the bunny over nonchalantly, giving the girl no opportunity to refuse. She curled her arm around it, slowly brought it to her cheek and squeezed, those eyes still set in a glare, but a dimmed one.

"What's her name?" Doug asked.

It would seem strange Mick didn't know, but there was no way around it. "Don't remember."

Mick had another gift. A secret weapon. After his mistake trying to win the girl over with a photo on his phone, he had thought this one through, twisted it around, looked at all angles. It could go two ways. It would prove Mick had been close to this girl's people, maybe even Waapikoona herself, depending on what the girl remembered. The other

way? In this girl's eyes, she might see this gift and think *this man murdered my sister*.

He'd hoped to make more ground with the bunny and not have to take this risk. But with that glare still in place, he figured he had nothing to lose. Reaching into his jeans pocket, he withdrew the two beaded earrings Waapikoona had left on his bathroom sink. The same ones he tried to return to her that night in the mausoleum just before he'd kissed her. She refused to come forward and take them on her own, so he decided to keep them instead. And since that day she left, they'd lay on his bathroom sink as a reminder of what he lost, and what he vowed to find.

He was sore with need for her. This girl in front of him needed her too. And now, she was needed to bring about a miracle, possible only if he found her.

Bright against his palm, the earrings needed no introduction. He held them there, let the girl look. She tipped forward, rising to her knees in an act of getting closer she seemed unaware of.

All at once she was on her feet, craning to look past Mick, twisting to check the door. Mick caught his hasty reach—grabbing her would be a bad move. He lowered his arm, tried to relax. She wasn't planning to dart. She was looking for someone.

He extended the earrings closer to her, jingling them in his palm. "You want 'em?"

This was how creeps lured children, and to her, he was a creep. The processing of that thought was cut short by the girl stabbing a finger into his hand that held the earrings, rapid fire.

"Yeah. Waapikoona's, right?"

She ceased stabbing to look at him, lips tight, eyes frantic.

"You'll stay with me and I'll find her. I'll bring her home. Can you—"

But she was frowning now, focusing on his words but looking very lost. This language barrier had to somehow be overcome for any of this to work. He pointed to his chest then the earrings. He shaded his eyes as if looking across a great distance and scanned the room. "I'm lookin' for her."

All it did was make the girl stab his palm more frantically.

"Hey, Dougie, can you draw a quick sketch? Somethin' that'll show her I'm lookin' for her sister?"

Doug got up and sat beside Mick on the couch with his sketchbook balanced on his lap. He drew a tall stick person next to a short one. "How d'ya spell Sarah's other name?"

As Mick spelled it out, Doug wrote it above the tall figure, but halfway through Mick realized that was all wrong. "Draw two people the same size. Well, one just a hair bigger than the other, like a kid her size next to a bigger kid. She ain't gonna remember her sister as an adult."

"For real?" Doug flipped to a new page. He sketched two figures, one slightly larger with long hair and Waapikoona's name written above. The other he drew with bangs and hair cut blunt above the shoulders. He pointed to that one then pointed to the girl. "This one's you."

"And I," Mick said, pointing to himself, "am looking for Waapikoona." He repeated his pantomime from before, following it up with a finger on the taller stick figure.

The girl gripped his sleeve and yanked—hard. Her need for him to get up and go wouldn't have been more clear if she'd yelled it in English. And now Mick had to do exactly what she demanded, but the get up and go would only bring her to another strange house nowhere near Waapikoona. It would look like a trick. He'd have to figure out a way for it not to.

While Doug packed his stuff, Pop got the girl into the coat. She refused the zipper and the hood, but that was good enough for Mick, especially with that faux spring outside. Doug's dinosaur pajamas would keep her warm. She resisted the sneakers until Doug put on his own. Then she slid her feet in and tested them one at a time against the floor. Pressing, lifting, pressing, seeming to enjoy the squish of the sole and the slight squeak.

"You never worn sneakers before?" Doug had stopped shoving stuff into his backpack to watch. He caught Mick's eye, but the question on his face was too deep—too observant—for Mick to answer now. Or ever.

Mick picked up the pink bunny and handed it to her. She took it without malice. He was getting somewhere. Finally, things were working out.

They got her outside as far as the driveway before she put on the brakes, her gaze narrowed on the GTO sitting in the sunlight. It was afire, a Brazen Orange monster crouched among dripping trees. If she expected horses, a carriage, a train, then what sat before her was a spaceship.

Doug walked up beside her, watching her face. "Ain't it almost like she never seen a car? Never seen sneakers? And you shoulda seen her when Grandpop turned the TV on."

"She's just green to society, like I said."

"Aw, really? Never seen a car or a TV?" The no-bullshit cock to his head, the hands on his hips—there wouldn't be any fooling this kid much longer.

"Let's get inside and show 'er it's okay."

The girl had started backing toward Pop's front door. Doug took her hand, gave her a gentle tug toward the car. Mick opened the door and folded the seat forward. Doug would have to ride in back with her to keep her calm. The startup sound was going to scare her back to death. Had he been thinking, he would have borrowed Kari's docile old Buick for this trip.

The girl had planted her feet a few yards from the open car door, and Doug's coaxing had lost effect. The way she was squeezing that pink rabbit had Doug's prediction of decapitation looking truer than ever. He opened his free palm to Mick in a *what now?*

Mick had no idea what. His Saturday was slipping away, and that mental list was nowhere near complete. Picking her up and strapping her into the backseat would dissolve the inch of trust he'd gained, and it would take twice the time to earn back. His free time was too valuable to be spending on things done wrong.

If this car was a spaceship to her, maybe she needed to see a demo run. He needed a guinea pig.

He turned around, waved to Pop who was watching through the window. When the door opened, Mick called, "Hey, Pop, would ya mind lettin' Spot out? We're gonna take him with us."

Pop whistled, and the dog came barreling toward them and hopped straight in the back seat as if he knew the drill. Mick folded the seat back and said to Doug, "Cover her ears, will ya?" As Doug cupped his hands over the girl's ears, Mick got in and closed the door. He stuck the key in the ignition and shook his head. "She's gonna bolt."

He closed his eyes against the startup roar of engine and exhaust. Kept them closed as the engine found its idle, willing his eagle down because if she ran, he'd want to shift. The image of a fleeing underworld creature pulled a trigger in him so deeply he had to shove it far away. Let her run. He could catch her as a man like he had last time. He let the memory of it fill in, proving to his eagle he could do it. She'd be caught. There was no need to shift.

When he opened his eyes and risked a glance, he found the girl still in place, Doug's hands slowly lowering from her ears. Mick shifted into reverse and eased the gas, backing down the driveway as he watched the kids for any sign of failure. Spot nosed his window, so he opened it and called out, "All okay?"

Doug gave a thumbs-up.

He backed to the road then shifted into first and returned to his spot by the house where he killed the engine. He got out and let Spot out, but he hopped right back in, determined to have his ride. Mick called him back out and walked to the kids, whistling for the dog to follow.

"See?" he said when he closed in. "Spot wants to go again. You want to ride with him?"

The girl wasn't listening. She was too focused on the GTO behind him. What had he done with those earrings? He checked his pocket—there. He pulled them out, held them in front of her. "You have to ride if you want me to find Waapikoona."

At that, the girl looked straight up at him.

If he got her in the car, she'd be expecting Waapikoona at the end of the ride. This whole thing was going to blow up in his face. As if cued by that thought, the girl went forward, strangling that bunny in the crook of one arm while pulling Doug along with the other.

"Holy cow, it's workin'," Doug said.

Spot made it in the backseat first and the girl followed, stiff with her step like she didn't know where to place her feet. Mick went around to open the passenger side and found her crouched, wet sneakers on the seat next to Spot, following the dog's lead. Mick tugged Spot out. Inside, Doug had slid over to force the girl into Janie's booster and was now tapping her feet to show her where he'd put his. She unfolded hers and let them fall over the edge of the seat, so Mick pulled out the seat belt and stretched it across her.

She cried out. Mick ducked just in time to avoid a thrown elbow. An electric blow to his bad leg had him clamping down on every curse word he knew. He bent, catching himself against the seat, muscle memory sending his hands to shield the leg. The seat belt zipped back into its holder.

"It's okay! It's okay!" Doug was shouting as he got ahold of her arm. It was her legs that needed to be restrained. That kick, right into his bad shin, took him back to a place he visited in nightmares. Dry leaves shuffling across stone floor. Bound wrists. The ripe metallic smell of his own blood, the stench of his burned flesh. And Waapikoona's chilling laughter as she lay broken on the floor, baiting Jeremiah. Her haunted, helpless eyes as she pleaded for Mick to find his eagle.

Mick shoved out of the car and slammed the door. Fingers tapped his shoulders, his head. He spun, worsening the pain shooting through his leg. No one behind him. A drop of water hit the roof of the car, another plopped onto the hood. It hadn't been fingers but water dropping from the trees. *Breathe, Mick. Get a grip.*

All air released from his lungs, he took a huge gulp of it. Spot was circling the car, looking for a way in. The torture in that mausoleum was long gone. Mick was here, in Pop's driveway, on this new, bright day. He opened the car door.

"She don't like the seat belt," Doug said.

"Fine. No seat belt." Mick unfolded the front seat and let Spot in. "You put yours on, though." He slammed the door and limped around to the driver's side. Anger was damn well misplaced here—that girl didn't intend that aim. She was afraid for good reason. Didn't matter it was over a damn seat belt and a damn car ride. To her, he may as well

be chaining her to the back of a fire-breathing dragon. This called for sympathy, not anger.

Didn't stop him from being pissed. The world was out to get him, right in his fuckin' shin that took some sadistic asshole's knife a couple months ago and would never be the same. And he'd just gotten this girl in his car on a promise he couldn't fulfill at the end of the ride. Or may not ever fulfill. Waapikoona could help him three times over right now, but if the world was out to punish him, then he'd never find her. She'd be lost in it forever.

"Cover her ears." His voice sounded pissed. He had no energy to fix it. He turned the key and the GTO roared alive; he saw the girl flinch in the rearview mirror. He hit the door locks and backed to the road before she changed her mind. "And if there's any way you can get that seat belt on her ..."

Doug went to work and Mick tuned out. He had to figure out how to show her he was trying to find her sister, that he wanted—*needed*—her just as badly as the girl did. That it was going to take time, and she'd have to be patient, and trust him, and stay in his apartment, and not cause any trouble every day and night he was at work. It was a lot to ask of any kid her age. He was going to have to lean on Old Mae, and he didn't want to do that. But it was better than leaning on Kari.

"We gotta give her a name," Doug said.

"Give 'er one."

"Has to be something cool, 'cause Indians always have cool names like Walks With Wolves or somethin' like that."

"I ain't sure that's—" Mick didn't know why it was wrong, it just was. It seemed a name like that would be given by her own people, not by them. "Just don't seem all that appropriate for us to ..."

"You think she has two names like Sarah does?"

That seemed likely. And Waapikoona couldn't condemn them for giving the girl an English name when Waapikoona used one herself. "I bet you're right there, Dougie."

"You think she'd tell me if I guessed it?"

Mick had to chuckle at the optimism in that. "Worth a try." He heard the seat belt click and glanced in the mirror to find the strap crossing the girl's chest. His eyes met hers in the reflection. Her look was that of icy distrust put on temporary hold due to a promise he'd made—and might not be able to fulfill.

CHAPTER
10

SEVERAL DRIVEWAYS AWAY from Sam and Josie's, Waapikoona killed the Jeep's engine and coasted to a stop. Rain had taught her this trick in a different Jeep many years ago. The house slept but the door was unlocked, so she let herself in, trading the sharp bite of the wind for a toasty warmth that soothed the prickle of her winter-stung cheeks. She found her old bedroom by feel in the dark. The scent of dollar-store fabric softener in the fresh bedding sucked her back in time, and she closed the door behind her and stood there soaking it all in. That smell was absolution. It was medicine, just as it had been so many years ago. As a child she'd burrow in those sheets and imagine herself underground with her sister. Her arm linked with Pinepakatwi's imaginary one, she'd promised to someday find her and bring her back just like someone had brought her back.

She needed a safe, stable place like this for her sister as soon as she revived her. Not a drafty tomb with cold stone floors and the stain of Mick's blood. Not the old spider-filled hunting cabin with broken windows she'd found after that. Not a cave, or derelict RV, or empty foreclosed mansion, or cheap motel room. A home, legal and permanent. She'd have to backtrack and unearth all her stashed money. She had enough to buy a cheap plot of land outright, with a trailer like Rain's, far from modern civilization. Maybe she could buy Rain's. Pay for it with real money so no one could ever tell her to leave. Following the white man's rules to keep her sister safe was a compromise she'd make.

She felt along the wall for the electrical outlet and found it still held a night-light. She flipped it on—the same shooting star night-light Sam had bought her when she was eleven years old. *Someday you won't be afraid of the dark*, he'd told her. *And then you won't need this.*

She'd joined the dark.

And she'd found a man who knew this and was willing to die for her anyway.

Hands on head, fingers woven into hair, she tugged, ready to rip it all out. If Mick didn't get out of her head soon, she wasn't sure she'd have any hair left.

The decision had been obvious in that tomb and was still obvious now. Refusing to see him die had put her sister's chance at a new life in a very bad man's hands. At the time, there had been no way out of it. Now she knew Mick was a liability she couldn't afford. He meant too much. As much as her sister? Impossible—but for the question to exist at all meant there was some chance it could be true. She'd been pushed to choose between them, and in failing to, she'd nearly destroyed them both. Mick had to be put away, left behind, relegated to another part of her circle of time. She knew this; she'd decided this. So she couldn't understand why he kept coming up like some unresolved matter.

He was born alive and she was undead, yet he was the one haunting her.

After stripping off her boots, coat, and jeans, she burrowed into the clean sheets and thought of anything but him.

Sleep came in unsatisfying fits, too erratic to be considered rest. Even while dozing she felt awake, her dreams too vivid to be the work of an unconscious mind. The faint trickle of morning sun crawled across the curtained window. Cars with bad mufflers started up outside and drove off. She rolled out of bed and found a robe and slippers in the closet. Even though she'd been half awake enough to hear each time the heater hummed alive, the house had taken on a chill overnight.

In the kitchen, the west-facing window over the old cast iron sink was still dark. Yesterday she hadn't considered this room, or how little it had changed, right down to the joyous yellow towels hanging on the oven handle and the hummingbird suncatcher suction-cupped to the window. Something about that turquoise and gold bird had reminded her of her mother when she came here as an orphan. As much as she wanted to touch it, to feel its weight in her palm, she feared her touch would cause it to fall and crash on the floor. Its presence linked this life to her life with her people, and she couldn't stand to think it could be so easily broken, so she left it alone and never told a soul how much it meant to her. Perhaps it was time she started talking. She flipped on the light above the stove and found a note on the counter: *Stew in fridge.*

That had been dinner she'd missed. She hoped Sam and Josie hadn't waited up for her. The intention hadn't been to stay away for most of the night, but that's what had happened. She needed to do better.

"Eggs and toast?" Sam's gravelly pre-coffee voice from the doorway.

"Let me do it," she answered. "You sit."

"I'll get the coffee going."

There was no reason for any of this to remind her of prepping breakfast with Mick. Of his pillow-smushed hair and heavy-lidded eyes or how he'd teased her about eating the horned serpent he'd caught and she'd teased him back. The ghost of that day's belly-tingle fluttered through her, desperate for notice. She knew some ghosts had to be ignored until they gave up. And speaking of ghosts …

"You didn't tell me about Rain."

Sam smeared a hand across his forehead. "I had it in mind to. We're a bit torn up still. It's not the easiest thing …" Although he was looking at her, his attention drifted away, to a place she didn't want to follow him. He raised a shoulder, wiped his eye on it. "We wanted to call you when it happened, but had no way."

She was drawn away a moment, wondering what she would've done when hearing that news. Drop everything and go home? Run farther away?

"Why don't you give me your number—" Sam had retrieved his phone from its charging cable on the counter and was thumbing through screens. "Well isn't that funny. Rain's father's house burned last night. It's a total loss. And he's missing …" His gaze slowly raised to meet Waapikoona's.

Alibis weren't something she ever needed. If things got too tricky, or she made too much of a mess—like burning a house to the ground in a close-knit community—she'd simply snag a set of wheels and move on. The town of Wyona had kept her longer than any other place, only because she'd gotten so tangled with Mick.

Instead of lie to Sam, she'd have to avoid it. "I don't have a number to give you. I don't have a phone."

Sam looked up from his screen, reading her face for a lie, finding none. "You should get one. It's a convenient thing to have."

A phone would make her accountable. Trackable, findable, a permanent fixture in people's lives. Once her sister was raised she couldn't avoid that with her, and having or not having a phone had nothing to do with it. She planned to be the rock her sister could stand on. "I know."

He set down his phone. "You went to see Rain last night."

She met his eyes calmly, kept her face steady. "I tried to. His trailer is boarded up. I met his neighbor, and she gave me the keys to the Jeep. He left it for me." Saying those words moved her so much she felt her throat lock up.

"Meredith?"

To use the neighbor as an alibi, she'd at least need her name. It was almost like Sam was helping her out. Where had she left the urns? They were damning evidence she had to destroy.

"You don't remember her, do you?" Sam asked.

Killing people was a lot easier in places where she was anonymous. Practice hadn't made her good. It had made her sloppy.

"She was probably a little girl when you left. Rick and Savannah's kid."

A match struck deep inside the cavern of those memories. Baby Meredith. Premature, nearly bankrupted her parents with hospital bills. The three of them had to move into Sam and Josie's basement for a few months after they lost their house. "I didn't remember, but I do now."

"She married a Blackfeet. Good guy. Does handyman work for the Tribal office sometimes. He's paying her way through community college. She wants to be a journalist, add some Native perspective to the news."

It was a nice endeavor, so full of hope and progress and the potential to invoke real change—until The Silent One flooded the land with his demons.

"Is the guy from around here?"

"Nope. He doesn't give away much either. Doesn't seem to have any family but Meredith now."

"So you really have made peace with the Blackfeet." She smiled so he'd know she was only ribbing.

He gave her hair a gentle tug. "You know it was only one Blackfeet I had no peace for."

"You should've had no peace with me, for running away with him."

"I could never be angry like that with you, girl."

She watched the eggs wiggle in the skillet and imagined what would happen if she relayed everything she'd learned from Jeremiah—things about herself, where she'd come from, whom she'd agreed to serve, the people she'd killed for him, and for what purpose. She could go even further and tell him about Mick and how she'd betrayed The Silent One. How she'd been involved in Jeremiah's death. It was all too heavy, too outlandish. He'd never believe her, and if he did, he'd never again sleep at night.

One of those things pressed her to speak of more than the others, and she had the sense she could do it without roaming out of Sam's world. She flipped the eggs and decided to test the waters. "What do you know about our Thunder-Being legends?"

"Not a lot. You need to speak to the elders."

She felt like an imposter around the elders. Like somehow, they'd know she wasn't one of them. As a child it had only been a feeling with no weight except for the one in her heart.

Now she had the knowledge and the unearthed memories to prove it.

He scooped the eggs from the skillet onto a plate. "I see your face. You can't still be afraid of the elders."

"Not afraid. Just—"

"Just pulling my arm out of the socket in the opposite direction when it's time to say hi to them or hiding behind me anytime they're near—"

She laughed, full into her belly. "I was eleven!"

"And twelve and thirteen—"

She socked him in the arm, nearly spilling both plates. As he righted himself her laughter died, the high it gave her flipping to the darkest low. It left behind a sobering desire for absolute confession. All of it—her past life, her current, The Silent One, her sister, Mick. "I never felt like I belonged here."

"Waapikoona—"

"I know, it's stupid. Makes no sense because of how much you did for me."

"You knew *Myaamia*. Before you remembered how to speak English."

"Only some words. They could've been overlap words from other similar languages. And we're a mixture of tribes, displaced by the white people. Our history is—"

He took her arm, waited for her to look at him. She didn't remember being on his eye level before. Her image of him had always been strong and tall. Her rock, her monster slayer, her protector. "Then that's true for all of us, and none of us belong. But we gather as we can, and we've made a decision in this time to be one people."

"I met a man in Missouri, different from any man—" Random, completely unrelated. Those thoughts that had pressed her before were now stampeding, and she'd lost control. "I feel like I grew roots there that I didn't plan and don't want. And can't break."

Sam pushed down the lever on the toaster, a slow, deliberate, contemplative mash of plastic. "Tell me about this man." His voice took on the tone of what it sounded like when he spoke of Jeremiah.

"A nice man. Too nice. Kind. Hard-working. Simple, until you get to know him." She had never met anymore more complicated than Mick.

"Did you get to know him?"

"Not as much as I wanted to." No, that was wrong. "More than I wanted to."

"He have a job?"

"Two jobs." Also wrong. He said he had three. That was the day she saw him after taking his Pontiac. Standing there in his coveralls, smelling of car oil and grease, with a smudge across his cheek. He'd been so bristly, his eyes so harsh in the sun she'd wanted to stand there in the cold wind and stare. She'd pissed him off so much he threatened to kill her, and she nearly accepted, just so he'd get close enough to try it.

"Kids?"

"Just a niece and a nephew he dotes on like crazy."

"I'm not hearing any faults here, girl."

"He's white."

"And you have a problem with that?"

She knew her hatred was based on a life lived so far from this time, but it was near to her and as vivid and relevant as anything that might try to counteract it. Ripples of that past plagued this present. A wrong hung in the air, invisible to some, ignored by others. It didn't seem to matter her hatred might be unfair. Many things were unfair. But then she'd met Mick, and none of her labels would stick. "Not ... anymore."

"So?"

"So he's not—" She couldn't explain the depth of the 'so' without taking Sam for a ride into a world he'd think was supernatural and would never understand unless he saw things firsthand. She didn't want him to see things. "He's not from the world I come from."

Sam poured coffee and gestured at her to sit at the table. "I bet you don't have to look all that hard to see these worlds you talk about aren't as different as you think. What matters is what's in the middle of the Venn diagram."

With Sam, things like this were always science and data. A pros and cons list, a graph, a diagram—it was a solution to be worked out on paper. To her, there was nothing to compare. All she saw was contrast. Virtuous Thunder-Beings against venomous flying demons, sunlight against darkness, life against death. People born from their mothers versus people raised from their own dead bones. These opposites might not matter if she hadn't bargained with the mightiest demon, hadn't contributed resources to his war against Mick's world.

But then … she'd strayed from that. She'd brought a Thunder-Being into The Silent One's den. She was having serious thoughts about mutiny. And if Soto was right, she seemed to be a scrupulous murderer. Mick had crossed over to her side just as she had to his. His Thunder-Being had killed mother-born men with her, had traveled into the underworld and made it out alive. Together, she and Mick *were* the overlapping piece of a Venn diagram of their two worlds.

She took a hasty chug of coffee, burning her tongue and throat all the way down. This line of thinking would only make things worse.

So desperate was the need for a change in subject, she picked out the hardest news to surrender. "I have a sister."

"What?" Sam said, joining Josie's voice from the doorway.

Josie slid quickly into the chair beside her. Early morning revealed the age on her face normally hidden by Josie's constant motion in her always busy day. She was the hummingbird in that kitchen, flitting around so much a person might never lay an eye on her. "A sister you remembered? Or was it one of those online DNA tests—"

"Yes, I remembered." She had no way to explain this safely. She had to think.

"Where is she?"

"In Missouri. I'm ... waiting to be reunited with her."

Sam slapped the table. "Well what's the wait? I can drive—"

"No—" *Think, think, think.* "I'm not going to see her until I've brought the man who abused her to justice."

"Oh." The excited light in Josie's eyes darkened. She found Waapikoona's hand, covering it with her own. "How old is she?"

"Eight."

"A little girl?"

Sam made a short, low grumble in the back of his throat. "Who's the man?"

Waapikoona knew better than to link her name with Hammond's, even with people she trusted. That kind of secret only weighed down the people she loved. "He might be going by a different name than the one I know."

"White man?"

She nodded, even though she hated tagging him with the same label she'd used a moment ago on Mick. They were the same color, yes, but one was a guardian of the upperworld, and the other was a skin-covered pile of waste with an immeasurable debt to settle. An efficient blade to the neck was not what she had planned. His payment would take a

115

long time to work off. She'd dreamed of the things she'd do to him in not one life, but two.

The grumble that came from Sam meant he had some ideas of his own—ideas his high moral stance would never allow him to carry out. Waapikoona was thankful she'd left her morals back in her old life and was glad to be away from Mick and the inconvenient influence of his.

"How can we help?" Josie asked.

Waapikoona withdrew her hand from under Josie's. "Giving me a place to crash is help enough."

No one could help. Finding Hammond was her job to face alone. Jeremiah's people had to be keeping him, and the only leads she had were here in Oklahoma. She had no idea if these people he spoke of were Blackfeet like him, but it was the only clue she had to go on. She had to visit Meredith again and speak to her husband.

Solitary work had never felt so lonely.

CHAPTER
11

"**E**DNA?"

Doug had found the top one hundred names in the year 1890 on Mick's phone and was reading them to the girl in the backseat of the GTO. He'd asked Mick if he remembered anything about her name, and Mick figured there was no harm in a little shrouded truth so he told him it was an old-fashioned name, one from the late 1800s. Even though Mick could not remember Waapikoona saying her sister's name, he knew if the girl had an English name it had to come from that time period.

Doug had gone to work. He'd established their names—Doug, Mick, Spot—and the girl seemed to understand. Mick was halfway to his apartment and hadn't come up with any ideas for how he was going to get her inside and keep her there once they arrived and the girl saw no Waapikoona waiting.

"Mabel?"

In the rearview mirror, Mick saw the girl shake her head.

"You think she can write?" Doug asked. "Maybe if I write our names, she could write hers."

For Doug to think an eight-year-old girl couldn't write meant he'd caught on to a lot more than Mick had explained. "Maybe."

Papers shuffled as Doug flipped to a new page in his sketchbook. He wrote 'Doug,' 'Mick,' and 'Spot,' saying them again while pointing them out in the car. Then he turned the paper toward her.

Mick slowed for a turn. Now they were five minutes away from his promise blowing up into nothing. The girl's name was not important now. He needed her to understand this promise would not pay out at the end of this drive. "Hey, Dougie, do me a favor? Draw a picture with ..." Waapikoona in a box—no, too much unintended meaning. Waapikoona hiding, or in a car, with them in a car following—no, the girl had no experience with cars. Waapikoona lost, somewhere not too frightening. "Draw Waapikoona in the forest and me lookin' for her."

"She's writing. I think that's—is that an *I*?"

"And draw the girl waiting in my apartment." Mick saw the turn-in for his driveway ahead.

"*I-S*—"

"Draw you waitin' with her. I need you to—"

"Isabel!"

The girl's movement caught in Mick's peripheral vision, and he hit the brakes as a shudder tore through his bones. The dashboard lights turned rainbow, kaleidoscopic. Road and forest sharpened, every piece of gravel, every pine needle, every curled dead leaf. It was surreal without his eagle's field of view, and that was proof he hadn't lost his human form.

He concentrated on the feel of his jacket against his skin, of his foot mashing the brake pedal. He reached for the gearshift and found first gear, fixating on the clunk in the belly of the GTO, the mechanics of it, how it looked from his back on the creeper. The road ahead was now overlaid with two scenes—one belonging to eagle, another to human. He centered himself on that inferior human version and heard Doug calling his name.

"You gotta keep her still, Dougie. She can't be jumpin' around like that."

"She's just excited I got her name."

A thunder rolled from Mick's head to his toes as his eagle retreated, the vibration of it so pronounced in his ears he worried it had reached into the real world. "Yeah, but I gotta drive this car—"

"Sorry."

Mick checked the mirror, found the girl's seat belt across her chest and her surprised eyes hard on his. "You don't gotta be sorry, just …" He couldn't have close calls like this around the kids. He'd been a fool to think he'd mastered shifting. It was the lack of underworld creatures in his life that had allowed him to maintain control, not him learning to control it. And if this girl had just figured out what he was, she'd never stay in his apartment. He stopped in the middle of the driveway. Ahead, Old Mae's house glistened in the daylight, having shed its skin of ice.

"And 'Isabel' ain't that old-fashioned," Doug said. "There's two girls named Isabel in my class at school."

Mick turned around in the seat to look Doug in the eye. "This girl expects her sister to be here, and she ain't gonna be happy to find she's not."

Doug's mouth made a silent *Oh*.

"Her name really Isabel?"

The girl sat straighter. Doug said, "I think so," and turned his sketchbook page to face Mick.

ISABEL was written in block letters, large and spaced apart like the work of a child who'd just learned to write. This was good—finally something to help Mick out. If she could write she could read. He took the page and wrote, *Your sister is not here. She is missing.*

He turned it back to her.

She stared, her face blank. The understanding Mick hoped to see—not there. He pointed to the words he wrote. She shook her head.

He flipped a page and drew the picture he'd asked Doug to draw. Quickly sketched trees, a stick-figure Waapikoona standing among them, her name written above her head. Him, labeled with his name, standing far away. The girl, Isabel, standing inside a house with a wide porch and peaked roof just like Old Mae's.

"Mick, Isabel, this house." He pointed to all three as he named them. "Waapikoona, somewhere out there." He gestured to the woods beside the driveway. "I am going to find her." He walked his fingers from his image on the page to the image of Waapikoona in the trees.

He didn't have time for any of this.

"Keep drillin' that in, Dougie, and I'll get us to the house." He handed the sketchbook back to Doug and put his foot on the gas.

As he parked the GTO, he noticed the house's long shadow darkening the lawn behind. Checking the time proved it was well into the afternoon. He still had to get the girl settled, feed everyone including himself, and search the mausoleum before his U-Fill shift. Two of the three couldn't be rushed.

Spot invaded his lap when he opened his car door, eager to lead the way. Mick let him out, got out, and folded the seat forward for Doug.

"Get a good hold of her hand, would ya?"

He wished he had a leash to clip onto the girl. Minutes ticked away as they negotiated her out of the car. The farthest they got her was to the edge of the seat. Mick had to restrain himself from taking her by the arm and lifting her onto his shoulder. This wasn't Janie throwing a temper tantrum in the grocery store and needing to be removed to save everyone's hearing. It was an orphaned girl, awakened in a new time, stolen from the safety of the woods, brought to the home of a stranger who looked very much like her enemy.

"I'm gonna unlock the door," Mick said, backing away.

He was her enemy in more ways than one. In her time as the invader. In this time as the protector of the upperworld whose job it was to exterminate underworld beings like her. Could she be considered the invader in this time? No—it was different, somehow, and trying to think it through left the idea spinning in a catch-22 he couldn't dedicate any time to.

Above him, gutters ticked with the melted snow trickling off the roof. The low winter angle of sunlight stroked his back through his jacket. The day was losing light; soon that mausoleum would be too dark to search. A flashlight's beam would be consumed by the shadows inside.

Feathers littered the steps down to his apartment door and clung to the welcome mat. This was the mess he'd made ungracefully shifting back to human after searching for Waapikoona as an eagle. He'd walked over it enough times to get used to it. He should have thought to clean it up before he brought the girl here.

Isabel. It seemed to be the only word she could read or write, the first and only one she'd learned. It had to be her name.

He glanced across the yard at Dougie, still hanging on to the girl's hand even though she was stubbornly glued to the GTO's seat. The gentle sound of Doug's coaxing voice carried across the yard. There was time. Inside his apartment he found a broom and dustpan and made quick work of the feather mess, dumping them in a trash bag he hid under the porch at the rear of the house. If she was like Waapikoona, she might be able to sense them if he'd brought them inside. He glanced again. She had one foot out of the car.

Up the steps, down the walkway, he worked. With everything wet from the melt, it was tougher work getting the feathers unstuck from the grass. How many feathers had he lost? He kept one eye on the broom and the other on the kids at the car—not an easy task without his eagle's foveae and mix of monocular and binocular vision. Doug had taught him that about eagles. Mick had lived it. He was still a long way from accepting it permanently. Temporarily? He had no choice. He hadn't thought through his life deep into his future, and right now he couldn't. It was a day at a time.

And this day was getting away from him fast.

He dumped the contents of the dustpan and stashed the broom. Doug had Isabel out of the car on two feet. Her eyes were trained to the highest peak of the roof; Mick shielded his eyes from the sun and looked.

A red-tailed hawk perched on the glossy peak, watching them.

An ordinary bird or one of his kind? He had no way to know in human form, other than a wild hunch that was telling him right now a thunderbird would have a good reason to watch him offering shelter to a girl born from the underworld. His work was solitary, but was it for all of them? Did they gather, communicate, work in teams? Could they recognize his eagle when he walked as human?

Yes—he'd been trailed by them after ditching Waapikoona in Illinois. He'd gotten out of the car and hollered at them, chucking rocks like a crazy person until it had forced them on their way. That was when he'd made a pledge to himself to leave both her and his eagle and not look back. It was a different lifetime, when a decision like that had felt like an option.

"We need to get inside," he said to the kids. He ignored the gruffness of his voice and the look it prompted from Doug.

Isabel was already aiming for the cover below the porch, sneakers slapping through small puddles as she dragged Doug by the arm. Doug steered her to the steps leading down to Mick's apartment; Mick got there first and opened the door.

"That was easy," Mick said, flipping the lock behind them. More to close the girl inside than to keep anything out.

Doug shook his abused arm, toeing out of his shoes. "Not really."

"Easy at the end, I mean."

"You see that hawk? You think she has a phobia of birds or somethin'?"

"Maybe."

"Not that the one at Grandpop's house should count, though. Anyone would be afraid of that big ol' thing. And it was chasin' her—"

"Hey, help her get out of them shoes before they mess the floor." He didn't like to interrupt Doug, but this conversation could not take place now.

"And there was this freak thunderstorm, like, thunder and lightning with no rain. Is that normal for winter?"

"Not really, but the weather's been weird lately. The shoes, Dougie?"

"Yeah, sorry." Doug went over to Isabel, who had backed into the wall by the door and glued herself like she'd been

to the GTO's backseat. He ripped the Velcro free, held the shoe, and looked up at her. "Okay, step out."

Mick could leave Doug in charge of that. He had to deal with food. Then figure out how he could leave the two of them alone.

Outside, three short bursts of the hawk's call were answered by a long shriek of its mate, gaining in volume as it dived from the sky. Mick couldn't stop himself from meeting Isabel's big dark eyes across his apartment, their shared recognition like an admission of guilt on both their sides. Hers for being the underworld creature who shouldn't be welcome above ground and his for sheltering her and betraying his allies in the sky.

She trembled but straightened her spine against it. One of The Silent One's raised, accepting shelter from a thunderbird.

"It's all gonna be okay," Mick said.

And that thunderbird, not performing his duty to destroy her.

CHAPTER
12

I F I T W A S possible to overdose on carrots, this girl was
about to prove it. Mick had made a full meal. She'd dissected the sandwich and picked at the soup. When Doug
mentioned she'd eaten carrots at Pop's, Mick handed her
the whole bag from the fridge, and she'd eaten so many he
had to take it away from her.

"So, I gotta step out for a couple hours. You think you
two will be okay watchin' TV until I get home?" Mick had
his back to the kids at the table while he rinsed dishes in the
sink. He didn't want to take the time to clean up now, but
he also knew he wouldn't have time to scrub dried cheese
off plates later. Instead of hearing Doug's reply, he got a
hard tug on his sleeve.

Isabel had come up behind him. Her face was locked in
impatient determination to see the promise met. They didn't
need a common language for him to understand she wanted
Waapikoona now.

"Isabel," he said, wiping off his hands. At the sound of her name, she took in a quick breath. He dug into his pocket for Waapikoona's earrings and pressed them into the girl's good hand quickly enough that she had no time to pull away. He held her fist, closed inside both his own, and waited for her eyes to meet his. "I need you to be patient. But I'm gonna find her."

And in affirmation of that promise to her, he made it more than a vow to himself. He would find her. Even if he had to surrender his human self to his eagle. Even if he lost himself trying.

FOR ONCE, THE old cemetery wasn't empty of the living.

It was a sad place of unkempt landscaping and faded, ancient gravestones marking the lives of those who had been dead long enough to have been abandoned by the living—except for bored teenage boys who had nothing better to do in a small town than run along the tops of the graves, nearly braining themselves each time they slipped. The local stories about this cemetery normally kept even the foolhardiest kids away, so this was a change of pace.

Mick was glad he'd hammered a two-by-four over the door of Waapikoona's mausoleum. The thought of these jokers gaining entrance to the place where he'd nearly died, where he'd last looked into Waapikoona's eyes, where the little girl in his apartment nearly lost her second chance at life … it made him angry enough to be unfit to be around other humans. He wasn't sure what he'd do, and these boys jumping gravestones were wasting his limited time.

He sat in the GTO with the engine running and waited for the kids to grow tired of the game. They'd be real tired of it as soon as one of them slipped the right way and took a gravestone to the balls. They'd spotted the car as soon as he rolled up. Now that they had an audience, a likely grown-up who'd be annoyed by their antics, they had an added level of defiance which upped their game and turned them more brash. With each surly look cast Mick's way, they dared him to get out and stop them. No part of him needed to be dared.

One of them slipped, scarcely avoiding a crack to the spine that sent the others into a fit of macho laughter. Because spinal damage was funny? *Enough.* Mick killed the engine and got out. Maybe it was envy that his teenage years had been spent working long hours after school and mourning his mother, but he wanted, *so* wanted, to shift in front of their smug faces and chase them off with his talons. If they outed him, no one would believe them, but they'd be awake to a new terror that might give them some manners. He released a heavy sigh and got the crowbar out of his trunk. He'd brought it for the two-by-four, but it would come in handy here too. After slamming the lid, he headed toward them.

In their faces he could see them calculating odds. Three of them, one of him. Younger, slighter, and unarmed versus what they saw as one old man with a crowbar. What Mick saw was the reality—three lanky adolescents with budding muscle they hadn't yet learned how to properly use versus a guy who could carry a twenty-inch rim with tire in each arm across a parking lot and had no money to indulge in junk food. He didn't even need a weapon. He started closing the distance between them, minimizing his limp the best he could.

"Ya'll need to get lost."

Two of them backed up, one elbowing the other. The third one jumped off a headstone toward Mick. "Says who?"

Mick weighed the crowbar in his hand. If this kid really wanted to go up against a crowbar, Mick didn't want to hurt him. And if he did cause a concussion or break a bone, it would be human laws that determined consequences. No laws could touch his eagle.

"You really wanna do this?" Mick meant it for himself, but he said it aloud. Shifting in front of strangers? There really was no other quick option?

"Yeah, dickhead. Let's do this."

All right, but he had to lose the clothes. He was done with ruining shirts and jackets, and he couldn't always count on his pants to fall off cleanly. He couldn't afford to replace another pair of talon-gouged jeans. So it all had to come off.

He shrugged out of his jacket and lay it on the ground. Stripped off his shirt. The kid followed with his own coat but paused at the shirt. It seemed strange in the middle of winter, and maybe it was—but the kid went through with it since it seemed stripping off shirts was a natural part of a fist fight. When Mick went for his belt buckle the kid took a big step back. As Mick pulled his belt from the loops the kid shuffled sideways, knocking a knee against a nearby grave. His friends were hollering at him to run, *the dude's crazy, he's a pedo, get outta there!* And Mick didn't even have his zipper halfway down before the three of them were scrambling through the headstones like prey from his eagle, and he hadn't even shifted yet.

Was it a bad time to laugh? Too bad, because he was— so hard he had to bend in half, lean against a gravestone, wipe his eyes. This dude? Surely crazy.

He replaced his belt, shirt, and jacket. Picked up the crowbar. Then he crossed the cemetery far enough to confirm the boys had made it all the way to the road. They had, and they were still running, the slap of their sneakers against the pavement traveling all the way to him in the crisp air.

At the boarded mausoleum door he remembered what he'd done the last time he was here. His human self had stripped the clothes from the eagle-shredded flesh of Jeremiah's corpse. He'd saved the keys from the pockets before tossing everything on a hot fire. He'd driven Jeremiah's old Toyota sedan as deep into the woods as it would go. Then he'd returned to the mausoleum, turned eagle, and carried the corpse piece by piece far into the Ozarks where he'd dropped it into waters infested with horned serpents. It was a cleanup task; it was a warning. *This is what's done to your kind who escape your graves, your dark caverns, your underwater dens. You will be hunted. You will be destroyed.* Those serpents took care of that corpse under his orders because disobedience might allow strange body parts to wash ashore and alert the upperworld of their presence too soon. Even if they recognized the bribe, they still had to obey. Mick's eagle wasn't petty enough to get a kick out of that, but Mick was.

As he wedged the crowbar under the two-by-four, he remembered what still stained the stone floor beyond this door. His blood, Jeremiah's blood. Beside it, the rope that bound Mick to the wall, preventing him from fighting Jeremiah man-to-man. The ash from Waapikoona's fire that had kept her warm on those cold nights, her pallet she slept in. The residue of their kiss that found him in dreams—and in daylight as he worked under cars, prepared breakfast, folded his laundry. And as he lay in bed alone at night.

The two-by-four popped off; the door swung open. Mick stepped into the musty, still air hanging on to the night's deeper chill. His eyes adjusted to the shadows, and he saw it all. Circle of ash. Frayed rope. Stone floor stained with

old blood. He'd survived this. There was no reason it should haunt him so deeply.

The pallet by the fire was nothing but a ragged sleeping bag and a few blankets, but he shook them out, one by one, just to make sure. He moved on to the pile in the corner. There he found a fleece jacket. Hoping to absorb something of her, he pressed it to his nose and inhaled, smelling the wet stone and faded wood smoke she sometimes brought with her. It was a more intimate scent he craved—her skin, her hair. He checked the pockets and found her mica crystal, the one that had guided him to the entrance to The Silent One's cave.

"Bonus," he said, sliding it into his own pocket. He tucked the jacket under his arm. He'd wash it and return it to her when he found her. No use in wasting a good jacket.

The pockets of a pair of jeans gave him a bundle of twenties he fanned in his hand—looked to be over two hundred dollars—and a switchblade that matched the one she'd tried to cut his throat with in his apartment on the day he met her. Dried blood crusted near the handle—was this the knife she'd used to kill Leo Boyle? He couldn't remember. Even if it wasn't, it had probably been used to kill countless others. It was evidence—he couldn't keep it. It was Waapikoona's. He had to.

So he slid it into his pocket next to the crystal and kicked around in the pile of dead leaves in the corner, searching for more because what he'd already gathered would not help him find her. Unearthing two crushed throwaway Ramen cups sent a jolt straight into his bad shin. He ignored it. One purple knit glove surfaced; he picked it up, kicked around for its mate. The slant of late afternoon sun coming through the high window suddenly waned. He took the jacket and jeans to his car and returned to the mausoleum with a flashlight.

In the bright beam of light, he spotted a white piece of paper against the wall. This was his break. It would have an address, a phone number. Something—anything that could help him. He fished it out—a receipt. He squinted to read the faded print and recognized the last four digits of his own debit card number on his bill from Lucky's Tavern. It must have fallen out of his pocket when he was fighting those ropes. That was evidence he was here, linking him to the night Leo Boyle was last seen at Lucky's. He needed to come back here with a gas-powered blower and a pressure washer. But why? Any forensics team could find his blood soaked deep into the cracks of the stone floor. He was here looking for connections that would lead him to Waapikoona, but would anything here connect him to the missing guy no one yet knew was murdered and devoured by demons? Did Jeremiah's blood or his car abandoned in the woods connect to Mick, or Leo, or anything that might land him in hot water? The involvement of law enforcement in this seemed like a joke, but Mick had to pay attention—and be careful. His goal for the future was to shed the eagle, not the man, and he didn't want that man convicted of murder and sent to prison.

He checked the clock on his phone—nearly out of time.

Kicking through the dead leaves lining the walls unearthed a shallow dish of water that Waapikoona must have set out for Spot. After taking one final look around, he slammed the door, retrieved a hammer and nails from his trunk, and replaced the two-by-four across the entrance.

One edge of sky blazed gold with sunset, setting off the deep cobalt blue of the opposite horizon. Hazy slender shapes floated around the graves until he fixed them with a direct stare and they ducked away. He had only a few minutes to find the car in the woods and search it. If he

couldn't find a clue to lead him to Waapikoona, he'd find one to lead him to Jeremiah. Even if he was dead, he'd have family, and Mick had to use what he could get.

Standing on the dirt-packed driveway beside his parked GTO, he tried to return to that day. Jeremiah's old Toyota had been parked in about the same spot. Mick had backed it up, turning on the narrow drive to aim it toward the woods. He'd considered stashing it behind the mausoleum for better cover, but the ground had been too soggy and the necessary path slightly uphill, so he'd instead turned a bit wide and plunged nose-first into the trees, steering around the thick trunks that would cleave the car in half. He walked a few paces behind the GTO's bumper and looked for ruts in the earth. It had only been a few months.

He found twin dips, muddier than the rest of the ground. That's where a front-wheel-drive car would have dug in. He headed into the woods in that direction and found snapped young trees, a grazed trunk of a 100-year-old oak, and a piece of torn slate gray Toyota bumper. Ahead, the forest was too dusky gray itself to find a gray car. He raised the beam of his flashlight and caught something reflective. A tail light, a license plate, and the hunkered frame of a tilted broken car.

When he got up to it, all the windows were missing. Automotive glass sparkled against the forest floor. He opened the driver's side door and found a void where the stereo had been. The glove box open, spilling its contents onto the seat and floor. Someone had found it, had ravaged it. Might have taken something that would help him find Waapikoona.

"Fuckin' meth-heads," he said, banging a fist against the roof.

Losing his cool would not help him right now. He checked the clock on his phone. He needed to be heading back to the kids. It had been too long. He needed to get them set up for the night. He needed to get cleaned up and headed to his U-Fill shift.

He needed to find Waapikoona yesterday, though.

Ignoring the strain in his leg, he swung into the driver's seat. Glass particles crunched under his jeans. Through the litter he searched, pocketing the legible receipts and wrappers. Anything could be a clue. He found an envelope half opened—Oklahoma vehicle registration. He stuck that one in his inner jacket pocket. A couple parking tickets, car repair invoices—he had no time to look now, so he took it all. He tore through the backseat. Empty soda cans, a roll of duct tape, and a purple knit glove matching the one he found in the tomb. There was no time to hold that between both hands and close his eyes, but he did it anyway.

She'd been in this backseat, probably bound with that duct tape.

He could kill Jeremiah all over again. Cut him up in a thousand little pieces. Toss him off a cliff. He could turn eagle and dissect him slowly, eating an organ a day starting with the least essential, making it last until that day no longer haunted him.

He pressed the trunk release and walked to the rear of the car, bracing himself for what he'd find.

It wasn't too bad. Spare tire, snow boots, two history books with library stickers on the spine which he tucked under his arm. He pushed a heavy winter coat aside after checking its pockets. Underneath the coat he found a plastic zipper bag full of photographs. With no time to skim through them, his curiosity would have to wait until later. He shined his flashlight around the trunk one final time and found an empty cardboard box with a half-peeled shipping label. He smoothed the label back on the box, dumped the books and bag of photos inside it, and slammed the trunk. Through the

woods he sprinted on his complaining leg, box in hand, and jumped into the GTO and burned rubber home.

THE SIGHT THAT greeted him in his apartment threatened to choke him up good. Dougie had found Janie's stash of picture books and was reading them to Isabel, his finger trailing each word like a learn-to-read program on TV.

"I know she's gotta know English," Doug said to Mick as he came in the door. "If she can write her name, somebody taught her somethin'."

"You have any trouble with her?"

"Nope. Been doin' this the whole time. I think she remembers, just doesn't want to talk to us yet."

Mick ransacked the kitchen, looking for snacks that would serve as dinner for two kids while he was at work. "Hey, come on over here a minute."

Doug handed the book to Isabel and went to Mick's side.

"Here's what I got for ya. Microwave popcorn, applesauce, bread and American cheese for sandwiches." He opened the fridge and pointed. "Plus carrots if she wants more of them. I'm gonna leave my phone here, so if you run into any problems you call me first. Don't bug Old Mae or your mom unless somebody's bleedin'. We good?"

"Can we make chocolate milk?"

"Yeah, if you can find the mix. I gotta scoot. You stay inside, no matter what. Even if someone knocks on the door, you don't answer it."

Mick set his phone on the counter. He slapped a piece of that cheese between two slices of bread and grabbed a soda out of the fridge. "Bedtime is normal time—"

"Aw, can't we stay up?"

"Okay, but ten is it. You think she'll be okay sleepin' next to you in a bed?"

Doug shrugged. "If she ain't, I'll make us a bed on the floor like we did at Grandpop's."

"You know the U-Fill number? Here." Mick jotted it on the back of a piece of mail on the counter. "You're the man, you know that?"

"Yeah, I know it." Big grin.

Mick ran out the door. Before he made it to the GTO, his apartment door opened again. "Hey, Uncle Mick?"

"Yeah?"

"Would you mind checkin' under the bed? In case another one of them aliens got in?"

There was no time but he had to do it, partially to ease the fears of the boy and partially to ease his own. So he jogged back inside on his stupid leg, found a dust bunny and Doug's missing toy Lamborghini under his bed, locked the door behind him, and ran to the car. As the GTO kicked gravel on his way to the road, he hoped Isabel didn't carry demons in her palms like her sister.

CHAPTER
13

THE BORROWED NAIL puller made neat work of the board across Rain's trailer door. There wasn't a soul around to hear each nail as it shrieked its release into the morning. Meredith's driveway was empty, and no cars had passed on the road as Waapikoona tore each nail free. The cold was keeping people indoors. She leaned the board against the wall, tucked the nail puller into her coat pocket, and opened the door.

The inside was in better shape than she'd ever seen it. Aside from a layer of dust and a few spiderwebs, the whole place was tidy and spotless. She plopped onto the battered little sofa and watched her breath cloud the air as the cold-saturated cushions froze the backs of her legs. She sank into it, hood up, hands shoved into pockets. After such a restless night, her eyelids grew instantly heavy, but she couldn't submit to a nap now. She had things to do.

First up—time to snoop. It wasn't the right word. The dead no longer needed the secrets of their earthly life.

Without a living person to tie them to, nothing mattered. And she already knew Rain had no secrets. He was the most upfront, easy to read person she had ever known.

Except for the part about being suicidal. That had been hidden—or perhaps she'd been too self-involved to see it.

In the kitchen she found a few cans of soup not yet expired. She tried the stove—nothing. She put the soup back because she'd eaten her share of cold canned soup and couldn't do it today after that hot breakfast at Sam and Josie's. Granola bars, expired, but it was all she had. She didn't want to leave and risk missing Meredith. She raised the shades on the two tiny windows, hoping the sun might chase away the night's lingering cold.

Tires popped gravel on Meredith's driveway across the road. Waapikoona went outside but found it was only the mail carrier. As she turned around to go back inside, her attention snagged on a group of people standing at the edge of the woods beyond the tall grass behind Rain's trailer. Four people, slim and tall, every face angled straight at her.

Sister. The word wasn't spoken but it fell into her just as if it was.

"I'm not your sister," she bit back. It was a sore word, and she had no interest in anyone calling her that right now. She headed for the trailer door.

You were raised like us. We are all children of The Silent One.

The only other raised person she knew had been Jeremiah—and now Hammond, the only white man raised by some trick of Jeremiah's. She didn't know how many of her people had already been raised. Thousands? Millions? The goal was many more, and the increase was exponential. The more who worked for The Silent One, the more could be raised. One thing she always got hung up on was

how many of them wouldn't care for The Silent One's war, that they'd be more interested in being returned to the quiet of their graves. And she'd never been interested in seeking them out or teaming up. Mutiny tempted her, but did she have time? Not right now, not until she found Hammond and raised her sister. And then—would she want that kind of struggle in her sister's life?

It was coming anyway, whether it was underworld against upperworld or The Silent One against her mutinous people. It was too much to think about right now. She came here to get answers from Meredith, and here they were looking for her. No matter how good or helpful they might seem to be, she didn't like surprises. None had ever worked in her favor. And these people had somehow mastered some kind of telepathy, maybe more advanced in their undeadness than her. They'd expect her to be on their side, and she didn't want them to find out otherwise.

"Fine. But I work alone."

For one dark moment she considered that telepathic voice. She was undeniably tied to The Silent One, able to surrender her form to him anytime she pleased. If they were raised, so could they. If it was The Silent One's voice speaking through them to her …

She went back inside the trailer and latched the door behind her. Shut the window shades she'd just opened. She'd always figured once her quota was met she could sever herself from The Silent One, but what if that wasn't true? Jeremiah said she was a slave for life. It may have been a lie, but if it wasn't, then she had no choice but to choose: fight with The Silent One or against him. There was no retiring to a hidden plot of land. No bringing her sister up in a new life of peace. She'd be stuck fighting a war she didn't want, and her sister would be bound to the same fate.

Rain's bed looked warm and she was so cold. She tugged off her boots and lay down, stifling the rot in her heart and quiver in her breath, missing the clear light of Mick's presence more than she should ever admit.

THE CRY OF a raptor woke her. She sat up fast, her eyes expecting daylight seeping into the trailer's windows but everything was shades of gray. It couldn't be dusk. That meant she'd slept the day away and may have missed Meredith.

The bird called again, the sound traversing across the sky above the trailer, so clear the roof may have not even been between it and her. In her newly wakened state, her mind thought, *golden eagle, Thunder-Being, Mick*, and she snapped out of bed, earning a head rush and a banged knee.

If it *was* Mick outside, she needed to stay inside, hope he didn't sense her, pray he left.

She went for the kitchen sink and flipped on the faucet. No water—of course. Her stomach tumbled, growling loud enough for that eagle—or whatever it was—to hear. So there was no point in hiding, and she could go outside and see what it was.

Lamest excuse ever.

She pulled on her boots and went outside anyway.

An army of shadowy clouds stretched across the sky, choking out the waning sun, turning its dying light blood red in the west. Behind the trailer, lightning scattered through the clouds over a forest so dark it appeared in silhouette. Far beyond its rolling edge of black, a raptor fell like a bullet, talons open as it breached the highest limbs. Waapikoona didn't know whether it was hunting natural prey or supernatural prey, but the lightning gave her a clear guess. There was only one Thunder-Being that would give her a free pass. Across the road, Meredith's trailer gleamed like a refuge. With one last glance at the sky, Waapikoona crossed the road, willing her legs not to run. A coward would run, and she was no coward.

At Meredith's door, she knocked, ignoring the prickle up her spine now that she'd offered her back to that bird hunting the woods beyond Rain's place. The door opened faster than it should have, startling her enough to have to stifle taking a step backward.

A man peered down at her. Dark hair like her own lay against both shoulders of his fleece hoodie. A beaded leather necklace hung tucked inside the collar. His eyes strayed from hers, searching the sky as if it was second nature. "Can I help you?"

"I'm here to see Meredith."

He returned his attention to her. "And you are?"

She hesitated on which name to give. Just being Native didn't make him one of her own, even though The Silent One, Jeremiah, and the whole damn country liked to squish them all together into one homogeneous group. If he was with the ones who'd joined up with Jeremiah, she didn't want him to have her real name even though Meredith already knew it.

"A friend of Rain's."

"Waapikoona?" he asked.

That made it simple. "Can I come in?"

After a thorough look at the feathers hanging from her ears, he stepped aside, holding the door. Waapikoona looked past him into the depths of the home. The view from outside had tricked her into thinking this home was smaller. It was a double-wide, with an interior more complicated than Rain's simple trailer. Walls, rooms, doors—

Suddenly she remembered the ambush in the cemetery. The men, the cars, the duct tape over her mouth, the lid of the trunk slamming closed above her.

"Is Meredith here now?" If she wasn't, Waapikoona would gladly wait in Rain's trailer instead of this house.

A raptor cried behind her; cold flushed down her spine. She glanced over her shoulder. The bird flapped down onto Meredith's mailbox and folded its wings. Its head swiveled to aim an eye straight at her. She sensed the man's face leaning out beside her, his frame going still as he spotted the bird now looking at both of them. He clutched the shoulder of her coat and yanked her inside. When she jerked from his grasp, he was already shutting the door.

"It's ... cold out there," he said. The stare-down that followed was a bargain laid before her. Apology for the rough handling. Empathy for the threat they'd both witnessed. A promise to keep it all secret—if she'd award the same to him.

Waapikoona put it together. Meredith's husband, Blackfeet like Jeremiah, possibly someone Jeremiah might have raised. Not from here but married in, and neither Sam nor Josie knew anything else about him.

"You're raised," she said, her voice low.

He said nothing, just maintained his stony stare, a silent showdown.

"Babe?" Meredith called from around the wall.

"She doesn't know?" Waapikoona whispered.

Slowly he shook his head. She sensed him going through scenarios of how to get rid of her without alerting his wife.

If he was raised, then he was bound to The Silent One just as she was. "Are you working for—"

"I do the minimum."

And just like that she had her answer. Meredith's husband *was* raised and working for The Silent One, or some other underground demon. Probably knew Jeremiah and would know where to find Hammond. Doing the minimum suggested he wasn't all in, might know how to game the system so she could distance herself from all of it. He wasn't just a lucky break. He was *the* lucky break.

"I think we need to talk."

Unmistakable desperation fluttered across his face, tightening his mouth, shining in his eyes. "You say nothing to her."

Waapikoona had seen the same force of desperation on someone else not too long ago. She lived to forget it.

"Oh, hi. Jeez, babe, let her come in." Meredith came forward to give Waapikoona a warm hug. "You want something to eat? We're about to sit down to dinner. I saw the Jeep over there when I got home but thought you might've left it …"

"I accidentally fell asleep in Rain's place. Didn't have the best night last night."

Meredith took a moment to read Waapikoona's meaning and seemed to understand some kind of deed had been done. "Join us for dinner, then. We never have guests. My husband is so anti-social."

At that moment, he flipped the door bolt home with a loud click like an exclamation mark on the end of her thought. He grinned at both of them.

"And afraid werewolves are out there every single night. I never get to sleep with the windows open, even though we live in the middle of nowhere. Can he take your coat?"

Waapikoona slid it off. Meredith looked pointedly at her husband and shuffled away in fuzzy bunny slippers.

"Werewolves, huh?" Waapikoona handed him her coat.

"She reads too many fantasy books."

"Sounds like she's reading the wrong myths. What's your name?"

He hung her coat on a hook by the door. He took the nail puller from the pocket and looked it over before putting it back. "Nathan."

"English name."

"It's all I remembered." He left her for the doorway to a bedroom where once inside, he lowered the shade.

Waapikoona followed Meredith into the kitchen. She had just a minute to establish her alibi for the previous night, but the smell of oil in the skillet snatched that thought away. Vegetables dropped in, hissing as they hit. The oven's light illuminated something baking in a glass pan. She'd lived too long without the regular schedule of hot, home-cooked food, and she'd never take it for granted again.

"Where'd he go?" Meredith said over her shoulder. "He needs to finish setting the table. And he's supposed to be watching that quiche."

"I can do it." Waapikoona arranged the dishes that had been set out. She found a third plate in the cabinet and silverware in a drawer. Then Meredith directed her to an extra chair in the other room. As she scooted it into place at the little table against the wall, she remembered one of her reasons for coming here. "I might need to have been here a bit longer than I was last night. Depending on who asks."

Meredith paused in her sautéing but kept her eyes on the pan. "Because you had a lot to ask me about Rain."

"Yes. And you had a lot to tell me."

Meredith looked up. "Makes sense to me. Nathan worked late. He didn't get home until about ten."

Waapikoona guessed it wasn't a respectable job he was working that late. There simply wasn't enough of that around. They didn't even have a 24-hour gas station like the one where Mick worked. Killing people for The Silent One was work best done late at night. If the guy wanted to lie to his wife, even if it irked Waapikoona, it was none of her business. His working late would give her an opportunity to talk to him about things she couldn't ask in front Meredith. "Does he always work that late?"

"Only when I have to," Nathan answered behind her.

She turned, catching the warning in his look behind Meredith's back exactly as he'd meant her to.

"What kind of work?" She faced him head-on. Perhaps it wasn't wise to piss off the guy whose help she needed, but she couldn't stop herself.

"Janitorial. Two towns over." His look gained a new level of caution.

"And he doesn't even have to," Meredith said, raising to her toes to reach for a bowl on a shelf. "He just does. I keep telling him student loan debt is good debt, but—"

Nathan took the bowl down for her. "I don't like debt."

Waapikoona didn't like debt either. Buried so long in it—and now double buried, due to taking over Jeremiah's work—she was ready to see sunlight. If she was forced to continue her work for The Silent One after her sister was raised, then soon she too would be lying to someone she loved. Her ire for Nathan's warnings fizzled away.

All she had to do now was figure out how to get him alone.

CHAPTER
14

THE THAWING WINTER day had lured so many people out of their homes that even as evening hit, business at the U-Fill remained heavy. All the stuff Mick had gathered from Jeremiah's car waited in a box on the floor behind the counter. He'd nearly tripped over it two times already while stepping between the cash register and the lotto machine.

Here was the one night he wasn't longing for more business to pass the hours faster, and he had a line at his register that reached halfway down the center aisle. He couldn't remember the last time he'd had a line. These people didn't just want to pay for their fuel and beverages and leave. They wanted to make small talk. Which slowed the line, and grew the line, and made the box at his feet more incessant for his attention because at this pace, he'd never be able to touch it.

He didn't watch the clock, but the clock watched him. It announced each second in a bullhorn aimed straight at his ear, adding time to the count for how long Dougie and the girl had been alone in his apartment, allowing time for

Waapikoona to get farther away, stealing time from Helen's life. And he was here, pressing buttons and making small talk. Bills didn't go away, even when your niece was dying. Even when you were a thunderbird.

"We see you."

Mick felt the statement like a sucker punch but knew it couldn't be meant for him. "Pump number?"

His fingers hovered, ready to ring up the sale and get this customer out of here and move on to the next. There was no answer. He focused on the face that should be giving it: a man with a stare too direct to be simply buying something. On any normal day, customers couldn't be bothered to take their eyes off their phones as they swiped their card. And even though the warm weather had brought more engagement out of people, from the expectant, near threatening look in this guy's eye, he wasn't there to make small talk.

"Pump number?" Mick repeated. Playing stupid might end this quicker. He had no time for this.

Two women walked from the sidelines to stand beside the man. With all the business, Mick's night clerk vigilance hadn't kicked in yet, but here it landed fast and hard. This was the body language he was always looking out for as he worked a cash register alone at night, the stiff set of shoulders, twitchy fingers, and overactive eyes.

He took his hand off the register and flattened it against the counter—a distraction to feel for the always ready baseball bat with his other hand. It never got there. Because all at once he saw the unique build of their faces, their straight black hair. They were Native. Not unusual—he knew better than to think this now—but unusual for Wyona. They could be passing through like a lot of folks who stopped here, but people passing through had no need to size him up like this, no need to say the words that now echoed in his head.

They weren't just normal Native people. They were brought back, just like Waapikoona. Caught off guard, his eagle screamed inside him, proving just how right he was.

"Say it again," he said, low enough not to scare the other customers with the grit in his voice.

The man smiled. Mick clenched his fist, his whole arm. An overhead light flickered, turned to a strobe. Mick's eagle thrashed; in his tightening fist he imagined holding its legs, letting it flap all it wanted because it would not be freed, not in front of all these witnesses. Not pushed into it by these messengers from the underworld.

"Hey, are you payin'?" It came from the rear of the line. "'Cause I got somewhere to be and ..."

Mick couldn't address anyone else right now, couldn't be sure a human voice would come from him. All his energy was being fed into restraining his eagle and holding that man's eye with all the force he would have been using as thunderbird, diving from the sky to tear out throats.

The man dropped his smile and jabbed index and middle finger toward his own eyes, leaving them in position as if Mick was too slow to comprehend what he'd said. He turned for the door. One woman followed. The other stayed behind, making a quick lunge to smack a hand on the counter. It was meant to make Mick jump, but he caught her wrist instead, surprising both the woman and himself.

Twist it. Break it.

He let go. She jerked away, spat on the floor. One last glare, and she was out the door with the others. Watching them get away—he couldn't let his eagle see it, had to divert—

His head spun. His legs trembled. He closed his eyes. Human things brought him back from this. He forced his mind to visualize ...

Shoveling snow from porch steps. Scraping ice from a windshield. Wading into a river in the summer, catching crawdads, slipping on slimy rocks.

And Waapikoona, biting down on a smile she couldn't keep from shining in her eyes. Her arms around his neck. Her lips, her tongue.

"You okay, man?"

Mick mashed palms against his eyes, feeling the pressure hard on his cheekbones, seeing the smeary, perfectly human vision it left him with. He blinked against the light, found the overhead had quit its flashing. "I'm fine. Pump number?"

He pushed shaky fingers to move faster on the register so he could get through the damn line. Five minutes alone was all he needed to digest that encounter, file it away, and breathe the threatening shift completely out of his blood. Every rejection of a shift drove the next one further from his control. There was a threshold known to his eagle but unknown to him—how many times his eagle would allow him to deny it before removing human choice from the process altogether.

Somehow he had to learn to control it always. Over and over. Forever. No matter the circumstance, no matter how many consecutive shifts he'd need to shut down, no matter what creature stood in front of him.

As if he'd snapped his fingers and wished it, the store was empty. He moved to the window and peered out at the pumps. Two customers, one swiping a card for self-pay, the other tearing off a receipt and heading back to her car. A plastic cup skipped across the lot as a hard gust of wind hit the window and rattled the vents in the roof. A cold front blowing in, hopefully pushing everyone indoors.

Mick's stomach grumbled into the newly empty store as he grabbed the mop from the closet and cleaned up the woman's spit. All the commotion had made him forget what a lousy dinner he'd had. He rang up a frozen burrito and bag of chips and stepped into the back room to use the microwave. The box of stuff behind the counter couldn't wait four more minutes while he waited on that burrito, so he went back out front, lifted it to the counter, and dug in.

The last thing that would help him were the photos, but that's where he went first. He sifted through landscapes and sunsets until he stopped on a woman sitting on the trunk of a beater Volkswagen, cowboy boots propped on the bumper. It was her. A younger Waapikoona with a shy, uncertain gaze, her hair blowing across one cheek. Shoulders curled in, hands shoved into her pockets, the body language of a woman he didn't know. He pushed around the other photos, looking for a similar one that might show the person who took the picture. It had to have been Jeremiah. He wanted proof, an image to focus his hunt, a head on a pike.

He went back to the pile and found another. Young Waapikoona's shoulders crunched by Jeremiah's possessive arm as he grinned broadly beside her distant stare. Her cheeks had that soft look of youth, but her eyes were lost, troubled, a thousand years old.

It wasn't simply jealously that made Mick want to kill Jeremiah all over again. There was something in this picture, a wrongness between the two of them, a crime that had gone on too long before receiving its sentence.

This was dwelling. He shouldn't be. Jeremiah was dead and that part was over, but he did need to use his things to find Waapikoona. If they both came from the same place, Waapikoona may have returned there. While munching his burrito, he sorted through the remaining photos, separating useless scenery from possibly useful images of people

and places. A few even had legible signs he could look up on the internet.

He dug into the box and brought out the two history books. Inside, they were both stamped with the same library name. He got out his phone and tapped the name into the search. What came back was a town in Illinois not far from the Cahokia Mounds site where he'd gone with Waapikoona to dig up her sister's bones. It didn't fit with all the other clues—the phone call from Oklahoma, the vehicle registration ... and hadn't Waapikoona told him she was from Oklahoma? It would make sense for her to go back there. He retrieved the envelope with the vehicle registration from his coat and opened it. Same make and model of the car he drove into the woods by the mausoleum, but instead of Jeremiah's name it listed a Lenora Black with an Illinois address in the same town as the library. So the car was stolen, and those books had probably come with it. That fact wasn't a surprise, knowing the character of the man who'd been driving it. What didn't fit right in Mick's head was it had been stolen so near where he and Waapikoona had gone.

So Jeremiah had been there. Following them? It seemed like a stretch. More likely, Waapikoona had buried her sister's bones in a place near where she'd been living—with him. Could this be where Waapikoona had gone? But then there was the Oklahoma phone call ...

He got a bargain orange soda out of the cold case, rang it up, and popped the top. This diet of an overworked, overtired person was going to kill him, but right now the hit of sugar was worth it.

The landline rang. He grabbed it before its second ring. "U-Fill."

"Uncle Mick?"

Oh god something happened. "What's up, bud?"

"Isabel threw up two times."

Vomiting was normal kid stuff. Nothing to worry about. He'd babysat a sick Doug and Janie often enough to have a dedicated bucket just for that. "Did you find the yellow bucket in the closet?"

"Yeah. I just—should I do somethin'?"

"Just get her on the couch. Give her sips of water. Remember how we always do?"

"Okay. But what if she don't quit?"

"She'll quit. Did she eat anything earlier?"

"Just popcorn and applesauce. She wouldn't eat the sandwich. Oh, and she had two glasses of chocolate milk. Maybe I shouldn't have let her have two, but she liked it so much and—"

"It's okay, Dougie. You did good. Just get her comfy on the couch and keep that bucket close." The bells on the door jingled, and Mick looked up to see a man and woman enter. He lowered his voice. "Hey, I gotta go. Janie left a movie there she might like. Pop that in and maybe she'll fall asleep to it."

"Okay, bye."

Mick said goodbye and hung up. He returned the box to the floor behind the counter and kept an eye on the couple while sipping his soda.

The girl's stomach might be sensitive to milk. In her time, her people probably didn't keep milk cows. She'd be sensitive to all dairy, which disqualified a ton of kid foods he had on hand. Grilled cheese, mac and cheese, pizza. He'd have to go shopping in time he didn't have. Tomorrow, because the store would be closed when he got off his shift tonight. And what to buy? He had no knowledge of the diet she was used to in her first life, but it sure wasn't the processed stuff

people ate now. He'd get her some turkey and some bulk nuts. Potatoes, squash, fish …

In the security mirror in the corner of the store, the man put his arm around the woman's neck and dragged her in for a kiss. Mick wished they'd get what they wanted and go. The man went to the cold cases to analyze the energy drinks, and the woman picked up a magazine and flipped it open. Staring at them only seemed to be making them dawdle worse. They didn't have the body language of thieves; it seemed more like they had time to kill. So he moved his box of stuff from the floor to the end of the counter where it was mostly out of view.

He fished out the invoice from an automotive shop in Oklahoma and smoothed it against the countertop. This document was in Jeremiah's name but had no last name or address—those fields contained a random splattering of letters like the computer required input Jeremiah wouldn't give so the mechanic just typed nonsense to get through the screen. There was a note: *Customer refused phone number, will return in one hour.* The first line item was a tire puncture. The second was a starting issue, only in wet weather. They replaced the plugs and wires and patched the tire. It was dated late November of last year. Not much before Jeremiah had tried to kill Mick and found death by eagle instead.

Mick felt eyes on him and looked up. The guy stared at him from across the store. On his face lay something between shock and epiphany—he was probably on something. Mick gave him a nod. The guy headed straight for him.

"You're the mechanic that works in the shop on highway 29, right?"

"Yeah?"

"Just the guy I need to see. Didn't think I'd catch you until Monday. Name's Raúl." He stuck his open hand over the counter. Behind his shoulder, the woman set down her magazine and walked toward them.

Mick took a quick look at the guy. Late thirties, five foot six, shaved head, sturdy like a power lifter, some kind of ink on his neck. Didn't fit anyone he knew. He wasn't in the mood to shake a stranger's hand and sure as hell wasn't going to be diagnosing cars on U-Fill time.

"Sorry, but I ain't on the clock for that right now. Come by the shop next ..."

He lost the thought for how intently the woman was staring. He met her eyes—hazel, with a gold outer edge. That detail alone proved he did know *her* but wasn't sure how. She'd locked her elbow around the man's outstretched arm and drew herself against him to speak clipped and hushed straight into his ear. Mick couldn't make out a word. It didn't seem to be English. Now the woman had a grip on the man's jacket as she attempted to pull his bulk toward the door.

With her face turned away, Mick couldn't collect any more clues to figure her out. She had to be a customer at Virgil's, but he couldn't connect her with a car which was how he normally identified customers. The memory of her face echoed deep inside him like a penny plunking into water at the bottom of a mile-deep well. The answer came from so far away, by the time he had it the door had jingled their exit and the store was empty again.

Those same hazel eyes, thick glove on one arm, breath clouding the night air under stark parking lot light. Beside her, a black car glossy with rain. It was the same 300ZX Waapikoona had vandalized here in Wyona, spotted by his eagle in a random motel lot in Oklahoma the night he searched for her.

Mick hopped the counter and burst through the door. A black 300ZX pulled away from him onto the road, exhaust pipes roaring against the wall of night.

"Hey!" he shouted, giving chase even though human legs versus twin turbos was futile.

All the details flooded him at once in Waapikoona's voice over the phone. *Hispanic, muscular, tattoo of a* maneto *on his neck*. The guy Waapikoona had called to warn him about. A guy who knew of her, might know where to find her. Mick couldn't let him get away. He went for the top button of his flannel. An eagle could catch them, find out where they were going. His fingers moved in opposition to his brain as he spun toward the U-Fill's fluorescent glare. He couldn't leave it. The store would be robbed and he'd be fired and he needed this job. More than he needed Waapikoona?

He dropped to a squat, growling like a caged animal, hands fisted in his hair.

He couldn't be away from the U-Fill phone either, in case Doug needed him.

The cold wind blew into his shirt, prompting him to button up, head inside, stand behind the counter, and watch the store without seeing it. That guy had come here to find him for a reason he might never know. The woman—she seemed on board with whatever the guy's plan had been until she got a good look into Mick's eyes. What had she seen that made her change her mind?

No way she recognized him from that night he'd seen her. She'd been human just like tonight. He'd been a goddamn golden eagle. And of all cars it was *that* car, the one he'd tried to save from Waapikoona's crowbar that day. It was the incident that started it all.

"Wait one second," Mick said to the vacant store.

A man had come at them from across the parking lot that day, prompting them to hop in the GTO and hightail it out of there. Bulky upper body, shaved head. Same car, same guy, hunting Waapikoona that day and, according to her phoned warning, hunting her still. Hunting—and finding—Mick, until called off by his girlfriend.

These two had answers. He'd had enough of waiting on people he couldn't track down. Let them drive all night if they wanted. It wouldn't stop him from tracking them down as soon as he had a couple hours free to spend in the sky.

CHAPTER
15

THE THIRD TIME Mick nearly faceplanted from nodding off, he peeled himself from behind the counter and went to straighten the candy aisle. *That car that woman that guy.* It cycled through his head on repeat, a hypnotist's swinging watch, a maze with no end. Even though it felt like certain elements had come full circle, the process was missing its sense of conclusion and satisfaction. Instead it felt more like he was the snake eating its own tail. Doug had taught him the word for that thing. Ouroboros. Mick knew all the stories about the ouroboros, also thanks to Doug. It seemed every ancient civilization had one. In Norse myth, the day the snake released its tail, the end of the world began.

It might be possible the kid needed to ease up on the monster myths. Soon he might come across the ones that were real.

Candy aisle in order, he moved on to chips. Some smartass had turned all the Fritos bags upside down. Or maybe he'd been the one to stock it and he'd been half in eagle mind—or half asleep.

That car that woman that guy.

If he didn't find out who they were soon, he'd be in full crazy mind.

And those three Native people who said they had their eye on him. What was that all about?

"Svendsen!" It burst in on the opening door. Brenda sometimes found it funny to shock him awake and scare the shit out of him. "Wake up and get outta here." She dumped her bag on the counter and got a good look at him. "You look like hell. Even more'n usual."

"Just tired."

"Well that's 'cause you're out here arrangin' chips when you should be behind that counter takin' a nap like the rest of us."

Stiff shoulders shrugged on his jacket. Hands that felt disconnected collected his box. There was something he needed to tell her, but it was too much effort to push through the fog in his brain. It was important though, he had to think ...

"Hey, there's somethin'..." He rubbed his forehead, the pads of three fingers hard against his skull, drilling in. Waapikoona. The phone. If she called when he wasn't here. "You happen to see that note the boss left? If a woman calls here lookin' for me—"

"Yeah I seen that. Give her your number and tell her what a lady pleaser you are."

"I'd appreciate that."

She grinned. Too late he heard the end of her reply.

"The first part I mean." He swatted a hand in the air and turned for the door. "Or all of it. Don't matter what you say as long as you give her the number and tell her it's real important she call me."

Exhaustion didn't stop his heart from its predictable spasm at the thought—and memory—of her voice on the phone. Since he could now predict it, the spasm shouldn't happen at all. His damn heart had a mind of its own ... or no mind at all. Primitive impulse gone haywire. He felt sick and high at the same time.

"Anyway, I gotta get outta here." He walked outside into a gust of wind that nearly stole the box from his hands. The cold was so thick now it was as if the spring temps from hours ago had never been. He zipped his inadequate jacket, got in the GTO, and dialed up the heat. All he had to do was stay awake long enough to get home.

The task proved easier than expected. The deranged circle of events and people tying him to that day he met Waapikoona had too great a hold on his consciousness. It was an unfinished 1000-piece puzzle containing all the answers and the room where it sat was on fire. No time to complete it, no time to move it to safety, no way to get the answers before his world got destroyed. He couldn't hunt the 300ZX and Jeremiah's trail at the same time, so which was more important? Which would lead to Waapikoona quicker?

He let off the gas for a curve in the road. Motion flared at the edge of his headlights and he slammed the brakes, grinding to a stop. A whitetail bobbed into the darkness on the opposite edge of the road. His brain caught up to the vision—a massive buck, shoulders higher than his line of sight, out here trying to kill him. He waited, working to choke his heart back into his chest. There were always two. And there she was, a female hopping directly into the spread of his headlights and then off the other side of the road.

Shock left him so shaky he could barely find first gear. His legs ached with it. The bad one tightened, threatening to lock up. There would be no way to drive if it seized. He was too tired for this kind of near-death experience, and the last drop of energy he needed to get home was all used up. He leaned forward for better view past the A-pillars and found the seat belt locked against him. All the way home he fought with it. His mistake was taking it off, because he couldn't get it back out of the holder. If another deer tried to take him out, that would be the one he'd not see in time, and it would crash into the windshield as he crashed out of it. No one walked away from that.

The sight of his driveway turn-in was too good to be true. Halfway to the house, he stopped. He turned on his high beams. The objects flitting around couldn't really be there; they were spots on his overtired eyes. He blinked, leaning over the wheel for a better look. Bats swarmed like this in the summer when the air was full of insects to eat. He'd never seen a swarm like this, even when the mosquitos were in full force. In winter? It had to be a hallucination.

But the weather had been weird. Springtime to deep freeze in a matter of hours. It was making the animals weird. He didn't need to think about the truly weird creatures that Waapikoona had introduced him to. The ones that came from her palms and devoured humans, the ones in the cave, the ones that shape-shifted from the false image of a child into their true form, with venomous fangs and barbed wings. Even though that's what he was seeing right now, perched on his hood, hissing at him, fangs white against rubbery black flesh and those shiny sharp talons. It was just a premature nightmare. He was seconds from his bed. His brain was done, so done, and getting started early.

He eased the gas and drove through the swarm. Flipped off his high beams so they wouldn't shine into Old Mae's windows. Parked in his spot. Killed the engine. Fisted his hands and closed his eyes against a shift he knew could only

be stalled. His human form was spent, his eagle voracious since being denied. These creatures were too great in number, too close to the people he had to protect.

His human side also knew if he got out of the car, he'd be attacked. The bite from one winged demon had almost killed him, and this here was a hundred. There was no Waapikoona ready to lead him through the cave to her healer and no way for him to pass from car to apartment as a human without taking on a bite from one of these things. They weren't going to go away. They were there for him.

Quick, move, because his eagle wasn't waiting and another set of clothes was about to be ruined. *Move—now!* He'd say it aloud for motivation but knew his human voice had already dissolved. He struggled out of his jacket and tore through the buttons on his flannel. Belt, button, zipper, jeans shoved to his knees. Boot laces—he reached, but they'd be fine and it was almost too late. He needed his human hand to work the door before—

Wings caught the air and he pushed out, landing on the swinging car door. A demon coming at the car diverted; the eagle took off in pursuit. The screeching beast stayed ahead of his talons, so he flapped high and dived, catching it in one talon, then a second and third in the other. He crushed, released, and watched all three hit the ground. The swarm split, shrieking. The noise would draw attention he didn't need. He targeted the loudest, heard the snap of bones in his grip, and watched them fall beside the others. One pile of corpses would be easier for his human to clean up.

Three attacked at once, their voices ringing close. He banked then flapped high. One bite was all it would take for the venom to enter his blood, and both his forms would be compromised. The hunt for his human's woman remained unfulfilled. More urgency wasn't what his human needed.

He circled, higher than the creatures dared to fly. They preferred the shadows that hung against the land, thinking circling thunderbirds could not readily see them. He could always see them.

Exhaustion weighed as if he carried heavy prey. The wind pushed and pulled, requiring too much of him to remain stable in the air. He aimed for the peak of the house and perched. There was a force inside him, one different from talons and hooked beak. It was the kind of attack he needed now. He tilted his head, saw the tumble of dark clouds blowing in from the west. Soon they'd arrive for his use, but his energy faded each time the wind shoved against him, catching his tail feathers, working to unsteady his grip. If he waited, he'd have the means to destroy the swarm with one swift blow. And during that wait, he could be feeding.

He leapt and snatched the closest creature, a strong one, larger than the others. This one he didn't crush but took it up to the roof peak with him, slit its soft underside and tore its insides out. Feeding the hunger turned him new again—his frame steadier against the wind, vision clearer, talons holding tighter. His meal's screams sent the horde into a frenzy, so he hooked his beak against its throat and ripped until it lay quiet. Clouds filled the sky as he fed, ripping out soft insides and dropping pelts into the pile. He could spend all night at this, taking out demons one at a time, sating his unending hunger. But the human side needed rest.

Clouds dipped low, heavy, teeming with power. He discarded his last pelt and surveyed the swarm. It had dispersed around the building, seeking ways to catch him off guard. He swooped low, tempting them with a chase that scooped them into a concentrated bundle, and then he shot upward into the clouds. His cry brought forth a strike he sent through the bodies and into the pile of corpses, scorching them all.

The earth shuddered with the impact. Particulate cracked in the air now saturated with burned flesh. A gust of wind carried it across the land, dispersing ash, cleaning the mess so his human would not have to.

Light flooded the opening to the house. A figure appeared in a window. He'd made too much noise. He had to shift back—now. He soared to the ground by the car, shaking himself, calling to his other half. But his human was weak, his thoughts too far away. His human needed to be reminded. He flew over the car to the open side and hopped in, flapping to find purchase on the odd shapes and angles unfit for talons. This was a human space, comfortable and familiar to his other half now beginning to slide in.

Here, I'm here. Tires chirping against sunbaked pavement in July. The roar of redline, the jerk of the arm when shifting into second, the force pressing body against seat. Human feet, legs stretching into the floorboard, an elbow against the center console. A pounding heart. That tang of demon blood, so repulsive to human taste buds. Grabbing for his clothes, Mick shivered but not from cold. He brimmed with unshed electricity, lightning trapped in a human body and unable to get out. He fumbled with his jeans. His fingers were too weak to grip his boots so he forgot them. Shoved one arm into his shirt then the other. Ran a sleeve across his mouth to reduce some of the nauseating taste. Fell out of the car.

Like *hell* he was going to pass out before he made it to the apartment door. He latched on to the GTO's sill plate and hauled himself to his feet. Caught himself before falling headfirst into the car. Leave the boots, leave the jacket. The box— had to leave it. He grabbed his keys and slammed the door.

Old Mae's face in the front window—forget it. Couldn't handle it now. Talk to her tomorrow. She saw; she knows. Damn it all.

Stumbling toward the house, he fell to his knees a thousand times. Dragged himself up each time. His bad leg was gone, a ghost. Doug and Isabel inside, have to make sure they're okay. Bed, have to go to bed. He fell against the apartment door. Too noisy, would scare the kids. Couldn't be helped. His hands shook as he searched for the right key with blurred vision. Somehow it found the lock, and he landed inside his apartment on his knees. Shut the door. Breathed.

The kitchen overhead cast harsh light across the front room over upset couch cushions, a spray of fallen papers and books, the coffee table on its side.

"Doug," he whispered. Not a greeting, but a prayer.

Blankets and pillows—what may have been a sleeping pallet—tangled and thrown all over the room. Two plastic cups on their sides on the rug. No children to be seen. The kitchen light flickered, went out. Mick scrambled for the switch by the door, flipped it on. All it did was reveal more mess, the result of a chaos that rolled through his apartment.

Around him the room shifted in pieces, fragmented into impossible angles and dimensions. Eagle vision joined to human vision, leaving his tired brain unable to make sense of it all. He backed into the wall, bracing his hands against cold stone foundation. He'd just come out of eagle form. He couldn't go into it again. But the residue of whatever happened here sank through him, calling upon the part of him that carried the strength to fix this.

"Uncle Mick?" It was muffled—through the ceiling? The wall?

"Dougie?"

The bathroom door was never closed but it was closed now. Mick crossed the room and tore it open to find Doug huddled under a blanket against the toilet, Mick's phone in hand. Too relieved for words, Mick held on to the sink to

lower himself down. Doug hiding in the bathroom, Isabel gone, the house swarming with demons outside. It had to mean—what? What did it mean?

"That sound," Doug whispered. "Just now."

"Lightning. It's okay."

Doug's voice quivered. "Something happened to Isabel. I called you but the lady said you'd just left. I couldn't call my mom—" His voice cracked.

The frigid grasp of deadly failure gripped Mick by the throat. Fathomless regret threatened to swallow him. He left them here alone and should have known better. Waapikoona had been locked in the trunk of a car that had turned down his driveway in search of her days before. Those people knew this house. It didn't matter he and Waapikoona had killed every man that night. Of course there were more of them. He should have stashed the kids somewhere those people had never come, but he'd been too occupied by other things, too careless to think it through. He should have left the girl with Pop. She'd been safe there. He should have trusted that. He closed his eyes and thought of Waapikoona in the trunk of that car. The men, the guns, her fighting for her life.

Now they had Isabel.

Mick trembled with the urge to shift. He tensed his arms, fisting his hands against the cold floor tile. He knew they'd be too far gone to find tonight. His eagle disagreed. Even if his two sides were in agreement, he couldn't do it here with Doug—

"I had to lock her in the bedroom."

"She's here?"

"She … I dunno if it's even …" Doug cupped both hands around his eyes like blinders, as if prepping to shield them from an image too disturbing to recall. "She turned into this …"

Mick didn't need to hear the rest. He needed to see. His bad leg strained as he straightened up. Pushing off the wall forced it into working because he sure as hell wasn't going to fall down. Doug trailed him to the bedroom door and warned him to wait, but Mick was already turning the knob and pushing it open.

Translucent white wings spread before him and flapped, stirring the air. Not a girl but a raptor, lifting from its perch on the end of the bed, tucking legs, and aiming straight for him. The human in him tried to duck, but the action fell onto the wrong body parts as his own wings spread and lifted him into the room, crashing against the glassy falcon.

The human inside him screamed. The eagle was too busy to care. This opponent's talons would wound him just as badly as those demons outside, perhaps worse. She was thunderbird, yet born from the underworld. An abomination that must be destroyed.

No. A word from his other side, strong and unyielding. Only a human moral would be so irrational.

He darted into the dark corner of the unlit room and folded his wings, tilting his head to take it all in. The falcon, making its escape from this holding cell. The boy, ducking just as his human had tried, but now looking up, eyes reflecting the light in their wide stare. He flapped for a better position and landed, watching the boy, waiting for the falcon to settle on a perch. All while his other half called out to preserve this underworld prey just as he had before. Chase it, capture it, do not kill it.

His human asked too much.

The boy fell back, elbows against floor, kicking his feet to gain some space. His head swiveled from eagle to falcon and back again. Darting in the opposite direction took him

away from both until the falcon took off, crossing the room in search of a larger escape.

The eagle couldn't let that happen. Soaring from the dark room into the larger lit one sent the boy scurrying in another direction. The falcon attacked, talons bared. Eagle and falcon clashed in a space too small for battle. A dark hole emerged at the edge, through it sailed the night's wind. The boy held the door open, and the falcon spared no time. Out it flew into the night and the eagle followed, one eye trained on the hunt, the other aimed at the boy, mouth agape as he watched both birds lift into the sky.

CHAPTER
16

WAAPIKOONA HAD NO smooth opportunity to ask about Jeremiah or Hammond at dinner, but when Meredith insisted her husband walk her back to the trailer across the road, she knew it was the perfect chance.

"You feel like a long-lost sister," Meredith said at the door as she handed Waapikoona her coat. "I know that's so Indian of me. But Rain was like a big brother, and now you …"

It may have been the look on Waapikoona's face that made her trail off like that. Sisterhood … Rain … These two things tumbled like stones, pounding each time they cycled around. Mick was in there too, as an unyielding brick; instead of rounding out, its edges chipped off, creating new shards that stung in different ways. She'd put Rain to peace. She'd grieve and get over him and that stone would smooth out. The pain from her sister's absence would drop out of the spinning circle as soon as she could raise her from her bones. But that brick and its shards—she wasn't sure they would ever go away.

"He was right to say you're just like him," Meredith said. "Sorry. That must upset you. Nathan, will you get your shoes so I stop ruining our nice night?"

Waapikoona raised her hood, zipped her coat. "Meredith." The need to preserve this new friendship was like a struck match. Natural, expected—but still surprising. Waapikoona wanted to let it burn, even if it reached her fingers. Even if she had to fight against blowing it out. Honest explanations were part of friendship. It was the mistake she'd made with Mick. But here, she chose to make it happen. "I'm not upset with you. I'm angry with Rain for doing what he did. I don't forgive it." She turned for the door so she didn't have to see Meredith's reaction. Someone so sweet and hopeful would never understand how far away her forgiveness was. It was the truth, but she almost wished she hadn't said it. "Thanks again for dinner."

Nathan led the way out. Beyond the pool of light from the porch spread a night so black and silent Waapikoona felt she'd just stepped into The Silent One's cave. Above, the sky was opaque; absent of moon, stars, and light pollution, it could be the ceiling of the great demon's den. For a breath she steadied herself, focused on the murky reflection of this home's light in the windows of Rain's trailer across the road.

Nathan drew a flashlight from his pocket and switched it on. "I've found they target me less if I have a light. Almost like it tricks them, like they think normal humans carry flashlights, demon-raised ones don't. They're growing in number, you know."

She didn't need to say it, but she did anyway, just so he knew she understood. "Thunder-Beings." She also knew the reason they grew in number was because her kind did the same. It was an attempt for the earth to find balance, to level out an ecosystem that soon would be too out of control.

He stopped, flashlight aimed at the ground, a hand on her coat sleeve. "I have to tell her."

If he was seeking advice, she had none to offer. The only experience she could draw from was her relationship with Mick, and he'd found out about her the quick and easy way—by her releasing her Helpers into his apartment before putting a knife against his throat while possessed by The Silent One. Everything after that had just been a step at a time deeper into the truth, helped along by Mick's own shape-shifting. It was visual, physical proof, not one person sitting another down and telling a fantastic story.

"She wants a baby. And I have to tell her ... I don't know what kind of creature I would put inside her."

To remain so reserved through dinner, only to confide in her, a complete stranger, in the stolen minutes of a walk across the street—this was not a man casually lying to his wife. He was buried under the weight of his secrets, deep in debt, alone. Just like her.

"I kill—do you know how many? Too many. I'm a slave to a demon. She wants me to be a father? How could I do that, even if it was human?"

Waapikoona spotted Meredith's shadow moving against the glow of their home's windows and dragged him by the sleeve across the road. The distance necessary for this private conversation left them without cover from the birds. She surveyed the veil of sky, the dimly etched tree line, and saw him doing the same. If he was part of Jeremiah's group, he was not fit to be a father. But if he was like her, working alone, killing in the hope of being free of the debt, then somehow, they had to find a way to get there.

She walked forward, expecting him to follow. "I need to ask you something. I'm looking for a white man named Gilbert Hammond who was raised like us. He's—"

"A white man—raised?"

They stopped on the shoulder of the road on Rain's side. Mist hung low against the sloping land behind the trailer. The hint of upright shapes formed a small gathering of spirits, wandering close, unsure of their welcome. "Yes. Either by some trick or some favor to a Blackfeet named Jeremiah."

All the anguish and desperation fell from his face, sobering him fast. His answer was stiff, cautious. "I don't know Gilbert Hammond."

That wasn't the name that had stripped him of all the emotion over Meredith. "But you do know Jeremiah."

Nathan took a breath, turned away. "Used to. Don't know anything about him now. I need to get back—"

"I can help you with Meredith." She wasn't sure how, but she would find a way. "I need to find Jeremiah's people to find Hammond. So if you have any information—"

He spun toward her. "Why? That's—Jeremiah—it's a place no one should go."

"Hammond hurt my little sister, and I have to kill him. The last time I saw him was a couple months ago in southern Missouri. Jeremiah handed him over to someone he called a friend."

"Why not ask *him*?"

"He's dead."

Nathan's gaze found the group of spirits, lingering long enough to prove he saw them as more than just fog and a churn of air. "You killed him."

Not exactly. Mick's eagle had killed him, but she'd ordered him to. "Someone I trust killed him for me."

Trust. The emotion blazed through her. She trusted so few people in the world, and with Mick that trust was made up of an element so sharp and pure it hurt her to think about it. And she didn't just trust Mick the man, she trusted his eagle too. Forged onto her was the trust of two beings she should never trust.

"You know this? You saw him dead?"

"I saw his throat ripped out and his heart torn from his chest."

"I have some names. I can't give them out. If they find me—" He glanced at his home across the road before turning serious eyes back on her. "I can't be dragged back into that."

Ratting him out wasn't a possibility. She'd kill, or die, before that happened. And Nathan wasn't onto it yet, but now that she knew his secret and his reluctance to tell his wife, it'd be easy to force his hand.

She wouldn't do it. "I need to find where they're keeping Hammond."

He walked away, toward Rain's trailer. She watched him cross the front yard, take a seat on the front step, and turn his face skyward. A walk across the road shouldn't take this long, and Meredith had no reason to be suspicious, but any normal person would wonder. So she followed him and stood in front of him, waiting for an answer.

"Here's the problem," he said. "I don't know you, don't know who knows you. Don't know what you've left behind for someone to link to you."

That was fair. She'd never been too concerned with the tracks she left, so she couldn't assure him her trail was clean. "Jeremiah only knew my English name. The group of his people who saw my face—all dead. Their flesh has been delivered to The Silent One."

"And who's this person you mentioned, the one you trust?"

She held his gaze, resisting the urge to look away. The answer to this question would not win these names from

Nathan. They would push him so far away. What could she say about Mick? Both white man and Thunder-Being, who knew everything about her but had more reason to expose her than guard her—

"He's killed some people for me. That's it."

"That can't be it."

Waapikoona took the time to arrange the right words in her head before she spoke them aloud. "He's a man who's no threat to me or you." His eagle should be a threat, and could be, if his human half wasn't so strongly ... Mick.

"What tribe?"

Damn it—he had to ask that. She couldn't lie. "White."

He huffed a breath. "Somehow, that's better here." He got up, brushing himself off. "I need to sleep on it. Give me your number and I'll—"

"I don't have a phone. Or email."

Reaching for his pocket, he paused. "Really? Well I haven't written a letter since, like, 1879."

Funny, because it was probably true. The joke was so unexpected and out of place, she laughed. Urgency struck her like a punishment. "I need this info now."

"I can't give it now."

She watched him walk away, cross the road, go inside his trailer and shut off the porch light. An unnatural wind hit from above, too similar to the gust from a giant bird's wings for her to remain comfortably outside. She found the keys inside Rain's trailer and locked up, hopped in the Jeep and started the engine.

As she turned around in the yard, the headlights swooped across the land behind, erasing the spirits so desperate to connect with her. Whatever they wanted would have to be taken elsewhere. She'd done her good deed for Rain and his mother. She had no more left in her.

When she arrived at Sam and Josie's, she saw they'd left the porch light on for her. Inside, Sam graded papers at the kitchen table while Josie cleaned up another dinner Waapikoona should have spent with them.

"Cold night to be out in," Sam remarked without looking up at Waapikoona's entrance. This was his attempt at small talk, his effort not to judge that came off exactly the opposite way. Always worried but trying not to inflict the pressure it brought. And failing.

The teenage version of herself would have bristled, only hearing the judgment and not the worry. "You know I like the cold."

"Tea?" Josie reached for the kettle.

"Sorry I missed dinner again. I ended up eating with Meredith and her husband."

Sam raised his eyebrows in a *well?*

"He might be able to help me find the man I'm looking for. So I'm not sure how long I'll stay in Oklahoma."

"Is this guy you're looking for dangerous? Someone the police might be able to handle—"

"No," Waapikoona said. And she would tell Sam no more than that.

"We're glad to have you here, even if it's not for long," Josie said.

Waapikoona pulled out a chair next to Sam and sat. Sitting beside him while he graded middle school science papers and Josie made tea felt like a leap backward in time. She should be doing homework of her own, in her flannel nightgown, while Josie brushed her hair. Her foster siblings would be doing their own thing—homework, video games, music. A house full of noise and life, and the whole time she'd been undead and didn't know it, except for the crippling feeling of being so out of place.

"You call that man of yours?"

With Sam still marking up the papers in front of him, the question hadn't been pointed. Waapikoona just heard it like that. She had told him about Mick, hadn't she? So free with her secrets, she barely recognized herself. It would take a while to get used to something like that being out in the open. Too long like this and it might start feeling natural when she knew it couldn't be further from that.

"I don't need to call him. I said goodbye."

Sam's red pen inked the grade at the top, and he flipped to the next paper before he looked up at her. Another attempt to be cool, make all this appear lighter than it was. "Goodbye doesn't always have to be forever."

"This one does." She tried not to think about how she'd left Sam and Josie, whether she'd said goodbye then. If she had, it proved Sam's point. Here she was, back again, certain she'd never say—or not say—goodbye to them again.

"I wonder what *he* thinks."

"What he thinks doesn't matter." With effort she'd slowed the words down to make sure they didn't snap.

Josie put a mug in front of each of them. "She's right, Sam."

Sam put his pen down. "Okay. Full disclosure. Life's too short to deny yourself happiness for silly reasons like—okay, I'll say it. Race. If that's all this is."

"It's not all it is."

He reached for her hand, squeezed it hard. "I can't stand to see you find someone else, someone like Jeremiah again. There are too many bad guys out there, and you're still young, and I worry—"

She had to smile at that. "I'm not so young."

"You'll always be young to me. Our little snow bunny, found in the snow."

Snow bunny. It was her nickname for so long. She held her breath against the water in her eyes.

"Where's the tea?" She got up. A lame escape. A childish one. There was nothing wrong with crying for memories of a child's harsh fear, and rescue, and love so rich it felt undeserved against that child's other life, her mistakes, her painful past she could never speak of for fear it was nothing but imagined. And the realization later that all those nightmares were real.

"Coming," Josie said.

That was the trick of her feelings for Jeremiah. He was special because he understood her past, he gave the explanation she'd sought for so long and never found.

It was also the con of her feelings for Mick. He was the only person in the world who knew the truth about her. Her unguarded past, her present battles. It led her toward something that felt like the longing of love, when really it was the longing to be herself, free of all secrets. With Mick she was free, for the first time since she lied to her sister in their first life and taken Pinepakatwi to the top of that cliff. *Before we hit the ground, we'll turn to birds and fly into the sky. Give me your hand, we'll do it together.*

Mick even knew this secret. In vague terms, but he still knew it. Why had she told him so much? She knew it was a mistake but couldn't find the regret that proved it was.

She remembered. His friendliness, his rural charm—that wasn't for her. He gave it to everyone. His strong arms and wind-blown hair and bluest eyes—also not for her. That was just his build, not something he could control. His anger, though, that was for her. It aimed and shot true, and she caught it and shot it right back. She had to admit that was special and rare, something he reserved only for the people who could work it out of him.

"What are you smiling about?" Sam asked.

She felt it, strong in her cheeks, tight in her eyes, too late to cover.

"Can't see it'd hurt anything to check in, let him know you're thinking about him."

It was exactly what she hadn't done when she'd left them. It wasn't meant to be a blow, but she couldn't stop herself thinking she deserved it.

She dunked her tea bag. "I'll call him. Someday."

Someday when the wound of leaving him had healed into a faint line no one could see but her.

CHAPTER
17

THE EAGLE PURSUED the falcon into the trees, noting the unnatural flap of one wing, an extra fast stroke working double to compensate for the inadequate range to match the other. An injury to his advantage. Her flight was erratic, dodging limbs she should have soared over, banking too late for obstacles he had already avoided. His plan to drive her back to the house so his human could lock her in a cage was quickly failing. She was too nimble, too hard to predict. The added complication of keeping her alive made his attacks too hesitant to be fruitful. If his human wanted her dead, it would already be finished.

He'd chase her to exhaustion, then. The night would be long. His human would not be pleased.

Up she darted suddenly, breaking through the cover of limbs into open sky. Her silver moon coloration ebbed, turning her night-dark, the outline of body merging with black sky. The eagle pushed power into flight to overtake. A view from above would put her outline against earth and

give him better sight of a creature about to vanish before his eyes. This was not a familiar hunt.

Just as he regained vision of her, she dived into the trees. He followed—stronger, faster, anticipating her angle and meeting her in the air. She flapped against him, her eye on his. He could've killed her. She knew this and spared him from her talons as he had spared her of his. She drifted to a low limb and folded her wings—one flat against her, the other curved at an odd angle. He chose a tree nearby, catching the limb near the trunk where it would support his weight.

He called out. She tilted her head but did not return the call. She was confused, just like he'd been on his first flight. Unsure where to go, what to do, how to recover her human. He could not help her with that. His human floated far away, too underpowered and used up to reclaim his space and shed the eagle. If he didn't have a fledgling thunderbird to watch, he'd be out hunting demons for more nights than his human would have ever allowed.

Soon he'd lead her back to the boy to be locked up, but not yet. He'd sit with her, make her see he was the one to follow. He stretched one wing, then the other, and cast his view across the forest. Night creatures scared away by the chase tested the ground below them, sensing danger, unsure if it was directed toward them or for others. Right now, the falcon appeared too disoriented to hunt even upperworld prey, and he had never bothered. There were too many more satisfying creatures to hunt.

Eagle and falcon watched each other and waited. The sky opened into great depths, revealing white moon and two bright, brave stars. Clouds whisked by and wind called through the trees. The night creatures resumed their business below. The falcon settled her weight on the limb in rest, the language of a truce. She may not trust him if he approached, but she did trust from a distance. He'd let her rest, prove no harm. Then she'd trust. She'd follow him. It could take longer than chasing her to exhaustion, but his human wouldn't return soon. He settled on his own limb, ruffling his feathers to allow the crisp air to cool him. One eye on the falcon, the other watchful of sky and land. The moon sneaked across the sky. Time flowed like water, a spring feeding a creek, rolling across land, over rock, through a crevice underground. From one world into another and then back again, never ending.

He called to her. *Awake, and follow.*

Below them, a different creature cried out. The boy's call reached into him, seeking out his other form. In his rest he hadn't noticed his human working his way back. The boy cried again from below, another language he could almost recognize …

He stretched his wings, catching air before he knew he was falling. His human yearned for the safety of the ground. Against him he wrestled; feathers spiraled around him as he flapped against the human form quickly overtaking him. This was wrong. A miscalculation. The falcon would leave. He would fail this duty. She would be lost. Called forth by the bond of kin, his human fought hard.

"Uncle Mick!"

Tree bark razed human skin as he flung himself, shedding wings and talons and finding arms and legs in their place. One last impact knocked him to hands and knees. He panted, a growl forming low in his chest as he worked to find his human voice. "D-Dougie. I'm—" The rasp made him cough. "I'm—I got to—"

Take a minute. Catch my breath. Figure out what's up and what's down. Put on some pants.

Something hit him in the arm. He looked—his jeans. His legs nearly bent backward but he managed to get upright and shove feet into holes.

"Holy cow, Uncle Mick. I—did you—?"

"Yeah, just gimme a minute." Mick fell back against the tree, razing his back a second time, but he had to remember what was so important. He'd been perched in this tree, keeping watch. Not winged demons, not horned serpents. A different kind of prey that was half one of his own kind. The underworld falcon. The *girl*. Isabel.

He planted a hand against the tree trunk and pushed off, looking up. "Where'd she go? You see her?" He squinted into the tangle of black limbs and blacker shadow, the moon too low at the far edge of the sky to be helpful. Human vision was shit. "Did she fly off or did she shift back too?"

"Shift back?"

"That a flashlight you got there?"

An object in Doug's hand aimed a beam of white light against the ground. He looked down, unseeing. "Shift, like … like what you done? Is that, I mean, can you—"

Mick took the forgotten flashlight out of Doug's hand and shined it into the canopy of hibernating winter limbs above. And there, just where he expected, sat a large bird with an eye trained on him. He took a needed breath. She hadn't fled. There was hope she might be coaxed down, might find her human form.

Doug stuttered words, no sentence completing before it was interrupted by a new one. Reality sat hard upon Mick. His nephew had seen him as eagle. He'd seen him shift into, and out of, a supernatural form. There was no explaining himself out of this one. Mick put a hand on Doug's shoulder to quiet him.

"This has to be a secret, bud. I need to count on you."

"I can't—I don't even know—" Doug looked up at him and shrugged, helpless against too many words trying to get out at once.

The forest floor's cold had passed into Mick's bare feet and was quickly working its way up both legs. Soon he would buckle, a victim of the winter freeze and his own fatigue. The adrenaline from the shift carried him; he had little time before he'd collapse, and he had no idea how far they'd traveled from his apartment. Human needs began to take form. He took inventory of Doug—winter coat zipped to his chin, hood raised, pajama pants, snow boots. "You warm enough?"

"I'm good."

"Any chance you got more clothes for me?"

Doug turned around. Mick shined the light, landing it on a pile of clothes a few yards back. He found the clothes he'd been wearing earlier along with his coat and boots, socks shoved inside. He struggled into them, feeling the strain deeply in every bone. The girl's pajamas remained; he shook those out and tucked them under his arm. "How'd you know to bring clothes?"

"That time you left. That night. You came back with no clothes."

"Good thinkin'."

"I had to go back for 'em. I came out to look first and got past the old barn and—all of it made sense and I remembered—"

"Okay, okay." If he didn't stop him, they'd be out here all night. "We can talk about all this later, I promise. Right now, we gotta get the girl outta that bird and back to my place. Any ideas?"

Doug stared at him. Overtired, overwhelmed but wired from the excitement. Eyes as big as the roundest moon.

"I need your help here, bud."

"You was that giant eagle that chased us at Grandpop's."

Mick tucked the flashlight under his other arm and took Doug by the shoulders. "We really gotta focus here."

"I'm focusin'."

Mick aimed the flashlight into the trees. "See there? That's her. She's tired and afraid, and we need her down on the ground so Isabel can imagine her feet there and come back."

Doug walked to the tree that held the falcon, lay a hand against the bark, looked up. "Can you lift me?"

"You ain't climbin' up there."

"Not all the way. Just up a little so I can talk to her better."

Mick didn't like this at all. He joined Doug by the tree and surveyed the climb himself. There was no way for a man his size to do it. Even if he had the energy for it, his weight would be too much for most of the footholds. And the falcon wouldn't be comfortable sitting there while he advanced.

"Come on," Doug said. "I climb that big tree behind my house all the time."

Mick had no better ideas. He put the flashlight down and lifted Doug to the lowest limb, catching his legs after he grabbed on to push him upward. Strength came from some forgotten place. His muscles strained, heat blazing double-sided all the way down his backbone. He was going to pay for that for days. The monster of a head rush that followed made him grateful for the tree trunk so he could hold on until the white noise faded from his ears and his vision returned. By then, Doug was high enough for his voice to sound far away. Not the thing to think about when he was helpless here on the ground and his nephew was high in a tree in the middle of a dark night, coaxing a mistrusting undead thunderbird out of tree. After spending who knew how many hours alone in that apartment, scared out of his mind then walking the woods by himself to find the adult who should be home with him. *Uncle of the year.*

The blame was all his. The situation? He wouldn't own that. It could've been the fatigue threatening to crumble him to a pile of skin and bones, or the bleary-eyed exhaustion fogging the view around him, but something was working to fill all that in with anger instead. A fiery, justified anger, ramping through him like the electricity his eagle had ripped from the sky. It cleared his head. It empowered him. He heard Doug's gentle conversation to the bird above as background noise to the voice in his head.

She caused this. She left this mess in your backyard and ran away. Left no contact information, took no time to call and check in.

The one call didn't count. She didn't let him get a word in. Even if he had known about her sister at that time, she'd have hung up before he got two words out. And it wasn't just the girl's bones she left, knowing they were due to revive. She'd left *him* a mess. She'd turned him into this unnatural creature, brought criminals and demons to his doorstep, and walked away.

Kari was right. He was a sucker.

But what to do? Turning the girl in to the police could be as simple as dropping her off and driving away. It could also put eyes on him. He had no murderous blood on his human hands, but those same hands dragged bodies. Pillaged clothes from a dead man. Drove a stolen car after watching its driver be killed by an undead woman and devoured by demons. His eagle soared with righteous justice while his human self staggered under the burden of the guilt. If it came down to it, he couldn't lie to any cop. Hell, he'd be lucky to get through the whole thing without going eagle.

"Hey, help me down."

Mick nearly took a foot to the face. He grabbed hold of the ankle to steady it and looked up to find Doug attempting to slide off the lowest limb—with a translucent falcon attached to his shoulder.

"Kinda like a pirate." The boy grinned.

Mick grabbed his hips and lowered him to the ground, avoiding the falcon's gaze. "You're too good, you know that?"

A cool-kid shrug. "Had a superball in my pocket. I told her I'd give it to her if she came down."

"I ain't sure if I can trust her to stay with us if she stays like that. Why don't you see if you can set her on that log, and maybe she can go back to being a girl." Mick took off his coat and shirt, replaced the coat, and held out the shirt. "Here, let me put this over her."

As if she could understand, she hopped off Doug's arm onto the fallen tree and tilted an eye toward Mick. He draped his shirt over her then took Doug's hand and turned him around. "Might take her a minute."

"What if she flies away?"

"Then you'll probably hear me say a couple bad words." The anger had faded to a hum inside him. Now given thought it sprouted hot in his chest, but he was so tired the end result felt more like nausea. His eyelids were closing on their own; his head snapped, chin against chest. If he didn't get to his bed soon, he'd be flat on the forest floor, human and helpless and freezing to death.

"You hear that?" Doug shook Mick's arm.

"Mm?" He still had the boy's hand, and he wasn't going to let go. If he did, he might fall down.

"Sounded like somethin' happened."

Mick turned them around. Found a girl hunched behind a log, wrapped in his shirt. Carried her clothes to her. Turned them back around. Doug was talking but he couldn't make sense of it—parts of his brain were shutting down. He got his shirt back, the girl got the superball, Doug got the girl's hand. They trailed through the woods, Mick's navigation somewhere between eagle memory and autopilot. He had no gauge for how long it took because he was sleepwalking. The apartment door was worthy of worship. The heat inside was bliss.

He got all three of them inside and locked the door. He tried to look at both kids, but his eyes were half closed. "Listen up. If I don't get to bed now, I'm fittin' to drop. I need—" He squinted at the clock. *Holy god.* "What's tomorrow?"

"Sunday," Doug said.

Day off. Mick nearly cried. He did the math, weighing need for sleep against time needed in the day to get stuff done. It was the only math a man with three jobs could do while half asleep. "I need five solid hours of sleep before I hear a peep outta either one of you. Think you can help me out with that?"

Through the slits of his eyes, he saw Doug's expression freeze into a look of *oh my gosh you said we could talk about the bird thing and I didn't realize you were going to make me wait until morning because if I have to wait that long my head is going to explode.*

But Mick was already halfway to the bedroom, kicking off his boots, falling onto his bed. As he grabbed the edge of the blanket and rolled into it, his anger lay heavily upon him. Its urgent, unsatisfied need threatened to keep him from shutting his eyes—just like Waapikoona herself—and he'd be damned if he was going to allow either of them to steal a minute of his five hours of desperately needed sleep.

CHAPTER
18

WAAPIKOONA WOKE CLEARHEADED and alive with purpose. In sleep, troubles had untangled and plans had formed. She was now sure Nathan was the quickest way to the information that would lead her to Hammond, but he needed an incentive to give it out. She knew what offer she could make. Answers traded for answers.

The first one awake in the kitchen, she started the coffee. There was a time not long ago she'd drink a cup upon rising and then fast until the sun had long set. Part laziness, part bravado. She'd known her body needed fuel just like any other living human, but without the appetite to convince her she found more satisfaction in believing herself invincible. Her younger body forgave her. Even though Sam believed her to be young, lately she felt far from it. Weary, drained, lost. Near to giving up. Today was different. She had found the path again, and she was ready to climb it.

"Good morning," Josie said, joining her. "I don't feel like cooking. Let's send Sam off for some donuts." She reached for a mug from the cabinet and Waapikoona filled it.

A soft bed, a hot shower, and treats for breakfast. This was a different life than the one Waapikoona had lived for years, and it wasn't wise to get used to it. Killing scumbags to fill her quota didn't easily follow a morning like this. And neither did the task she'd planned for this day.

SOMEHOW, SHE DRAGGED herself from the warm kitchen into a harsh February cold that chapped her face and froze her jeans rigid. The Jeep started roughly. If Rain had been there, he'd be apologizing to it for forcing it to work in such a hostile early morning cold. Waapikoona did not talk to Jeeps. But she did talk to underworld demons who could give her answers she could trade for answers she needed. She just had to find an opening into his realm and a way to phrase it all without giving anything away. She was surely breaking rules for which punishment would be death—a second, more final one. It was a danger of her lifestyle she could accept, if it didn't leave her sister forever dead as well.

She cranked up the heater and backed out. Josie and Sam's cozy home and loving hospitality were making her weak. Comfort made discomfort less bearable. Her tomb—no, she could never go back there. Not after what happened inside. Not for how close it was to Mick. She could find a different tomb in a different town. Yes, that would be added to the plan. Talk to The Silent One, talk to Nathan. Track down Hammond, kill him, find a new tomb to continue working off her quota.

At some point she'd have to go back to Wyona and dig up Pinepakatwi's bones—but not until her quota was filled and she was ready. She wouldn't risk going to Wyona until then.

Overcast skies loomed overhead, smothering the sun. She drove far from town, long enough for the Jeep's heater to match the comfort she left behind—a mistake she'd pay for as soon as she found her stop, which was proving harder than she expected. Walking the line between the upperworld and underworld made it easier to fit into either. The further she sunk into one, the longer she was from the other. And that soft bed, hot shower, sugar-coated breakfast, and laughing over memories with Sam and Josie were doing her no favors now. The Silent One felt far away, her sense of him untethered. Finding a hole into the underworld shouldn't be this hard. They were everywhere. There had to be one closer than the one she remembered. Her sense of direction broken, she decided to head toward the one she knew.

She drove south, to where the farmland ended and the trees grew thick. On a road trip long ago, Jeremiah had taken this route, with her in the passenger seat waiting to be introduced to her new life full of knowledge and power. He didn't mention the burden she'd take on, or the contract she'd sign as soon as she set foot in The Silent One's cave. As she drove, she allowed herself to relive it all. The day she said goodbye to Rain and fled with Jeremiah. His hard grip on the back of her neck as he pointed her toward the entrance of the cave and sent her in to face The Silent One alone. The terms she'd agreed to but had no time to weigh. A drive across state lines to rob her sister's grave. Acting as lookout while Jeremiah killed. His victims were not so carefully chosen as hers. Thinking on all this did not help digest it, but it did help distract her from other things.

Other *people*.

She couldn't blame Sam for bringing him up. Mick was always there, hanging in the periphery. All she had to do was turn, and she'd see him. Eagle form, gliding on the breeze above, his shadow roaming the ground. Human form, glaring at her across the U-Fill store from his perch behind the counter. Catching her arm as she tried to escape his Pontiac, his eyes intense in the dashboard lights. Bleeding to death in her tomb. Giving up, until she begged him not to.

She'd spoken the words to save him, but she was the reason he was in that death-filled tomb to begin with.

So she didn't turn. She kept her eyes tight on her way ahead. Seeing him would disrupt her, and she had no time for that.

The road gained a shoulder wide enough to park, so she pulled off and sat with the engine running. Pavement stretched in front of her, bending out of sight past the edge of winter-bare woods, not a breeze touching the branches. She turned the key. A ticking sound from under the hood slowed then cut off. The silence engulfed her.

Loneliness couldn't touch those who preferred to be alone. Yet here it was, hanging against her, so heavy she felt she'd never shake it off.

You call that man of yours?

"He isn't mine," she said, jabbing her seat belt release.

Chaos erupted from the woods to her right. She ducked as a cloud swooped against the Jeep and across the hood, one large mass of individual objects moving separately yet together. She straightened, leaning forward for a better view when a hard smack against the passenger window made her duck again. The creature rolled off, leaving a smudge of black goo. Not birds or even bats. Demons out in the day like this, though? It was—

A raptor's screech tore the sky. She covered her ears too late—through her body the sound rang as if its payload had been aimed into her rebuilt bones, knocking her askew. All at once she felt hunted, fragile. As ancient as centuries-old bones should feel. She tightened her fists against a tremble in her chest that threatened to run the length of her. A second hawk swooped low, one eye on her as it banked, catching a demon in its talons before flapping away. The dark swarm moved across the road and disappeared into the trees, the two hawks on its tail.

She released her fists, shook out her arms. This could be good for her. If the local Thunder-Beings were busy chasing an unearthed nest of flying demons, they wouldn't be interested in following her. It also suggested she was right about this spot and the opening to The Silent One's cave was indeed nearby. The bad feeling souring the plan was nothing but residue from that Thunder-Being's call. There was no wrongness here, nothing that should stop her progress. Demons out in daytime was unusual, but the sun was little threat to any creature on such a gray day.

Quiet restored, she slid out of the Jeep, slammed the door, and fell fast through time.

Sarah?

Shh! Don't call me that!

I have to. They hit my hands if I use your name.

They're not here, are they?

No, but they find out. They always know.

They lie. They make up reasons to use the paddle. Here, get under my blanket before she sees. You remember what I said? Tomorrow, after breakfast ...

Waapikoona regained her footing, her tangible space on Oklahoma land in her present day. She saw her own face reflected back at her. Hazy, darkened, overlaid with the interior of the Jeep. Staring into the window, back in her present, the memory so ripe she was in two places at once—

She choked, a palm against her chest. No breaking down, not on this day that had started so positively clear she barely recognized it as her life. Her old life would not intrude. She had things to do, well-planned steps forward with no diversions. It didn't matter how exposed she felt on this empty road, how crushed she was by the low hanging sky and a town where Rain should be but never would be again. This gloom would pass if she gave it no space to settle. She was here to speak to The Silent One, force him to give her answers for Nathan and an answer for herself—a number she could start counting down to the rebirth of her sister. Once they had each other, neither would be alone again.

The thought plunged through her. Nothing mattered. Her sister's revival was too far away, the quota unreachable. It was how The Silent One kept them working. Promises made only because they'd never be fulfilled, the steps necessary to reach them too impossible to achieve in one lifetime. It's why Jeremiah had tried to talk her into mutiny ...

Two hands against the Jeep, she sagged, her cheek against the cold glass. Rain's Jeep. He should be driving her here, but he was dead.

"Dead," she whispered. And an unquiet spirit until she'd taken him to a place of rest. Not her fault he'd been in torment, but if she hadn't stayed away so long she could have fixed it sooner. If she'd returned before he'd died, she could have prevented it. She sank to the ground, knees against pavement, sharp rocks digging through her jeans. His death, her failure, her regret. Tears and grief wasted energy, but now they wasted her, on a road so lonely not one car had passed. It gave the grief more courage as she bent beneath it, fists and forehead against the pavement.

The swarm of flying demons, the Thunder-Beings ... she needed to get up, get walking.

Tomorrow, after breakfast, you and I will get away from here. We don't have to be afraid anymore.

Promise?

Death for her sister. Death for Rain. Only one she could undo. She reached for the Jeep's door handle and hauled herself up. The gloom and its torpor would never win. The loneliness had a good grip but soon she'd shake it. Being with Mick had weakened her. Without him, she'd heal. Companionship was like comfort—the more she became accustomed to it, the harder it was to live without.

Rocks scattered as she took the steep embankment down into the woods. She broke through dead underbrush and found a ridge of limestone that led straight to the cave's opening. Dry leaves clogged the narrow slot so it looked more like a step of rock than a place to slide yourself into. Nearby, a thick, straight branch lay against the natural rock steps leading uphill. She couldn't believe this was the same stick Jeremiah had used when he brought her here so many years ago. As she stabbed through the leaves to find the entrance, she felt like she'd fallen through time.

Feet-first into the hole, she lowered herself until her boots caught solid ground. Water pelted her back from above. Crouching in the dark void, she breathed in, feeling the body of the cave fill her until she knew it like her own. She could close her eyes and walk the tunnels by heart, but doing so required her to give too much of herself over. So she drew the flashlight from her pocket and flipped it on, holding a piece of the human world in her hand like a lifeline back. It also happened to be a piece of Mick. She needed to buy herself a new flashlight and leave this one in her next motel room.

Once she reached The Silent One's yawning chamber, she found the driest spot and sat down to wait. The bloat of darkness reduced her flashlight to a powerless finger of light. She switched it off, closed her eyes, and listened to the cave as it breathed and dripped around her. Time released its steady hand. Past and present regrets mingled with future ones, a shackling of spirit she felt too worn to fight. She'd never be free of this. She owed her life to the powers that revived her, and she planned to commit her sister to the same fate. How long could someone raised by The Silent One live without doing his work? If she hadn't had a sister to raise, would she be living a life ignorant of the underworld? Or would it eventually find her?

Questions like these would have to remain unanswered. She couldn't muddle the more urgent ones.

In the dark, she emptied her boots of leaf debris from her descent into the cave. She finger-combed and braided her hair. Waiting was both a chore and a respite. And again, she thought of Mick. Near him, lust almost broke her apart. Away, she was warped by something worse. It pounded in the deepest recess of her heart, thunderous, desperate, painful. He could be dead for how her spirit mourned.

"I'm here," she called out, pushing to her feet. She couldn't sit idle like this. If she traveled farther into the cavern she might find the great demon faster. If not, at least she'd be up and moving and not alone with only her thoughts for entertainment. Not many could endure a meeting with The Silent One in tighter inner tunnels, including her. It was a thought disturbing enough to displace the gnawing sensation in her heart.

For now, she thought. It would be back. If she could figure out how to permanently banish Mick, it would be next on her list.

A shuffling sound echoed off the far wall. She turned on her light and swung it toward the opening where the shadow rippled. Upright shapes loomed against the adjacent wall, row upon row of them, unmoving. If there hadn't been so many she might have convinced herself they were some strange cave growth or rock determined to form itself into many human shapes, similar enough to trick the imagination into seeing a human army in stasis, erect but asleep. This was no trick of darkness and illusion. Her light moved from face to face, revealing Native men and women in all stages of adulthood except for the very old. These were The Silent One's Raised, stored away like machines ready to be powered on. She'd come in here and killed time, unaware she shared this space with so many bodies. At once the sound of a hundred legs filled the cavern, and a shiny exoskeleton slid into view to encircle her before she had a chance to step away from its reach.

"Identify yourself."

"Waapikoona." He wouldn't hear how she'd blurted it or how unsettled she was. His mind was all demon; she'd been joined with it enough times to be certain he had no human intuition. The spoken human language was a facade.

"Douse your torch."

She switched off the light, taking a breath, distancing herself from the shock of his unusually quick entrance and the affront of being ordered around—and those bodies standing against the wall. He might be superior over the others he'd raised, but he wasn't to her. She could walk away as soon as she had what she wanted.

But there would be no escape right now. The hard plates of his body segments swished against the sleeve of her coat. She shifted away to avoid further contact on that arm but gained the press of his body against her other side. His laugh carried high above her, raspy yet broad with power. She hated how it froze her in place. She used that feeling as fuel. "I need some answers."

"Your need is not my concern. Your work lags."

"I've been traveling. You know I can't stay in one place too long."

"Your job is to not stay in one place ever."

"My job is to send you flesh. How I go about that—"

"You've become delinquent."

This wasn't at all how she wanted this to go. It seemed to be spinning off in some erratic direction of which she had no sight. His many legs fluttered against the cave floor. So close they sounded, she sensed him coiling tighter around her. As he moved, his smell filled the air. Musty, damp, metallic … and something else, some tinge so alien and so *off* it spoke a word in her ear: *run*. In the absolute pitch-dark, she saw nothing. The space around her could be a void going on forever if it weren't for this demon wrapping his body so tightly around her. Instinct called her to extend her arms to prove what her ears and nose sensed, but she shoved her hands into her pockets and closed her eyes instead. It took the struggle out of seeing when seeing was impossible. Her ears burned hot under a rapid pulse. The movement of all those legs created a breeze against her jeans, sending a tingle on her skin all the way up to the back of her neck. She imagined the stories-high ceiling above her, the walls too far away to touch. Not this creature building an inescapable box around her.

"I'm hoping you'll tell me how far from my quota I am."

"Too far for you to be asking."

"A hundred? A thousand?"

"What are we measuring, Waapikoona?"

"Corpses."

"We do not count corpses."

Well, *she* counted corpses. But to be fair, they didn't exactly arrive at The Silent One's den in one piece. To come back at him again would make all this sound like petty bick-

ering. This was not an everyday difference in opinion. It was her life. He wouldn't be badgered into answering with the truth. What he'd said was all he would say, and she had to move on.

"I have a question you probably don't know the answer to." Baiting him to prove his knowledge in order to elicit the truth—this was a tactic for a child, not a great demon.

"Again you waste my time."

"So you have no answers, then. It sounds like I'm wasting *my* time." It took all she had to remove her hands from the safety of her pockets and lay them against his cold flank until his tail end passed by her and she could step through to an outer coil and find her escape. That otherworld scent sharpened as the rings of his body bumped under her palms. She pressed her nose against her shoulder. Her eyes tricked her with imagined green sparks too close beside her to be coming from him. The coiling slowed. She walked against him, hoping to find the exit sooner.

"State your inquiry."

Her game couldn't have worked so easily. "What happens if a person raised from bones has a child with a mother-born person?"

"You long to be a mother."

If she claimed to be asking for someone else, he'd know she'd broken her agreement not to befriend one of her kind. "No, but I'm curious. For the future."

"My children I raise from death are as human as their previous mother-born selves."

"And a child born from—"

"Don't you think if I could pair you up and create more soldiers for our cause, I would? Do you think me a fool?"

There was her answer. His Raised were human enough to have children, but those children would not belong to him like those raised from bones. His slippery exoskeleton fell away from her hands, and she quickly stepped through, hands out to brace herself against the next coil.

"You've grown too bold, Waapikoona."

"I have to go."

"You will go when I'm through with you."

Those words matched a snippet of her past. Jeremiah, blocking her at the door to a hotel room. Her wrist, caught, twisted—

She shoved, but instead of warm human body she encountered cold millipede. He hissed, drowning her in an emission of that metallic musk. Where her hands had contacted him they stung as if electrocuted. She sensed the aftermath of a strike rather than the strike itself. Off-balance, swaying, the weight of her own body too much for her frame. Confused, she reached for her right mind in the muddied distance— might it be another memory? Was she—

"You have wandered from your ..."

She covered her ears, stinging palms leaking viscous liquid onto her face. His words continued, all around and inside her, toxic, angry, punishing, too painful to take with unprotected ears.

"... an important lesson you learn. This ..."

Although her wrists and ankles remained free, she felt a terrifying sense of being shackled. It awoke a deeper memory, one long before Jeremiah and his games. Real shackles. Terror that reached past her to family and friends. Not a game but a war. Invasion, genocide, captivity. The images pushed her further off center, spiraling and coiling like The Silent One's body around her, a prison she couldn't escape by simply reaching forward and finding the end.

Hands and knees against stone ground, she breathed. *In through the nose, out through the mouth*. Silence cradled her.

The dark sat calm, its menace retreated. *Nose, in. Mouth, out.* Alone—but worse than that. A new kind of isolation, it felt more like being cut off, disconnected. A puddle spread beneath her hands. Blood, sweat, or moisture from the cave, she wasn't sure. The new ache in her bones felt permanent. Not an ailment but a disease. Sitting back on her heels set her head spinning, so she breathed more. Focused on only the act of drawing and releasing air, making each slower than the last. She could get up and leave soon. The Silent One was gone. Alone should have been a good thing in this moment, but the starkness and totality of it draped her in sadness. Never had she looked upon her future and seen it so bleak.

Working for this creature—alone.

Carrying out justice against Hammond—alone.

Raising her sister—alone.

Why did any of it matter? Against the mass of the world, she was nothing. Time, endless. Her life, an insignificant blink. All these things that meant so much to her carried no weight in the world without some way to share it. She could go on denying it—and she would—but here in the dark she allowed the thoughts to rise and take their fullest shape. All her plans, her victories and failures, meant more with someone by her side to share them. Someone who understood, who fought beside her. A warm body to share the space, to care, and worry if she didn't come home.

She'd told Sam someday she'd call Mick but now, sitting alone and broken in the dark chamber, she recognized the poison in that thought. Left inside her as a future possibility it did nothing but plague her. She couldn't have him. Could never call him. Wouldn't see him ever again. She didn't need to figure out how to banish him. She would bury him, here and now.

So she got up. Dug Mick's flashlight out of her pocket, switched it on, and set it on the cave floor aimed at the tunnel that led to the entrance. She removed the golden eagle feathers from her earrings and crouched to lay them on the cave floor. Leaving a piece of Thunder-Being in The Silent One's den seemed wrong, like a bad omen. And hadn't she angered the great demon enough for one day?

With the feathers tucked into her boot she backtracked, the beam of light shining against glossy walls. Her every muscle ached. She trailed fingers along the ceiling when it lowered, saving her skull from impact while straining an already sore arm. A slight corner in the tunnel muted her light; another turned her path too dim for human eyes to navigate. She paused, connecting with the cave's body as she had when she arrived. Its presence hung too far away to grasp. Weakened, tired, she would soon be lost. One hand feeling for a drop in the ceiling, she lay the other against the wall and let it lead her out. After two cracked shins and a banged knee, she glimpsed a hint of daylight, knowing it could be a trick of tired eyes, praying it wasn't. With each step the cave filled more thoroughly with light, adding confidence to her steps. Crawling out on her belly into the day stole the last of her stamina, and she lay there in the cold.

This dreadfully weakened state could not be as permanent as it felt. She'd go home, warm her muscles, rest, and be new again in the morning. She dug her nails into the earth. She needed to claw a hole in the soil, bury those feathers, and not look back. But the ground was more frozen than she remembered, and her hands felt too fragile for the motion. She dragged herself to her feet, bracing against a tree trunk until her head cleared.

The Jeep sat ahead. Soon she'd be there, turning the engine, cranking up the heat. She'd drive home, sit with Sam and Josie over a table of food in the warmth of their little kitchen. Later, she'd visit Nathan. She had what she needed for this next step in her plan, and it was these thoughts that guided her to the road. Tree roots snagged her boots, rocks tripped her, hard bark skinned more flesh off her already torn palms. Through the bare branches above her, a beam of sunlight broke through the clouds, and she stopped in its glare, feeling it warm her deep into the marrow of her human bones. As human as she'd been in her first life, as human as a person could be. The Silent One had confirmed it and she would believe. It powered her forward. New strength carried her up the embankment, and she shook out her sore arms and fished the Jeep's key from her pocket.

As she rounded the fender, a woman stood from a crouch beside the driver-side door.

"Hi."

Waapikoona gathered the strength she'd just found and held it tight. She had no friendly greeting for a person who ambushed her.

The woman took a step closer, coolly blocking the Jeep's door. There was nothing cool about her black combat boots set wide apart, balanced, ready to deliver or block blows. Or the flash of teeth some might mistake for a smile. "You must be here to visit the same one I visit."

"I'm leaving."

"Can we talk?"

Another attempt to recruit her into mutiny, then. It couldn't be more obvious. Native people were common in this area, but this woman couldn't be local. No one raised by The Silent One would dare to expose their own people to the secrets they all kept, and to admit anything this close to home gave Waapikoona a feeling more suitable to snapping a person's neck and beckoning her Helpers for cleanup than having a friendly chat on the side of the road. The Silent One would end her if she killed another one of his soldiers.

200

She had to lie. "About what? I had to pee. Call the cops if you want." For half a second she considered dashing around to the passenger door and sliding into the driver's seat on the inside. It seemed like more trouble. Confrontation was quicker. "Now move away from my Jeep."

Waapikoona wasn't as ignorant as The Silent One. All Native people weren't her people. All raised by The Silent One weren't her sisters and brothers. And if it came down to it, she'd have no problem delivering punishment to this one who stood in her way.

CHAPTER
19

DOUG TRAILED MICK from waking to bathroom to breakfast prep to shower and the questions did not show any signs of ending.

How long have you been able to—?

Since December. That first time, when you were stayin' the night.

Can you control it?

Sometimes. Sometimes not.

Why sometimes not?

Haven't figured that out yet.

Mick was honest but brief, ending every bout of questions with a reminder to keep all of it locked and guarded—for now. They wouldn't lie to Doug's mom, but right now, she had too much stress to take this on. If Mick hadn't already showed her the stills from the video he took when he was trying to figure out what he was doing at night before waking up naked outside, he might feel like he was keeping something from her. For now, she'd been clued in. She didn't believe it then and wouldn't believe it now if told the truth.

The kids got dressed as Mick cleaned up breakfast. The break from Doug's questions allowed him time to frame out his day. Time off work *should* be for chores and grocery shopping, checking on Pop, and paying bills—and the long mental list of overdue maintenance on the GTO that always seemed too superfluous for his meager hours off. Especially now that he had new tires, the most urgent thing had been crossed off. Finding the woman who'd bought him those tires was more important than shocks and struts and a trip to the junkyard for a factory radio to fill the ugly gap in his dash. He'd never get so lucky to find one anyway. He needed to give it up and start saving for a new one. Or use the empty space as a storage shelf because who was he kidding? A radio was a luxury he had no spare time or money to afford.

At least a guy could dream.

A guy could also reminisce about his no-time-to-breathe previous life, the one before he'd turned into a demon-slaying thunderbird, the one filled with normal work and errands. The one he planned to return to really soon.

He ripped a sheet of paper off a pad on his counter and took a pen over to the kids.

"Isabel?"

Her dark eyes caught his. He brought the paper within her view and drew a crude picture of a bird. Hooked beak, talons—and a big X through the whole thing. Pointed to her then pointed to the picture. "No shifting today, right?"

She nodded. He doubted she had the strength for it after last night's drama followed by only five hours of sleep, but sometimes that lack of strength was what caused the shifting in the first place. "Okay, Dougie. You got three more

questions and then we gotta quit that for now. I'm leavin'
you with Old Mae for the day so I can get some stuff done."

All that normal life stuff would have to wait. He had a
300ZX to hunt.

Doug snatched his sketchbook and read from the page.
"When you chased us at Grandpop's were you trying to kill
us? Do you talk to other birds? And do you think when I'm
your age I'll be able to do it?"

He had a written list now? *God help me.* "No, yes, and
I hope not."

"Why do you hope not?"

"Because it ain't as cool as it seems. It's a real hard thing
to deal with." Mick wanted his damn normal life back now.
"Put on your shoes and grab what you want to take upstairs.
Both of you."

Mick went in search of his own boots. That clipped tone
wasn't normally how he talked to kids. All night he'd had
anger as a bedmate, and now it was following him around
his apartment. He had to get out, set himself on the way
to finding the woman who deserved that anger instead of
these innocent kids. Too much time he spent looking for his
boots before remembering he'd left them behind in his car
last night, along with his coat and that box of stuff, because
he'd been too exhausted to drag anything but himself inside
after ridding the house of a swarm of winged demons.

As they finally took the steps up from Mick's apartment to
the yard, he sensed Isabel hanging back. One glance got her
in gear, and he wondered if his anger had turned him frightening and she was obeying out of fear. Or—and he didn't
know how he felt about this—her own thunderbird remembered his eagle and followed because of that. He didn't need
any more reasons to rely on his eagle.

On the stairs up to Old Mae's front porch, Isabel stopped hard. Mick reached for her hand—she shied out of his reach so abruptly she nearly lost her balance. Too late he realized he'd gone for her crippled one. A defect that felt like his own doing shouldn't be so easy to forget, but his mind was too many steps ahead of him. This couldn't be the start of another game of getting the girl from one place to another. His patience was all out. He had one day to make some progress on finding Waapikoona. One slim chance that couple and their 300ZX were still close enough to track down. One prayer that he'd make some small breakthrough. Negotiating this girl into Old Mae's wasn't on the agenda. But she hadn't moved an inch, and her eyes said, *I'd like to see you try.*

He sat on the step next to her knees and looked out across the yard. Winter's gray hand had a tight grip. Nothing stirred, not even a breeze. The bare tree tops fanned across the flat featureless sky, beautiful in the sleepiness found only at the far edge of winter. He could see every tiny detail of the highest reaching branches, black against matte gray. Some craggy and twisted, others delicate, each tree as unique as a fingerprint. His eagle had taught him that. "I ain't gonna be able to find your sister from this porch, you know."

The creak of the door told him Doug had made it inside, and Old Mae was no doubt standing in the doorway staring a hole in Mick's back. Damn, he forgot he'd have to face Old Mae after what she saw last night. Spot bounded out at them, all wiggly dog body and flapping tail. Mick ducked away from the wet tongue. "See? Spot's cool with Old Mae's place. You want to go in where it's warm?"

Another reach for her hand would be too much too fast, but it was a risk he would have to take. There was no spare time. A glance over his shoulder showed Old Mae staring him down just as he suspected; he met her eye as directly as she gave it. The only way to win this would be to admit everything. A person did not lie to this woman and live.

"All my heat's gettin' out," she said.

As Mick stood, he slid his hand around Isabel's good one as if she were Janie and had no reason to balk. His upward motion added diversion, and he had her crossing the threshold before any sign of resistance. By then it was too late to refuse because he'd already let her go. Spot pushed past them, aiming for the kitchen where Doug had already started unloading his arms of books and games onto the table in some kind of Doug-specific order.

Isabel looked up at Mick. For a second Mick thought she might speak, but her eyes held on to his, her mouth set in the smallest frown.

"You're good, go on." Mick put a hand on the back of her head and pointed her forward.

Once the girl was out of earshot, he faced Old Mae. "I'm lookin' for her sister. The woman who was stayin' with me."

"You gone and got yourself mixed up in that?"

Mick rubbed the back of his neck, a nervous tic he couldn't subdue. "Don't figure I had too much choice in it. I hate droppin' them on you like this, but I got nowhere else to take 'em. Kari—"

"Hush. They're fine with me as long as you need to leave 'em."

There was something else riding on those words, a deeper meaning he sensed but second-guessed as soon as it fired in his brain. Old Mae said what she meant and that was it. She didn't hide meaning in talk. He was placing it there because he knew what she saw last night. Or did he? Maybe he imagined her there, looking out her window as he morphed from eagle to man. Maybe he dreamed it. If he didn't confront it now, he'd be nagged by it every time he saw her.

"I feel like you know what's goin' on around here," he said.

"I keep to myself."

"And I'm tryin' to keep my problems away from here but … they're gettin' a little outta hand."

"Seems some of it will always be outta your hands."

"I'm tryin' to fix that."

"You're only one man. Come upstairs, Mickey."

"I don't …" … *have time to be chewed out right now.* If he complained, he'd only get it worse, so he followed her upstairs to the dark second-floor hall where the doors to all the rooms were kept closed to keep her heat in the heart of the house. This big house was too much for an old woman, with the steep, slippery wooden steps and the many unused rooms filling with cobwebs. She would never leave this house, no matter what he or Kari had to say. A new owner might not want Mick living in the basement, so it wouldn't do him any good to argue reality.

Cold air fell against them as she opened the door of the bedroom that faced the yard opposite Mick's apartment side. It wasn't the stagnant air of a closed off room. It smelled of wet earth and the far-off scent of burning leaves. Old Mae drew the curtain away from the window. Through the glass, a long stretch of fascia dangled. It caught the wind and banged against the window frame outside.

"A good breeze is gonna break that through my window pane."

And before that, it would keep bringing weather into this already drafty house. Mick had no time for a handyman job, but he preferred it to the scolding he thought he'd receive up here away from the kids. "I'll get the ladder."

"I'll introduce the little girl to my cats."

Mick followed her down the stairs, her bony hand tight on the railing, her footsteps doubling up on each step. The slow pace worked Mick's bad leg harder than if he'd hopped down them two at a time. A warning to her to be careful entered his mind, but he held his tongue. He'd avoided the scolding he'd expected and didn't want to bring forth a new one. Those anti-slip stair treads he'd bought but hadn't had time to install yet—where'd he stash those? They had to still be in the bag from the hardware store. He went outside and dragged the ladder out of the crawlspace and hauled it around the house, adding up time in his head. Ten minutes to hammer some nails in the fascia, thirty minutes to install the stair treads. Then he'd be out of here.

At the top of the ladder he found more than damaged fascia. Parts of the soffit had been peeled away as if someone had latched on with a pair of pliers and torn a way in. He descended the ladder for hammer, nails, and a flashlight because of course he had to check that hole before he closed it up, even though a voice inside him was telling him not to. Squirrels chewed. They didn't bend wood. Whatever had gotten in could still be in there, hiding under the roof with Old Mae and the kids unaware in the house below.

What he found in the hole was exactly what that inner voice told him he'd find—a dozen of the winged demons that had escaped his eagle last night, sleeping away the day-light hours. He got down off the ladder. Considered his eagle form, decided against it. He'd get them out the human way—brains and high-powered tools. In daylight he counted on them to flee, not attack, and he wouldn't give the time to any thoughts otherwise.

From his apartment he gathered a compressor, hose, and extension cord. He moved fast, aiming to stick to his ten-minute time even with the added work. Exertion warmed his core, bringing the winter's bite on his fingers and ears to his attention. He found his hat in his pocket and pulled it on. Work gloves would protect his hands from the cold and from a demon's bite, so he grabbed some from his apartment. With the extension cord plugged in and strung across the yard, he flipped the compressor's power switch. If its noise didn't scare those creatures out of the roof, a sharp blast of air would. He climbed the ladder, hose in hand.

A dark form burst from above. He ducked, bracing an arm against the house to keep the ladder from sliding. The creature's shriek carried away. When Mick had regained enough balance to look, he located the thing flapping halfway across the yard, low against the ground, heading toward the woods. He stayed in place, a few rungs away from the height he needed to reach the hole, and waited.

"Come on, you little shits." If they'd come out now, it would save him time and the risk of getting bitten.

All above was quiet. He couldn't think too much on this or he'd discover the insanity of it. He climbed to the top, stuck his hose in the hole, and pressed the trigger. The sound of blasting air was all he could hear. Demons waking would be muffled. Impulse jerked his arm from the hole; he turned his face away from a rush of flapping bodies, slick yet barbed, an erratic mob. The compressor hammered into the air as demon shrieks filled his ears and head then pushed against the heart of him, into his eagle. The ladder slid. He kicked a leg out—his bad leg—it caught against the window frame and held, his weight straining its damaged bone.

Another demon bite with no Waapikoona here to help him would mean his death. But this day had no time for his eagle. He dropped the hose, put both hands against the house, and righted the ladder. Released his leg, now inflamed with a splintering pain. The compressor shut off. Above him, the loose fascia banged against the house like a final call to get those creatures out.

He readjusted his feet so he could turn and look across the yard. The landscape mirrored the matte, unmoving sky as if all life had dissolved and he was looking into a snapshot of time. This scene was too gray and dull for a swarm of fantastical creatures to be released upon it, and the day mocked him for it. It was vicious in its dullness, as if its blind eye to his troubles were an act, when instead it was waiting for something to happen.

Forget the damn day and all its silent expectation. He called the shots, and he had other crap to do.

With plywood he patched the soffit, and he hammered the fascia back into place. In spring he'd fix it correctly, once he got his normal life back. A look at his phone told him thirty minutes had passed. He'd have to make up for it.

He found the anti-slip treads and started at the top of the stairs. Like a machine he worked his way down, alternating staple gun with hammer and nail when a spot in the wood proved too stubborn for staples. Even though the treads were rubber-backed, he didn't want to turn his slipping hazard fix into a trip hazard. The amount of holes he'd put through her staircase was surely overkill.

"My cats are just gonna tear that up." Old Mae had used his one and only sweat-wiping break to give him shit.

"Good, it'll give 'em somethin' to do. You got a towel I could use for my face?"

She left and returned with one, wetted with cold water from the sink. It felt like heaven on his flushed skin. He hadn't even spared the time to take off his flannel, and now his undershirt was soaked in sweat.

"I get the hint you think I'm unfit to use my own stairs."

"Nah," he said, lining up the last piece. She'd have to be okay with eyeballed measuring; he'd had no time for anything better. "This is for me and my dang limp."

"Ought to get that looked at."

"I look at it every day."

A few nails later he was stepping out the front door. The GTO held the box of stuff he'd collected from Jeremiah's car, but those clues seemed stale compared to the man and woman in the 300ZX. With the receipts and papers he at least had a starting point, something concrete to hold in his hand. With the 300ZX, he had no idea which way to go.

Raúl. Not a common name around here. He couldn't go around town asking about him, though. Waapikoona had called to warn him, and he wouldn't take that lightly. Which way had they headed? North. His eagle knew that car and if they were anywhere within his eagle's flying range, he could easily spot it from the sky. A day spent as eagle? Not again. He'd become too reliant on it. Was there any other way?

If Old Mae expected him to leave, he needed to get the GTO out of there. He got in and started the engine. Halfway down the driveway his phone dinged. He stopped, knowing he shouldn't look. It would only deter him from what he needed to do.

Visit Mom. His calendar, reminding him each month to do what he should remember himself. And he would, if time would stop passing him by so fast he'd for once have the opportunity to think to do it. Right now, it seemed he'd just been at her grave last week. He wouldn't put this off. It would turn it into what it had been for so many years— denial that his mother was dead. If he didn't talk about it, didn't visit her, didn't think about it, then he wouldn't have to care. He needed to care.

"Fifteen minutes," he said, turning onto the road in the direction of the cemetery. It wouldn't take any longer than that, even with stopping at the store for a small bouquet of flowers. And the release of fifteen more minutes of his day made his idea of eagle mode more necessary. It was the only way to find that car on fleeting time.

HE'D VISITED THIS grave enough times since Jeremiah brought him and his mother's stolen spirit back here as blackmail, yet every time he drove through the gates he remembered the rope around his wrists and the corner he'd been backed into. And his stubborn fight against his eagle which could have ended everything then and there.

It was a pointless thought. How it ended up was how it should have, with his mother gently returned to her grave. His eagle's presence would have disrupted that, may have pushed Jeremiah to do something worse than what he did. If the worst part was his bad leg and Isabel's crippled hand, he should be happy. Jeremiah was dead. The people he cared about were alive. His mother rested in her grave. It was a better ending than the one he'd have predicted when he was tied up and bleeding to death in the mausoleum, even if Waapikoona was still missing. It was only a matter of time before he found her.

"Hey, Mom." He cleared last month's flowers from his mother's grave and set the new bouquet against the head-stone. "Kari says hi. She'd come, but she can't leave the baby's side. Helen's not good. Don't got much time left."

Cold air came in on his inhale, tightening his throat. His eyes watered. He should be crying, but he wasn't ready to do that for Helen. It didn't seem real that a girl so little could be dying and there was nothing anyone could do about it— except for him, and Waapikoona, as soon as he could find her. If his idea worked he'd never need to cry for Helen.

"Pop's doin' good. Like I always say, he's happiest on the days he remembers you, and those days seem more often now. Not sure why that is but suppose I shouldn't question. I put some carpet treads on Old Mae's steps so she don't slip, and she gave me a hard time—"

His phone was ringing. If time had been on his side he'd be in the sky right now, unable to hear it. He shouldn't pick it up, didn't have time for whatever it was on the other end. But there were too many things that could be more important than what he'd planned for this day.

The screen said it was Kari. Probably just checking on Doug. "Hey."

"I need some help today, Mick."

He closed his eyes. No time for anything else right now. But there was no way he could decline. "What's up?"

"Can you bring Pop over to see Helen? I'm afraid if we wait, she'll get worse, and ..."

Mick saved her from having to finish that. "Yeah, no problem." He rearranged time in his head. Twenty minutes to get there, get Pop, get to Kari's. He could leave him there then go do what he needed to do. It would tick off his check-on-Pop responsibility for the day and help out Kari. "We'll be right there."

CHAPTER
20

WALKING INTO POP'S kitchen, Mick realized his mistake. The drive between his mother's grave and picking up Pop would have been enough time for a person to get dressed. But if that person hadn't been called, he'd still be sitting in front of his TV in his robe and slippers just like Pop was when Mick showed up.

Mick hadn't called because he hadn't had room for the thought. The lists in his brain were overlapping, the uncompleted tasks battling one another. His head had turned into a field of combat, overloaded, an unending white noise of directives all drowning each other out. Instead of the quick stop he'd planned, he'd have to hang out while Pop shaved, showered, and combed his hair.

The last chance Mick had an opportunity to hang out anywhere had been so long ago he'd forgotten how. Pop's chair in front of the TV stood empty and waiting, but the idea of sitting idle gave Mick an urgent sense of danger like he just might explode. Pacing between back window and front window was doing nothing but wear out the floor.

The clock on the microwave incremented minutes in super speed like some sick game. Mick grabbed the TV remote and flipped channels, if only to satisfy the need to fidget. Sports, old movies, home shopping, news—and a name hit him in the back of the head.

Cahokia Mounds.

He'd already passed it up. He flipped backward in the channels and found a reporter standing outside the visitor center of the historic site in Illinois where he and Waapikoona had climbed the steps to the top of the great mound and connected like two opposite beings should never connect. And there it was, that mound in a panned camera shot, the land as bare and wintery as he remembered.

The reporter was now interviewing a woman in a state park uniform. "… only one percent of the site has been excavated. Many mounds were destroyed for housing developments. Other parts of the site simply haven't been studied. So unfortunately, we're not exactly sure what's been taken."

Shots of disturbed earth cycled across the screen as the woman continued to talk about lack of funding and highway development stalling excavations in years past. A wide view of a large field pocked with muddy holes. Close-up images of torn turf and gouges in the earth filled with rain. The scarred side of one of the mounds, skin of dead grass turned under to the dark earth. Mick thought of Waapikoona's reason for needing to go there. She'd buried her sister's bones, and she needed to dig them up to move to a safer place.

A police officer filled the screen. "At this point we can't consider it a grave robbery. There's no evidence any of these holes contained any bones."

Back to the park ranger. "Many of these mounds served as mass graves. This was a huge civilization. There's no doubt in my mind we're walking on human remains as we speak.

What I don't understand is why someone would want to steal history like that."

Pop joined Mick's side. Together they watched locals give their own theories for the mysterious new holes all over Cahokia Mounds. The report ended with a phone number to an anonymous tip line.

"That's a national news channel," Mick said. He'd have to figure out why that made him so uncomfortable because right now, all he could do was stare at the next segment without seeing it.

Pop sat to put on his shoes. "You and I know that ain't grave robbers."

Then what? And why had Waapikoona picked that site as a temporary holding spot for Isabel's bones? If others like her had buried then unearthed their own family members, someone would have noticed. The place was a state park and landmark visible from a somewhat busy road running through an area more populated than Wyona. That Illinois land was so flat, grave robbers could be spotted from a mile away.

Mick powered off the TV. Pop's shoes remained on the floor alone. "You ready, Pop?"

"Ready for what?"

"To visit Kari, remember?" It had been so long that Mick had to remind Pop of something, he forgot to not tack on the 'remember' at the end. It just confused Pop and made Mick feel rotten. If dementia had stolen the thought, of course Pop wouldn't remember.

"You gotta warn me of these things, Mickey. I need to get dressed."

There was no need to point out he was already dressed, hair combed to perfection. "You look good. Just need to put on them shoes."

Pop looked down like he didn't expect them to be there. "Well ain't that convenient. They're waitin' for me."

Mick found Pop's coat and stood by the door. He couldn't stomach the microwave clock anymore, with its hurry to count time that shouldn't be passing so fast. Out on the driveway, Pop stopped to stare at the road, chin angled in the manner of a person looking for something. Mick opened the passenger side of the GTO and took a breath, hoping to clear the impatience from his voice. "Hop on in."

"Glad to see that car ain't back."

With Pop in the seat, Mick closed the door and went around to his side. He reached across for Pop's seat belt and buckled it. "What car?"

"That old Toyota. Fella who left it there looked to be up to no good."

Mick backed off the driveway into the road, straightening out and hitting the gas before a semi had a chance to come around the turn and clobber them. The maneuver was a lot quicker than turning around in the narrow driveway but riskier. Sometimes the GTO V8 came in handy. "Did he come to the house?"

"Nah, but I watched him through my binoculars. Dragged another fella out of the woods and shoved him in the car."

Mick looked over at Pop, surprised. "The woods on your property?"

"Hard to tell. But pretty dad-gum close."

The house was too remote for anyone to be walking around on Pop's land. "Why didn't you call the cops? Or at least call me?"

"I reckon these ain't police matters. Same reason I didn't call 'em on the woman who showed up lookin' for her missing sister."

A surge of adrenaline, the impulse to slam the brakes. Just like when the deer had jumped in front of him that night, only this time there was no deer. He steadied himself. No use in driving them off the road over something that could be nothing, but nausea had rolled in behind the adrenaline, promising to deliver if Mick got a certain answer to the question he had to ask. "What woman?"

"Indian woman. Knocked on my front door. Said her sister was missin' and asked if she could check my woods."

He couldn't drive and make sense of these words. It couldn't have been her. She'd been right about her sister's bones being behind the house—had she put them there? Did she track down Mick's father as she'd tracked down Mick?

"Expected her back to warm herself up, but she never came. And them two guys sat so long in the car I got tired of watchin'."

Mick hit the brakes—he'd almost missed his turn. He couldn't be mad that Pop hadn't called the cops. That would have been trouble for Mick. He could be mad Pop hadn't told him this before, though. "You sayin' that car was there the same day as the woman?"

"Yeah, and she said she knew you. Didn't stay long enough to ask how, but I put it all together when that little girl—"

"Gray Toyota Corolla? About an '03? Rusting around the wheel wells?"

"Sounds about right. You know those fellas?"

He'd killed one of them. The other might know where Waapikoona was, but who was he and whose side was he on? "This happen last December?"

Pop took a moment to ponder that. "Seems right. Before Christmas."

When Waapikoona had still been in town and Jeremiah had still been alive. Could Jeremiah have found her here that day of Mick's almost death in the mausoleum, shoved her in the car and brought her there with him? "You sure that other person was a man?"

"Ain't no doubt."

She and Jeremiah had spoken of another man that day. She'd said a name, told Jeremiah he was just like this person. Mick had been far away, watching Jeremiah threaten to crush her sister's bones, distanced from the knife Jeremiah had put in Waapikoona's hand and ordered her to finish him as he lay dying on that stone floor. If he could remember, he might have something to go on.

"You don't watch the news much, do ya?" Pop asked.

Soon Mick would be alone and he could dig in his brain for that damn name. "Can't remember the last time I had my TV on."

"People goin' missing all over. No one can decide if it's terrorists or aliens or some kind of conspiracy. Then there's some sayin' it's nothin' at all, just more eyes on something that's been goin' on forever. Government wants to put the military on it."

"That dog won't hunt." Mick spoke it before he could censor himself.

"You got that right."

Mick hoped he'd leave it at that. He had no willpower to determine how much Pop knew or how much of this could be discussed.

Pop's voice lowered, even though they were the only ones in the car. "Only a matter of time before they know what we know—"

"Let's not get worried 'bout that—"

"I ain't worried."

Mick turned into Kari's driveway and slowed to a stop. He'd ask Pop not to bring any of this up inside, but he didn't feel right about adding more weight to a topic he wished would go away. Since Pop's memory had a high chance of losing the request, it seemed better not to say a thing. With a glance at the clock on his phone, he got out and waited for Pop at the nose of the GTO. A huge chunk of the day now gone, he'd done no looking for Raúl and hadn't found any more clues to help him find Waapikoona. Both of them could be moving farther out of both human and eagle range. The good news was that 300ZX would catch the eye of any person half knowledgeable about cars. He had to ask all the guys at Virgil's, all their friends. See if he could catch anyone at Lucky's Tavern who might've seen it.

Pop had made it to the porch, and Kari was opening the door, grim-faced and bleary-eyed. This was more important.

Grief fractured Mick's resolve; he forced his good leg to take a step then his bad one. Not facing death meant he could forget it, push it behind a wall like he'd done with his mother. He was young and stupid then. Too scared to learn how to cope, too selfish to see he wasn't the only one torn in two. This time he wasn't feeling his own fear. He was feeling the deep chasm of Kari's, having to watch her baby girl die. Of Pop's, helpless and burdened to hold the whole family's strength. Of Doug's, angry and grasping for reasons. Of Janie, soon to be the youngest, no longer the big sister, confused by a world that shouldn't be so unfair. And he couldn't forget baby Helen's own fear, feeling the door slowly close when it had just opened, the unknown of what lay beyond.

He was going to change that beyond. He needed Helen's bones and Waapikoona by his side to lead him into that cave. Not much to ask for, but it seemed like so much.

The last to enter Kari's front room, Mick closed the door and backed against it. Kari sat on the edge of the bed. Pop leaned over Helen's small bundled form, his hand on her head, his eyes unspeakably sad. Machines beeped and whirred all around. Kari took hold of a little foot and looked across the room at Mick. Even though he saw a different end than the one they saw, he couldn't stop the clamp against his throat or swell in his eyes. His plan may not work. His baby niece might die, forever.

It was so bleak he stepped away, letting that thought linger in the space against the door he'd vacated. The coward's space. The one inhabited by a person too afraid to confront death. He was a thunderbird. He tore demons from the underworld and split them apart in the sky. Death had found him, nearly taken him. He'd fought it and won. He was in love with a woman who'd seen the inside of a grave and was now here in his world, in the flesh—somewhere he would soon find. Death did not scare him.

He put a hand on Kari's shoulder and tilted his head toward the kitchen. "Talk a minute?"

Janie had found Pop and was now crushed in a hug. The kitchen would be free.

Kari followed him. He found the kettle in the cabinet and filled it with water. He set mugs, tea bags, spoons, and sugar on the table and pulled out a chair for her to sit. Seeing her standing there so wooden and lost would very soon steal his nerve.

"This'll sound crazy."

She moved her unblinking gaze up to meet his. The skin under both eyes so dark, for a second he thought they were bruised.

"And ..." There really wasn't a word, but he had to think of something. "Insensitive."

She shrugged. It was clear such things were beyond her level of feeling.

How to say this? In what order? With how much explanation? The longer he stared at her the more her eyes welled, and if he didn't get it out quick he'd soon be the one crying.

221

This had to come out strong and sensible. "I'm askin' a favor that you trust me and not think too much about what I'm gonna ask."

Tears trickled down both her cheeks. He got a napkin from the table; she let him dab her face like she'd lost the capacity to care about wiping her eyes.

"When the baby dies, don't tell no one but me. We need to bury her on Pop's land until …"

Until I can find my undead friend to escort me into the underworld and beg a great demon to revive baby Helen from her own bones.

"… until I can find the woman that can help her."

Kari's eyes narrowed. "Help who?"

"Help Helen."

She repeated those two words, half disbelief, half prayer. "No one can help. Not now. Not after she's gone. What are you—"

"I'm sayin' I know someone who can, after she's gone. But I gotta have her bones—intact—and no one can know. So when she comes back—"

"Comes *back*?"

The kettle overflowed, water hissing against the hot burner. He'd left the spout cover open so it hadn't had a chance to whistle. He turned off the stove and brought the kettle to the table, taking a chair across from Kari.

"I saw it happen to another little girl."

"Have you lost all—"

He reached across the table and took her hands in his. "See, this is the favor I'm askin'. Don't think. Just trust me. No funeral. When she goes, just call me and I'll …"

Kari's voice lowered. Disappointment, outrage—the *you-oughta-be-ashamed* tone she used on her kids when they stepped too far out of line. "*Mick.*"

At that moment, the reality of what he'd just requested brushed a cold hand down his spine. There would be a body. A child's corpse. The lifeless form of his sweet little niece he'd have to carry in his arms, transport in his car, bury in the ground, all by himself. He couldn't do it but somehow he would have to. Another thought unfurled. What if Helen's disease was reborn inside her the second time? Could he ask Kari to suffer all this, all over again? He closed his eyes and rolled that bad idea back up into itself. Baseless worries would not derail him. And worries were just that; they rarely came true. This would work out. It had to. "If anyone asks, you gotta lie, tell 'em she's doin' okay—"

She tore her hands from his. "Have you lost your *mind*?"

A shadow fell over them, and they both looked up at Pop, who'd entered the room with Janie behind him. "Kari, you need to have faith in your brother."

A deep, angry line formed between her eyebrows. "Now you're both …" Noticing Janie in the doorway, she tilted her head, reaching for her. The anger on her face softened as she pulled Janie onto her lap.

"I know I don't get a lot of things right no more and forget more things than I remember. But what Mickey's sayin' … Kari, it's crazy. But he ain't crazy like me. And whatever's goin' on, he's in the know."

Kari looked across the table at Mick. Her jaw had dropped a bit, but a new light shone in her eyes. Her face showed the same thought in Mick's head—Pop had never recognized his condition. The dementia came and went, but when it came, Pop was fully in its grasp, never seeing it for what it was. And when it went, Pop was the man he had always been, untouched by lapses of memory or understanding and offended that anyone might assume he needed help. Dementia couldn't be cured and wouldn't go away, but this

moment was a bridge between the father they used to know and the man he'd become, and the words born from this felt too much like a miracle.

Still regarding Mick, Kari pressed her lips against Janie's hair. Mick didn't need agreement or acceptance. He didn't even ask for understanding. But if she could just give him trust, and a little time, he could offer her proof she could see with her own eyes. Her own child, once dead but now awake, alive, cured, a second chance. If he could give Kari that she wouldn't need to believe the crazy things he was saying. She could move past it and pretend it never happened. Their memories of Helen's sunken eyes and weak breath, of that metal bed surrounded by machines and the medicine bottles cluttering the table, and this impossible conversation tinged with a request to believe something so absurd it bordered betrayal … it could all disappear like the memories lost in Pop's mind.

Mick feared the answer, but had to ask one final time. "Trust me?"

The slightest nod. It was enough.

Mick gathered himself, got up, and lay a hand on Pop's shoulder in gratitude. Duty rang through him with the force of his thunderbird. He held Helen's hand, kissed her forehead, whispered in her ear. "Go in peace, sweetheart. We will see you real soon."

Outside, the sky hung low. The grayness all around said, *Your confidence is unfounded. Failure is possible; this loss will destroy you.* But failure wasn't an option, not after what he just promised. He found the GTO key in his pocket and pressed the unlock button. As the door locks clicked against dead air, a name sprung from deep, dark memory into active thought.

Hammond.

In Waapikoona's voice, inside that tomb, the day he almost died at Jeremiah's hand. Deep in his half-human, half-eagle core, he recognized that name for the one he needed, the clue that would lead him to her.

CHAPTER
21

THE SHAFT OF sunlight that had warmed Waapikoona a moment ago faded away, choked behind clouds flattening the sky once more. The woman was not moving away from the Jeep like Waapikoona had demanded. The strength gathered from that slight glimpse of sun had left her, and now she felt the crawl through the cave in every joint. More unsettling was this new weariness, this uncertainty. Before this visit to The Silent One's cave, her goal was clear. Now she felt chained in a new way, burdened by a new weight pulling against her with each step forward.

Wind gusted across the road, lifting her hair, pushing the stranger's hair away from her face to reveal a deep scar arcing across her forehead. *Join them now, before they break you down. At least then it will be your choice.* On this bleak day in the numbing cold, the thought had fangs. Waapikoona wasn't even sure it was her thought it felt so unfamiliar. She felt out The Silent One's ever-lingering presence, found it strangely absent from inside her. New fear wound around her, unlike any she'd felt in this life. It worried her.

Not enough to back away from this meeting, though.

The woman had no gloves against this terrible chill, but her hands remained loose at her sides. "I hear others have tried to talk to you."

"I told them I work alone."

"There's no option for that anymore. You're either with him..." she angled her head toward the woods, in the direction of The Silent One's cave "...or with us."

"I guess I'm with him, then."

"Then, I have to kill you."

Tires scuffed gravel on the road behind Waapikoona. An engine droned closer, a slight squeak of brakes slowing to a stop. If this woman had called her friends for help, Waapikoona would kill them first to illustrate the screwup then leave the woman alive so she could explain to the others exactly what 'no' meant.

A door opened. Closed. Waapikoona restrained the urge to look behind her. The woman hadn't changed her stance, but her eyes were on this car and they weren't welcoming.

"You ladies having some car trouble?"

The woman's gaze returned to Waapikoona's face. "Isn't it great when they come right to you?"

This woman had just admitted to not being with The Silent One. "You don't work for him."

"Oh, but I have to. If I stopped, that would tip him off. And sometimes I enjoy it so much."

Too often Waapikoona had also enjoyed it, but it seemed a weird thing to admit out loud. Especially since a random good Samaritan didn't seem to deserve death and delivery to The Silent One. She turned to look at the guy. He headed toward them, flipping his collar up against the cold. He

had the smooth-faced look of youth, and a friendly smile that shot her through with an image of Mick. Earnest, hard-working, ready to help a stranger on the road.

She had to stop this.

The woman had already made it past her to meet the guy between the cars and was gesturing, mentioning something about a tire on the other side of the Jeep. Now she was leading him over there, to the cover behind the Jeep where a person could be murdered and shoved down the embankment until the body could be cleared away.

The woman bent, arm extended toward the ground. Two Helpers rolled off her palm and scattered into the grass, heading down the incline toward the woods. The good Samaritan had bent for a better look at the tire and had missed it all. Waapikoona rounded the Jeep and latched an arm around the woman's throat just as she swung. The young man grunted, head snapping to the side—her blow had still made indirect contact, but she wouldn't get a second because both her hands were in use against Waapikoona's tightening arm, locked against the other, a perfect hold. The woman's body sagged as she fought; Waapikoona threw her against the Jeep, ignoring the fingernails digging into her wrist, her cheek. The strain in her arm carried electric pain into her neck, exploding in her head. She closed her eyes against it and kept her hold. Soon the woman's oxygen would be depleted, and she'd keep her arms locked a little longer, just until the heart stopped.

Another person raised by The Silent One and killed by Waapikoona. She'd never be able to show her face in his cave again. She held on as the woman kicked and flipped. She should let go, let her live. She released an inch. The woman gasped a hoarse breath. Waapikoona swiveled, allowing a better angle to see where the young man had gone. There he lay, crumpled against the dead grass after having rolled halfway down the embankment, one arm twisted underneath his body.

"Will you behave if I let you go?" Waapikoona said in the woman's ear.

She thought of Mick and what he'd say if he was here. He'd be begging her to stop, to release the woman, even though Waapikoona felt freeing her could only be a mistake.

Rigid in the chokehold, her arm didn't want to release, but she gave enough room for the woman to drop out and hit the ground on all fours. Gasping, she cursed Waapikoona using slurs created by the white man.

Maybe Waapikoona had gotten it wrong. Maybe this woman wasn't Native. But she knew of The Silent One even if she hadn't mentioned him by name. She carried his Helpers. Waapikoona scanned the edge of woods for the creatures, thinking she imagined it. She was still out of breath and tired, so tired. She felt for the Jeep key in her pocket. She longed to get off this road and go home.

Now upright, the woman unzipped her coat. Too late Waapikoona saw the release of a blade, too short was her reach, too slow her lunge, too clumsy her boots against the sloped embankment. A red slash across the young man's neck, a weep of blood, bright against the gray of landscape and sky. The body shuddered, fighting death even while in its undeniable grip. Now Waapikoona had her own grip of coat and hair as she wrenched the woman off, spinning her, reaching for the wrist of the hand that held the knife—and caught the blade instead.

Waapikoona held on, steel biting so deeply into her palm she lost all feeling to it. She twisted her wrist—that scream, it must be her own. The wind picked it up, cycling it around her before casting it across road and field and forest. This

pain was her punishment for failure, for thinking of Mick's conscience as if it had any bearing on her. It only worked out for him.

Now she had the knife freed. So much blood, her grip turned slippery. She tightened her hold on the blade, through the searing anger of her ruined hand and jabbed. The handle caught the woman in the temple, snapping her head to one side. Another jab—the nose, a burst of blood. Now the woman fell. Waapikoona opened her hand, but the blade had become a part of her. She wrapped her other hand around the handle. A yank, another scream carried by the wind. Down on her knees. A second slashed neck bubbling blood into the gray.

Quiet. Stillness. Waapikoona's ruined palm throbbed fire into the cold wind that hissed through the dry grass where two bodies lay. The ground passed its freeze into her shins, her legs, her belly. She would never warm this cold. It would live in her until her own death filled her.

On the road above her, a semi passed, pushing air down the slope against her. She had to clean this up, had to get away. Her hand—oh how it bled. She could feel her energy draining away. Good hand planted against the ground, she shoved herself up, breathing until her head cleared. The taste of blood in her mouth was false, just her mind in shock and trying to make sense of the open wound. There was no reason to throw up. She needed something to wrap her hand. A piece of cloth. A scarf, a glove, a sock. She eyed the dead man's boots and imagined him being gobbled by her Helpers while missing his boots. No, it wasn't right. His attacker's socks? She'd rather not take a piece of that woman home. So she yanked off her own boot, biting down against the rush that traveled from the beat of her heart into her ruined hand, and removed her own sock, wrapping it tight around the fissure that surely revealed her bones, and locked her fist. Boot pulled back on, she released her Helpers. Across the ground a second team of Helpers ran and joined her own, one pair of jaws at each end of each body until they met in the middle and burrowed into the ground, leaving only fresh dirt in their wake.

Waapikoona wiped her eyes and got up. Inside the Jeep, she made a loose knot in the sock and tightened it with her teeth. She pulled onto the road thinking *accelerate, steer, drive*, waiting—pleading—that soon all would go numb.

Too many thoughts kept her from that need. A tremble began in her legs, feeding a continual shiver up her spine. Blood dripped on her jeans, leaving warm wet spots that quickly turned cold. She tried to think of the turns in the road and the place she'd arrive, but instead she thought of how she no longer had two quotas to fulfill for The Silent One. Now she had a third. She would never get her sister back. She had a thought that had been easing its way in, building a case in the idle space of the day. In sleep and dreams, in every failure and loss.

She could leave her sister in her grave. Let her remain at rest. Decide not to push her into this grim world where war built underground and violence hunted her above. She could return to her own grave—for good this time. Every day it seemed more and more like she would have been better off never leaving it. It wasn't surrender if she decided the fight was no longer worth her time.

With every step toward raising her sister, new obstacles were being built in her way. To have to fight so hard—maybe what she wanted wasn't meant to be.

And everywhere she looked she saw the lifeless green-gray eyes of that young man, his carefree walk toward her, his sincere smile so much like Mick's. Someone would be

missing that young man as much as she missed Mick. They'd search and never find him and feel as broken as her.

TINY SNOWFLAKES WHIRLED against Waapikoona as she crossed the road between Rain's trailer and the soft glow of Meredith's curtained windows. In the hours she'd waited in the dark on Rain's frigid sofa, she'd done nothing but watch the driveway across the road. Nathan's car arrived first—a strike of luck for which she could spare no gratitude. Meredith did not need to see the woman reflected in the trailer's little bathroom mirror. Face gouged by fingernails, red-purple bruised cheek, blood-caked sock clenched tight in her fist that she'd had no will to properly bandage. And a look in her eyes of failure and grief so ghoulish she looked exactly like a soul raised from a grave. For the first time she felt truly powered by evil, by underworld war and age-old revenge. Her lifestyle had never felt so inescapable. Never had it been so branded on her spirit. She had killed. She would kill more. So many more.

Don't forget the other option. You could always just give up.

She'd tried to save that young man and failed. Maybe it was no coincidence he reminded her of Mick. Maybe this was the universe showing her where this path led if she continued on it. The things she wanted, never reached, only pushed further away behind new obstacles. The things she feared, coming true at every turn. What kind of person would keep going?

Nathan opened the door before she could knock. The face she'd studied in the mirror hours ago made him take a grip of the door frame and lean out past her, scanning the road for danger. He extended an arm to help her up the step, caught sight of her ruined hand, and froze.

"I'll live." She stepped across the threshold, pressing him back. "I have info to trade for info."

"Okay, but not until you put a proper bandage on that. Hang on." He flipped the deadbolt on the door and left the front room as if on a mission.

Waapikoona took in the little living room with its pretty floral couch and color coordinated throw blankets folded in matching squares across the back. It was no place for a woman covered in dead grass, dirt, and congealed blood. She looked at her boots. Mud-caked, blood-splattered, they needed to come off before they ruined the clean floors. It didn't seem she could muster the effort.

"Those are fine." Nathan had caught her looking. "Just come in the kitchen. I can mop before Meredith gets home." He set a case of first aid stuff on the table and pulled out a chair for her.

She sat. He sifted through white boxes and tubes and set a few things out on the table.

"You're going to have to lose the—what is that?" He eyed her blood-caked hand.

"My sock."

"Mind if I …?" He took hold of her forearm, gently twisting so the fingers of her closed fist faced upward. "Can you open your hand?"

When she didn't answer, he looked at her face. His deeply brown eyes brimmed with kindness. She had built powerful armor against hate and violence but carried no ready defense against unconditional compassion. She thought of the good Samaritan on the road, stopping his day to help strangers in the cold. A pang struck her in the chest. She took a breath and unclenched her fingers, welcoming the stab of pain to push that young man's dead eyes out of her head.

Nathan sucked air through his teeth as he picked off the soaked sock. Despite his steady fingers, her palm felt ripped open a second time. So long in one position, the coagulated blood flexed free, scab undone, cool air rushing over inner flesh that should never feel air.

Nathan turned his face away, collecting himself. "I need to drive you to the ER."

"I won't go. Just put the sock back—"

"That's not … sterile."

"Okay, then give me a bandage. I need to go home before Meredith sees me like this."

"She's with her study group. Listen, I think I—" He turned away again and coughed. "I think I see bone."

Suddenly light-headed, Waapikoona hardened herself against her body's reaction to an injury her brain was apt to handle. Instead of gaining control, she shuddered involuntarily. The reaction brought her outside of herself, watching a person she didn't know.

"How much blood have you lost?"

The question gave her an image. Mick, on the stone floor of that tomb in a lake of his own blood. He could've been dead just like that young man on the road, his bright eyes clouded by death. She was to blame for that. As much as she yearned to see him, hear his voice, rake her fingers through his hair … she was the reason he'd been there, and she'd never put him that close to danger again.

Nathan lowered her hand to his knee and tore open bandages and gauze. Her vision lost focus; she closed her eyes. A cold liquid against the wound—she brought her good fist against her mouth as her stomach twisted.

"Don't throw up," Nathan said. "If you do, I will, and…"

This kindness was going to kill her. She had to find a distraction. "You don't need to worry about being a father."

He looked up from his work.

"The Silent One told me himself. Our babies are human."

"He could be lying."

"He has no reason to. He said if our babies were part of him like we are, he'd be—" She had to swallow, gather herself. Whatever he was doing to her hand sent an electric prod straight into her guts. "Be pairing us up to make more soldiers."

He turned her hand, started wrapping it with gauze. "Has he tried that?"

"No. He wants us separate, beholden only to him. We only know about each other because we've found out on our own."

Nathan ripped a piece of tape off the roll with his teeth. She could see him weighing this new knowledge, working to find a hole. With the tape stuck to his thumb, he stopped to look at her again. A grim shadow fell across his eyes, and he worked his jaw as if to clear away a tightness. "Did he do this to you?"

Funny how she had to think about that. Remembering the earlier part of the day, the time before she'd sat in that state in Rain's trailer, simmering in grief and darkness, failure and blood—the details before that seemed impossible to recall as if it was another past life. A second one, when now she was living her third.

The answer came from some other part of her. "No."

"Then who?"

All she saw were the staring eyes of the young man. His blood, smeared up his chin, staining the chest of his coat. The youthful cheeks that would never again be kissed by his mother or stroked by his girl. A life bled out, flesh consumed by demons to deliver to The Silent One so he could tear spirits from their graves against their consent and rebuild a clash between peoples that should be fading out, not given new life.

Her voice, so low, it grated the words. "One of the mutinous ones. She killed an innocent man, so I killed her."

"Oh shit," he whispered.

She watched as concern turned to fear. Not of her, but for her. It was a feeling she should find in herself, but she'd lost the common sense that dictated that kind of thing long ago. Fear was no ally. It undermined and sabotaged and slowed her down. Maybe it was a healthy part of a human existence, but she was far from healthy. The Silent One had said those he raised were all human, and she would accept that for Nathan. She would not accept it for herself.

"It's fine. No one saw me."

"You can't keep rocking the boat like this. If he finds out—"

"He already knows." Some forgotten instinct traveled from her belly to dry her throat, and she remembered, there in the cave, with The Silent One's voice going on and on— had she lost consciousness? Something had been done to her. Something had changed her. And that instinct—what was it? Shame? Regret? It made her feel small, sad, and angry, like a child punished. Now wasn't the time to figure it out, though. "Someday I will no longer serve him."

He watched her one long moment before he spoke. "That's not possible."

"It will have to be."

"I was told, if I ever stop working for him, my own Helpers will come for me. Eat me alive and leave no trace. And then go after every person I care about."

She'd never heard this. But then, she'd never asked. "You believe that?"

"I've never known anyone to break away from him. So, I don't have much choice over what to believe."

No one had these answers. Not yet, anyway. She might just have to be the first to try it. Now wasn't the time to be thinking about it. She had other things to do. "If you still want to tell Meredith the truth, I'm willing to vouch for you. If that would help."

He covered his face with both hands and dragged them slowly down. "She'll just think we're both crazy."

"Until I show her my Helpers."

He grunted, looking off into the room at nothing. A slow, steady throb began in her bad hand, threatening to build into something worse if she didn't take it easy. She had to go. And with that lost look in his eyes it was clear he'd need a little prodding to produce the answers she hoped to win in this trade. "I'd love to have that info on Jeremiah, if you've decided to give it."

He dug a folded piece of paper from his pocket and held it up, just out of easy reach. "I was on my way over to give it to you when you came to my door."

She reached and took hold with her good hand.

He didn't release his grip. "You can't go there. There are too many of them."

"I have The Silent One on my side."

"Yeah, and so do they."

With a jerk, the paper pulled free. She shook it open. He'd written a Missouri address with a question mark, followed by a list of turns and landmarks.

"Address is a guess based on what I found on the internet. Jeremiah's people set up a little commune at an abandoned mine just outside of that town. They're not there all the time. They come and go. But if this guy Hammond is being held by them, that's where he'd be."

Elation nearly made her forget the chaos that was going on in her bandaged hand. "Looks like I'm heading back to Missouri."

It was exactly where she didn't want to go.

CHAPTER
22

MICK DROVE THE GTO back to Pop's and parked in the driveway. He checked his phone one last time before powering it off. All the people who might need him were taken care of. Doug and Isabel with Old Mae. Pop with Kari. And if Kari needed anything, she had a strangely lucent Pop there to help her and Amanda a phone call away.

Afternoon had arrived quickly. The day was fading. His human body, limited by gravity, roads, and hunger would be inefficient. He got out of the car and stripped off his clothes. Cold winter air and modesty were temporary problems that no longer concerned him. He couldn't decide if he was getting good at this shifting thing or bad and careless at it.

No time to think.

With his clothes, keys, and phone tossed in the backseat, he slammed the door. He bounced in place, pissing off that bad leg—another temporary problem. It used to transition into eagle form, but lately he no longer felt it once he was in the air. His prey: a shiny black 300ZX. His human mind translated the memory from his eagle, the night he'd spotted the car in the parking lot. Now with a fresh picture of that prey, he needed a trigger to shift. He put himself back on that ladder, face-to-face with those roosting winged demons he cleared from Old Mae's, and took off on human feet. Sharp, cold gravel replaced with brittle grass and yard, unyielding ground—then air, lifting him up. He pumped arms—wings—and tucked his legs. Treetops now below him, the space around him wide, unending.

This time his prey was not demons and serpents. He'd waste no time on them. His prey was a machine that prowled the treeless land smoothed by humans. This was a hunt without a kill. He needed this machine to lead him to *her*, the woman from the underworld, his human's mate, his guide.

Human time bound him. He must return to this place before the land grew dark.

MICK DRESSED BESIDE the GTO. His eagle had searched many towns over in every direction and returned to Pop's driveway focused and undeterred. Now back in human form, he worked to hold on to that feeling. The search wasn't a failure; he had simply eliminated areas. The next search would be more direct. Defeat crawled all over him, but he shook it off. His eagle wasn't defeated, so neither was he.

He got behind the wheel and started the engine. He got back out to throw up in the driveway.

There had been a few meals as eagle, small horned serpents found in a nearly dry creek. The taste of their blood mixed with human bile nearly sent him back out of the GTO a second time, but he grabbed a half-full bottle of water from the cup holder—he'd learned to keep one on hand just for this reason—and rinsed his mouth out. For once the water wasn't encapsulated in ice.

The sky was pure black on one edge, gray on the other. He floored the GTO backward to the road and headed toward Kari's. She'd be wondering what took him so long to return, and he didn't have a reason he could tell her and wasn't going to lie. *Please trust me* wasn't going to last long.

It was Sunday night. He had another full week of work starting in the morning. And today, he'd gotten nothing.

Pop came out of Kari's before he'd shut off the engine, so he left it to idle and got out. Kari stood in the doorway, looking too tired to even ask the question he expected. With no truths or lies to give her, Mick simply wrapped his arms around her. She was stiff, unbreathing, but she turned her cheek against his chest and stayed there.

"It's gonna be okay," he said.

She took a tiny breath. He let her go so she could take all the air in her lungs, the same air that held him in the sky, healed him, made him feel so undefeatable.

"Good. Now another big breath, bigger than the last." He filled his lungs, let his chest nearly pop with it, and watched her mimic him. "Keep doin' that until all this is past us. 'Cause it will be."

She nodded, her eyes filling so they shined in the porch-light. Pop was already in the car, so Mick got in and drove.

By the time he got Pop settled at home, the night was in full effect. Without his eagle's vision the road back to Old Mae's was a black tunnel lit by high beams that swooped around the curves in their forward-facing, single-minded intensity that proved so inadequate against the faded presence of eagle vision. The human ability to move so fast, even if aided by machine, seemed at odds with such limited senses. Obstacles could be lining up outside that beam of light, and he'd never see them until they were right in front of him. He remembered the deer from the other night and dropped ten miles per hour. Invincibility belonged to his eagle half. And he didn't want to wreck this paid-off set of wheels. He'd not be able to afford another.

Money used to be his only worry. Deep in a new set of life-or-death problems, he was still hounded by it.

Finally home, Mick could now address every screaming muscle in his back and neck, and the smarting shin bone in his bad leg that felt newly chipped. A hot shower was a must. Choosing between aspirin or a beer was the hard call he'd have to make before that. He trudged up Old Mae's front steps, knocked, and let himself in.

The only light came from the kitchen, so he followed it and found two kids and an old woman sitting at the table playing cards. A cat peeked over the tabletop from Isabel's lap, noticing him before any of the humans did.

"You kids ready to wrap it up?"

"Aww," Doug said. "We gotta play through. I'm winning."

"Isabel's winning," Old Mae said. "And I'm out." She tossed her cards on the table and unbent herself, one bone at a time. "Come 'ere, Mickey."

He followed her to the far cabinet where she pointed at the top shelf she couldn't reach.

"Them glasses right there. Both of 'em."

He got them down.

"Now open that cupboard up there." She pointed. "And get that bottle down."

Exhaustion made him do it without asking why. She took the bottle from him and poured two neat glasses of whiskey.

It looked like he wouldn't have to choose between pills or liquid. She was doing it for him. And this wasn't the cheap stuff he'd buy. It was the fifty-dollar-bottle-on-the-top-shelf stuff, out of reach physically and financially. "I ain't …"

She handed him a glass. He looked down into it, wondering how much he'd pay for this tomorrow when he was on that damn creeper at Virgil's.

"I don't waste this on varmints. But you're the only one of age here to celebrate."

He raised his glass to clink against hers. "Okay, but what are we celebratin'?"

"Your nephew got that little girl to laugh."

After the second sip, Mick had to sit down. The time to savor a drink didn't exist in this day, but that no longer mattered so much. Tight muscles released him, head to toe. Leaning back in the seat, he crossed his arms on his chest and his legs at the ankles and watched the kids finish their game while Old Mae braided the girl's hair in two tight rows on the back of her head. It wasn't long like her sister's, and he wondered about that.

In the morning it would be straight to work for him, school for Dougie, and no idea what he was going to do with Isabel … but he let it go. Tomorrow would work that out.

By the time he got up to take the kids to bed in his apartment, he felt he was swimming through the air. His shoulders were loose, his spine asleep, his bad leg pleased with itself. Distantly he heard Old Mae tell him to bring the girl back in the morning, and he agreed, expecting to feel guilty, but the notion never settled. Spot followed them down, and he tucked two kids and one dog into his bed and then found eggs and a dish of chopped onion in his fridge like they were treasure. Between the three-egg omelet and the hot shower that followed, he was nearly asleep, so he got on the couch

and drifted away before the whiskey wore off and allowed his pains and worries to bar him from much-needed rest.

It wasn't the creeper that punished him the next day but a couple of unexpected visitors. His head was still fuzzy after two cups of coffee, and the suspension job he was working on seemed more stubborn than it should be.

"That's Monday for ya," the junior mechanic had said after giving it a second set of eyes and determining Mick was on the right path, just had to fight a little harder. "And old cars with rusty old parts. Take a break, man."

His break came with two uniformed visitors blocking the coffee maker in the office. He held up greasy hands to avoid a handshake. A confrontation from the cops at his place of work wasn't making him feel too friendly, and after the fruitless day yesterday and the pain-in-the-ass job he was working on now, he wasn't sure what would come out of his mouth.

A customer sat in the waiting area, eyes now glued on him and the two cops instead of the TV. Mick jerked his head toward the door and elbowed his way through it into the parking lot without seeing if they'd follow.

They did. "We just need to ask you a few questions."

"You got me for a minute. I gotta get back to work." All the illegal things he'd witnessed and committed seemed far away now, but he reached for them, hoping not to be stuck here saying the wrong thing. That group of men he'd helped Waapikoona kill—but that was his eagle, not him. The one who'd dragged bodies, though, that was him. Watching Waapikoona kill Leo Boyle behind Lucky's Tavern, the corpse removed by her demons—that had been him. Accompanying her to dig up human remains in Illinois—also him, but he'd left before the actual digging. Jeremiah's death had been performed by eagle, the stashing of his car in the woods—human.

"We'd like to know if you've heard from Leo Boyle. He and two other men are missing."

Leo and two men—had Waapikoona killed more than just him? Thunder rumbled in his ears. For a moment he panicked, thinking his thunderbird was coming out but no, it was just blood pressure and nerves and his heart beating triple. He swallowed against it.

"I ain't seen him."

Cold ripped down his spine. That was a lie. He couldn't get caught in a lie.

"Well, I seen him on the road driving away from Amanda Coulson's a couple months ago. He paid her an unwelcome visit. Gave her a fat lip. You gonna catch that piece of shit and put 'em in a cage where he belongs?"

Too much. They'd suspect him if he gave them too much anger.

The cops had shared a glance and were now looking back at him. "Virgil told us a minute ago that Leo came here lookin' for you."

"I got nothin' to say to him."

"Sounds like you do."

"I might if he touches Amanda again or gets anywhere near my sister and her kids." Damn it, where was his cool? "But I'd rather leave that job to you. Ain't you better suited for catching criminals that assault people?"

"What's your relationship with Amanda Coulson?"

None of your business. He caught himself before he said it. "She's a friend of my sister."

245

One officer slid a small notepad from his coat pocket, consulted a page, and looked back up at Mick. "You familiar with Blake Pritchett or Charles Elmsworth?"

"I went to school with Blake. Never heard of the other guy."

"When was the last time you saw Mr. Pritchett?"

"Couple months maybe. I see him around town. Far as I'm concerned, he belongs the same place Leo does." Too much, too much, too much. This other missing scumbag had to be Waapikoona's doing, independent of both him and his eagle, and he didn't want to go down for it.

"What makes you say that?"

"He beats on his wife and kids. Surprised you don't know that."

"That somethin' you might want to address yourself?"

Mick took a moment to let his blood cool and let reason find him. He kept his eyes level and easy on the officer's. Confident, honest, relaxed. Not judging, not angry, not brazen. All human. No eagle. "No, 'cause like I said, that's your job."

The shop door jangled open behind him, and Virgil's voice rang out. "With all due respect, officers, but you got my best mechanic out there, and time is money here."

The cop put his notepad away. "Don't go too far away, Mr. Svendsen."

With the way Mick's stomach fell a little, that statement was more official than it sounded, and he couldn't accept that right now, not with everything else. "Ain't got any plans to."

What they didn't know was his eagle followed no laws.

Back in the office, he thanked Virgil, who swatted the sentiment away, and said, "I'll be out back for a bit."

"Take your time," Virgil said, no longer so concerned about time and money.

Not a drop of sunlight had touched the shadow behind the building. The air hung heavy with the previous night's dense cold. Tucked in his pocket was the paid invoice for the car repair he'd found in Jeremiah's car. He drew it out, along with his phone, and called the number on the top.

A man answered. "Steel Town Auto."

"Hi, I'm hopin' you can help me nail down an issue I'm havin' with a car. Previous owner had it serviced there, and I was hopin' to get his info so I can ask him what he knows about it."

"We can't give out that kind of information."

"Yeah, I figured that. But I don't got a lot of money to throw at this thing, and it would help me out a lot."

"Sir, I said we can't—"

Desperation pushed him. "Do you know if the guy lived around there?"

"Look, are you some bail bond guy or something?"

Mick had to laugh. It's exactly what this sounded like. "No, nothin' like that. I'm just a broke guy with a car that won't start and not a lot of time to fix it. If I could just talk to this guy—"

"Give me the VIN. It might not even be in the system."

Mick called it out. From the tapping on the other end, he could tell the guy was going through screens, looking to see what he could give him.

"Looks like we did spark plugs and wires last November. That's all I got."

"You got a phone number or address?"

A long silence followed by more tapping. "Strange, I have no contact info ... hold on, I remember this guy. He wouldn't give us a phone number or anything. Real intense

kind of guy. After he left we got to thinking, and my boss called in the VIN. That car's stolen, my friend."

"Stolen." Mick knew this, but he said it just to keep the act up. "That's my luck."

"Sorry, man."

Mick thanked him and hung up. He stared at the paper long enough to let it sink in. This was a dead end to Jeremiah or whoever Hammond was. No help in finding Waapikoona. He wadded the paper, his frustration so ripe he had to slow himself down before he found something to punch. As the paper crushed he spotted an image on the back side, almost as if in eagle vision. He remembered, every time he folded and unfolded there had been something on the back he'd never given any time to, but now, it glared at him.

He unwadded the paper and spread it flat against his knee. There in front of him was a crude hand-drawn map. His human brain recognized the labeled roads. His eagle recognized it from a different view. Looking down on the curling ribbon of pavement through the trees, powerlines strung straight in their own gouge, an old rusted water tower throwing a long-legged shadow across a plot of cleared land, a group of buildings beyond it.

Inside, his eagle said, *Yes*.

By that evening he needed to decide which was the more urgent hunt. The 300ZX, or this place that just woke his eagle.

CHAPTER
23

ON HIS DRIVE home Mick determined the place on the map with the old water tower wasn't going anywhere, but the 300ZX would, and he had to try one more time to find that man who had a direct connection with Waapikoona—and a voice to give Mick information. The place on the map could be nothing, and if there were no people there, it could not speak to Mick.

His eagle would have to be patient.

He collected Isabel from Old Mae and unloaded his groceries in his kitchen. The girl lingered beside the couch, regarding him in the same way as that cat had upstairs—the same one that had been on her lap the day before. Like he had already been sized up and figured out and now, or very soon, he'd prove their judgments correct.

It didn't just remind him of that watchful cat. The girl was too much like her sister.

"Got you a piece of fresh salmon. Cost me an arm and a leg, so I hope you like it." He lifted a sack of red potatoes from the bag. "And these. You like these?"

No answer, not even a blink of her eyes.

He found the cashews he'd bought, opened the lid, and set them on the table. "Here," he said, pulling out a chair. "Start on this and I'll get the salmon going."

When he returned to unload the rest of the bags, he heard the chair scoot and the cashews can slide across the table. Looking at her might ruin the progress he'd just made, so he ignored what he heard and started on dinner. He suppressed the urge to fill the silence between them with conversation. If she was happy munching cashews, he'd leave it at that. Without Doug to ease the tension, he didn't want to add any pressure from the language barrier—if it even existed. She could know perfect English and just be choosing silence until she figured him out. He was okay with that as long as she didn't attempt another escape.

Once the food was ready, he made two plates, set one in front of her, and took the seat across from her. She watched him as if waiting for a cue.

"Dig in." He did so himself. He was starved and still had a full night ahead of him.

She ate every morsel. He took the return of her appetite as proof he was doing something right. He'd picked the right foods and made her comfortable enough to eat it, all without Doug.

"So, I don't know if you understand me, but I gotta leave you here for a few hours. Will you be okay by yourself?"

She set her fork down and looked at him. He got up to get a pad of paper and pen and sat back down. He drew a bird, flying out of a house. Pointing to himself, he said, "I'm going to change into eagle and search for your sister. Waapikoona. Remember?"

Her eyes changed from scrutiny to hopeful interest.

"You…" he pointed to her "…stay here." He drew a smaller stick figure inside the house. "Okay?"

A very determined shake of the head.

"You can't come. It ain't safe. And I just can't ask Old Mae to keep you again. She's an old lady and needs her rest."

She took the paper, snatched the pen from him, and drew a second, smaller bird next to the one he'd drawn.

"No. Ain't gonna happen." He took the pen, crossed through her bird, and circled the stick figure in the house hard enough to gouge the paper. "You stay here where it's safe." Once he left, how would he know she'd stay? She could open the door and shift and be gone forever—or killed. Waapikoona would never forgive him. *He'd* never forgive him.

"Look, I can't find Waapikoona if I can't count on you bein' safe. You know what safe is, right?" He gestured all around, hands spanning the walls of the apartment around him. "Safe inside. I'll even let you watch TV until you fall asleep. I know Janie left some movies here."

And Spot. She'd need the dog for company and protection. He went outside and whistled; seconds later paws pounded the ground, and Spot blasted inside. Isabel got up to see him, and Mick cleaned up dinner then found every blanket in the place and loaded it on the couch. Settled in a nest of blankets with the dog, her stuffed pink bunny, and the can of cashews, Isabel held Mick's eye. He remembered how her sister had tricked him, how he'd settled that woman on the couch with the agreement to speak of important things the following morning and she'd conceded—until he went to bed. That next morning she was gone, couch and blankets untouched.

He turned on the TV and started the movie. Isabel appeared to already be familiar with the remote as he demon-

strated how to increase and decrease volume. "You get tired, you just fall asleep right there. I'll be back in a few hours."

Her attention had been stolen by the cartoon. It could also be an act. With the night slipping away, he'd just have to trust her. He went outside, locked the door, and hid the key in a crevice in the stone foundation. Leaving his clothes in a pile, he flew into the night.

HIS HUMAN NEEDED more clues before seeking out the place in the picture. It would be another setting of the sun before they made it there, but it would be a better hunt if the human first found his bearings. He didn't want his human to walk into a place lacking the predator's certainty. Human doubt only created disaster.

The eagle's job was the hunt. His human would handle what followed. Symbiosis between the two would prove a success. He had to tolerate his human in all its inefficient complexities as his human had to tolerate him.

He climbed higher into the sky for a better view and scanned the earth below him, remembering the places he'd scouted the night before, analyzing the probable movement of a pair of humans in their shiny black machine. Humans were more predictable than any other creature that roamed the land.

One cluster of light after the other, he searched, ignoring the slither of a horned serpent through the grass, another across a ridge of stone. A swarm of winged demons dispersed at the sight of him, each creature unaware he could end them all before they could reach the cover of trees. Some other night he'd come back and do the work he was meant to do. Tonight he worked for his human.

He turned into the breeze, heading for a lone building in a circle of yellow light. His eye had caught a glint of that certain color, so like the surface of a still lake on a moonless night. Now focused on that patch of black, he knew he'd found the car his human sought.

It sat at the edge of the pavement, closest to where the hibernating forest would resume its battle to retake this human-cleared land once the season changed and the sun began to warm the earth again. Other cars sat in a line against the building. He glided down to land on a sturdy branch closest to that black car. His human needed to process this scene. His eagle mind would not gather the right clues. But his human would be cold and naked and unable to do much unless he found something to wear.

Halfway down the long building, a door opened. A woman came into view—the same woman he'd seen beside that car before, again with her thick leather glove covering her to mid-forearm. She scanned the sky. The eagle stayed still. He blended well enough for human eyes to miss him, but he didn't want to take any chances. His human would need the element of surprise on his side, once he could figure out how to get him down there.

Headlights slid through the trees and turned into the lot. Seeing this, the woman went inside and closed the door. The car stopped and went silent. A man got out, took a bag from the rear, and set it on the ground.

His human could use this.

He dived from the tree, catching the bag in his talons. The man shouted but the eagle and his bag were already reaching the trees. Soaring low to remain in shadow, he

carried the bag deep into the forest where he dropped it and landed beside it.

Not a bag, Mick thought as he regained his shape. A giant rolling suitcase that probably cost a fortune and was most likely filled with high-dollar brand name clothes. He shook out his limbs and stomped his bad leg to regain feeling. Winter's cold arms encircled him. If only he had the skill to keep his feathers until he'd found some clothes … that would be something to work on. He unzipped the suitcase, hoping that his thieving would at least pay off with some clothes that fit. The shirt he found stretched tight against his back and shoulders, but he managed to get it buttoned. With the sleeves rolled no one would notice they were too short. He shoved aside the dress pants that would surely pinch his nuts and found a pair of cotton pants with an elastic waist that would be more forgiving. They were probably the guy's pajamas, but in the dark of night they wouldn't be so obvious. Having pants at all was a plus. He zipped up the suitcase and took off barefoot. Scoring a pair of shoes was beyond his luck.

Reaching the motel, he saw no sign of the man he'd robbed other than his parked car. Good, because once this was over, maybe he could return the suitcase. But first things first. He had to think himself back into eagle mind to see which door the woman had gone into. He saw the scene again, so clear and bright it tricked his human mind into thinking it had occurred in daylight. Fourth door from the end, next to the only lit window. He took a breath, walked up to the door, and knocked.

A shadow passed across the curtained window. Something shuffled against the inside of the door like someone had put a hand against it. He smiled at the peephole. A human voice on the other side uttered a short, harsh word. Some kind of curse, no doubt. He held his smile, feeling it fill him. Finally, for once, he had the damn upper hand.

The door opened against the security chain. A woman's voice, slightly accented. "What do you want?"

"Just to talk. In there, if you don't mind. My feet are fittin' to freeze off out here."

She looked down. Maybe the bare feet would help him out by buying him some sympathy and a ticket inside.

"I'm not sure that's a good idea," she said.

"Please, ma'am. It's real dang cold." His breath steamed in the slant of light coming through the door as if to prove his point.

Her eyes returned to his face.

He raised both hands. "I got nothin' on me. No weapons, not even a phone."

She closed the door. More curses traveled through from the other side. She opened it again, all the way this time, and stepped aside so he could pass. "Raúl is not here."

"Is he comin' back?"

"Eventually."

The room was tidy, barely used. Bedspread flat and tight, plastic cups still in their wrappers on the counter. A laptop sat open on the little table by the window, and two rolling suitcases smaller than the one he'd stolen clustered side by side against the foot of the bed. "Mind if I sit?"

She crossed her arms on her chest and shrugged. He pulled a chair from the table into open space by the door and lowered himself down, trying not to call attention to his bad leg, stiff from the cold. "I get the impression you don't like me."

She shrugged again. "I don't trust you."

"Can't figure why that would be."

She said nothing.

"Okay, well I'm hopin' you can get over that for a minute and help me out." Suddenly worried he might botch this up, he took a moment to think through all the things he knew about this woman and Raúl. Months ago Waapikoona had trashed their car, which was now fixed. Raúl had come across the parking lot toward them that day; Mick had no idea if he'd tried to follow them once they'd fled in the GTO. Then more recently, the phone call from Waapikoona, warning him about Raúl. Mick's eagle finding the 300ZX and this woman in Oklahoma, with a high chance they were with Waapikoona or hunting her. Finally, their visit to the U-Fill. Raúl's interest in talking to him. And this woman's eyes on Mick, her strange assessment, or recognition, or whatever it was that caused her to drag Raúl out of the U-Fill and speed away.

Soto. It came to him in Waapikoona's voice. But in the U-Fill, the guy had introduced himself as Raúl. That detail gave Mick the idea he shouldn't use Waapikoona's real name.

He returned his attention back to the woman, who had tilted her head in a confrontational slant, like his silence and her silence were some kind of battle.

"Sorry, just tryin' to get my head around this. I feel like you, Raúl, and I are all lookin' for the same woman, and I'd like to know if you had any luck finding her. I'm runnin' out of time and could use some help."

"We can't help you."

"Why not?"

"I know what you are."

That had to mean what he thought it meant. She *did* recognize him, bird form to human form. He wasn't sure how that was possible. He wasn't sure where next to go with this.

"And you," she said, "… and that woman …"

Her pointed look at him meant it was his duty to finish the sentence, but he had no idea how to. He'd knocked on the door outside thinking he had the upper hand, but here he was, in way over his head. He hadn't come here to play guessing games. He needed information. "We're both talkin' about Sarah Clarke, right?"

"Yes. You are one thing and she is another. You need to leave her alone and do your job."

His *job*? His job was what the hell *he* determined his job to be, and right now that job was finding Waapikoona. He, and especially his eagle, answered to no one. This was the closest he'd gotten to some useful information, and he couldn't let this woman anger him, which was clearly what she was trying to do. "I know Raúl found her. I need to know where."

"Why?"

"It ain't important why."

"It's important to me."

Damn this conversation that kept drawing him into this back-and-forth game that could go on forever. He'd just have to kill it with clarity and straightforwardness, but he didn't think it was safe to mention Isabel, and it sure as hell wasn't right to mention his plan to bring Helen back from the dead. So he shoved all that aside. The only reason that remained was silly and selfish, but it was true and completely unthreatening. "I'm in love with her."

This caused a flutter of surprise on the woman's face before she wrestled it down.

Maybe he was a fool but he went on. "I can't live without her."

"That makes no sense."

Mick had to smile at the truth in that. "Sure don't."

"You're lying."

"I ain't a liar, ma'am."

The tight hold of her crossed arms loosened. Her shoulders softened, and she looked away as if this meeting had not lived up to expectation and she needed to regroup. Past her hip, the heavy glove she'd had on earlier lay on the end of the bed.

He didn't want to derail the conversation but he had to ask. "Are you a falconer or something?"

"He found her the same place you found her."

The motel parking lot in Oklahoma.

"Okay, but I lost track of that. You seen her since then?"

The woman shook her head and reached for the doorknob. "We can't help you."

He needed to get something—anything—before he got kicked out. "Okay, what about a guy named Hammond. You know anything about him?"

She pulled her hand away from the door and put some space between herself and him. "That's trouble best handled by your other side."

"My other side don't feel like handlin' it." And since she really did know about his other side, she'd know the power he held. He could use that. Not a threat, just a little encouragement. "Do you know where I could find Hammond?"

She crossed her arms again. Tightened her jaw. Okay, fine. He'd draw her a picture. He got up—she angled her body around him, like he was some kind of physical threat—and snagged the paper pad and pen from the phone table. From memory he copied the crude map he'd found on the back side of that auto repair invoice, the roads labeled with their state highway numbers, the old water tower, the powerlines. He tore the sheet off the pad and handed it to her. "You familiar with any of this?"

She watched him a moment before taking the page. After a quick glance, she handed it back. "Yes."

"So, is that—"

"If that's the kind of trouble you want, that's where you'll find it."

He wanted to grab her by the shoulders and hug her. It wasn't the best idea. Instead, he tore up the map and walked past her toward the bathroom, where he flushed it down the toilet.

"You're going to get yourself killed," she said, opening the door for him.

On the pad he wrote his number and tore off the page. "If you happen to see Sarah will you give me a call?"

"I'll think about it." She took the paper from him.

It was the best he'd get. Her face and posture told him this conversation was over, and pushing her now might convince her not to call him with news of Waapikoona. They were better at finding her—they'd found her twice, at least—and he couldn't ruin that chance.

"I didn't catch your name," he said, stepping out to the sidewalk.

"The turn-in isn't marked. It's right beside the powerlines, where it's cleared. And you don't need my name."

The door closed hard behind him. He wished he knew the nature of their business with Waapikoona, if they were friends or foes ... and if he needed to find her before they did.

HE WAS LATE for work the next day because Isabel wouldn't stay put. He'd dropped her with Old Mae like he had the day before, but she was dead set on going with him.

The fierceness in her eyes meant she'd lost patience with his promise, and she was ready to look for her sister herself. The second time she came out after him, he dragged her back to the front stoop by the arm—gently, despite his own diminishing patience—and bent to her level while holding her in place by the shoulders. "If I lose my job there ain't gonna be any food or heat for us, and we'll die before we find your sister."

Did she even understand modern work and bills? He doubted it. She poked a finger into her chest then pointed to the sky.

He took hold of her hand and held it, firmly enough to communicate his seriousness. "Big trouble if you do that, Isabel."

At the sound of her name, her eyes caught his and held.

"Come on, girlie," Old Mae said behind them. "It's a lot warmer in the house."

She didn't budge.

"How's it possible you're more stubborn than your sister?" Just mentioning Waapikoona gave him a cramp in his heart. It felt too close to mourning someone dead, and he didn't like that at all. She'd called him not long ago. He heard her voice. She wasn't dead. "Look. I want to find Waapikoona just as bad as you. But I still gotta work. You help me by stayin' here and bein' good for Old Mae." He trailed a finger across her forehead to brush her bangs aside. They needed a trim.

She lost her fight against a frown so sincere Mick felt her troubles compound his own. A tear escaped down both her cheeks. She scrubbed them away with her good hand, angrier than any child should ever be.

"God help us," Mick said, straightening up to look at Old Mae. "I can't take her to work with me."

She cackled. "Looks to me like you're about to."

At least then the girl might understand, might find a little more tolerance for the things that interrupted his search for Waapikoona. She'd get bored sitting at Virgil's, in the plastic chair chilled by a gust of winter wind every time a customer came or went, and tomorrow morning might not put up such a fight against staying in a warm house full of friendly animals and all the sweets she could ever want. Kids often misbehaved because they didn't understand things. Come lunchtime she'd understand and be begging to come home.

"All right. In the car."

He helped her into the back of the GTO and buckled her up.

The highway noise around the shop earned him a tight grip on his coveralls as they crossed the parking lot. Inside, she still clung, wide eyes still misty from her fight on Old Mae's porch.

"Brought yourself a helper?" Virgil said.

"Wouldn't stay put with the babysitter. I'm hopin' she gets bored enough by lunchtime that I can take her back there."

"She a friend of Janie's?"

"Belongs to a woman I know. I'm keeping her while she's out of town."

Mick uncurled her hand from his coveralls and led her to a chair in the waiting area. Virgil got the remote and set the TV on a kids' station. Doug and Janie had come in enough times lately for this to be the drill. Guilt gnawed at him, but he told himself he wasn't taking advantage of Virgil. He was there to work and that was what mattered. Leaving a well-behaved kid in the waiting room for a few hours wasn't hurting anyone. He went through the door to the garage—and grabbed it, just in time before it hit Isabel on its closing swing.

"Shoot, Isabel. You can't follow me out here. Gotta sit there and let me work." He pointed to the chair. Anxiety rolled through him. He was the adult and she was the child, but he had no control over this girl. She could shift into bird form right here in the shop, and he'd have no way to stop it. What had he been thinking, bringing her here?

What he ended up with was an audience as he worked. When a task got dangerous, he made her stand against the far wall. But when it was just turning wrenches and pulling off wheels, she got right up there, watching with a curiosity only evident in someone born to fix and build. It pained him to think it. He couldn't do this job with one hand. Maybe that was his bias, though. Maybe she could or would learn a new way to. Pretty soon he was handing her tools and teaching her their names … and she was smiling, just a little, content and interested and looking at him like he was more special than he should be.

"Insurance company is gonna have my ass, Svendsen," Virgil called to him from the door.

"I'm watchin' her."

"If it ain't them, it'll be the child labor laws."

Mick laughed, startling Isabel. The pry bar fell from her hand directly onto his foot. As it clanged against the floor, she winced, shrinking away as if bracing for a blow.

"It's all right," he said, picking it up. "Steel toe." He rapped it against his boot a few times to demonstrate.

It was a very different sound than the one they'd just heard. That clatter of metal bar against concrete floor plucked a memory and threw it in his face. Waapikoona, dropping her crowbar the day he met her. The fragmented pieces of him absorbed that sound—this new one, and the memory of the first one—and fractured further. God, when he finally found her, the things he'd stored up to say and do—

He schooled his expression so it wouldn't give away the unexpected anger and yearning that clawed its way through him. His baggage had no place here.

Lunchtime came and he felt no need to drive Isabel home. He shared his packed food with her and let her pick two snacks out of the vending machine. She munched pretzel sticks in her chair against the wall while he tightened lug nuts and aired up tires. When the compressor kicked off, he noticed the blanket of quiet over the shop; he looked around and found all the guys had abandoned their work. A glance through the window to the office showed more bodies than normal, so he wiped his hands, told Isabel to stay put, and joined them.

Every mechanic was glued to a live press conference playing on the waiting room TV. Uniformed highway patrol officers stood behind the governor as she spoke about strange disappearances all over the state, seemingly disconnected. Now other states were reporting the same. Aside from the police, a university research team had mapped and studied the missing, and no one could draw any conclusions from the data. Law enforcement was working, but asking for tips.

Mick was there in the room, sharing space with these guys around him, yet a great distance away. Answers to their questions lived inside him. He had the tips. He had the whole story, but no one would believe him. He was disconnected, floating high above, watching these guys as they stood around trying to make sense of something he had a top-level view of.

First it was the damage to Cahokia Mounds. Now, reports of missing people, nationally recognized in great numbers. What would be next? He felt called upon, called out, and

his back prickled with new sweat unrelated to the work he'd been doing out in the garage. The only person he could share this with had left him.

"This on its way out?" he asked Virgil, grabbing a tied bag of trash sitting behind the counter.

Virgil nodded, still watching the press conference.

Mick took it outside. In the lot behind the office, he took a long gulp of fresh air sharp with cold. The sun glared. Through the wind he felt its heat on the back of his neck like an oath. He found more trash bags waiting to be tossed in, so he flung the dumpster lid all the way open. Small black insects fell into the open bin, scrambled along the walls, dropped to the pavement. He stepped back, away from the crawling mass.

Snakes—but no, along all the writhing bodies was a set of fluttering legs. Millipedes, so numerous they blanketed the trash inside and spread down toward the emptier side, racing into the shadow created by the other half's lid. The whole dumpster could be filled with only the millipedes and no one would know the difference.

In unison, they hissed in the glare of the sun. Mick side-stepped one that had hit the ground. It circled and charged his boot. Its tail end sizzled, smoke rising. Mick saw fangs sprout from the front end, raised his boot, and stomped hard enough to jar his knee. Black goo exploded against the pavement all around his boot. The smell of scorched metal and sewage swirled against him as the breeze caught the fumes of those being cremated by the sun.

Mick flung open the dumpster's other lid. The creatures fried in the sunlight, shrieking, fangs open in the hope to infect any living thing before they turned to ash. He stood and watched, holding his breath against the stench, his eyes locked on the scene in front of him that would bring on his eagle if he let the slightest bit of control slip.

The underworld wasn't coming; it was here.

He couldn't fight it without Waapikoona.

CHAPTER
24

AN INVISIBLE PRESENCE had slung a rope on Waapikoona's ankle, keeping her from driving straight to the Missouri address Nathan had given her. For two days she'd made excuses in the long hours of night that should have been spent in sleep.

Can't leave Sam and Josie so soon after returning home.
Need to let my hand heal before moving on.
Don't want to leave without saying goodbye to Meredith.

The truth was too ridiculous to admit. She'd looked up the address Nathan had given her. It wasn't just in Missouri but dangerously close to Wyona, and she was afraid.

Long ago, she'd banished fear. It had plagued her past life; she'd found murder-suicide as the only escape. Reborn with it in her second life, she learned new ways to cope. Josie had taught her to fall asleep. Sam had showed her how to speak up, straighten her spine, and look a person in the eye. And then she'd found Jeremiah who undid all that. The more he tore her down, the more she needed him. Being returned to that kind of prison awoke her old fear, but this time it mutated within her and turned on itself—and then turned on him.

The fear that caged her now was something new. Every time she took Nathan's paper out of her pocket and studied the address, a profound unease settled upon her, tightening that rope and making up new excuses.

It's too close to Mick, and I don't know what I might do.

She imagined the return to Missouri, with a detour straight into Wyona that could be so easy. Mick wouldn't even have to know. She could sit in the Jeep outside his auto shop and watch him work through the glass garage doors. He wouldn't recognize that Jeep and would never guess a thing. He'd open the big door, back a car out, park it near her. She'd watch him walk back inside—earnest eyes, industrious stride, the sun and wind in his hair. She could hike through the woods to his apartment and wait in the shadow of the trees until he came home. That orange car shifting gravel along the driveway, slowing to a stop. A door swinging open, a breathless glimpse. She could sit and wait, see if he came back outside as man or eagle.

It wouldn't be enough, and she'd regret it. Nothing would ever be enough.

She'd just have to start driving and hope the damn rope snapped—and a new one didn't attach as she closed in on Wyona.

"I have to go back to Missouri," she told Sam and Josie over breakfast.

They'd been as alarmed as Nathan about her hand, and she'd told them the truth—seeking help in locating her sister's abuser got her around some nasty people, but she knew how to take care of herself. That was why she was alive with a wounded hand instead of dead. No lie would be that harsh,

so Sam and Josie asked for no more specifics. She wouldn't tell them what she planned to do in Missouri.

"You leaving soon?"

"Yes—today." She'd already repacked her modest bag.

Josie pressed her lips together like she did when she knew she shouldn't say something but was going to say it anyway. "I suppose there's no way to beg you to stay one more night and get some better sleep. You look very tired, Waapikoona."

"I wish I could. But I won't be getting any sleep until I see this done."

"Promise if you get a phone, you'll send us your number?" Sam knew when to change the subject.

"Promise," she said and held his eye the way he'd taught her.

Josie wouldn't let her leave without re-wrapping her hand and loading her arms with a box of spare bandages, tube of ointment, and bottle of aspirin. Then Josie was adding a sweatshirt and pair of socks to the pile and pulling an old backpack from the hall closet and filling it with other things. "I can't stand to see you leave with so little. I know you're okay with just the clothes on your back. You can toss this in the trunk and never even open it."

Instead of saying goodbye, she gave them both a hug. "I'll call soon."

She got in the Jeep, ignoring the bite of the cold seat against her legs and her new intolerance to it. Too much time spent in a warm home had almost ruined her. They waved as she backed out. Against the house, three orphaned Helpers hunkered in the shadow. Her own two had returned to her palm a day ago. She couldn't call the orphans into the Jeep on a morning so awash with sunlight. They'd have to catch up or find another of her kind to follow.

268

Small-town road turned into state road then interstate. In the glove box she found a pair of her old sunglasses to shield the glare of the highway stretching straight in front of her. She ached with the act of leaving, of moving forward. She finally had a solid clue, a clear path toward her goal ... but everything felt off-center, like this taut stretch of road was impossibly pitched. Heading straight to that Missouri address was the obvious decision—but she felt burdened, disoriented. Distracted, as if in a dream she knew was a dream and hoped she'd soon wake from.

A return to a place so close to where she didn't want to go wasn't bad luck. It was punishment. It was the circle of time, cycling her into an endless pattern of trials, failures, and regrets because she hadn't yet found the split thread and fixed it. She'd never move forward, never reach a different level until she corrected the problem.

The problem was Hammond. He shouldn't be here, should never have been raised. Jeremiah broke a piece of her timeline, and it was up to her to fix it. Her heart was broken and lost because she'd convinced her sister to die and couldn't give her a new chance at life until the man who abused her was scrubbed from the earth. The grief was for her sister, for past regrets. Not for Mick.

Her thoughts consumed the drive. She couldn't ignore when Wyona appeared on the highway sign, or the small amount of miles listed beside it. She couldn't stop watching that number count down, or find any damn thing to think about when she reached an intersection that showed Wyona to the right, her intended destination the opposite way. She took the left, disgusted by the heavy beat of her heart. She should turn around and go straight to Mick, sleep with him, and leave. Prove that was all this was. Lust, curiosity, rebellion. She'd never have to think about him again.

That new fear kept her driving straight ahead.

THE ROAD RUNNING along the southern boundary of the supposed commune showed no way in by car. Monster-sized power lines cut the block of forest in half. There were no features to suggest anyone lived beyond the line of trees that edged the shoulder and nowhere for her to park the Jeep without it looking severely out of place. She drove until she found a pocket of buildings a few miles down the state road and parked in a gravel lot scattered with rusted storage containers.

Exiting the Jeep, she turned into the wind. It had picked up on her drive, pushing so hard she had to hold tight to the wheel to keep the Jeep on the road. Her hair flapped behind her. Missing was the flutter of her feather earrings against her neck. She adjusted her flint knife on her belt, zipped her coat to her chin, and tucked her bandaged hand into her pocket.

A chill reached deep into her undead bones. If she'd been living this past week in an abandoned barn or cave, she wouldn't notice this cold or how fragile it made her feel. Her route was at least eight miles on foot—or more, if this place sat closer to the road that crossed through to the north. Soon it would be dark, but the sky was clear and a bright moon was due to arrive just after nightfall.

After finishing off a half-full bottle of water she'd left in the cup holder, she set off. The woods were brambly, thick with thorns and prickly low-growing branches that snagged her coat and scraped down her jeans. She angled her path, hoping to find an animal trail, but it only seemed to get thicker. She ducked and climbed and fought until finally she reached a cluster of mature pines towering so high and wide they blocked the sky. Brambles could not grow under these limbs, not with the carpet of dead needles that lay thick against the ground. High enough to walk underneath, the lowest branches quieted the world. It felt like a sacred place where she was unwelcome. Where Mick's eagle would be perched high above, watching. She followed the vein of these evergreens, breathing in the medicine of their crisp scent, worried at the path becoming too easy, like they were leading her the wrong way. Mother Earth wouldn't do that—but maybe she would to a person born from the underworld.

As if on cue, a throng of creatures startled and fled. Waapikoona caught sight of shiny black claws and studded tails as the things found new shadows to hide in. These forms were new to her, leaked from The Silent One's domain, now learning to adapt to life on earth. But so was she.

Where the pines ended she found the edge of an old dirt road. She climbed the eroded shoulder to stand on the rutted earth and looked in both directions. One side surely hit the state road that had brought her here, so she'd either missed its turn-in or it had been hidden. The other way was hers. It would take her straight to the old mine where Jeremiah's people stayed. Instead of walking the road so visibly, she picked her way back down the crumbling shoulder with the quick cover of trees ready to hide her should someone come by. She wanted her arrival to be under cover until she decided what to do.

Cold had breached her boots and collar. She felt it slipping against her neck, now so warmed by the hike. Her toes felt brittle. She increased her pace, wishing she'd brought an extra bottle of water. The sun slid down the sky. The faster she walked the warmer she became and the more

deeply she felt her thirst. And now, a little pinch of hunger in her stomach.

She thought of that dinner she'd shared with Mick, the one she'd crashed and he'd tried to kick her out, failing under the pressure of his good manners. Her disloyal memory had turned a simple meal in a tiny basement apartment into something magical.

As soon as she killed Hammond, she would return to the medicine woman and beg her for a cure to this longing before she found herself shattered.

Now the night had closed the door on the sun. She walked until even her undead eyes could no longer make out her path, and then she stopped to face reality. The only option was to sit and wait for the moon. This deep, gusty cold wouldn't be any fun to sit still in, but it wouldn't kill her. Looking for shelter would take her too far off course.

She found a fallen tree and sat. In any other situation she could call upon The Silent One, ask him to sit inside her while she drew within herself to not feel the cold. She could even ask him to walk her forward in the dark and continue to make progress while she waited for moonrise. He was hungry for time in the upperworld. But cluing in The Silent One might be cluing in Jeremiah's people. All those raised by the great demon were joined, whether she liked to admit it or not.

It was the whole point. One people, one army, all controlled by one leader.

If she thought too hard on it, she'd never ask him to raise her sister. She'd decide to leave Pinepakatwi's bones in the cradle of the earth, walk into this commune, and demand they finish what they'd started when they'd ambushed her at her tomb and thrown her in the trunk of that car. Forget ridding the world of Hammond. If such a thing as him was allowed to exist, the world was no good anyway. Let the underworld flood up and claim it all. She and Pinepakatwi would move on to the next life and be excused from this sorry time.

She bent and rocked forward, wounded hand pressed against her coat. These thoughts were no pep talk for what she planned to do here. *Help me. Give me strength.*

She could pray, but she wasn't sure what or whom she'd pray to. The sun, the moon, the rivers, Mother Earth.

The Thunder-Beings.

It was all forbidden now. She'd forgotten too much of her previous life and would do them no justice. Those raised by the great demon of the underworld had no gods. Perhaps she should pray to herself. She was all she had.

When the moon finally spread its light across the tree-tops, the numbness in her toes and fingers had migrated up her legs and arms. A strange lethargy covered her, making her wonder if she'd ever find the strength to get up and walk again. Now she was sure her physical hardiness hadn't just been weakened by too much time spent in Sam and Josie's warm house. The air was cold but not as cold as it had been on other nights she'd spent outside in the recent past. She felt irreversibly changed. The Silent One had withdrawn something from her, a protection she hadn't known she'd carried until it was gone.

She got up, stretching. It didn't matter. She didn't need it. Without it, she was more human—and less beholden to him. She could pretend it. She would believe it.

The forest floor now dappled in moonlight and swaying shadow, she walked.

A violent shivering took her over. She increased her pace to move blood and warm her core. Her head swam so badly she had to stop and lean against a tree. She swallowed

against the dryness in her throat. In answer, her stomach rolled, hollow and impatient. Survival on nothing had been so easy before. A spark of reality shot through her. Without food, water, and shelter, a person might not survive this night without The Silent One's protection.

No. So close to Hammond, failure was unacceptable. She moved forward, pushing off tree trunks with her unwounded hand to keep herself in motion. Time released its hold. Minutes, hours, days—it was all the same to her. Frost-edged bark and snapping twigs flowed endlessly past her. The moon glanced through spaces in the canopy. Dead leaves and ice crunched underfoot. Moonlight slowly waned and she stumbled in the dark, one hand reaching to catch hard wood before it caught her. Ahead, a halo of light. She staggered into the wide-open bleakness of the road she'd avoided earlier and discovered its end. Old buildings clustered in the washed-out unnatural brightness, some patched up and in obvious use, others forsaken. Sleek, shiny cars sat among others rusted and tilted on flat tires.

And coming down the road toward her were two men. So much for arriving under cover—her fight against exhaustion had led her in here blind. She gathered the last drip of her strength and took a purposeful step forward. She'd just have to work with it.

One of them stopped to swing a large firearm from his back and aim it at her. This was the point most people would raise their hands in the air, but she didn't come here to surrender to anyone. And playing the good-guy card—it just wasn't in her.

"Where's Hammond?" she yelled.

The man with the gun stalked closer and stopped, keeping the barrel trained on her. The other one calmly walked into speaking range. With the light at his back, it was hard to make out a face, but his beard was full enough to give his jaw a bushy silhouette. "Who's asking?"

"Where is he?" She locked her stance against a smack of bitter wind.

He chuckled, adjusting his knit hat so it covered the tips of his ears. "See, strangers who come wandering in here don't get to ask questions."

"Who said I'm a stranger?"

With a click, he swung a flashlight beam into her face.

She raised her good hand to block the light from her eyes—but not soon enough to stop it from temporarily blinding her. Black spots swam in front of her as watering eyes shed tears that nearly froze against her cheeks. He was close enough to get his arm twisted behind his back and an ankle kicked out from under him. The bulge of shoulder and bicep under his zip-up jacket meant he was muscular and would fall hard—but he'd be more abashed than hurt and call his friend over with that gun, and she'd be overpowered. His failure would then be taken out on her.

"How about you tell us your name."

"Not until I see Hammond."

"I don't like that answer." He turned off his flashlight and stuck it in his back pocket. "And I got work to do, so you're gonna have to come inside until we figure out what to do with you."

She weighed that. There could be heat inside and a chair to rest her legs, her back, her shoulders … and everything else, because everything hurt. Inside would also be closer to Hammond, if he was indeed here. She started walking, past the bearded man, straight toward the guy with the gun. "You can put that down. If you were going to kill me, you'd have already done it."

They caught up and walked her past the line of cars parked against the nearest building and into the dark. Light from beyond escaped around an aged water tower looming over them on decrepit legs. With the flashlight showing the way, they went toward the water tower and around, to a long building stretched out behind it. The bearded man took a set of keys off his belt and unlocked the door. Inside spread a pitch-dark unknown.

The other man leaned his gun against the wall and then grabbed her by the hair at the back of her neck and pulled her face close to his. "I don't just kill mouthy women. I cut them up first."

She smiled at him.

He twisted his fist of her hair so hard she had to lock her elbows to keep them from latching on to save her from the pain. Without the fight he wanted, he simply tossed her inside and slammed the door. Keys jangled outside then the lock sank into position. Only then did she allow herself to draw a fast breath at the flaring sting in her wounded hand—she'd caught her fall with both palms flat against the ground. Josie's last bandage held, as far as she could feel, but underneath—oh, how it felt like a fresh cut of the knife.

With her hand tight against her, she shuffled back to the door, leaned her back against it, and slid down to sit. Cold ground and hard steel were not the chair she'd dreamed of, but it would do for now until the shock in her hand subsided. Her eyes now starting to adjust, she looked around. Light escaped between door and frame and through many cracks in the walls. It was more a small warehouse than a building and obviously used for some kind of storage because all around her were the consistent shapes of stacked square and cylindrical objects. Voices carried in from outside. Shouts from working people. Someone calling out commands, others answering. None sounded female. There was something severely unbalanced about a communal group of people that excluded women. She wasn't sure how concerning it should be for her. It didn't feel like good news.

She would not admit to herself how cold she was. How hungry. How bone-deep tired. And how stupid it was to show up here in this condition with no energy or plan to defend herself.

Instead, she leaned her head back against the frigid door and closed her eyes.

MICK VISITED HER in a vivid dream, awash in filtered white light. As he spoke, his words drifted away so she could not hear, and he was changing before her, from man to eagle. His voice became more urgent but she was unable to call back, to ask him to speak up, to repeat it. The light turned his feathers white, and then he was gone, and a darkness fell across the scene and filled her with such dread she choked herself awake, fighting a rising scream.

For a moment she was lost, blind in the dark, unable to recall where she was or what brought her here. She cradled a hand against her ... yes, the bandage, the wound. With her other hand she felt the dirt floor, the cold metal door behind her.

Here with Jeremiah's people. The commune. Locked in a storage shed.

Car engines started up outside and droned away, leaving a grim quiet with not even a breeze to give texture to the dark. Before she'd seen light through the cracks, but now it was nothing, a void as absent of light as The Silent One's

cave with no flashlight. Maybe they'd forgotten she was there and vacated the place without her. She eased herself to her knees. It turned her pulse into a nightmare, her head into a throbbing block. With a hand braced against the wall she slowly raised to her feet, battling a nauseating dizziness that somehow spun complete darkness around her.

She'd known hunger in her previous life, a hunger fathomless and unrelenting, far worse than the one she felt now. This one would not overcome her. She felt along the door, felt its texture give way to wood. With a hand on the wall she extended a foot against the ground, shuffling until it hit something hard. A site like this would have no plumbing. They'd need to store water, and she hoped to find some here.

After slamming both knees and an elbow in the dark, she found a prize. She felt it up and down by hand a second time just to be certain—egg crates filled with gallon jugs stacked on a pallet. She twisted off a lid, sniffed, and found no chemical odor. She took a deeper smell and found no odor at all. A dipped finger encountered liquid that felt like water. She then raised the remaining drip to her lips and touched her tongue—yes. A sip from the jug—double yes.

This find would keep her alive.

After a conservative drink to test her stomach, she capped the jug and set it on the ground. She moved by feel onto the next pallet—boxes of ammunition—and the next she identified by smell—gasoline. Now too far away from her water, she backtracked, locating it with her foot before she tripped over it. She was about to move it along the pallets so it wouldn't get lost when she heard footsteps crunching outside. The clink of keys. The metallic slide of the lock.

Light spilled across the ground as she booted the water jug behind a pallet and crouched then lowered to the floor. By the time the bushy-faced man found her with his flashlight, she was leaning against a pallet of boxes like she'd just woken from a nap. No one needed to know she'd been snooping through their stash.

"Get up. Boss wants to see you."

"I'm not interested in seeing anyone but Hammond."

"Get the fuck up before I make you get up."

She couldn't see his face with the light in her eyes and couldn't gauge how tough he thought he was. She also couldn't see if he had a weapon. Testing him further wasn't going to win a thing, but she wasn't sure how she'd get herself up without showing how damaged she was.

CHAPTER
25

WAAPIKOONA TURNED AWAY from the bushy-faced man's harsh beam of light. "Could you not blind me?"

"I could. But I won't."

She braced herself and got up on feeble legs. The head rush blinded her in a different way, but she found mental balance and transferred it to wobbly legs and curling spine. A display of her exhaustion was the opposite of what this moment called for. She straightened her shoulders, raised her chin, and met the man face-to-face. He gave her a wary appraisal before leading the way out the door.

The bite of cold outside those thin walls surprised her. There had been no temperature change going in hours ago, but she had been so frozen for so long perhaps she'd been unable to feel. Of course that warehouse had been minimally heated. They had to keep their supplies from freezing. Now that she'd thawed the slightest, she felt her blood on its way to a refreeze. She couldn't take the pain of it a second time— but she had to. This was far from over.

Across the gravel lot they walked. The sky was a dark nothingness. Past the beam of the man's flashlight lay another skin of black, interrupted here and there by a passing stack of wooden pallets or a derelict car. She hadn't made note of any landmarks on her way in and was now hopelessly without bearings. Escape wasn't a certainty, but finding Hammond was. She'd not stop until she found success in that, even if she had to accept death along with it. Killing him now was more important than everything else—her sister, their future, her freedom from The Silent One.

Even more important than Mick? It hit from nowhere.

"Hey, no stopping." The man's voice sounded farther ahead than she expected.

She caught up the few paces she'd fallen behind. Mick was not a part of this anymore. Distracting thoughts were no more than a test of her grit. It seemed another side of her was dead set on running her through these trials, checking for the slightest bit of slip.

They finally stopped beside a brick building with plywood boards nailed inside the old arched window openings. In the scant light she saw aged tuckpointing and brick still sooty from a century ago. These buildings could be as old as her. The man selected a key and unlocked the modern steel door, his boxy flashlight tucked under his chin. It was the perfect chance to yank it away and break it over his face, but she held back, knowing she needed him. This boss of his could be behind five more locked doors, and speaking to the leader of this place seemed to be the only avenue to Hammond. As she stepped across the threshold, dry heat warmed her cheeks. This unexpected comfort would drown her, would strip the structure from every bone if she let it. She could so easily melt against the wall and let the pulse of her warming

limbs undo her, but she straightened herself against that need and followed the man into a dim hall.

Now she stood in a room with a scattered assortment of mismatched furniture and no recollection of the walk there. If it had been at all possible to walk hallways with her eyes closed, that was what she had done. She could also be sleepwalking, delirious, hallucinating. A man stood from a chair at a small table in the corner, stubbing out his cigarette. He gave a nod to the bushy-faced man, who stuck his head out the doorway behind her and whistled. More men piled in, forcing her forward. It got her closer to the man by the table. Time stuttered, like pieces were missing. She appeared a few feet away from where she'd been without sensing the walk there. People moved in disjointed motion. If that water she'd drank had been drugged, this would be its outcome—but no, she'd cracked the seal on that bottle herself. Her ailments were hunger, thirst, sleep deprivation, probably hypothermia. Simple annoyances to shove aside, if she could only remember how to do it.

The man who'd been at the table was now in front of her, eyes level with hers. Now she could see his features in a closer light, and it turned her exhaustion into something lit up and hyper aware of an answer when she'd entirely missed the question.

Older, thinner, and more weathered, but unmistakably Jeremiah. Internally she scrambled for memory of that night Mick killed him—was there any way he could have escaped?

"Sarah, right?" he said.

Jeremiah wouldn't have greeted her with any amount of uncertainty. He knew her as well as she knew him, wherever they were in the circle of time.

"I've heard some interesting things about you." He leaned to look behind her. "Somebody back there close the door. She's a slippery one."

At that moment she caught a glimpse of his tattooed forearm. It was not Jeremiah's tattoo of a rising sun, but something different. Horses running through flames, rearing up, bared teeth, bulging eyes. She returned her gaze to his face. She couldn't allow her attention to be drawn away like that.

Who the hell are you?

"I'm here for Hammond," she said instead.

"We'll get to that. First, you tell me something."

Again, she was seeing the resemblance to Jeremiah, but there was no way to safely ask. He couldn't be a descendant. Jeremiah had died too young in his first life to have any children. He'd never mentioned brothers. The trouble with raising the dead is there was no way to determine age or where they fit into the family line.

Red-black darkness flooded her vision; heat erupted against one side of her face. Off-balance and crumpled, she felt bodies against her back, hands supporting her arms.

"You listening now?"

She raised her head, feeling a trickle of blood slither down her chin. No smartass answer came to her, so she kept her eyes on his and her mouth shut.

"Good. Let her go, boys. See if she can stand."

She elbowed the remaining arm from her shoulder and straightened to her full height. Ignored the devastating spin in her head. Tried to inhale enough oxygen to dislodge the watery vision and find balance.

"I'll repeat the question. Whole group of guys dispatched to a little town called Wyona. Every last one slaughtered. You know anything about that?"

She laughed. This time she saw the backhand coming. She took it head-on, reveling in the hot-cold-hot sting on her skin, the fresh dribble of blood stringing off her bottom lip. The Silent One had helped her kill all those men without knowing they were hired by his own raised soldiers. He'd been so lost in the bloodlust that he hadn't noticed when Mick's eagle arrived either. God of underworld fighting alongside god of upperworld. Enemies, so easily working as a team. It proved how pointless the whole thing was. With killing as their commonality, in the simplest terms, they were interchangeable.

The comparison sickened her, squashing her amusement.

There was one monumental difference. She had respect for Mick's Thunder-Being. The Silent One was her creator, her partner. Some might say her master, but she'd never accept that. And for him, her disgust grew daily.

It wouldn't stop her from summoning him once again, to slaughter all these men like she'd slaughtered the others. But not before they told her where to find Hammond.

"All I care to talk about…" she dragged her sleeve across her mouth to clear the blood "…is Hammond."

"It's hard for me to believe all those men were killed by one woman."

"Then don't."

"And what *should* I believe?"

"That if you don't turn him over to me, you're a slave to the white man in your new life just as you were in your first." It didn't matter the white men standing behind her appeared to be enslaved by him. They wouldn't be here if they weren't adding to their power in some way.

"Tough words coming from a woman who knows nothing about what we're doing here."

"Wrong. But you can slap me again if that makes you feel like you're right."

He looked at one of the men standing behind her shoulder and shook his head to say, *no, not yet*. Taking a casual seat on the arm of a nearby chair, he fisted one hand into the other and lay them against his chin. As he studied her, a truth connected itself in her brain.

These men—at least, those raised from bones—had never allowed themselves to be possessed by The Silent One. It could be they didn't know it was possible. No one who'd done it, or knew it could be done, would be in disbelief that one undead woman could execute so many men at once. Anyone knowledgeable of The Silent One's possession would immediately jump there, know it was her or someone like her, and have no reason to follow this line of questions. Or was all this a game? Forcing her to confirm something they already knew—for what?

Perhaps they did know, but had never done it themselves. She could see men like these men around her fearing the loss of control. Fearing what The Silent One would do in their bodies with—or without—their consent. And unaware of the experience, they'd have no idea the power they were missing out on, and she had no desire to clue them in.

"This is all bad timing," the man finally said. "We have somewhere to be. If you tell us who told you how to find this place, we'll do you a favor and drive you to the road."

"I'm not leaving without seeing Hammond."

"He's not here."

It was a lie. She knew it, he knew it, and he knew she knew it. He smiled, vicious, patronizing. Daring her to call him out.

She smiled back at him and gave a lie right back. "Jeremiah told me."

His face fell. She tasted blood again, hot and slippery, so much more than before. Couldn't understand why the guys behind her were holding her up when she could take blows just as easily from the floor. As the final one landed, she reached for a painful memory from her first life to prove this here, this pain was not so bad; she'd endured worse and lived. This was nothing. She shrugged out of their grip, planted her boots against the swaying ground, and looked straight into his eye. She'd figured it out. This man could only be Jeremiah's father. Raised along with Jeremiah or raised later by Jeremiah himself.

"What he got…" the words slurred, outside of her control "…he deserved."

The look that passed through his eyes fixed him in a hardened calm. Her regret was leaden, permanent. She'd failed. She'd never get to Hammond now.

"Throw her in the woods," he said to the man grabbing her coat sleeve to steady her. "Let the birds eat her."

He means thunderbirds, she thought absently as they dragged her outside and threw her into the bed of a pickup. She curled for the landing too late. Forehead collided with cold unforgiving metal, and she hissed in a breath to stop herself from crying out. Voices around her, too much to make sense of with all she had inside her head. She'd watched Mick's eagle tear the throats out of bad men, carve out Jeremiah's eyes and heart. Would he do that, if he wasn't doing it for her? Was he doing that now to others like her?

Forget Mick. He was too far away. It was his Thunder-Being friends who'd attack her. They were the ones she should be thinking about.

The truck's engine fired up, doors slammed. All that was left was to summon The Silent One and get herself out of this mess. Over the jarring rumble of the road she reached—and found nothing. She tried again, gaining clarity from closing her eyes and closing out the noise and ache in her head. His response, missing. His presence, nonexistent. She was reaching into nothingness. A place once connected to her creator, to the compass that guided her to every cave mouth, every opening to the underworld, was so profoundly absent now, it was as if she'd stepped off the edge of a cliff once again and found herself in freefall with no hard earth to end it all.

She withdrew back into herself, terrified she'd reached too far and disconnected from her own consciousness too.

This was what she'd felt in her last visit underground. Cut off from tapping into The Silent One's ready power. Severed from her tether to the underworld. She wasn't stupid enough to think he'd released her from servitude too. It was the power he'd relinquished in order to punish her.

Her head bounced, hit hard against the cold metal bed. The road had become more pocked. They were indeed dropping her in the woods to die at the hand of the elements or be ripped apart by Thunder-Beings. She sat up to avoid another head smack, saw the deep black of the moonless night, the hint of passing trees.

She was lost. Misguided. She had been for a long time and hadn't paid attention. She was driven forward not by determination and purpose but by desperation, chasing something that led her away from a new, good place with a man who sealed her away from the cold world of her past and shined warmth onto her future. She his guide and he hers, allies, stronger together, one whole. Apart they were broken.

All was lost because she'd been a fool. Mother Earth had given her a once-in-many-lifetimes gift, and she'd been too stubborn and proud to accept it. She and Mick could help each other. As lovers or friends, it didn't matter. Even platonic teamwork made sense. Having a Thunder-Being at her call, ready to deal out the consequences for which he was created—it was better than dying alone in the frozen woods. Mother Earth had called them together, and she had spat in her face.

Now tree limbs were smacking the sides of the truck, and she ducked low behind the cab to avoid a smack herself. She could jump now to steal their satisfaction of tossing her in the woods to die. But the unknown lay all around her. There could be a slope, just enough to land wrong and break an ankle, twist a knee. She'd have no chance for escape then. A well-placed tree or rock could do worse. Her head had taken enough damage tonight. It was all a bunch of bull-shit to divert her attention from the truth. She did not have the strength to get herself over the side of this truck on her own. She raised up enough to peer over the side of the bed—and got another knock to the skull at the truck's hard stop.

Two doors opened. Two men hopped out. She scrambled to the tailgate to maintain power over her body, but they were faster. Her ankle snagged in one grip and her wrist in another. She kicked her free leg, but they caught that one too. Every movement too languid, too slow, too helpless. At their mercy. She knew very well how some men behaved in a situation like this.

She hoped they'd try. She'd rip their faces off.

Her backbone bumped against the tailgate edge. She twisted for relief, found it worse on her ribs, but then she took another blow to the head and found herself against the crunchy ground. One man released her and stood. The other one leaned in, knee digging into her stomach, two hands attached to the collar of her coat. A new surge of adrena-line flushed through her, clearing her vision, waking every sense. This one was going to try. She grabbed his forearms and dug her fingers in.

"Have fun dying," he said, his breath moist on her cheek.

The move she should be doing was caught under a net of pain and exhaustion. A twist of hips, a leg swung up and around his neck, a hard wrench down. With herself in control, she'd hold on until he choked to death. With The Silent One's added power and influence, she'd jerk hard enough to break the neck. She had no strength for any of it. She didn't even try.

She watched as his partner nudged him. He slammed her once against the ground. Her head bounced off packed, rocky earth. They retreated to the truck and drove off. In a puff of rancid exhaust, she lay there, unmoving. She thought of Mick, circling above her, coming to perch beside her. She should cry. She wouldn't.

Closing her eyes, she felt the cold settle in, the blood on her face freeze in its descent, her body sink into the earth. It was Death who really circled, calling her to him. She found him on her own terms in her first life. This time, it would be his.

COUGHING—CHOKING—GAGGING, SHE WOKE. Monstrous light against her eyelids. Reaching everywhere, trying to find some surface her hands didn't slip from. Even her boots slipped against the watery box she found herself in. She rolled, coughing, all she'd become was lungs on fire. The action tore her apart.

Eyes now open, she saw glossy white and red all around. Her sense of smell arrived, bringing mildew and blood. The scene flashed in. A blood-soaked bathtub, her broken body inside. Her head ached so deeply it had to be split open. *Yes,* the tips of her fingers told her brain as they touched soggy, sticky hair behind her left ear.

A creaking hinge, a man standing in the doorway.

"Awake," he said, a command issued after it had already been fulfilled.

With every move, her blood rushed harder to the weeping wound in her head. She remained still.

"You're not dead, not yet. They said I could have you if I found you. So now you're mine."

She closed her eyes to remember. Footfalls in the earth as she lay in the woods, rattling her awake. Hammond's face eclipsing the black of night. And her final thoughts before waking up here.

He ruined my first life. Now he's here to ruin my last. I didn't fight hard enough. I should have killed him.

Her boots slipped, slamming against the wall as she tried to sit up. She was too woozy to prepare a better plan than flailing around in a pool of her own blood. Wet heat gushed behind her ear, and she felt her elbow knock porcelain as an evil man chuckled and her vision shuttered away.

THE MUSK OF animals, the dry, woody scent of a barn. Straw scratching her neck, traveling down her waistband. The hollow *knock-knock-knock-knock* of a woodpecker strangely close by. She wiggled her fingers, found wooden planks as she dug them through the soggy nest. This was different than before. No porcelain cage, no blinding light. But the ache in her head had turned catastrophic. It upended her stomach, sent her retching into the straw beside her. Too weak to move, she remained on her side, grateful for the straw to absorb some of the bile.

The crust on her eyes kept them from opening fully, but she worked at it, blinking away the dried tears and blood that no doubt covered them. Her hands were useless on arms too limp to raise, and that old wound in her hand— it crawled with itchy pain. Those were rafters above her. Surely a barn. A large rectangle of deeply orange light hung like a movie screen far past her boots but was too blurry to see anything within it.

In the near distance a sound of an approaching car, getting louder. It was—could it? No, she was dreaming. It didn't matter what it sounded like. No one knew she was here. No one would find her. She was unrecoverable. She was dead.

Now that sound had cut off, replaced with something new and equally dreamlike. A man's perfect, sunlit voice— Mick? Speaking to someone. Pleasant words edged with fierce intent. Couldn't be. It was a cruel trick of a dying mind, a medicine to calm her as Mother Earth handed her off to Death's waiting arms.

Her muscles had their own mind, fighting to get her upright so her defiant voice could call out against her will. Her bones trembled, her teeth chattered. She knew it was all in vain. She'd lost so much blood. Her voice creaked, too faint to carry past her own ears. She fell back, her voice a corpse, her body seizing into a dreamless quiet.

CHAPTER
26

BUSINESS WAS SLOW enough for Mick to cut out of the shop early. He'd miss the pay, but the extra hours gave him a head start. Now he had time to search for the place on the map in a human body so he could talk to humans. The strike of luck gave him a wild high.

He took Isabel through a drive-through for a quick early dinner of burgers and fries. He showed her how to unwrap one side of the burger and transform it into a one-hand meal. She opened the whole wrapper and dissected the burger in her lap. Eating was eating, so he let her be.

When they got to Old Mae's, he had a ketchup-smeared bun on his floorboard and loose fries to dig from between the seats. The girl was fed, but worn out.

"She might need a bath," Mick said.

Old Mae appraised Isabel's smudgy face and dirty fingernails. "Think you might be right. Off to the tub, girlie." She watched Isabel go inside the house and scoop a cat off the floor before turning sharp old eyes back on Mick. "I'll get her snuggly in the spare room. Don't bother wakin' us if you get in late."

How she knew these things, he'd never know.

In his apartment, he scrubbed his own fingernails and changed into clean jeans and a hoodie. Slid his heavy jacket over it and stuffed his sock hat and gloves in the pockets. From the fridge he grabbed an energy drink and chugged half of it. God, he had to stop buying this crap. But some days it was the only thing keeping him upright.

He smoothed the hand-drawn map against the kitchen counter and looked up a map of Wyona on his phone. He zoomed out until he found the right roads leading to the intersection on the paper map. There were turns between Wyona and this area he wasn't familiar with, so he penciled in roads on the page and then plugged his own starting address into his phone to get an idea of how long a drive it was. Not bad. He'd make it before sunset. He folded the map and went outside, checking his pants for keys, phone, and pocketknife.

The GTO's trunk was already outfitted with a proper murder kit. Crowbar, duct tape, rope, pair of old work gloves, and a socket wrench large enough to break a kneecap and smash clean through a skull—dead or undead. He tossed in a box of black fifty-gallon trash bags then went back inside for his waterproof heavy-duty flashlight and an extra set of batteries. And a second set of clothes and boots, in case he lost his current clothes in a shift somewhere and needed new ones to drive home in.

His human self seemed a bit high-maintenance. His eagle could get the job done and not need any of this crap.

In the driver's seat he checked his fuel level—all good. With the GTO's engine still warm from his drive home, he gunned it on the road, taking full advantage of sun-warmed

pavement that would soon be back to its winter freeze. He should have checked the weather forecast for tonight—but it didn't matter. If he found what he hoped to find, nothing would stop him from what he needed to do.

Which was what? He had no idea. In the moment, he'd better be able to figure it out.

His route took him deeper into mountain territory. Roads rose higher in elevation then plummeted down the other side, in twists and hairpins even tighter than the roads around Wyona. No signs of human civilization, no cell phone signal. Tall trees blocking all view of land, laying dark shadows that hid oncoming cars unless they had headlights on. The sun was still above the horizon somewhere, dyeing half the sky in orange and purple. He hit a patch of straight road heading into a valley and knew he had one more turn. Past that would be the landscape his eagle remembered. Power lines strung in a clearing of forest, old cluster of buildings, rusted water tower.

He reached an intersection and made the turn. A mile later, power lines. It didn't look anything like a road as he turned off the pavement onto the narrow cleared spot beside the metal giants. Without the hazel-eyed woman's hint, he'd have never found it. The GTO's tires caught in grooves, jerking the wheel. He gripped with both hands and lowered his speed. Once he lost sight of the state road behind him, the path dumped into a wider one. It was slow going on a deeply rutted road not suitable for a sports car, but he wasn't about to pull over and go as eagle now that he was so close. If there were humans here, he needed to be able to talk to them before they met their death by thunderbird.

An old sign, clinging by one nail to its post, passed him. *Doe Valley Lead Mine, 3 miles.*

Three miles was a long time on a road like this.

He saw the old water tower first, peeking over the trees. The road curved and set him on a straight path for a cluster of old buildings, some intact, others in the process of turning to rubble. Human-eye view merged with eagle-eye view and yes, this was it, the place on the map.

Aside from a few rusted cars missing body panels and wheels, the place looked like it'd been abandoned a century ago. He pulled to the side of the road just outside the entrance and got out, stepping on fresh tire marks that weren't his own. So, abandoned recently enough for those marks to remain. It looked like he might be too late.

He got the socket wrench out of his trunk and slid it into his waistband under his jacket. Tugged on his sock hat. Checked his phone—of course, no signal. If he had to shift he'd ruin his best jacket, but the cold was too harsh outside the car to take it off, and the sun was on its way out. What body heat he had, he needed to keep. He wasn't sure what he'd find inside.

Passing between two buildings, he found a newer Chevy sedan, its trunk open and half full of boxes, parked outside the large open entrance to an old barn. A lazy breeze blew across the yard, stirring dust, whistling through old wood. He stiffened at a sound, abrupt in the barren quiet—knocking, just above. A woodpecker?

"Who goes there?"

He spun, straining his bad leg. Before him stood a man, a bit older than himself. Hair grayed around his face, spreading into his beard. A long coat, the kind a cowboy might wear. He had hands in his pockets, and Mick thought of his own knife and tried to remember which pocket it was in.

"Hi." Mick took a step, offered a handshake. Win his information with manners then summon his eagle to tear him apart.

The man made no forward move. "You looking for something?"

Offer the truth or play stupid? Mick was no good at games. He withdrew his hand. "I'm lookin' for a guy named Hammond."

A slight tightening of the eyes before the man's features smoothed again. "For what kind of business?"

"Is he here?" His eagle jolted, suddenly awake and alarmed. Static discharged down his skin, into the ground. He steadied himself. There was no danger yet. His eagle needed to settle down.

"I'm the only one here at the moment. Well, myself and one other. Nobody ought to be here, including newcomers."

It seemed the 'one other' had been tacked on to make Mick believe he was outnumbered. It would take more than two humans to outnumber his eagle.

"This place is closed down, so you best head out."

"I just need to talk to him for five minutes. You got an idea where I can find him?"

"You aren't very good at listening, are you? I'm the last working man here, and as soon as I'm done with my business, this place is closed." The man walked to the trunk of the car and lifted a box.

"So Hammond does come here?"

The man rested his load on the bumper and turned his attention back to Mick. The initial suspicion that had started this conversation had drifted away, but now it was back, more armed than ever. "You have about ten seconds to get out of here."

Mick's eagle shuddered inside him. There was more to this man that what he was seeing. Could he be raised like

Waapikoona? He was white, but so were some of those men he'd slaughtered with Waapikoona that night they'd thrown her in the back of the Chrysler 300. Skin color might not factor in to which set of bones the underworld wanted to raise back to life. This man here could be a member of that same group.

His eagle shrieked inside him. It wasn't just a restless call fighting against restraints. It was a wake-up, directed straight at Mick.

"You're Hammond," he said in the same moment he thought it.

"Look, brother. I'd like to help you. But I'm on limited time to get this thing done, and if you and I don't get out of here before the boss gets back, we're both dead men." The man lifted the box and walked it toward the barn. Over his shoulder, he said, "Come back tomorrow and maybe we can talk."

Mick watched him fade into the shadow inside the large door. Tomorrow was better than nothing. Static prickled his skin again, but he held his eagle steady. This man was surely rebuilt by the underworld for how strongly his eagle fought. A shift and a kill would end all chance of speaking tomorrow. If Mick could be patient, so could his eagle. He returned to the GTO, buckled himself in, and turned it around in the dusty lot.

Dusk darkened the rutted road, hiding potholes and ridges that Mick worked hard to avoid. The driving consumed all his focus until he reached the pavement of the state road. Only then was he able to reflect on what had just happened. He'd not only found the place from a crude map, but he'd found Hammond; moments before he would have missed him entirely. Every bit of bad luck in his life had been payment for this, and right now, it was worth it.

The whole encounter felt like a dream. A ghost mine at the end of an unmarked road in the middle of nowhere. The only signs of modern times were himself and Hammond. Nothing else moved, as if the whole scene lay in wait of some great disturbance. It was so vivid in his mind now it was like waking from the dream, the realness of it so thorough he was desperate to share it with someone and transfer it to actual life.

Tomorrow he'd return. He'd speak to Hammond. He'd learn where to find Waapikoona. The end was a day away.

Black storm clouds ushered the night in. The closer he got to Wyona, the harder his eagle fought. Two hands on the wheel, gripping hard, and he felt any moment a giant zipper running through his vertical center would start to pull apart. Slow breathing became a struggle; he pulled to the roadside and got out for fresh air to help walk it off. At the rear of the GTO, he put his palms against the trunk lid and breathed deep. Everything felt upside down. That scene in the old mine wasn't right, but what crucial thing had he missed? That man had told him to come tomorrow, but it was a lie—no one would be there tomorrow. Meeting Hammond at that exact moment had been pure, once-in-a-lifetime luck. There'd be no second chance. He'd wrestle the steering wheel down the three miles of that godawful road again and find no one at all, his dream snatched away, back to square one.

Too bad. It couldn't be helped tonight. He'd gone too far and was nearly home. He had work in the morning and a U-Fill shift in the evening—damn it, tomorrow wasn't going to work out for a second try at the mine even if he wanted to test luck a second time. Waapikoona needed a damn phone so he could call her. She needed to come to him. He'd done enough. He got back in the GTO and buckled up. Started the engine. Checked his mirrors and tore onto the road, his anger with Waapikoona and himself fueling the thrashing eagle. If he didn't get home soon, he'd lose his hold, shift, and fly through the windshield. This car would keep going unmanned, head-on into traffic.

Two more turns and then his driveway. He added the miles and calculated the time, decided anything over thirty seconds seemed like an impossible challenge. The backseat could be overflowing with demon millipedes like that dumpster behind Virgil's for how vigorously his eagle fought. When he took the first turn he thought, *here, this is where I pull over and give in. Here's where my eagle wins.* What was it he did to talk himself out of a shift? That skill was buried, too lost behind the fight going on inside.

Wait—the smell of cut grass in the summer. The pop-pop-pop of a V8 exhaust. Slipping a hand against a woman's skin at the small of her back, fingers migrating under the waist of her jeans. Throwing a ball hard across a field, feeling the extension of arm and hand, the twist in the body, the feet tight against earth. Popcorn and a movie, a big gulp of sweet tea, so sugary it coated the teeth.

He made it to the second turn. His headlights glanced off tree trunks standing tall, breaking up the dark wall against the road. Several sets of eyes reflected back. The deer would just have to stay off the road tonight. He wasn't slowing down. He remembered the night he'd come across the fake Janie in the road who'd turned into a flying demon and bit him—the thought undid all the work he'd just done to regain human power over eagle, but it didn't matter because there ahead was his driveway. He'd made it.

But he paused in the road, turn signal flashing in the instrument panel, engine thrumming. His body and mind reached a startling, illogical calm. Upon viewing his hand-

drawn map, Raúl's hazel-eyed companion had warned him of danger, the kind to get him killed. That expectation must have thrown him off, had raised his alert enough to discount something more underhanded and devious. Now the scene of that old mine came alive once again, and he found something new—an element lurking, waiting, boiling under the surface. His eagle had sensed it. He should have listened. He should have asked to look around, should have insisted tomorrow was no good and he needed answers today. He knew it had been a mistake leaving that place, but it wasn't just that. It was the end.

He could fix his mistake now or regret it forever.

Using the mouth of his driveway, he made a U-turn, fishtailing back into the opposite lane as he slammed the gas pedal to the floor. Time was his enemy now. His mistake could be remedied if somehow he made it back to that place in time to piece together what he'd missed. This time, he'd have to find that place in the dark.

THE RAINCLOUDS BLOCKED moon and starlight, and erratic wind added hazard to the curving roads. As he turned onto the unmarked road beside the row of power lines, fat raindrops fell through his headlights and speckled the dust on his windshield. The rutted three miles to the mine punished the GTO. His eagle punished him. He was grateful for the extra set of clothes in his trunk. A shift tonight would be inevitable. At this point his only hope was to delay it.

He parked in the same spot as before, but the scene was slightly different. The first two buildings were edged with light shining from behind, and everything else disappeared into darkness. Outside of the car he heard the unmistakable noise of a generator. He put on his sock hat and gloves, slid the socket wrench into his waistband. He retrieved the flashlight and crowbar from the trunk. This time, he'd carry a second weapon in full view. A gust of wind colder than the already frigid air shoved him in the back like a slap of encouragement. He zipped up, raised his hood over his hat to shield him from the random splatter of rain, and shook off the cold.

When he walked through the two buildings, he found a single floodlight illuminating the same Chevy sedan and same man in his long coat flapping in the wind. This time, boxes were being loaded into the trunk. The same boxes, it appeared, from the stack he'd made earlier just inside the barn door. So, he'd needed that trunk before, to transport something large or dirty or both.

"Hammond," Mick called.

The man looked up.

"Tomorrow ain't gonna work for me. We talk now."

Hammond brushed off his hands. His boots and several inches of his coat hem were coated in mud. "Sneaking up on folks is a good way to get yourself shot, brother. You're the wrong color to shoot in the street like an animal, though."

Real foul thing to say, especially to a stranger who might not share in the racist ideology. "I don't want trouble. But this can't wait."

"I'm still not quite sure what to make of you, but I can spare a few minutes."

But Mick was starting to understand what to make of Hammond and how he could work with it. "You're not really working for *these people*, are you?" Mick had encountered enough bigots in his life to put the exact tone on those words. Like that phrase, *these people,* was somehow ironic,

forced into political correctness when there were other words a person like that preferred to use. It was a coward's way to own his beliefs, but wasn't that what they were deep down? Ignorant cowards.

Hammond released a dry cackle devoid of genuine amusement. "I'll tell you, white man to white man, I'll pay in Hell for communing with these devils. But they run this show—for now—and it's the only way to get close enough."

"Close enough to …" Mick didn't want to be wrong or his act might fail.

Another cackle, this time laced with sadism. "Exactly. One at a time. In fact, I'm just coming back from putting one in an early grave. Loud-mouthed woman. Even higher marks for that, I figure, once I finally see our maker. Speaking of, you and I better take cover before this rain hits."

A raindrop fell between them, a slow-motion, whispering descent through the wind ending in a sparkling splatter against dirt. Eagle mind caught the rainbow reflection in each newly created drop as it broke apart in a circular collision around the first mini crater. Another came down beside him a few feet away. It all happened in different time to the thought that ricocheted from human mind to eagle then back to human. He entered a new dream—a nightmare—and spoke his terror aloud. "Sarah Clarke."

Hammond had been busily working to get his trunk refilled with boxes, but now he paused, studying Mick. "How'd you know that?"

Mick's response came from within that nightmare in which he played the repulsive role of this man's 'brother.' "Lucky guess. I was after her too."

"Is that right? Well, you'll be pleased to know she's back in her English grave where she should be. Where all these animals should be. Not sure how to kill a demon right, so she may not have been all dead when she went in, but she'll be dead soon."

Mick felt the crowbar in his hand, thought of how easily it could hook into this guy's neck, tear the artery out like his eagle's talons.

"If I could get some more guys, maybe guys like you, we could work together, wipe them out faster like they were supposed to be wiped out centuries ago."

The sky unloaded. Hammond shut his trunk lid and ran for the wide doorway of the barn. Mick stood as rain pounded around him and sprayed off the roof. He felt alone in a glass dome, untouched, outside of the same time as the rain and the barn and Hammond. He thought of that night his eagle had followed the Chrysler 300 and its entourage of cars from Waapikoona's mausoleum to that clearing where its trunk opened and Waapikoona had sprung out, battered but fierce, killing like the demon Hammond had claimed her to be. She was no demon. She was a battle goddess, an undead warrior. Revived, repowered, unmatched. She couldn't be dead and buried in her old grave. Her body was human, but her soul was so much more.

He couldn't be too late. He couldn't have missed his chance to stop this before. For life to lay a burden like that on him—it just couldn't be.

"You're welcome to come inside, out of that," Hammond called from the barn doorway. "I've got good whiskey in here, and they won't be back for ..." The rest was lost to the rain and wind, and Mick's gutting, fiery grief.

Mick had no time to kill him—as man or as eagle. He had to get to Waapikoona first.

CHAPTER
27

WRISTS BOUND BY biting rope, every bone bruised, no room to breathe. The air was too tight, clamped off, thick with a bad flavor no one should gulp in like she was now. She focused foggy thoughts: car exhaust. Her eyes opened into nothing. She raised a leaden arm to feel cold vibrating metal all around, tight like a box. An engine droned on. It seemed so familiar, so present. She was stuck in a repeat of time, never making it past the Chrysler 300's trunk, Jeremiah's cramped backseat, the trunk she found herself in now. Her knees pressed so hard against her chest she had to get a grip. Slow her respiration. Stall her head from exploding from the unstoppable need to stretch out her legs when stretching her legs was impossible. Or maybe it was, if she found miracle strength and kicked hard enough to go clear through the fender.

It was more likely she'd break both her legs. That would be worse. At this point, she wasn't sure if worse mattered.

She'd have to put herself somewhere else, even with her skull banging against the trunk bed and the taste of exhaust on her tongue and every appendage tingly and starved for blood flow. Remaining in her present would only stir up her already cracked mind.

She stood on a cliff's edge, her sister beside her. A little girl, but so was she. Together they looked across the land, the roll of trees wearing their autumn regalia. There in her mind, she lost sight of those trees for an older memory of her village burning. She didn't ask her sister what was in her thoughts. If it was as mournful as hers, she could not bear it. She took her sister's hand and held it tight. The fear of falling could be no worse than any night in that school— or any day. Pick one, and it would be worse. Lying still in pretend sleep, eyes shut tight, but not too tight. Breath slow despite the pounding heart. A pinch on her sister's arm beside her—she had to stop that tiny whimper, had to get a hold on that choky breath—and the boots' steps drew closer—

Falling and landing would be easier than that.

But had it been? She couldn't remember. All she had left was the trust in Pinepakatwi's eyes before they took that fatal step, her fingers slipping from her grasp, and the regret she'd been reborn with. She couldn't even remember her sister's name. She'd lifted a meaning from the language she thought she knew. *Leaves are falling.* A selfish act, to recast her sister as something other than a mangled body on the ground so somehow Waapikoona would be absolved. A fallen leaf would be caught up by the wind, laid to rest gently, intact and perfect. It wouldn't be some awful broken thing.

Now her sister was bones in a bag, buried behind an old white man's house where she'd stay until a glacier from

the next ice age dragged her body to sea. Waapikoona was now broken herself, and soon she'd be killed and turn to bones. Her connection to The Silent One severed, she had no backup to summon and fill her body with new power. She was woozy with blood loss, unable to walk on her own, barely able to see. She'd come into this new life alone, and that was how she'd leave it.

A rush of air, a jerk of her bones. She wasn't sure what was up or down, but there—that was a kneecap against earth, and that was the rest of her body falling after it. Hip, ribs, shoulder, head, an orchestra of bruising pain. Someone was talking, really running his mouth, but she had no capacity to understand language with the crashing noise in her head. She squinted and saw her own boots far away, her legs stretched long, bumping against the ground over stiff dead grass.

Dragged—yes, that was the reason for the numb pulling contact around both wrists and her arms lifted past her head. Through a graveyard it seemed, if her eyes were seeing right. And look, there were her Helpers, the new ones, the orphans, struggling to keep up while staying under cover. From the shadow of one headstone to the next, they bounded, as eager and loyal as her own. She could use them, but how? They didn't attack living people, only dead ones. If Hammond was dead right now, she wouldn't need her Helpers for anything but cleanup. Her mind might be working, but there was no hope for her body.

Her field of vision was shrinking, going gray. She wasn't sure how much longer she could stand having her arms wrenched back over her head without blacking out. The urge to support the ribs on her left side came on strongly, like the part of her brain that knew there was a crucial injury there had just been reconnected.

Gray swirled into black, and then she was falling. She hit—hard. Nothing like fainting. Nothing like jumping from a cliff. Too painful and jarring for anything but real life, and everything began to spiral away, but no—no—no. This could not be such an uneventful end. She would fight it, she'd breathe, she'd think of inflating her lungs, the sting in her ribs, the hot rush of blood back into her arms. Above her, a man toiled with something—swinging a door shut—right on her shins. The pain of it was bright, new, terrifying in intensity. She tried to bend, but her hands were still tied and the box—the casket—was too small.

"Didn't count on you not fitting, but it makes sense. We'll just have to make do."

So it was a casket. She'd been a child when she'd first lay in this. Now she was a woman.

And then the lid slammed again on her shins, and she just let the pain fill her to her head, fought to stay alert, denying herself the peace of a blackout.

Dirt crumbled around her, piling against her shoulder where it spilled through the gap held open by her legs, weighing down her hair. Then came a pattering on the casket lid as the sides of the grave caved in further. The first dump came down heavy, the pressure on her shins not heavy enough to put her into shock. She'd not go that easy. It would be suffocation, for how long she wasn't sure.

Long enough for her to think about how her choices had led her to dying alone in a box. The mistake wasn't her pursuit of vengeance. Her sister would not walk the same earth on which Hammond lived. Even now as each dump of dirt silenced her enclosure more and more, she held fast to that belief. There was a different misstep that had brought her here—pursuing that vengeance alone.

Now she saw all her options laid before her. Each one played in the pitch like a movie in short blinks and flashes. In the first she raised her sister and taught her all she knew then fast-forward to the future when they'd hunt and kill Hammond together. A second option—she joined her people in mutiny against The Silent One, made friends, convinced a team to help her find Hammond. If told his history, her people would join her. Soto's help could have been her third choice. The final option hurt her to see, even though she knew it was a flash of something to never become. It was the most immediate, the most fulfilling, the most perilous. The one imbued with so much detail it felt more like memory than vision. A new sound came from above—the slow patter of rain, building into a steady backdrop behind the hits of dirt. The weight on the casket lid against her shins had become too much. She strained and cried out with the effort of drawing her knees to her chest so that damn lid could find its proper closure. Now encased and insulated from the truth of what continued above her, she let her mind flesh out that last option in painful delusion.

She could see the Wyona highway sign clearly just like she had in real life on her way back into Missouri. This time, she followed it. In this vision it was night, hollow and cold like the most broken of hearts. She'd pull the Jeep off the road into Mick's gas station, around the side of the quick shop, sidling up next to the orange Pontiac. She'd go inside. There would be a customer at the counter pulling cash from a wallet, and Mick's gaze would move from that exchange to her. He wouldn't smile. He'd regard her in that way he had—watchful, curious, ominously inviting. She'd wait until they were alone. Then she'd approach the counter. His hair would be rough, like he'd run a hand through it. His eyes would be sleepy, and he'd be due for a shave. He'd cross his arms on his chest and wait. Desperate, wounded, just like she'd left him.

She'd say, "Hi, Mick."

He would say nothing.

"I need your help."

He'd chuckle, like he knew this was coming, knew she was here to use him, and knew he'd be unable to say no. "With what?"

"There's a commune not far from here. A guy I need to kill. Could be alone, but probably won't be."

Mick would put his hands on the counter, aim his gaze down, blow out a frustrated breath. "Why should I help you?"

"Because I need you." And that would snap his eyes back to hers. In her head the statement would be practical and innocent, but from her lips it would be a heavier truth exposed, and she'd never be able to take it back.

"I'll help," he'd say, stone-faced. "But there's one condition."

And she'd know what that was because it was her condition too. She'd hop to sit on the counter, spin to face him. He'd lean in as she'd wrap her arms around his neck, and then he'd stand up, bringing her with him. It would be like that kiss in the tomb, a grinding of body and soul. Necessary and unstoppable but so utterly unsatisfactory. The mutual press against one another would leave them at a standstill until she gave, letting him get a leg between hers and her body against the wall. With her pinned he would slow down and taste her, and she would feel him, solid and powerful in all the right places. They wouldn't stop. Not ever. And she wouldn't be here—alone, lost, dying. Delusional mind, fractured ribs, broken heart. A failure, mourning for what could have been.

How different this night would have ended had she kept him by her side as the ally he had been. He'd never abandon her like The Silent One had. They weren't meant to be, but they could've been … if she'd only allowed it.

Water leaked through a crack in the casket. Dripping against her neck. Water colder than her.

The world was sealed away. She could no longer smell the air or hear the rain, but she could still imagine. Waking against him in the morning, latching onto his body to keep him captive in bed. Riding beside him in his Pontiac on the twisty southern Missouri roads on a hot summer day, the car full of wind. Preparing meals, raking leaves, leaving muddy boots side by side at the door to go inside and share a shower after a long day of work. All those domestic things she'd never had the urge to share with a man until she met him.

She couldn't travel back in time to undo her mistake and try again, but she could lie there and dwell on it, let it subdue the fight her wasted body could not perform. Now with no chance of ever seeing him again, she could drown in that cold water and finally let herself miss him, and she'd do it until her heart's final beat.

CHAPTER
28

MICK SPED THROUGH the dark in the GTO, soaked roads reflecting his headlights back at him so at times all he could see was a curtain of sparkly rain. He lost his steering several times to an invisible sheet of water but had much practice driving an unsafe car in unsafe conditions. His skills tested too many times, slipping up turned from an if to a when. Finding death against a tree would not help Waapikoona. Wings would be safer, faster—he passed a gravel patch at the roadside, hit his brakes, and reversed into it.

He got out of the car and stripped out of clinging wet clothes and boots and shoved everything into the backseat. Now where to stash the key so someone wouldn't take off with his car—there, stick it between the backseat cushions. Even with how remote this road was, he wasn't taking chances with his stupid luck.

With a running start on the sodden pavement, he launched into the night sky, new feathers shedding water and darkness no longer so grim.

His shift back to human happened so hastily he fell six feet from the air hard onto his heels. The impact traveled his backbone and jarred his skull. Old Mae's house sat in shadow before him.

"Too old for this shit," he muttered, snatching the hidden key.

Inside his apartment he threw on jeans and a tee and ran outside and up the steps to Old Mae's front door. What time was it? The middle of the night? And shoot—Old Mae had told him not to wake them. He tried the knob. It opened. He followed the light into the kitchen where the old woman sat at her table with a mug of a steaming drink. She looked up at him, her wrinkled eyes steady, her mouth in a near smile.

"Isabel—is she—? I gotta talk to her right now."

She regarded him for a long moment. He remembered the exchange they had a lifetime ago, when he'd brought Waapikoona home from their trip through the belly of the underworld to find the medicine woman who healed his demon-bitten arm.

Your guest walks unholy ground.

It's under control, he'd replied.

I live a quiet life.

He'd been sincere when he told her he respected that, but since then, he'd lost all control. The magnitude of unquiet had reached new levels. He'd brought chaos down upon her secluded old house, and he wasn't sure what he could do, what he could say—

"Mickey."

"I'm sorry. All of this. It ain't—"

"Take a slow breath. You're pantin' like you run all the way home. Where's your socks and shoes?"

"Don't need 'em. Listen—"

Old Mae looked away from him, toward a shuffle in the hallway, and he followed her gaze. There stood Isabel, rubbing an eye with her good hand, her bad one nestled against her. Mick didn't think about what he needed to do, he just did it. Isabel, steered to a seat at the table. An opened letter—some kind of bill—snatched from the counter and flipped onto the blank side. With a pencil awaiting him on the table, he drew two headstones: one labeled ISABEL, the other labeled SARAH. This was all going to happen right in front of Old Mae, and he didn't have a way to get around it or the time to care.

"Isabel, you remember, the first time. I know you remember. You…" he pointed at her grave "…and your sister." He wrote WAAPIKOONA on the grave as well. "This is somewhere in Missouri. Has to be. Do you remember? Could you find it from the sky?"

Leaning over her, he drew two birds, one large, one small. Pointed at her, then himself. Circled the birds' eyes and slashed hard lines from the circles to the graves. She was squinting at him. He couldn't tell if she was thinking, or angry, or if the kitchen light was too bright for her unadjusted human eyes.

"This is real, real important right now." But how could she know the answer? He went through the scenario. Two little girls die a couple centuries ago and are buried in a cemetery. They're both unearthed, to be revived later from their bones decades apart. In Isabel's case, she'd been reburied in at least two places he knew of before coming back to life. She couldn't help him with this. She'd have no clue. What was he thinking?

"It had to be near your school, in your first life. Had to be …" He let the pencil fall. It rolled across the table until it stopped under the slow clasp of Old Mae's hand.

Another mistake. Another lost chance. He should have accepted Hammond's invitation into the barn and out of the rain. He should have broken the man's knees with a socket wrench and then extracted the cemetery's location from him, by whatever means.

He stood up. He would tear everything apart. Himself, this town, the world. He'd failed Waapikoona once, now twice. Living with this—it would break him to pieces.

A tug on the hem of his shirt—he started like an edgy horse. Below him, Isabel pulled harder and he gave in and followed her to the door. She walked out onto the porch, his bare feet following hers into the frigid spray from the rain. At the top of the steps she pointed due north. To speak would break this magic of possibility, so he crouched to her eye level and looked into her eyes. His were wet from anger and grief. Hers were watering in the cold.

She gave him a confident nod that lit up the world.

He ran down the steps to the cover of his apartment entryway, stripped off his shirt and jeans, and flung his eagle into the sky. Below him, a shadow tore across land through the rain, turning to a sparkle of white wings and his beacon of hope.

She knew, and she would lead him there.

The falcon's uneven flight slowed their pace. The rain slowed them even more. He could see an unnatural twist in her damaged wing as it carried her and knew pushing her for more speed would only tire her out. They crossed into a downpour they couldn't avoid and took temporary cover in the pines. Human anxiousness breached eagle patience. He moved limb to limb as the falcon rested. From a high perch he watched the rain ease; he called to her and they moved on. The lights from a human town passed below them, and the falcon banked, unsure. He followed her down. Halfway to land she abandoned the descent and gained more air. Their flight continued through patches of rain. He found a hole through the clouds, and for some time they flew in crisp moonlight. After passing another town the storm returned, harder, colder, nearly knocking the falcon out of the sky. He called her down for cover. She refused, fighting the wind toward a cluster of light ahead, then beyond, where she banked and landed high in an ancient tree.

He circled the area, wary. Spirits roamed below—he could sense them but not see them. He widened his patrol and there, just ahead, past the snaking road, he spotted a cleared patch of land dotted with upright stones. Leaving the falcon to rest in the tree, he dived, and yes, his human's underworld woman was here, somewhere, her presence muted by a layer of earth just like she ought to be. His human didn't believe; he demanded he take a look at each stone. Row after row. His human needed a detail to recognize, to confirm he and the falcon were right. He flapped to the final row, found earth mounded beside a sunken spot filling with rain. A human machine sat near the edge of trees, rusty scoop collecting its own puddle. His human called, *Go around! The front! Hurry!* He flapped over the row of stones and positioned himself in front.

Yes, his human said. *Go tell her then come back. Now!*

But the falcon had already flown in to perch on the first row of stones, near the road. The eagle told her what his human demanded. *You can't be here for this. Fly home. Don't stop until you're there.*

She cried back, resistant.

There was no time for disobedience. He opened both wings and lunged at her, talons aimed. She dodged and flapped into the air, making for the tree she had perched in earlier. Not good enough. He chased her, his size and talons no match for her, until she was far enough to send her off with a final order. *Do not stop until you are home.*

His human fought to get out of him. High in the sky would be a bad place. He landed just as his human clawed out, frenzied, violent, unstoppable.

Mick landed on hands and knees in the mud. Icy cold rain pelted his bare back. His hair lay in strings that dripped into his face. He ran a hand against his forehead to smooth the hair back, ran it across eyes to clear the water, but it didn't matter. Eagle vision had tricked him into thinking there was a touch of light here, at least enough to make out where he was, where her grave was, where that backhoe had been parked. All around him was nothing but shadow upon shadow. He closed his eyes, begging his eagle to map his surroundings, to lead him where he needed to go. In the dark shower of rain, he stood. His bad leg seized and folded, he fought back to his feet and hopped in place to get the blood pumped. She was here—his eagle had known it. *He* knew it. It wasn't too late. He knew that like a man going to war. Victory was due or he wouldn't be marching toward it.

The eagle's view from the sky rested into his conscious mind. He walked forward, blind, full of trust and belief in everything he'd wished he could deny that was now an unshakable part of him. He and eagle were one. His toes touched a slippery edge; he caught himself before falling in. Back on hands and knees he felt ahead, found the grave unfinished. Hammond had done half the job. Perhaps he thought it was good enough or hoped to get back to the commune before the rain hit. Mick felt around the grave—

there, a glint—he reached for it, felt it up and down, saw it in the dark.

A shovel.

He struck into the hole, plunging into wet earth. He could see—eagle vision or human vision, he wasn't sure and didn't question. Every hole he opened in the earth filled with rain. He labored below a waterfall. His toes sunk in the sloppy mud. She'd drown, if she hadn't already suffocated under all that sludge. He shoveled on, powered by every force he believed in. Truth. Integrity. Justice. He tasted sky and earth. He prayed to luck and fate and every god he knew. The god he'd been brought up to believe in. The demon god who'd raised Waapikoona from her grave the first time. If he was doing the work of this underworld god, his eagle chose to remain quiet, and he was grateful for that.

His shovel struck something solid. He hooked his feet into spongy ground and lowered his upper body in, feeling for an edge—there. He jumped in, landing against a mud shelf at the foot of the coffin. Hammond must have over dug then filled it in at the foot for how his feet sunk in loosened earth. He scraped the coffin's top with the shovel then tossed it aside to carve out the edge by his knees with his hands. As he worked, rain washed the coffin clean and eroded the edges. Now he could feel a gap where the lid would open. An old thing, just a simple box. It was a wonder it hadn't decomposed.

He worked his fingers around the edge and heaved it off.

She rested. But it was no image of peace. It was heartbreak and violence, torture and despair. It was the image of his warrior goddess in pained surrender. How it rolled through him as cold rain poured down and mud rushed in, and his soul tore itself in half. He was too late. He'd failed her. She was here, blood-caked and bruised, but gone forever.

She lay crumpled, broken, as rain traced lines against the dirt on her face. If he cried, this downpour would wash it away like his pain didn't matter. He had to get her body out of this godforsaken place.

With everything slippery with mud and rain, there was no easy way. He used her clothes as a grip, hauling her out like a limp thing instead of the powerful woman she once was. She landed in a grotesque twist made worse by rope-bound wrists. He righted her limbs, straightened her head, combed her hair away from her face. He had no knife to cut her free. Anger and failure numbed him. He should cry, even if this world cared nothing for it, and he would. But the tears were dammed behind a scream that continued to build even though he knew better than to bend to it. He couldn't lose his mind tonight. He had other work to do. There was Isabel, and Helen, and—yes. Okay, all right. He'd been dealt shit in life before. He could handle this. He could get up and move, do what needed to be done. He still had Isabel; she could lead him through the cave to The Silent One to raise Helen's bones. She was the living piece of Waapikoona that could get him through this. Not in the same way, but an equally important way. He could do this. He had to. He could take his hands from Waapikoona's cold dead cheeks and get himself up.

Fury shrieked through him, peeling him from his skin into eagle with wings flapping air and thunder rocking the earth. It sent him high, above the death of a woman so deeply ingrained he'd never live as human again. He couldn't bear a life without her. If she was dead, so was his human.

Into the clouds his anger carried him. Static from the storm fused with the charge in his heart. Power swelled, uncontainable. He released it, a strike so hot and wide it scorched the rain-soaked brush around every cemetery stone and rattled the air around him. His human didn't want to let go of this scream, but his eagle did. The sound tore through the pounding rain, a warning to every demon that this night would be their last. But not until he found the man who'd done this. He'd slaughter him into pieces and carry them here to dump in this open grave.

Her body—he wasn't sure. He'd have to do something with it later. Banking against the wind, he took a last look. This appalling scene, this hellish crime—

She did not lay as she should. Her knees were bent—raised—and her head—

The eagle flapped to the ground. As talons touched earth, human feet finished the landing. Mick fell to his knees beside her where threads of singed rope lay, her wrists now free. Her legs had fallen flat, but her arms, her shoulders, they had lifted her up, and her head turned, her eyes caught his in one breathless moment before they closed again.

"Mick," she whispered. "Don't leave me."

She fell back but he caught her, pulled her against him. He would absorb her. She would never leave him ever again. Real or delusion, he didn't care. He would bring her into himself, make her his, never let go. She sparked in his arms, a remnant of the static that had once been in the sky and in his eagle, discharged into earth, but not before it went through her first.

CHAPTER
29

WAAPIKOONA JOLTED ALIVE. Ozone mixed with ash—and flame. She tried to bend her legs to get up, but without vision or any sense of where her arms and legs were, she was lost to the feeling. The ground around her burned. She could smell it through the—rain? But how could there be fire and water, unless it had been lightning, and that was crazy because she was sure she was dead. Unquiet spirits could pass through earth and seep around stones. In rain and around lightning, they'd be untouched. This was her new existence. Alone and helpless for as long as time spun in its endless circle. She'd failed her sister and now she would roam. Without being laid into a peaceful resting place, she'd been doomed to walk the earth forever.

An outline of a figure soared above. Inside her, a heart thumped. A mistake—unquiet spirits had no blood. It was a phantom heart, like a severed limb that retained its feeling in the living. The figure fell beside her. Golden eagle, now man. *Her* man. The one she'd dreamed of as the dirt was shoveled on top of her while she lay in her casket. He was here—an unquiet spirit himself? They could stay together, roam time side by side.

But a mission lit his eyes. He was not at rest like her. He was leaving—

She begged him to stay. The words came, but she didn't hear them. Her strength had waned and her propped arms collapsed.

His body closed over her like a new burial. She smelled him, the purity of Mick, equal parts man, animal, and god. Earth-coated, sky-touched, rain-soaked. He leaked heaven against her; she wished he would hold her like this across all of time. The rain coated them, cocooned them. He drew her ever closer.

"You died," he said against her hair, a whisper in the roar of the rain. "This isn't real."

It wasn't. It was the death throes of her brain, the last neurons firing.

"Oh God," he said.

That was him—he was the god. He held her away, his hands, warm enough to feel through sopping clothes on her shoulders. His face, a light in the darkness and rain. Yes, these were the hands and face of a god.

"Mick." She had no strength to say any more before her eyelids closed and she fell away.

"No!"

Her head snapped; she felt a sting on her cheek.

"Stay awake. I ain't gonna lose you again."

She felt him rearranging her, pushing strong body parts under her arm, lifting her from the cold watery ground. The pummel of rain lessened, and she smelled pine trees and damp forest earth.

"Not much cover here, but I got to leave you and get the car. Just a few minutes. Stay up like this. Your head is bleedin' bad." He adjusted her against something cold and rough, holding her shoulders in place. "Don't die on me. Promise?"

She reached for him, found his warm hand, his bent head, his scratchy neck. Breathed him in. He kissed her bruised lips. Through the slits of her eyelids, she saw a flap of feathers. She felt a push of wind. To Mother Earth she swore, *When he returns, I will be here, alive. For him.*

A POWERFUL ENGINE broke through hazy half-slumber, and a new dream image filled her head. Heroic orange blazing across a landscape of grays. Rainwater spewing from shiny black tires. A bumper coming to rest inches from a headstone. She took a deep breath, tasted rich exhaust. He was here, and she was alive.

Now his shoulder was under her arm, and he was yelling at her to walk, move her legs, come on, before they both froze to death. He had clothes now, but they were as wet as hers. She dropped into the Pontiac's seat. He stretched the seat belt over her. The billow of heat that fell against her as the door closed could put her right to sleep.

"Hey," he barked as he got in the other side. "No sleepin'. Ain't that the rule? You get a head injury and you gotta stay awake so you don't die."

"Again," she whispered. Her lips were slow.

"Right." He released a long breath, and on it, "God damn it, Waapikoona."

She had died once. She'd almost just died again. Maybe she'd been overpowered. Maybe there was no chance to save herself due to the state she was in. But there was always a chance if a person didn't surrender, and in that cemetery that was exactly what she'd just done.

Mick leaned over her, into her face. "I *need* to be able to get in touch with you."

The strange note in his voice gave her reason not to look directly at him. She'd see anger worse than any she'd seen in either of her lives. Now was not a time to see Mick reduced to such things—all because of her.

She felt the car pushing forward but didn't use the energy to look out the window.

"Hammond," she said.

"Yeah, that sick fucker. I'm gonna—"

"Now—" She choked, coughed, tasted blood. But had to get this out. "I do it now."

"You ain't gonna do nothin'—"

She somehow found enough grit in her to grab his arm. "I do it now."

SHE DIDN'T NEED to tell Mick where to go. The rain had slowed to a sprinkle by the time the Pontiac's headlights found the buildings on the edge of the commune. He took the car out of gear and set the parking brake—and stopped her exit from the car with a warm hand over hers. "You stay here. I'm leavin' the engine runnin'. You need to get warmed up."

"I'm warmed enough."

He smoothed wet hair away from his face. "You can barely walk."

"I don't need to walk to cut that man's throat." It sounded stupid because it was, but she was going to kill that man herself. She jerked her hand away from his and opened the door. He had killed the engine and was out and around the car before she had a chance to stabilize her vision enough to get herself upright.

"I'll bring you back his head."

"Mick, move."

Instead of moving aside he clasped her hand and pulled her to standing. She swayed; he caught her, wrapped his arm around her shoulders. If he was here to lend strength, she would take it.

Mick walked her to the rear of the car, lifted her arm around his neck, and opened the trunk. While she held on to him he found a giant wrench and stuck it in his waistband. He dug out a switchblade—her switchblade, the one she'd left in the tomb. The one she'd held against his neck that first day long ago. He closed her fingers around it. "You might need this."

Her hand trembled with the effort of maintaining grip. Prepping for murder when so near death herself should be an unthinkable thing. But walking into this commune this time, she'd not be alone. He was here with her, like he should have been the first time. She'd been granted the redo she'd dreamed of in that casket, and she had no idea why.

He walked her in, and with each step she found new power. Past the first two buildings she could see a light glowing from inside an old barn. That was where she'd woken, bruised and disoriented. Where she'd heard Mick's voice. Where Hammond had spewed hate as he struck her—after binding her hands so she couldn't fight back. By the time they reached the doorway, she was walking on her own—weakly but steady enough for Mick to leave her and go inside, calling a greeting that sounded friendly but soon would prove to be something else.

Light shone down upon her. She looked up, saw the moon, clear and bright through a break in the clouds. Puddles glinted all around her, edged with crystalline ice. She could no longer hear Mick's voice, but it didn't worry her. He had this handled as man or eagle, either could succeed. A moment later she saw him coming out of the barn, dragging the other man, Mick's thick arm squeezed in a chokehold around Hammond's neck. In his free hand he carried that giant wrench. Hammond's legs moved from the hip but everything below both knees looked strangely loose as he fought to gain traction against the gravel. Mick's advance toward her did not falter even though she could see where the man's fingers gouged into his arm.

Mick tossed him to the ground at her feet. "Beg her—" The exertion had cost him some; he fought to find his breath. "Beg her for your life."

Hammond coughed without end, his breathing hoarse as he bent against the ground, his face unnaturally hued in the moonlight.

Mick put his boot against Hammond's back and shoved him toward her. "Beg her."

She gazed at Mick, remembering his anger with her in the car. If she didn't want to see him reduced to that degree of anger, she wasn't sure she wanted to see this either. Mick's purity and righteousness, tainted—because of her. She looked down at their victim as he looked up at her. She wouldn't wait for him to beg. She wouldn't give him any chance to be human, because he was a monster.

Onto her knees. A grip of hair, her blade across his neck. A scream tore through her bones but it wasn't his, it was her own. She felt the knife's handle in her grasp, but its cut was everywhere. In that moment they were one, children connected, underworld soldiers, slaves of the same great demon. Hive mind and body, working apart but as one. Cutting him was like cutting herself. Killing him was suicide. She dropped the knife, shoved him away. Her scream carried on. She felt, and remembered, the lash of his whip, the shame of his hands, the grief of losing her people, her home, her life. The rushing air at the top of the cliff, falling through it, crashing into earth, her hand no longer tight in her sister's.

"It's okay," Mick said. His hands on her shoulders planted her back in this time, his eyes clear and wild. "It's over. You're okay."

She sank. On their knees together, he held her up.

"Waapikoona. Say something."

Her throat felt raw and shredded. She wasn't sure she could speak, but she had to. For him. "Thank you."

He wrapped his arms around her, squeezed her against him. Over his shoulder she could see Hammond's body shudder to its end, the rush of blood across a pale neck joining the rainwater still puddled on the ground, turning the ice crystals to gemstones.

The gravel gouged her knees, but she couldn't get up, and she didn't need to as long as Mick stayed on his knees with his arms around her.

"This is bad," she whispered against his shoulder. "You and me. Look at this, these things I make you do. You're too good for this."

He released her and looked into her face. "None of that matters."

"It does—"

"I need you." He'd gone angry again, called to a task he seemed long prepared for.

"Why?"

Both his hands took violent hold of her shirt at the collar. To keep her from falling or from leaving him again?

He held her like that, unwavering in the bitter cold. His hair and clothes were still soaked, but warmth radiated through it. There was a darkening of skin under his eye and a bloody split at the corner of his lip. He knelt there in the moonlight, a pillar of endurance and hope. "You keep me unbroken."

IF THEY HADN'T been the words to perfectly express how she felt now that she was finally with him again, she'd have told him to go. To drive her to where she'd parked the Jeep and go home to his family.

Those words he gave her were inside her now, as true as they had been when his breath had steamed the frozen air with them.

As he backed the Pontiac to find the mouth of the road that would lead them out of there, her orphan Helpers bounded from the woods. Headed for Hammond's corpse, soon they'd transport his flesh to The Silent One. It would be another forbidden kill for her, another tally mark on The Silent One's list of evidence against her. He'd already cut her off for insubordination. She wasn't sure what he would do next.

But right now she would settle against the seat, close her eyes, let Mick hold her hand in the sanctuary of his car. The bumpy dirt road would turn to pavement, the steadier

vibration would lull her to sleep. She wouldn't question the joining of their worlds or what it meant for each of them. She'd save that thought for tomorrow, when she was out of these wet clothes and back inside her normal head again and ready to tackle the impossible.

CHAPTER
30

MICK THANKED THE dashboard lights for illuminating what rested in the seat beside him.

Waapikoona. Alive. Willing to come home with him.

As he drove he had to keep looking over to check. Yes, she was still there. Still beaten, bloody, and hypothermic, but alive. He wanted to let her sleep and heal, but he worried about that sticky wound in her head and the possibility of concussion. He had to warn her about who would be at his apartment when they got there.

If she had made it back.

Of course she'd made it back. Luck was on his side tonight.

A HEALTHY SUNRISE began to trickle against the night as Mick parked outside his apartment and killed the engine. He left Waapikoona inside the car to stick his head inside and check—no Isabel.

It didn't mean she hadn't made it back. It meant she'd come back and gone up to Old Mae's, and he wouldn't entertain any thoughts otherwise. Having her safe upstairs made his work simpler now. Waapikoona mumbled his name when he unbuckled her, waking just enough to lay flimsy arms around his neck so he could heave her up. Her boots dragged the ground on the way in. She cradled her head with her free hand. He took her to his bed and laid her down.

"Wait a second. I got to tell you somethin' before you go back asleep."

She was lying on top of the comforter and sheet, so he pried it from under her body to buy some time to find the right words. This couldn't wait but he wanted her to be able to rest afterward. It had to be gentle, undramatic. Sound like he had everything under control. She grimaced, fingering that wound in her head.

He stopped her from touching it. "Let me get somethin' for that."

In the other room he found his box of first aid. He applied gauze and an elastic bandage to her head. Everything needed to be scrubbed, but he was afraid to move her, and there was too much caked blood and dirt in her hair to spot clean while she stayed in bed. Her underworld constitution would have to see her through infection until she had enough strength for a shower. He helped her raise up for a sip of water. She drained it like she hadn't had water for days.

"Listen—this is gonna sound like big news, but it's more important you rest. It's about your sister."

She opened her eyes. Her fierceness shined through them even though she was nearly passed out.

"She woke up. We found her behind my pop's house. Wait—" Mick took hold of her shoulders as she tried to sit up. "She's with Old Mae now. She's fine. Been stayin' with me."

Her breath came fast, ragged. He gave her a little push, and she reclined back to the pillows.

"You should have …" She trailed off, as if realizing the accusation should be aimed at herself, not him. She was the one who'd left.

He guessed what she was going to say. "I did."

She closed her eyes.

He'd found her, and here, now, inside his apartment and away from that muddy grave filling with that pour of rain, he couldn't figure out how he had. There was no reason to it. He'd messed up, more than once. He'd persevered. The outcome shouldn't be so victorious based on only that, but it was.

"I need to see her now."

"She don't know you, Waapikoona. Not as you are now. It took a long time to get her to trust me."

"Please, Mick."

He went outside and climbed the steps to Old Mae's door, moved by the intensity of Waapikoona's tone. Finding her sister and raising her from the dead was her life's work, and he felt a calling to help her until the end. Up on the porch, he didn't bother knocking. He was still in his wet dirty clothes and too exhausted to raise his knuckles to the door. Inside, cats milled in the hall, and Old Mae's voice carried from the kitchen. He found her serving breakfast to the little girl who was hunkered under a thick blanket, shivering in her nightgown.

"You old dog," Old Mae said, spotting him. "Nearly got this girl froze to death."

He held a hand out to Isabel. "I found Waapikoona."

She got up fast, causing the blanket to fall. She put her hand in his. They rushed outside, slowing for the wet steps. Inside his apartment he put a finger to his lips.

"She's hurt. Very tired. A quick visit then you go back upstairs so she can rest."

She pulled away from him and followed the light into the bedroom. He followed her in, found her standing at the foot of the bed.

"Pinepakatwi," Waapikoona said.

"Isabel," the girl corrected.

Waapikoona put a hand over her mouth. Mick had never seen Waapikoona cry … had he? If he had, it wasn't like this. Big tears, welling in her eyes until they overflowed across both cheeks. He felt it infecting him. His eyes wet, he looked away, cleared his throat against a sudden tightness. It was not his place to cry.

The girl pointed. "Sarah."

"Yes." Waapikoona had somehow mustered a sturdy voice. She cleared her cheeks with a quick hand. "Do you remember our Indian names?"

Isabel shook her head.

"That's okay. We have new ones."

The girl risked a step closer then another, until Waapikoona reached a hand and Isabel met it with her own.

"Your other hand. Let me see."

Isabel released her crippled hand from its resting spot against her belly and held it out for her sister to see. Waapikoona took it, straightened the limp, bent fingers, and looked into the little girl's face. "I think it's okay. What do you think?"

The girl shrugged.

"*Tipeewe neeyolaani*," Waapikoona said.

Isabel started to cry. Shuddering sobs curled her shoulders as Waapikoona reached for her, but the girl was too overcome to move. Mick came forward, picked her up, set her on the bed so Waapikoona could embrace her. Waapikoona held her while she cried, and when she looked up at Mick over the girl's shoulder, her fierce gratitude seared itself into Mick's heart.

He shook his head at her. No, this wasn't his doing; he could not take credit for this. It was something else. God. Nature. The universe. He had no idea what it was, but it wasn't him. But her look only strengthened, saying, *Yes, you did this.*

He would have to explain how the girl had just showed up without any effort from him. And not only that. There was so much more. Isabel, not just a reborn girl but also a thunderbird like him. Baby Helen dying, and needing the underworld's help. The other Native people watching him, the dumpster full of demon millipedes, Raúl and his hazel-eyed woman who knew too much. Waapikoona had a bad habit of leaving unexpectedly, and he wasn't sure how to say the words that would keep her here.

Please stay.

Don't leave me again.

I'm in love with you, and I can't survive without you.

Instead, he laid a hand on Isabel's back now that she had calmed and said to her, "Let's get you back upstairs to finish that breakfast. Plenty of time to talk later, and your sister's got to rest."

Waapikoona wiped Isabel's eyes with the sheet and gave her an assuring nod. Mick took the girl back upstairs. As long as Isabel was in this house, Waapikoona wouldn't leave. But that was banking on Waapikoona not whisking the girl away alongside her.

Back inside his apartment, he locked the door and closed the little curtain against the rising sun. He picked at the dried mud on his jaw then gave up when he found it continued up behind his ear and into his hair. It was a lost cause until he could get himself under a hot shower.

Waapikoona stared into him when he re-entered the room. He stared back.

"You really are more god than man."

"Okay, and you clearly ain't yourself right now." He moved to her side to check her head wound. The blood on the gauze had dried. No fresh blood seemed like good news. She watched him, one eye darkened with a burst of broken vessels, the other rimmed in gore. Mick wet a washcloth in the bathroom sink and cleaned her face, neck, and hands, wishing he'd done this before he'd let Isabel see her. Waapikoona let him do it, stubborn, independent woman that she was. He found a nasty cut on one palm and cleaned and bandaged the best he could. He moved to her feet to yank off a boot then the other. An object floated out, falling to the bedspread. He picked up the feather—his feather—and looked past it into her eyes.

"I lost the other one," she said. On her face was the look of someone caught but thoroughly unashamed.

"I got a few I could give you."

"I'm not sure I need them anymore."

He didn't want to interpret that now. It could go too many ways. And right now he had her in his bed as a compliant patient, unresisting to the rest and care she needed. He stripped off her soggy socks, peeled off cold, wet jeans and underwear. She watched him through half-lidded eyes, the set of her mouth no longer so somber.

"Just bein' practical," he said, drawing the covers over her lower half.

Her eyes closed as he moved to her shirt and started on the buttons.

"Mick."

He had to bend her arm to get it out of the sleeve. She clenched her jaw against it, and when that side of the shirt was off, he could see why. A raging bruise circled her upper arm, the exact width of a man's grip. "Yeah?"

"Did you want me to spare him?"

He couldn't stand that note in her voice, the hardening against judgment, the hint of care for what he thought. He did not judge her, not as a man, not as a thunderbird. Both of his forms worshipped her. And now he had to steel himself against the judgment she might have for him, but he owed her the truth, no matter what she thought. The enjoyment he'd found in breaking that man's knees was too extreme to cover with any lie.

"I wanted him to beg for his life, and I wanted you to kill him anyway."

She raised her hand. He wasn't sure why. In agreement? To stop further discussion? For a high five? He took it with his own and wove his fingers into her frail ones, closing his hand and holding tight. He held her eye, unsure if the gesture meant the same to her as it did to him. Teamwork. Homecoming. Promise. Mutual responsibility for the crime they'd committed tonight and the many crimes it reconciled. It was hard to feel triumphant when the woman he'd fought for lay so lifeless in his bed.

"Sleep," he said, folding the cover over her.

He switched off the lamp and closed himself out of the bedroom. He looked around his apartment at the evidence of normal life spread before him. Folded laundry on the arm of the couch. A stack of unopened bills on the coffee table. The box of cereal left out on the kitchen counter. And the clock, telling him he had to be at work in three hours. Sleep wasn't going to happen for him. A shower and a meal would have to. But stepping back into life after fighting through such darkness seemed like an impossible feat. He looked at

the little window tinted orange with the dawn. Before he could mount this day, he needed to see real evidence of it.

He opened the door and went outside.

The sun was low but alive, burning like a vow. As much as he wanted to believe it, to let it fill him, he couldn't. Not yet. Across the yard, shadows slid and twisted into the woods, taking refuge for the day. Tonight they would be back, greater in power and number, more work for his eagle. He would never sleep again.

A car with an exhaust note he knew well slowed on the road as if preparing for the turn onto his driveway. He walked away from the house for a better visual and stood behind the GTO. The shiny black paint of a 300ZX headed straight for him, taking it easy on the gravel. As it neared he could see Raúl behind the wheel. No other passengers. He waited as it came to stop and shut off. The door opened; Raúl got out.

"I'm here to collect that favor you owe Teresa. I hear she helped you out."

The clue that helped him find Waapikoona—he could never repay a favor like that.

"I see my timing might be bad. Looks like you had a rough night." Raúl took off his jacket and tossed it in the back seat. "All I ask is you follow me."

"I can't really—"

"Thirty minutes, human time." Raúl pulled his shirt off over his head.

A strange comment, an out-of-place shedding of clothes, not so strange to Mick anymore. The light fluttered around Raúl, like a mirror catching the sun, and then man became bird and flapped into the sky. Mick identified him at once. The same peregrine falcon he'd met in the sky near Oklahoma, hunting horned serpents the night Waapikoona had called him at the U-Fill to warn him of a guy named Soto.

"Raúl Soto," Mick said.

The peregrine falcon called back to him.

Thirty minutes human time. Repayment for the favor didn't come close, but if they were going to make it this easy, he'd be stupid not to take it. He shed his clothes and fell ungracefully into his eagle, too exhausted for any kind of running start. Once he had his wings, new life pulsed through him. Not enough to carry him far, but at least his human could fade away and take a much-needed rest. Sunlight spread wider above the land. He could feel its warmth pressing against the breeze as he tailed the falcon over rolling valleys still holding the dark cold of night. Flat lakes blanketed in mist. Shadowed bundles of rock hiding entrances to the underworld. All crawling with so many demons and serpents it wasn't necessary to seek them out. Their numbers were so great, their hiding became unnecessary and impossible. He and the peregrine falcon could start the hunt now, but the moon would rise and fall, and the land would be nowhere near cleansed.

Inside him, his human understood the repayment for the favor had only just begun.

FOR DETAILS ABOUT THE NEXT BOOK, PLEASE VISIT

KAYCAMDEN.COM

DEAR

Reader,

THANK YOU FOR reading *Unbroken*! Please visit kayc-amden.com for details about the next book in the series and my other books featuring different characters and worlds. Once there, you can subscribe to receive updates on my writing progress and other news.

If you liked this book please consider leaving a review. All reviews help, and indie writers count on them because we don't have big publishers promoting our work. And please tell your friends!

ARE YOU ON GOODREADS? SEND ME A FRIEND REQUEST!

I LOVE TO HEAR FROM READERS! EMAIL ME AT KAY@KAYCAMDEN.COM

Again, thank you for reading. Our time is valuable and finite and there are far too many good books to read. Thank you for choosing mine!

—Kay

www.ingramcontent.com/pod-product-compliance
Lightning Source LLC
Chambersburg PA
CBHW020919110726
47900CB00001B/218